Pr
EVERYBODY RISE

NEW YORK TIMES BESTSELLING NOVEL

Praise for *Everybody Rise*

"An intoxicating blend of class, ambition, and money."
—*Entertainment Weekly*

"Stephanie Clifford's *Everybody Rise* delves into the world of social climbing in a way that's as insightful as it is hilarious." —*Goop*

"Drily observant . . . Evelyn is a believable character because she's as flawed as she is likable. Readers of this sort of novel do want all the juicy details about closed societies, and Clifford is able to provide them." —*The Plain Dealer* (Cleveland)

"An expertly told novel of manners . . . This relentlessly fascinating story of old money and callous ambition could very well be the most talked-about book of the summer." —*Star Tribune* (Minneapolis)

"If Edith Wharton were alive today, this modern-day class struggle would set her up for some stark rivalry. From the Lilly Pulitzer dresses to the debutante balls to the regatta competitions, *New York Times* reporter Stephanie Clifford expertly conveys the ambition of an outsider desperate to make her way into an untouchable world."
—*National Post* (Canada)

"A juicy, scheme-filled update on Edith Wharton, and it's *unputdownable*." —*Lenny*

"Pure pleasure . . . the age-old story of wanting what we can't have."
—Wichita Public Radio

"A compulsive, up-close-and-personal read about the first cracks in the greed-and-bleed U.S. economy that went flying off the rails so spectacularly a short time later." —*Library Journal* (starred review)

"A sharp and witty cautionary tale . . . Clifford's shrewd look at upper-class dynamics in modern-day New York society takes up the torch of Edith Wharton. And although her story is sobering in its scope, Clifford keeps it afloat with bursts of comedy; the end result is a thoughtful yet entertaining yarn that manages to bring to mind both *The Great Gatsby* and the Shopaholic series. Filled with scandal and schadenfreude, *Everybody Rise* will keep readers flipping pages."
—*BookPage*

"With a sympathetic main character and a fascinating look into how the other half lives, this astute tale is irresistible."   —*Library Reads*

"The complex relationships, authentic characters, OMG moments, and cringe-worthy exchanges will continue to stick in your mind long after you put *Everybody Rise* down."   —*Glamour.com*

"Gossip Girl fans, rejoice! Behold the literary version of a Jenny-esque-narrated story, had she met Blair and Serena in her mid-twenties. Cue lies, affairs, and mounting debt."
—*Marie Claire* (Summer Reads Roundup)

"The summer's most anticipated beach read . . . a funny, sharply observed debut novel about young one percenters in New York . . . a buzzy Tom Wolfe–meets–Edith Wharton novel of young Manhattan."
—*The Hollywood Reporter*

"Addictive: think *Prep* meets *The Devil Wears Prada*."
—*Good Housekeeping*

"Stephanie Clifford's writing in her debut novel *Everybody Rise* is as effortless as a summer day—and the perfect companion for an end-of-the-season trip to the beach. Set in 2006 New York City, Clifford drops the veil on a money-obsessed society at its peak, just before an economic crisis threatens their old-world lifestyle."   —*Audible*

"Clifford deftly updates *The House of Mirth* to show that belonging to the social elite is still not for the faint of heart. . . . Clifford's characters are complex and the choices they make follow intriguing paths in this engaging and moving story." —*Indie Next*

"Full of ambition and grit. Clifford provides sharp-eyed access to a moneyed world and its glamorous inhabitants."
—Emma Straub, *New York Times* bestselling
author of *The Vacationers*

"A boom-time dramedy of manners featuring a bright young cast of haves and desperately want-to-haves, all clinging to a very rickety social ladder. Clifford's lively and biting debut gets to the quick of ambition at its most corrosive."
—Maggie Shipstead, *New York Times* bestselling
author of *Seating Arrangements*

Everybody Rise

A NOVEL

Stephanie Clifford

ST. MARTIN'S GRIFFIN
NEW YORK

To my parents,
with thanks

EVERYBODY RISE. Copyright © 2015 by Stephanie Clifford. All rights reserved. Printed in the United States of America. For information, address St. Martin's Press, 175 Fifth Avenue, New York, N.Y. 10010.

www.stmartins.com

The Library of Congress has cataloged the hardcover edition as follows:

Clifford, Stephanie.
    Everybody rise : a novel / Stephanie Clifford. — First edition.
        p. cm.
    ISBN 978-1-250-07717-2 (hardcover)
    ISBN 978-1-4668-8912-5 (e-book)
    1. Young women—New York (State)—New York—Fiction.   2. Social mobility—Fiction.   3. Upper class—Fiction.   I. Title.
    PS3603.L499E94 2015
    813'.6—dc23
                                                                    2015017296

ISBN 978-1-250-07750-9 (trade paperback)

Our books may be purchased in bulk for promotional, educational, or business use. Please contact your local bookseller or the Macmillan Corporate and Premium Sales Department at 1-800-221-7945, extension 5442, or by e-mail at MacmillanSpecialMarkets@macmillan.com.

First St. Martin's Griffin Edition: June 2016

10 9 8 7 6 5 4 3 2 1

I was loved, happiness was not far away, and seemed to be almost touching me; I went on living in careless ease without trying to understand myself, not knowing what I expected or what I wanted from life, and time went on and on. . . . People passed by me with their love, bright days and warm nights flashed by, the nightingales sang, the hay smelt fragrant, and all this, sweet and overwhelming in remembrance, passed with me as with everyone rapidly, leaving no trace, was not prized, and vanished like mist. . . . Where is it all?

—ANTON CHEKHOV, "A LADY'S STORY" (1887)

That faraway shore's looking not too far.

—STEPHEN SONDHEIM, "OPENING DOORS,"
MERRILY WE ROLL ALONG (1981)

Part One

CHAPTER ONE

Sheffield-Enfield

"Your pearl earrings are rather worn down. They're starting to look like molars," Barbara Beegan said to her daughter, poking with a cocktail knife at pâté that was so warmed by the sun that it was nearly the consistency of butter. "Don't you ever take them off?"

Evelyn's right hand jolted up to her ear and rubbed at an earring, which did feel lumpy. She'd bought them as a prep-school graduation gift for herself, and over the years, wearing them during showers and swims and tennis games must have eaten away at the earrings' round perfection, but it wasn't something she'd noticed until now. "You wanted me to wear them," she said.

"I wanted you to look like you were dressing to watch the lacrosse game, not playing in it. You could at least polish them every now and then. People must wonder if you can't take care of your things. I think this pâté has salmonella. Can't you find something else to put out?"

Evelyn sidled along the edge of the 1985 beige Mercedes. Her mother had bought it, used, after Evelyn's orientation at Sheffield, her prep school, once Barbara saw none of the old-money mothers would deign to drive a fresh-off-the-lot BMW like the Beegans had shown up in. The Mercedes was parked just a few inches from the next car, an aged Volvo—there was hardly a post-1996 car to be seen on the field—and Evelyn opened the door to slide her hand into a picnic basket in the backseat. She groped wedges of warm cheese in Saran Wrap, warm wine . . . a warm container of cream cheese? No, olive tapenade; and, guessing that the tapenade was the least likely to cause food poisoning, retrieved that. A roar went up from First Field, a few hundred yards away; the crowd approved of her choice. It was Sheffield-Enfield, her prep school's version of a homecoming game, and the spectators were absorbed in the lacrosse matchup.

Shaking her hair forward to cover her earlobes, Evelyn side-stepped up to the table at the car's trunk, one of the freestanding tables lined along Sheffield Academy's Second Field, which had been transformed into a parking lot for the day's game. A few tables had special banners draped across them, SHEFFIELD-ENFIELD SPRING 2006; the alumni association gave these to alums who donated more than $10,000 a year. Tables to Evelyn's left held rounds of triple-crèmes that were melting onto their trays in the May heat. To her right, bottles of white wine and Pellegrino were sweating from the exertion of being outdoors. She noticed ancient alumni toddling by in their varsity sweaters, which they insisted on wearing even in May, and made a mental note. Her bosses at People Like Us would be interested in that.

She was turning to go to the field house when there was a squelch-ing sound, and she saw Charlotte approaching, waving two boxes of water crackers in triumph in one hand and a Styrofoam cup in the other. For such a tiny person, narrow hipped enough that she often shopped at Gap Kids, Charlotte was leaving enormous gullies in the ground as she took huge steps in her rain boots. Her hair was pulled back in a ponytail, but the humidity had created a walnut-brown halo of frizz all around her pale face. "Success!" Charlotte said, stomping toward Evelyn. "Babs would have sold me into white slavery had I not found these."

"She didn't send you for crackers, did she? I told her not to. Sorry, Char."

"Listen, at least water crackers are actually something I can find. I was worried she'd send me to root you out a husband." Charlotte stuck out her tongue, and Evelyn side-kicked her in the shins, but the rubber of the boots made her foot bounce off.

"Here," Charlotte said, handing over the Styrofoam cup. "Cider."

"In May?"

"In May?" Charlotte mimicked, in a British accent. "What, you've been working at People Like Us for a day and you find the common people's habits confusing?"

"I've been working there three weeks, Char, and my plan for signing up the nation's elite is already in full effect." Evelyn gestured toward the spectators. "It's basically People Like Us membership sign-up day today. The people here just don't know it yet."

"Ah, Charlotte, you located some crackers." Barbara Beegan had reemerged, casting a blockish shadow over the girls. Her pedicured toes were strapped into flat sandals, which merged into pleated powder-blue pants with sturdy thighs bulging within, up to a crisp white oxford. She ended in dry butter-colored hair arranged in fat waves and a pair of big black sunglasses. In her prime, after a diet based on green apples, Barbara Beegan had been thin; now she was the kind of stout woman who covered up the extra weight with precisely tailored clothes. She smelled, as she always did, of leather. She frowned as she examined the boxes. "These have pepper in them, though."

Charlotte made a silent Munch-scream face at Evelyn. "Well, Mrs. Beegan, they were all I could find."

"They'll have to do, I suppose," Barbara said, looking over Charlotte's head.

"Say thank you, Mom," Evelyn said.

"Yes, thank you," Barbara said listlessly, and opened a box to begin arranging the crackers in a semicircle.

"I live to serve," Charlotte said, bowing briefly. "Ooh, there's

Mr. Marshon from prep-year history. Do you think he's still mad at me from when I reenacted the defenestration of Prague with his snow globe? I'm just going to say hi. Back in a jiff."

Evelyn took the opportunity to slip away. Second Field's grass had turned muddy and choppy with tire tracks and Tretorn tracks— Charlotte was smart to wear boots—and Evelyn picked her way over the chewed-up terrain to the field house. She watched in amusement as one alum tried to rein in a toddler while wiping down a Labrador who had apparently been swimming in the Ammonoosuc, but when the alum looked at her, she quickly coughed and looked away.

In the eight years since she'd graduated, she had not been back to Sheffield much, not wanting to see her classmates boasting about their children and jobs and weddings while Evelyn muddled along at her textbook-marketing job. Barbara, on the other hand, had been a steadfast alumna despite not actually attending Sheffield, and every year would call up Evelyn, pushing her to go to Sheffield-Enfield, and every year Evelyn would say no. Evelyn's penance for this resistance was a recurring lecture about how she was aging and needed to meet someone soon and shouldn't give up chances to meet eligible alumni.

This year, though, was different. After the textbook publisher laid her off a few months ago, she'd managed to talk her way into a job at People Like Us, a social-networking site aimed at the elite's elite. Even Charlotte, who was brilliant about business, thought that social-networking sites were going to be huge, and Evelyn sensed if she was a success at People Like Us, she could choose whatever job she wanted.

In the interview, Evelyn had dropped a few references to Sheffield and, pulling from her memory of her upper-year class Novels of the Gilded Age, Newport. When the co-CEOs asked her how she'd access the target members, she'd bluffed, mentioning two Upper East Side benefits and making it sound like she'd attended them when she hadn't. The made-up details she'd provided about the parties, the flower arrangements, and the specialty cocktails came out of her mouth surprisingly easily, and though it had made her feel unsettled, she'd reasoned that everyone stretched the truth in interviews. For $46,000 and a lot of stock options—Charlotte said this was how it worked these days—Evelyn became the director of membership at People Like Us, charged with recruiting society's finest to set up profiles on the site. Now, three weeks after she'd started, she needed some actual recruits and had headed to Sheffield's homecoming for that reason.

She could hear the fragments of a cheer coming from First Field, where the game was in its third quarter. It was the same cheer she had learned when she had arrived at Sheffield as a prep, the school's term for freshmen. The cheer was a paean to the school's mascot, a gryphon. Hearing it, a stooped man with watery blue eyes looked toward the sound and valiantly waved a tiny Sheffield flag, as though he were expecting troops from that direction to liberate him.

The cool gray stone of the field house offered respite from all the sound, and Evelyn followed the familiar path to the girls' bathroom, past the hockey rink on one side and the water-polo pool on the other. Inside, under the fluorescent lights, Evelyn leaned over the gray-concrete slabs of the sink, which stank of beer (that was the recent alumni; she'd barely seen a beer among the older alums all day) and was littered with red plastic cups. She reached into her bag, pulled out a sunglasses case, flipped it open, and extracted a flannel lens cloth. Leaning so close that she could see the thin film of grease forming on her nose, she carefully rubbed one pearl earring to a Vermeer-like shine. It was pockmarked, she admitted, but in her usual self-examination that she performed before seeing her mother, she hadn't caught it.

She briefly made eye contact with herself. Precisely one time, when she was twelve, she was told by one of her father's law partners that she'd be a heartbreaker someday, but it had yet to come true. At twenty-six, she felt like she still hadn't grown into her features, and if she hadn't by now, she probably never would. Her hair was mousy brown and hung limply past her shoulders, her face was too long, her nose too sharp, her blue eyes too small. The only body part she thought was really spectacular was her pointer finger. She'd resisted her mother's suggestions—"suggestions" was putting it mildly—of highlights, lowlights, a makeup session at Nordstrom. "You're telling everyone around you that you don't care," Barbara liked to say.

At least at Sheffield-Enfield this weekend, she and her mother had reached a tentative truce. Going to the school was one thing Evelyn had done right in her mother's eyes, even if, as Barbara said, Evelyn had failed to build on it. Evelyn had made a promising start when she became friends with Preston Hacking, a Winthrop on his mother's side ("Fine old Boston family," Barbara said) and, obviously, a Hacking on his father's. She'd remained close with Preston, but she had failed to parlay that into anything useful, Barbara believed. Evelyn's other best friend from Sheffield was Charlotte Macmillan, who was the daughter of a Procter & Gamble executive and whom her mother still referred to as "that girl in the pigtails" after the hairdo Char had worn when she first met Barbara.

Evelyn rubbed at the other earring. Folding her upper body over the sink until she was an inch from the mirror, she rotated and polished the earring, then rotated and polished it again for good measure. Her mother couldn't get her on that front.

As she heard people approaching, she jumped back from the mirror and turned the faucet on, so when alumnae with maroon S's on their cheeks burst in, she had a plausible explanation of what she had been up to. "Good game," she said brightly, pulling a paper towel from the dispenser.

With the mud trying to suck off her ballet flats, Evelyn resumed her post at the card table behind her mother's car and spread olive paste in careful curves on one of the offending pepper crackers.

"Well, well, well. If it isn't my cheerful little earful."

Preston Hacking's voice was reedy and nasal and familiar, and, hearing it and seeing the edge of his worn-down Top-Siders behind her, Evelyn let the guarded smile that had been fixed on her face since she'd left the field house balloon to a full grin. She spun on her toes and threw her arms around Preston, who picked her up with a yelp, then set her back down, out of breath from the exertion.

Preston looked exactly the same as he had at Sheffield, tall and thin, with thick, loosely curled blond hair, red glasses, and lips that were always in a half smile, the fine features of someone who had never gotten into a fight and instead had politely submitted to the hazing imposed on the well-bred boys as preps. Evelyn remembered hearing he'd been duct-taped to the statue of the Sheffield founder for several hours and, upon release, had offered his tormentors a cigar that he had in his sport-coat pocket; it was a Cuban. An ancient, scratchy-looking Sheffield sweater was hooked over his elbow—his grandfather's, or his great-grandfather's, Evelyn couldn't remember.

"Pres! I thought you were leaving me with the geriatric society. What took you so long?"

"I had, and still have, a massive hangover, and felt I could not take the cheer and school spirit of people such as you. Good God, woman, what was in those martinis last night?"

"Maybe they roofied you."

"If only. Perhaps it was the bathtub gin they seem to serve at these things. I knew I should have brought something up from the city. You can never trust the liquor service in rural New Hampshire. Would you get me a Bloody?"

Evelyn brought out one of the cut-crystal glasses her mother had brought up from Maryland and mixed a bit of vodka from a leather-covered flask with tomato juice. She wondered where her mother had obtained all these bartending accoutrements. They had shown up en masse when the family moved from their exurban ranch house to the grand and crumbling old house in Bibville when Evelyn was in elementary school. With that came aristocratic airs and fine glassware, she thought as she watched the vodka glug out from the flask. "I think my mom brought celery, but she's run off somewhere. And there was ice, but it's all melted. You might have to have warm tomato juice."

"Horseradish. Poppycock," Preston said. "More vodka. More. More. More. Good. If I don't get a drink in me soon, I might have to regurgitate all over this pretty picnic." He gulped down a long slug.

"Now that your thirst is being quenched, why don't you make yourself useful? Babs and I have been trying to sort out how these chairs unfold, and we clearly have not been able to master it," Evelyn said.

"Yes, we all remember your ill-fated forays into manual labor. Put me to work. I've always dreamt of being your handyman." Preston balanced his glass on the car's bumper and was crouched, fiddling with a washer, when Barbara Beegan returned. He jumped up. "Mrs. Beegan, what a pleasure," he said.

"Preston, what a delight. Evie said she saw you last night, during the young people's outing, but I'm glad I got to see you myself today."

"Well, not so young anymore. Did she tell you we're now in the middle-aged alumni grouping? Once you're more than five years out, it's all over."

Evelyn elbowed him in the ribs and tried to make it look like an accident in case her mother was watching, but it was too late.

"She's almost thirty. It's not surprising," Barbara said.

"I'm twenty-six, Mom. I'm not almost thirty," Evelyn muttered. When she'd walked by the current students, though, she'd realized that, to them, she was one of the sea of vaguely old alums who meandered through the dorms during Sheffield-Enfield and talked about what color the carpet was in their day.

"Almost twenty-seven," Barbara said, turning to look at her daughter.

"Nearly twenty-five," Evelyn said.

With a kick, Preston got one chair, then the other, into place. "Done and done. You both look like you've found the fountain of youth. Your daughter has me hard at work as usual. Is Mr. Beegan here as well?" he said.

Evelyn returned his drink to him. "For your labor," she said. "No, Dad had to work this weekend."

"Ah, well, I'm sure he's sad to miss it." This drew no response, so Preston picked up a cracker. "I read about a case he was involved in, in the *Journal*. I think it was a lawsuit against a pharmaceutical company in—"

"Aren't they all," Barbara interrupted with a bright tone. "It's been ages since I saw you last. You've been in London?"

"Just moved back to New York," Preston said.

"That's wonderful. Isn't that wonderful, Evie? I always tell her she needs to keep better track of her old friends. How are your old friends? That darling Nick? And that handsome brother of yours? Are they single?"

Evelyn handed her mother a cracker with cream cheese on it. "All right, Mom, we don't need to review every single person Preston knows for marriage eligibility."

"I'm just having a conversation, Evelyn. She can be so sensitive. Now. Tell me about you, Preston. You must be dating someone."

"The course of true love never did run smooth, Mrs. Beegan," Preston said.

"Of course, you have ages before you need to settle down," Barbara said.

Evelyn rolled her eyes and stuffed a cracker in her mouth. To Barbara, Preston asserted that New York life was treating him well, and his work as an independent investor was going swimmingly (though Evelyn had never been able to pin down exactly what it was Preston did or invested in). He said that Evelyn was doing terrifically in the city, which Evelyn thought he lied about rather nicely, and Barbara raised her sunglasses to the top of her head, her albino-blue eyes brightening with the compliment, which Barbara accepted as though it were about her. Exchanges complete, they separated, stepping away from one another as smoothly as if they were finishing a minuet. Barbara completed the encounter by saying she would find them all seats in the stadium, and she walked off.

A bellow from three rows of cars away arose, with a "Ha—CKING"
an octave apart. Then a "Beegs!"

"Oh, good Lord," Preston said to Evelyn.

The caller, whom Evelyn finally diagnosed as Phil Giamatti, a kid
from rural New Hampshire who'd overdosed on caffeine their lower
year, trundled over. To the untrained eye, Phil appeared to be dressed
even more snappily than Preston. His checked purple shirt, Evelyn
guessed, was Thomas Pink. His pants were Nantucket Reds. He wore
sockless Gucci loafers. Evelyn remembered when he'd arrived at
school in his oversize chambray button-downs and jeans. He smacked
of price tags these days, and he was drenched in cologne, some brand
that no doubt came in a black-leather-encased bottle.

"How are you guys?" He grabbed Evelyn with meaty hands to
lean in and smash his wet lips on her cheek. "Nice to be up here out of
Manhattan, huh?"

"It's always nice to be at Sheffield," Evelyn said flatly. She hadn't
liked Phil in high school, where he was always trying to copy Charlotte's tests, and she liked him even less with money.

"I know, right? Good to leave work, too. Banking is crazy, man."

"So I hear," Evelyn said.

"It's like, when you're doing deals the way I am, it's just nonstop.
It's like up at five A.M. and in the office till one A.M. But it's work hard,
play hard, right? Models and bottles?"

"'Models and bottles' is not exactly my scene," Preston said
haughtily.

"Models not your style, Hacking?"

Evelyn felt heat in her ears; she hoped Phil was not going where
he seemed to be going. "Pres's style—" she began.

But Phil continued. "You need male models and bottles? That
better?"

Evelyn didn't have to look at Preston to know that her friend
would be scarlet. "Preston *is* a male model, Phil," she said icily, which
wasn't the greatest of retorts, but she couldn't think of anything else.
"Good luck with your banking."

"Hey, I was just joking," Phil said as they walked away. "Hey, hey, Hacking? Hey, Beegs?"

Evelyn strode back to the card table, where she rearranged some of the cocktail knives to give Preston time to compose himself. Finally, he swallowed so hard she could hear it. "I don't know what he was talking about," Preston said.

"Me, either," Evelyn said evenly. She refilled his drink, armed with a topic change. "So, would you rather?"

"Ooh, what?" said Preston, seizing on their old game.

"Would you rather have to spend every dinner party for the rest of your life seated next to Phil Giamatti or have an aboveground pool in your front yard?"

"So elitist, Evelyn, my dear. What's the website you're working for now? Not Our Class, Dear?"

"Very funny. You know I'm going to sign you up."

"Nay! I eschew technology."

"You're going to have to embrace it. You have lineage and a respectable old name and, presumably, alcoholic uncles leaving you grand fortunes. You're exactly who they want. Don't worry. I'll help you make a charming profile."

"The answer, by the way, is aboveground pool. Dinner parties are too precious to spend with the likes of Phil."

"Agree," Evelyn said.

"What are we talking about?" Charlotte had skipped up and thrown her thin arms around both of them.

"Phil Giamatti," Evelyn said.

"You're not recruiting him for PLU, are you?" Charlotte said.

"Dahling." Evelyn held her nose and looked down at Charlotte. "He is not PLU caliber."

"Dahling, I wouldn't have ventured. Certainly not PLU," Charlotte said in her British voice. "I think Ev gets bounty-hunting points the more ancient the family money she signs up."

"Well, if People Like Us gets Evelyn back to Sheffield, I'll accept it," Preston said. "It's good to all be here together."

"I mean, of course we couldn't get our act together to hang out in New York," Charlotte said. "Isn't that New York, though?"

Evelyn tightened the cap on the vodka flask. New York when you're young, everyone in her hometown of Bibville said with reverence when they heard where she lived, having never lived in New York when they were young. Evelyn tried to love it, and sometimes did, when she was wearing heels and perfume and hailing a cab on Park on a crisp fall night, or when the fountain at Lincoln Center danced in the night light, or when she watched Alfred Molina as Tevye sing "Sunrise, Sunset" from her seat in the second balcony and felt her brain go still. The city hummed in a way Bibville never had, and the taxis were hard to get because everyone had somewhere to go, and it was invigorating. And then it became grating: the taxis just became hard to get.

She'd learned how to live in New York. She knew now never to eat lunch from the hot bar at Korean delis, never to buy shoes from the brandless leather joints that popped up in glass storefronts in Midtown, that there was more space in the middle of subway cars than at the ends, and that the flowers sold at bodegas were usually sourced from funerals. Yet she wasn't living a New York life. Despite her grand plans, she'd spent most days plodding to work and home from work without moving her life ahead. It was crowded, and loud, and dirty, and too hot, then too cold. It required an enormous amount of energy and time just to do errands like getting groceries. She was always sweaty after she got groceries.

She had expected to feel more at ease now that Charlotte and Preston were both back in New York. She thought the three of them would hang out all the time, a merry band of Sondheim characters working at love and life from their tiny apartments, all getting together on Sundays to punch each other up and drink wine on the roofs of their buildings. Instead, Charlotte, after working as a Goldman Sachs analyst—a year in which Evelyn saw her friend maybe once every two weeks and all Char talked about was how much she was working—had gone back to Harvard for business school. Charlotte had been back in the city almost a year, working for the intense private-equity firm Graystone, which meant her nights and weekends were mostly spoken for. Preston, meanwhile, had submerged himself into his preppy set upon his return from London. Evelyn had kept up with the few friends from Davidson College that had moved to the city, but their lives were starting to take wildly divergent directions. One was an actress and had just moved to Bushwick, and it would take three subways and, probably, the purchase of a shiv for Evelyn to navigate there safely. A second had gotten engaged and was moving to Garden City, Long Island.

The four years since her Davidson graduation had gone by at once too slowly and too quickly, and Evelyn found herself in her mid-twenties without the life she had expected to have. Girls her age were either forging ahead in their careers or in serious relationships that would soon produce rings and engagement parties. Her mother had offered to pay for Evelyn to freeze her eggs, and she hadn't turned down the offer right away. It wasn't so much that she wanted a husband and babies. But it would be nice to have a place for once, to have people look at her and think she was interesting and worth talking to, not to have them politely fumble for details about her life and instantly forget her. (Murray Hill, right? No, the Upper East Side. Ah, and Bucknell? No, Davidson.)

People Like Us could be her chance, even if her parents didn't see it that way. Her father said that that group hardly needed another way to cut itself off from everyone else. And her mother's response when Evelyn had told her about it was, "So rather than bothering to get to know the interesting social set in New York, you're now acting as a sort of paid concierge to them? This is why we sent you to Sheffield?"

She conceded she'd long been intimidated by the group of people she was now supposed to recruit. Earlier at the game, she had scouted out some of them, wondering if this social set would get its comeuppance as time went on, the guys devolving into thick-stomached drinkers, the girls becoming haggard. That would prove that her mother hadn't been right about the appeal of this group. Yet the girls looked great, easy and free with just the tiniest hint of private-beach tan, enamel Hermès bracelets clinking on their wrists, and the guys looked handsome and self-assured, bankers and lawyers and politicians-in-training. Eavesdropping, she'd overheard them dissecting an etiquette violation at a San Francisco private club and had initially backed away, worried they would pass her over and make her feel like nothing. Given her new job, though, she forced herself to talk to a couple of them whom she knew through Preston, and she'd managed to line up a few candidates for PLU. Evelyn was determined to make this work, to prove to her parents and to the people who'd overlooked her that she was someone. The city thought she wasn't going to make it. The city was wrong.

Preston had been sidelined by a friend of his father's, and Evelyn and Charlotte started heading toward the stadium. Another cheer started, and the girls did their accompanying hand motions in unison:

> *When – we fight – we fight – with literary*
> *Tropes – and themes – and leit – motifs because we*
> *Are – the school – that's known – for melancholy*
> *Wri – ter types – and po – et laureates and*
> *If – lacrosse – is not – our forte then we*
> *Urge – the oth – er team – to try composing*
> *I- ambic – penta – meters, allusions,*
> *Ripostes, similes*
> *And puns!*

Close to the end of the cheer, the Sheffield side lost the rhythm, but they screamed out "puns" in unison, as though it were the ultimate insult to the other team.

Barbara, taking up half a row of seats with a giant stadium blanket, waggled her fingers at Charlotte and Evelyn. Sheffield got the ball and the crowd started shouting as Evelyn squeezed in.

"Your earring looks smudged," Barbara said.

"Mother, I am going to throw the earring into this crowd if you do not stop harping on it," Evelyn said as she heard a snort from Charlotte.

Barbara rearranged herself on the blanket, and the crowd howled a mass downward arpeggio when Enfield took the ball back.

It's all right, it's okay, you're gonna work for us someday, rose the cheer from the Sheffield side.

CHAPTER TWO

Next Stop, Lake James

Evelyn looked at her bed, strewn with dresses, sweaters, jeans, boots, sandals, and Patagonias, and tried once again to narrow down what she'd need for an Adirondack weekend.

She flipped open her ringing cell phone. "Hi, Mom," she said.

"Are you bringing the Lilly?" Barbara said.

"Honestly, Mother, you're calling me to see what I'm packing? I've been to Preston's place, remember? You haven't."

"You'll never regret bringing a Lilly Pulitzer dress to a summer weekend," Barbara said firmly from the other end of the line.

Evelyn was headed to Preston's summer house in Lake James, in the Adirondacks, for Memorial Day, with the goal of recruiting more People Like Us members. Upon starting the job at People Like Us, Evelyn had waited a few days for the co-CEOs, Arun and Jin-ho, to tell her what the membership goals were and how she was supposed to achieve them—go to Spence School pickup with a sign-up sheet? They hadn't, though. People Like Us was a true start-up: an unrefurbished office in Chelsea, folding tables serving as desks, beige IBMs salvaged from some previous start-up.

The idea for the site, and the funding, came from a Swiss septua-genarian who was a Habsburg and wanted to connect with people of his ilk as he traveled to Dubai or the Maldives. He had hired Arun and Jin-ho, Stanford business school grads, and had left the rest up to them. They, in turn, seemed to be leaving the membership strategy completely up to Evelyn.

Evelyn started by studying the website New York Appointment Book and the social pages of the *Times*, trying to get a feel for who was who in society and who People Like Us might want as its American members. Her notion was that PLU should start with top-tier members to create buzz and exclusivity.

At the top of Evelyn's list was Camilla Rutherford. Evelyn had seen Camilla in person only once, when Evelyn was at the bar at Picholine, passing time with an overpriced Old Speckled Hen until *Barbara Cook's Broadway!* at the Vivian Beaumont started. The maître d' was on the phone with someone for a good twenty minutes, giving the person turn-by-turn directions from Chelsea. When Camilla walked in, the waiters hushed as though Madonna had arrived, and the maître d' apologized for having given such unclear directions. Evelyn, who had overheard the whole thing, thought they were perfectly clear and wondered why the man was so contrite. Then she glanced at Camilla, and just the fact of the girl's confidence, not to mention her beautiful hair and perfectly pressed silk blouse, made Evelyn feel wrinkled, her hair greasy, her toenails ratty.

Babs was well aware of Camilla, and had pushed her as a friend even when Evelyn was at Sheffield. Evelyn had heard of her at Shef-field, of course. Camilla-from-St. Paul's was a conversation topic when-ever Preston's New York set returned from vacations. Camilla was now an associate director of special events for *Vogue*, a job reserved for the beautiful and the chic, women who added luster to parties simply by showing up. On Appointment Book, the one social site that social-ites actually read, Camilla emerged as the clear center of Young New York. In a tiered dress the color of milky coffee, Camilla Ruther-ford lounging on a bench at the Met for its Egyptian-wing party. At the Young Collectors Council for the Guggenheim, in a black silk blouse and zigzag skirt, holding champagne. In a flamenco-looking getup that Evelyn would never have been able to pull off at For Whom the Belles Toll, a Spanish Civil War–themed fund-raiser for the New York Public Library. Identifying Camilla as a prospect was easy. Signing her up as one was the challenge.

That's when Evelyn remembered that Camilla had a camp in Lake James, where Preston had his summer place, and she'd known what to do. The way to attract these people was on their literal turf—not on city streets, where any huckster or green-energy evangelist with a clipboard could approach them, but at their hard-to-get-to summer homes where Evelyn's very presence would show she belonged. She'd e-mailed Preston to see if he was spending Memorial Day at Shuh-shuh-gah, his Lake James camp, and he'd e-mailed back, "Comme d'habitude."

"Can I crash?" she'd replied, and his response was a simple, "Oui." Things with old friends were so nicely simple.

Earlier in the week, she'd done a membership-strategy presentation about her idea, showing Arun and Jin-ho pictures of the Belles Toll event and a few others. "Look at how the people are interacting," she'd said. "Why has anyone come to this fund-raiser, other than a love of the library? It's because their friends asked them. 'Buy a table.' 'Give at the Supporters level.' That's how this world works. There are people at the center, and they are the influencers. They set the trends. They're the ones who are dictating what parties to go to. Where to vacation. What sites someone might want to sign up for," she said. "Focusing on numbers instead of quality is a surefire way to lose any credibility we have with this group. So. We'll take a page from their own playbook. It's going to be one-on-one recruitment, one-on-one appeals, just like we're putting together a library fund-raiser. A quiet sell." She'd ordered cards for People Like Us, nice card stock, and handed them out to the staff members who were headed to Nantucket and Martha's Vineyard and the Hamptons and Aspen for

Memorial Day to give to the right sorts. Arun and Jin-ho had been impressed.

Barbara was still jabbering away, and Evelyn walked to her window, where she swiped her finger across the thick grime-dust that had accumulated overnight. "I hadn't seen Preston in so long before Sheffield-Enfield. Whatever happened with the two of you?" Barbara said.

"Nothing happened. He was in London for, what, three years? So I barely saw him."

"His brother, too," Barbara was saying. "He was a nice young man. Sheffield turns them out well."

"Bing went to med school in the Virgin Islands because he couldn't get in anywhere in the States. And he has, like, an eight-year-old."

"Well. Don't rule out men who've been married. Divorced men would be very grateful to have someone young and pretty on their arm."

"Mother, there is an end button on this phone, and I am not afraid to use it." Evelyn jammed the phone between her shoulder and ear and began tossing clothes in her duffel. Her train was leaving soon.

"I always thought you and Preston would get married," Barbara continued. "His manners are lovely and he's so good at tennis. A man like that would make life easy, Evelyn. Think of how easy it would be to entertain, or go out to parties, with a husband like that. Who actually enjoys social interaction and always has such funny things to say. Preston's always the belle of the ball. The beau of the ball, I suppose."

Evelyn folded a thick wool sweater. She had considered it, too— the simple math of her and Preston marrying, leading their lives like a figure eight, doing their own activities during the day, coming together at night for parties and dinners, separating again afterward, presumably taking lovers on the side. She always screened her life-with-Preston scenes in black and white, accessorized with tiny round martini glasses and long cigarette holders. What she could not imagine was a night alone in the same house—without even getting to the mechanics around avoiding sleeping together, she shuddered at the awful intimacy of his wet toothbrush.

"What is your plan for the summer, Evelyn?"

"Lake James, at the moment." She knew her mother was asking about the rest of the summer. Some marketing people at her former employer, the textbook publisher, had gone in on a summer share on the Jersey Shore, but even if Evelyn had had the money for that, she didn't know what to say to those people, who made frat-boy jokes about dirty Sanchezes and quoted *Caddyshack*. On the other hand, staying in New York in summer wasn't all that appealing, either; last summer had meant lots of Sam Adams Summer Ale by herself on hot weekend days when it seemed like just her and the Dominican Day parade.

"You're doing that so you can do your website sales. At any rate, you can't just rely on Preston's mother's hospitality every weekend. A single woman is a strain on every hostess. It's a struggle to find a single man for a dinner partner."

"Mom. I'm already going to Lake James. Take your victories, okay? And, for the fourteenth time, it's not website sales."

"Did you pack the Lilly?"

Evelyn shook her head. "Good-bye, Mother." She tapped the phone on the bed, then stuffed the Lilly Pulitzer dress into her bag.

Evelyn dragged her duffel to the creaking elevator and through her building's lobby. She lived on the Upper East Side, in an apartment she could barely afford despite its being in a "troubling" part of the neighborhood, as her mother put it. When Evelyn had rented it, she had never lived in Manhattan before and didn't realize desirable real estate changed midblock. This had landed Evelyn in a building called the Petit Trianon, on Seventy-fourth Street on the wrong side of Third. When Barbara sent letters to Evelyn, she always addressed them to Evelyn Topfer Beegan, Le Petit Trianon, as though Evelyn resided at a country estate.

She passed the plants fighting for sunlight in the lobby, overcast with a fluorescent-green tinge. The victor these days was an aloe vera whose giant tentacles lay despondently on the tiled floor. Some time ago the plant had spawned, and a young handyman had put the babies in tiny planters, with FREE TO GOOD HOMES signs in front of the makeshift nursery. When Evelyn had returned from the bodega that morning, a homeless person had already peed on them, leaving a dark and stinking puddle around their bases.

When Evelyn stepped off the train at the Lake James station seven hours later, the sky was veiled with low gray clouds and held the threat of snow. In May, as the rest of New York bowed to summer, the Adirondacks clasped winter as tightly as they could. Winter was their season, and they weren't going to let go of it so easily. Evelyn shivered. The train hooted away, and though Evelyn knew the station was close to the road, she couldn't even hear car engines.

Preston was having a whole crew up this weekend. Nick Geary, Preston's best friend since middle school who had gone on to Enfield and Dartmouth, for one. He was in the consumer-products group at Morgan Stanley, so Charlotte dealt with him all the time in her private-equity job, where she worked on consumer-products acquisitions. There was also some acquaintance of Nick's from Morgan Stanley whom Charlotte also knew. Charlotte had decided to come last minute, after nonstop harassment from Evelyn, and then Bing, Bing's girlfriend, and Bing's kid were also up. Evelyn thought she could get at least a few of them onto the site, and she wanted to find other recruits at Lake James parties.

Lake James was gorgeous; she had to give it that. Even the train station was. In front of her was a small blue station house, the short concrete length of the platform, and, beyond, green trees in every direction. The wind picked up sharply, then quieted just as suddenly, and the trees rattled their leaves, an imitation of the sound of rain, but then they, too, settled into silence.

Evelyn had dressed for "summer" rather than "mountains" and pulled her cotton cardigan close around her. Looking to her left, to the other end of the platform, she saw a tall black-haired figure in a dark suit. He looked about her age, but his shoulders rolled forward, giving him the stoop of a much-older man. He was staring out at the trees and looked lost.

They both turned toward the station house and got there at the same time. He grabbed for the doorknob, fumbling with it, but managed to open the door for her. He was around six-three, with correspondingly exaggerated features that reminded her of a Croatian basketball player she had once seen when forced to watch a Lakers-Knicks game, and small dark eyes that peered down at her. She stepped in front of him to the small square waiting room, with blue walls and simple brown wooden benches along the sides. She looked at him carefully again, trying to match him with any of the Lake James people she had done research on. Evidently she had been studying his suit too closely.

"I came from work," he blurted, pulling at his tie.

"I figured," Evelyn said, smiling. "Either that or Lake James is becoming an important business center."

He half smiled, but it did nothing to wash away the nervousness on his face. "So, I guess, you're Evelyn? Nick said you'd be on the same train."

Nick's friend, then. Preston hadn't said anything about him other than he worked at Morgan Stanley, but this guy didn't strike Evelyn as a Nick cohort—he seemed unpolished, even kind of nice. "Evelyn Beegan. You're staying at Preston's?"

He reddened as he shook her hand. "Yeah, he didn't, ah, mention it? That we'd be on the same train? Sorry. I work with Nick, and he thought it would be fun if I came. Up."

"Right. Well, I'll bet it will be. I'm sorry—I didn't catch your name," said Evelyn. The guy's awkwardness made her feel at ease by comparison.

"Oh. Gosh. I'm sorry. Scot. Scot Tannauer." He held out his hand, then withdrew it just as quickly and shook it out as if he had carpal tunnel syndrome. She couldn't tell whether he was attracted to her or terrified of humans. He took a look around the station house. "I've never been to the Adirondacks before. I read up on them."

"I didn't know there was much reading to be had on them."

"Oh, yes. Yes. The history of the mountains, and the great camps, and the Vanderbilts and the other families who came up here."

"Bankers came even then," Evelyn said with a light laugh.

"Oh—yes—I get the joke," he said, looking down at his suit.

"Oh, no, I didn't mean—"

"Sorry. Just. No. I'm just—"

"So you were saying? The great camps?"

"The architecture is really something. It's an interesting style that was replicated in some of the national-park lodges, but really nowhere else."

Evelyn began to ask about who the architects had been, but the station house door opened and Nick Geary stepped in wearing white tennis shorts and a white polo shirt. His hair was still chocolate brown and perfectly floppy, his eyes the same dark blue, his skin perfect, and his lips a deep red that girls would've killed for. His nostrils were the only problem, large and quivering; they had no doubt seen their share of coke, Evelyn thought as she smiled and kissed his cheek. "Nick!"

"Evelyn. It's been ages. How's the singing?" he said, not as distantly as Evelyn had expected. "Sir," he said to Scot. "So I've been deputized as your chauffeur for the day. Hop in. Evelyn, how much luggage do you need for a three-day weekend? Jesus Christ."

"The singing?" Scot asked.

"I was really into musicals when I first met Nick. I'm surprised he remembers."

"Oh," Scot said, sounding like a horse neighing.

CHAPTER THREE

Shuh-shuh-gah

The stores of Lake James Village topped out at two stories, crowded together on one mile of the three-mile-circumference pond in town. It looked, comfortingly, exactly as Evelyn had remembered it from her first and only other trip there, the summer after Preston's Sheffield graduation. Though years had passed, no Walmarts had arrived to suck the specificity out of the village, and there were not even any chain drugstores, as those were relegated to the road leading out of town. Instead, it was Just Bead It and Custard Mustard & Ale and the confusing promise of the Steak Loft.

Even the smell of the air through the rolled-down windows was familiar after all these years, wet leaves and burning wood and muddy grass. Evelyn, who'd decided to sit in the backseat to let Nick handle conversing with Scot, watched as the light green of the trees whirred by. It was quiet but for some chirps of birds and the rumble of the ancient Hacking Jeep along the road.

Though it was late May, the local clothing store, the Sweater Haus, still had thick Irish sweaters and Wellies in the windows. Even the Gap and Bass outlets, part of an aborted attempt on the part of the town elders to make Lake James into a discount-clothing destination, showed what remained of winter gear in their windows: puffy jackets, raincoats, heavy leather hiking boots. The Lakeview Inn's A-frame chalkboard promised seven-bean soup and grilled cheese sandwiches and weather that was fifty-five and cloudy.

Evelyn looked over James Pond, which the Lakeview sat on, remembering the first time she'd seen it. All that talk about Lake James as a summer playground for the rich and well bred, she remembered thinking, and it was a rinky-dink middle-class vacation town with a tiny lake and wooden bears surrendering with their paws up outside every third store. Then she'd followed the directions Preston had given—the same directions Nick was following now—and taken a right between two stone pillars with a hanging wooden sign that read Mt. Jobe Road—Private Drive, and perceived her error. Here was an unfinished rough dirt road, and glimpses of an enormous lake to the left, and the suggestion of very nice houses, as implied by the trees in front of them that hid them from view.

"Oh," Scot said from the front, having the same realization Evelyn had had years earlier. "There's another lake? I thought the lake was the one in town."

"That's the pond," Evelyn said. "James Pond. All the tourists come here and think it's Lake James and take a paddleboat out or whatever and then go home thinking all the fuss is about this pond. Lake James is huge. At least ten times the size of the pond. You can't see it from town."

"Why can't you see it from town?"

"Private drives, friend," Nick said, hurtling up Mt. Jobe. "Get with the program."

"I'd think the residents would object to that," Scot said.

"The residents all live on the private drives," Evelyn said with a laugh. "They're the ones keeping everyone else out."

"Such communist ideas, Evelyn," Nick said.

On Mt. Jobe Road, each house was marked with a modest wood

post and slightly madcap letters, naming the places with a mix of hom-
age and play—THE AERIE, CAMP TAMANEND, TOE-HOLD, WEOWNA
CAMP.

Preston's parents had bought their place, Shuh-shuh-gah, in the
eighties, after Jean Hacking had a falling-out with her sisters and
decided they would henceforth stop going to Osterville. Mrs. Hacking
fit soundly into the social scene with her headbands and fleeces and
creased pants, her pantryful of good red wine, her patrician East
Coast roots, her competitiveness in hearty summer sports such as sailing and rowing, and her pronunciation of "hurricane" as "hurriken."

Though the Hackings had only been there three decades, a batch
of newer arrivals had turned the Hackings into something of the old
guard in Lake James. On the hill side of the road, away from the
water, were people from Los Angeles and Florida and South Carolina who had bought plots of land without water rights just for the
privilege of saying they had Adirondack camps. They had installed
gravel drives and granite statues of bears or eagles and were forever
fighting with the town's zoning board over adding satellite dishes to
their camps.

Making a screaming left turn, Nick bumped into a wooden ditch
and back out again, and Evelyn watched with some alarm as Scot's
dark head nearly hit the roof.

Around the last turn, at the bottom of the hill, Evelyn spotted
Shuh-shuh-gah's welcoming brown-wood boathouse with its green
window frames. The Hacking house at Lake James was part of an Adirondack great camp, one of many built by railroad, banking, and tim-
ber barons in the late 1800s. It was initially a hunting camp, with
separate platform tents for cooking, sleeping, and drinking. Once
upper-class women started joining their husbands in the Adirondacks,
trading up from the passé getaways of Saratoga Springs and Cape May,
the tented buildings were turned into wooden structures, though still
with a rustic, unfinished quality that tried to make visitors feel like they
were still living in nature.

Only a handful of the camps had been kept in one piece, and the Hackings' was not among them. What served as their main house had once been stables, and their boathouse was grand, with two covered docks and one open dock and sleeping quarters upstairs. The other parts of the original camp were now cut off from the Hackings' portion by copses of trees.

The first time Evelyn had come, it was raining when she'd arrived, a silver Adirondack storm, and she'd slipped down to the boathouse porch before joining Preston's graduation party. Thin pines that were bare for the first sixty feet of their trunks ended in thick daubs of green, like those in a Japanese silk painting. Through the gray, she could see only a few lights of houses across the lake, and the only sound was of the rain hitting the wooden railing and the dock below her. For a moment, Evelyn felt like everything was quiet.

Then she went to the party. Preston's older brother, Bing, had a bunch of his friends up, and they were drunk and arguing about rugby. The girls were pretty and mean and made jokes that Evelyn couldn't follow. Nick Geary, whom Evelyn had met several times by then, kept calling her Sarah. There was a regatta that Preston's mother shanghaied Evelyn into helping with, and Evelyn had rigged one of the boats incorrectly and was publicly chastised by Mrs. Hacking, and then it was one dinner on the lake followed by another dinner on the lake where Evelyn was clearly the dud guest. Everyone had worn embroidered whale belts; everyone but Evelyn.

This time, she had a whale belt—a never-worn birthday gift from Babs—and she was prepared. She could see the edge of the main house down a stone path to her left. Evelyn opened the car door and hopped out, removed her duffel from the back, and set off on the wide stone stairs toward the house's kitchen entrance.

The Hackings' Scottish deerhound, Hamilton, after Alexander, who was always having to be fetched from neighbors' houses after he paddled up to their shores on long and unauthorized swims, nosed open the screen door from the kitchen and greeted Evelyn with a welcoming snout jab. Evelyn followed Hamilton inside, where Preston sat on a stool next to the kitchen's central island, holding a bunch of grapes up to the light.

"Ah. Greetings to you, Evelyn Beegan," Preston said, rising. He wore an extremely old pink oxford, dark khakis, and monogrammed velvet driving slippers with a giant moth hole over his left little toe. He shook the cluster of fruit in front of her. "Would you care for a grape?"

"I'm good, thanks." Evelyn swung herself onto a stool. There wasn't a dish, clean or dirty, visible in the entire kitchen, just the photo-shoot-ready bowl of fruit.

"Where are your travel companions? And what is happening with your hair?" Preston asked.

"Coming down in a second, I think. And I straightened it. Thanks for letting me crash. The People Like Us recruitment continues."

"The drama continues here this weekend, too," Preston said, tossing a grape into his mouth and looking amused. "You remember Bing."

"Sure."

"He's now divorced."

"You told me. I'm so sorry."

"Don't be. Better all around. He made the rather ill-advised decision to bring his girlfriend up this weekend. She works at"—Preston stopped and chewed the grape deliberately—"an advertising agency. Promoting canned tomatoes, at the moment. And went to, I'm not sure. DePaul? DePauw? Somewhere decidedly third tier."

"Doesn't DePaul have really good soccer?"

Preston fixed her with a look. "Soccer? Evelyn."

"It's a sport."

"Barely. Here, take a grape. They're very good. Seeds, though. Be careful. She calls herself Chrissie."

"Is that because it's her name?"

Preston smiled. "Perhaps. Perhaps. Chrissie is up for the weekend, and I cannot say it is going swimmingly."

"How long have they been dating?"

Preston considered this. "Three months. Four. But she's no spring chicken, clearly eager to reproduce, and currently she's showing off her maternal skills with Pip—you remember my niece? They're racing together in the Fruit Stripe on Sunday. Pip is not pleased."

"The Fruit Stripe? The regatta? That's this weekend? I don't have to race, do I?"

"There's always a chance. If Mother recruits you, you do know you can't turn her down."

"Pres, when I was here before, your mother almost deported me because I got a knot wrong on the rigging."

"You're from the Eastern Shore. You're supposed to know these things."

"Yes. So says my own mother, but I managed to avoid sailing camp summer after summer. So Chrissie sails?"

"Well. The Fruit Stripe switches every year. The founder chooses what sport we'll do. Sailing, rowing, kayaking, canoeing. All boating, of course. Chrissie is apparently an excellent kayaker—she's from the West Coast—and Mother thought she'd be a ringer for this year. Then the race was deemed to be sailing again, not kayaking. So here we are."

"Your mother is not going to take a mediocre placement in a water-sports event very well."

"No. Nor is Bing. It's going to break them up. Which is perhaps the point. It should be a fun show, I suppose."

Hamilton nosed Preston's thigh as Nick and Scot entered. "Nice to see you again, man," said Preston to Scot, his tone now all urban masculinity.

A door at the other end of the house banged, and Mrs. Hacking came hurtling through with a sheaf of papers in her hand, her curly gray hair bobby-pinned above her ears. Evelyn had never seen her in anything other than sensible all-weather clothing that could take her from fixing a motorboat to a committee meeting to a brisk walk around the lake with Hamilton, and, in her L.L. Bean Norwegian sweater and ankle-length khakis, she did not disappoint.

"Hello! Everyone! Hamilton, sit. Evelyn, hello, the Fruit Stripe is sailing again this year so you won't be helping on the rigging. You must be Scot, welcome. Nick, thank you for doing pickup. I'm on my way to the Fruit Stripe meeting and then I have to stop by the town library before it closes. Preston, will you call the librarian and have her keep it open for me until six-fifteen? And it will be drinks at six-thirty, dinner at eight."

In Boston, where Preston's parents lived most of the year, Mrs. Hacking had joined a highly competitive masters' rowing team called Mildred's Moms and had taken to doing weight lifting. She was an excellent gardener, and had recently enrolled in a landscaping course. She had a fine memory, as evidenced by her vivid recollection of Evelyn's rigging error from years ago. She was a fierce hostess, and had been one of the top fund-raisers for Romney for Governor. The one thing Mrs. Hacking did not do was dishes.

The phone rang, and Mrs. Hacking picked it up and began arguing over how many trays of crudités the Fruit Stripe would require. Evelyn peeked into the living room, where Mr. Hacking was sitting in front of the fire with a thick hardbound book, and Bing, a hearty, doughy type, was telling a story about the Porcellian to the room, though no one appeared to be listening.

Toward the window, which looked out onto a porch and then down to the ice-calm lake, an anxious-looking red-haired woman with a thin ponytail was pacing, talking at eight-year-old Pip, who was curled up in a chair with her eyes closed. "Do you think I should practice? I'm afraid it's going to rain. The weather report said it would rain earlier in the day, but it didn't, and I should take a boat out, but it looks like it's going to rain. Don't you think it looks like it's going to rain?" Chrissie, Evelyn knew without having to check with Preston.

Evelyn took this all in, then looked back to Mrs. Hacking, who held up one finger as she listened to the other end of the line. "Margot, there are thirty-three boats entered this year, so that's at least sixty-six people in need of sustenance—fine, fine. Very well." She hung up the phone, then clapped at the group. "Now, let's see. Evelyn, you'll be on the second floor in the writing room, and Charlotte will be just down the hall. Nick and Scot, I'm sorry to say that you'll be in the maid's quarters this weekend, at the back of the house; we're simply oversubscribed."

"Mrs. Hacking," Evelyn said, realizing she needed to atone for the rigging error if she wanted help with PLU introductions this weekend, "I'd love to be in the maid's room. I think it's really charming. And it's Scot's first time here—he should have the view. Charlotte and I will do the maid's room. Really."

"All right. I can't say anyone else volunteered," Mrs. Hacking said, reassessing Evelyn and then leaning toward the living room to look pointedly at Chrissie. "Good. Thank you."

Evelyn picked up her bag and walked through the kitchen, through the pantry, and into the maid's room. She heard Mrs. Hacking saying, "Chrissie, why don't you stop worrying about whether to sail and just sail? Yes?"

The room had whitewashed walls and two twin beds that took up nearly the entire space. A big leather duffel was at the end of one, which must have been Nick's; she heard him clomping behind her.

"Hey," he said. "Thanks. That would've been gay if I had to sleep with Scot."

"A guest's duty, Nick," Evelyn said, floating her hand into the air.

He grunted as he picked up the bag and left.

Dusk was approaching, and birds whittered and cawed. Charlotte was snickering as Evelyn changed into a pair of white slacks and a navy cable-knit sweater; when Evelyn added a string of pearls, Charlotte fell back on her bed laughing. "Oh, come on," she hooted.

"I think I look grand," Evelyn said, baring her teeth in the mirror as she pulled the choker around her neck.

Charlotte kicked her feet in the air; her soles were dirty, as Charlotte had been chasing Hamilton on the grass all afternoon, with Hamilton and then Charlotte alternately jumping into the water to escape capture. As they had shrieked around, Mrs. Hacking shouted at her to be careful of getting the dog too riled up, and Charlotte had given a thumbs-up, then kept on chasing Hamilton. Charlotte had enough money—had always had enough money—that she didn't have to worry about her behavior. Charlotte's father had been one of the top marketing executives for Procter & Gamble, specializing in global markets, and Charlotte had been pulled from kindergarten in Cincinnati to live in places like Hong Kong and Russia and Chile. Charlotte was fluent in Cantonese, Arabic, French, and Spanish, decent at Turkish and Russian, and conversational in about ten other languages that she insisted on ordering in when she dragged Evelyn to outer-borough ethnic restaurants. While she'd grown up in rich expat communities, gone to sleek international schools, and had plenty of money, Charlotte didn't think money alone made people interesting.

Charlotte's father had gone just to Harvard B-School and was enormously proud of his daughter, the first of the three Macmillan kids to do double-Harvard. Charlotte liked the power of being a female among men, whether it was sparring with her brothers or hopping on planes with moguls or winning enormous amounts at the Belmont Stakes with her father or being the only woman on a hot acquisition at Graystone. Evelyn could guess how much money Charlotte made—somewhere between $200,000 and $400,000 a year—but Charlotte lived in an Ikea-furnished basement apartment in Midtown because it was a five-minute walk from her office, and most of her wardrobe came from the Gap.

Charlotte's four years at Sheffield had been the longest she'd lived anywhere to that point, making Preston and Evelyn her closest friends by default. With little time to cultivate a social life these days, she ended up doing what Preston and Evelyn were doing. When they went to places like Lake James, Charlotte was fine with it. She'd spent her youth going to rich people's events in cultures that weren't hers and was perfectly comfortable doing so still.

"I forgot to tell you," Evelyn said, fumbling with the necklace clasp. "Phil Giamatti, at Sheffield-Enfield? He basically insinuated Pres was gay while Pres was standing there."

"Really?" Charlotte said. "He should've seen Pres sticking his tongue down that girl's throat at Dorrian's that one time after we spent all Saturday at the Boathouse."

"That was two years ago," Evelyn said.

"So?"

"So that was the last time he kissed anyone, as far as I know. I'm not sure he would come out even if he were gay, as his family has such strict ideas of what he should be—or, more to the point, he thinks they have those ideas. The thing is—" She stopped herself, noticing that Charlotte was picking at her feet and remembering that Charlotte hadn't hooked up with anyone in a year or two, either. Evelyn flushed, feeling even more like an idiot when she remembered the unspoken Charlotte and Preston incident: In college, they had all met up one weekend in New York, and had ended up in the lobby of the Royalton after a long night of drinking. Evelyn was coming back from the bathroom when she saw Charlotte pull Preston's face down to hers and kiss him soundly on the mouth. Evelyn froze as Charlotte leaned in for more, but Preston pulled back and, not unkindly, patted Charlotte on the head then offered her some water. When Evelyn shook off her shock and rejoined them, both were settled into the Royalton's deep white chairs, conversing about where Preston could find cigars. Neither Charlotte nor Preston had ever mentioned it. Preston kept so much under wraps that that wasn't a surprise, but Charlotte never talking about it made Evelyn wonder how significant that kiss was in Charlotte's mind.

"Anyway, I'm not sure we need Phil Giamatti's take on it. Like, thanks, thought police," Evelyn said.

"Here, you're going to break that." Charlotte rose to fasten Evelyn's clasp. "I think Preston's just not into the whole dating thing."

"Right," Evelyn said. "Right."

"Want to know my opinion of Preston's demons?" Charlotte asked. "I think it's that he doesn't have a real job."

"Good work with the clasp, Char," Evelyn said, adjusting the necklace slightly. "Doesn't Pres manage his family's money?"

"'Independent investor'? I love Preston, but it's the modern-day equivalent of flâneur or saloniste or something. What rich boys do to amuse themselves."

"He's so smart, though."

"Right. He is. He's super smart, but since he doesn't have to work, it's like there's nowhere for that smartness to go."

"Oh, the curse of money."

"Yeah. Tough life. So, G and Ts on the boathouse porch?" Charlotte said, laughing as she slipped on her flip-flops. Evelyn headed down to the boathouse along a side path, Charlotte skipping ahead of her. The sun had finally appeared just in time for golden hour, and it perched on the crest of the mountains across the lake, lighting everything and everyone with Hollywood rose-gold. Preston stood behind a wooden bar in the corner of the porch, mixing drinks. Chrissie had made the mistake of finally deciding to take a sailboat out, but too late, which meant she would miss drinks, which meant Mrs. Hacking would be angrier with her than she already was. The rest were settling into their roles: Preston the attentive host, Nick the caustic friend, Charlotte the tough single girl, Bing the booming frat boy, Mr. Hacking the quiet intellectual, Chrissie the person they were all apparently siding against. And Evelyn, the perfectly pleasing houseguest.

"So, Evelyn, was the train up with Scot killer?" asked Nick. "I'm impressed you're still responding to verbal cues."

"I thought he was your friend," Evelyn said.

"Scot's the man Nick wants to be, basically," Charlotte said. "Pres, can you get Ev a little something-something?"

"For fuck's sake, Hillary, he's not the man I want to be." Evelyn had forgotten about Nick's moniker for Charlotte—Hillary, after Clinton.

"Whatever. Matter of time. Scot's much adored at Morgan Stanley, Ev—a protégé of David Greenbaum—so Nick thought he'd take him to see the sporting life for the weekend," Charlotte said, then made exaggerated kissing noises.

"Who's David Greenbaum?" Evelyn said.

"The head of the media group, which Nick has been trying to get into. Greenbaum's probably going to be the next chairman of Morgan Stanley and then the next Treasury secretary someday."

"You want to do media?" Evelyn said to Nick.

"I want to do power," Nick said.

Evelyn widened her eyes at Charlotte. This was why she generally avoided seeing Nick.

"The kid's from, like, Arizona and presumably has never seen a lake. I thought it might be nice. A little Fresh Air Fund," Nick said.

"I don't think a VP at Morgan Stanley is in need of your Fresh Air Fund, Nick," Charlotte muttered.

"No one asked you, Hill. So you've been hiding from the social life, Evelyn. What's new?"

Evelyn hated answering this question, since she rarely had much new to report—would he like to discuss whether she should get the Crate & Barrel couch in the sand or in the snow fabric? This time, though, she was prepared. "I just got a new job, actually," she said.

"Oh, yeah? Too bad, I was going to give you a book idea. You wanna hear it? It's on why Bernanke sucks."

"Right," Evelyn said. She had worked in marketing at a textbook publisher, doing research on market trends and creating presentations for buyers, but no matter how many times she had told that to Nick, whenever she saw him he offered lame ideas for business books. "The site is pretty interesting. We're in stealth mode, so I can't say too much." She had heard Arun refer to the site as being in stealth mode and had thought it sounded absurd but predicted, correctly, that this would pique Nick's interest.

"Stealth mode?" he said. "Do tell."

"Well, I have to be careful about what I say—our backer is high profile—but think a super elite Facebook. It's pretty restrictive in terms of membership, though—oh, excuse me for a second, would you?" Evelyn walked off, hoping she'd left Nick wanting more. Charlotte had gone to the bar, standing on her tiptoes and talking to Preston, and Evelyn joined them.

"Beer? We have Ubu, though be warned it has the alcohol level of straight liquor," Preston said.

"Gin and tonic," Evelyn said.

"Gin and tonic?" Preston repeated, surprised.

"Yes." Evelyn could see Charlotte's questioning look but ignored it. They then heard a crash, as Scot had apparently tripped and caught himself on the screen door. His face was deep red as he clung to the flimsy wood-and-screen frame.

"What's his story?" Evelyn asked Charlotte quietly, as Preston cut into a lime and the rest of the group pretended, kindly, not to have seen anything amiss.

"Scot? I don't really know him, but he's really smart. Graystone would hire him in a second. Undergrad somewhere random, HBS a couple years before me, where he met Greenbaum through some professor. I can't remember the story, but Greenbaum recruited him and made him a VP in a hot second. Single, obviously. He's brilliant on deal analysis, apparently. Nick can't stand him, though—Scot's a level above him now—but he's smart enough to get Scot on his side. Blatant suck-up-ery."

"Hmm." Evelyn turned to Preston. "Pres, could you make that two G and Ts?" She stepped into a pool of sunlight and put what she hoped was a placid look on her face.

Charlotte snorted when she saw the beatific smile Evelyn was displaying. "Ev, why do you look possessed?"

"Not possessed, Charlotte, dear. In recruitment mode." PLU was going to need up-and-coming people on the site at some point. It would be smart to at least make the connection now. With the fresh gin and tonic in her hand, Evelyn approached Scot and offered it to him. "I thought you could use a drink after the long train ride," she said.

"Oh. Gosh. Thanks. Thank you." He wrapped his large fingers around it, sloshing some over the side onto Evelyn's hand; she let the liquid sit there rather than wringing it off and risk making him feel even more ill at ease. "I was late because I thought Hamilton's dog treats were cookies and ate some," he blurted.

Evelyn gave him an it-happens-to-everyone smile.

At dinner, served at a long wooden table with antler candelabras, hunting-themed place mats, and stiff wooden-wicker seats, Evelyn practiced. A dinner party with old-money sorts was a series of hurdles that Evelyn had to clear if she wanted to come away from this weekend with PLU members. She remembered much of the etiquette that her mother had burned into her once they moved into Sag Neck, and as she flirt-talked with the ancient neighbors seated on either side of her, she revived her muscle memory to scoop her soup spoon away from her.

Still, she felt like an interloper. She was constantly afraid of using the wrong fork or overreaching for the salt or making some other mistake she wasn't even aware she was making. Like Scot, on the opposite end of the table, who was failing miserably. Evelyn had assumed that he'd have gone through enough HBS and firm dinners to pick up the rules of this set, but she detected as she watched him that he didn't know what he didn't know. He picked up his fork for the appetizer and dug in before anyone else, prompting a loud, "I have picked up my fork," from Mrs. Hacking several moments later. He buttered his bread in one piece; he passed the saltshaker without the pepper; he didn't seem to have any idea what to do with the fish knife during the sole course and left it at the side of his plate.

Part of the game, Evelyn thought as she watched the rest of them separating the sole's flesh from its spine with their fish knives, was to prove that they all knew the same code, that they'd all grown up in the same great country houses using fish knives every night. They hadn't, of course—no one did anymore—but without any actual aristocracy in America, the best those who wanted to be upper class could do was create systems of exclusivity and codes of conduct. She wondered how well she was passing as she used her fish knife to lift a delicate flake of sole from the spine and turned to Mr. Desrochers to inquire about how iron-ore mining had changed in the last decade.

During dessert, Scot used his spoon to break into a chocolate torte and then dumped milk into his espresso shot, earning a sharp cough from Mr. Van Borgh on Evelyn's left.

Scot soon made himself welcome to at least Mr. Hacking, though, given the homework he had done.

"Shuh-shuh-gah is one of the great camps?" Scot was saying.

"It was once," Mrs. Hacking said. "Split up and sold for parts when the Levelings needed money."

"We'll see one of the great camps tomorrow," said Mr. Hacking, an even thinner model of Preston who spent minimal time in the great outdoors but for golfing. He was taking dollhouse-spoon-sized bites of his torte, chewing each bite so mildly and slowly that Evelyn feared they would be at dinner for hours longer. "Camp Sachem. They're having the dinner for the Fruit Stripe."

"I read about that camp," said Scot with excitement. "It was a Rockefeller camp, wasn't it?"

"Thank you for not tipping your chair," Mrs. Hacking said to her husband, who righted himself quickly.

"No, you're thinking of Wonundra," Mr. Hacking said. "Sachem was owned by, among others, the Stokes family, the merchant line. A daughter inherited everything and then married into the Hennings, who, of course—"

"The Beech-Nut fortune!" Scot said, unable to contain his excitement.

Mr. Hacking looked immensely sad that his punch line had been stolen, and he gave a dour nod.

"The Beech-Nut fortune was a grand fortune," Mr. Van Borgh opined through what sounded like ounces of phlegm; Evelyn tried to shield her torte from his spray. "Built much of the Erie Canal. And the Henning girls always married well. A Vanderbilt here, a Hunt there. Smart, I think, to limit the breeding. Kept it in the family."

"What do you mean?" Evelyn asked.

"Primogeniture. The Hennings kept it at one child per generation. One reason why the camp was never carved up between fighting siblings. Direct inheritance. No fuss. Sachem über alles. That's the ticket."

"Hold on," said Charlotte. "They limited the number of kids they had so they could keep the camp in one piece?"

"Yes. Rather clever. Of course, Souse, who owns the camp now, didn't hew to that, did she? At least she had two girls, not two boys. Less of a fuss. Do you sail, child?" Mr. Van Borgh said.

Charlotte looked taken aback by this turn in conversation. "Not really. I mean, I can, but—"

"The Fruit Stripe, that's the Hennings' legacy as well. Souse runs the thing. You ought to race in it Sunday."

"Fruit Stripe? Like the gum?" Charlotte said.

"It's a Beech-Nut gum," Mr. Hacking said. "The company gave a chunk of money for the race years ago, when Souse threatened that either she was going to run for a board seat or the company had to fund this race."

Something snapped into place, and Evelyn turned to Mr. Van Borgh. "Beech-Nut," she said quietly. "Are they related to Camilla Rutherford?"

"Yes, yes," Mr. Van Borgh said, wheezing away. "That's one of the daughters. Camilla is the elder, Phoebe the younger."

Evelyn licked her lips, surprised at the whirr of excitement she was feeling. Camilla had been her top target for the weekend, and here, with barely any work, Evelyn already had an in to meet her. If she could land Camilla Rutherford as a member, she could make Arun and Jin-ho certain they'd hired the right person. "So the Fruit Stripe, that's their thing? The Rutherfords'?" she said.

"Yes, it's always been Souse's event, and she chooses what manner of race it will be each year. Participants have to have a boathouse full of all manner of boats; one year she chose Adirondack guide boats and only a handful of the camps had them at all and could participate. Indeed, Souse even changes what weekend it will be held every summer. When it's a May race, as it is this year, it's dreadful for the poor racers. So very cold. I prefer an August Fruit Stripe, myself," Mr. Van Borgh said.

"Understandably," said Evelyn. Of course the inhabitants of this world, she thought, would constantly change the rules of their race.

CHAPTER FOUR

Camp Sachem

On Saturday, Evelyn roused herself at eight. No one else was up, or rather, those who were up were already gone, pursuing some character-building goal; Charlotte was on a run, and Mrs. Hacking had left a "Help yourself!" note in the kitchen, next to a big bowl of fruit, a thermos of coffee, and a good-looking walnut bread. Evelyn chewed on a piece as she rifled through the *Journal*, which was also sitting there, trying to position herself as an interesting conversationalist tonight; she wasn't sure what Camilla and her ilk would want to talk about. She marched through a story on the teetering housing market and the exurban housing developments that were now in danger, particularly in Arizona and California. Next was a personal-finance story about why adjustable-rate mortgages made sense for middle-income consumers. Finally, the Marketplace section, and a story that Walmart, encouraged by the economy, was trying to go upscale with more expensive milk, neater aisles, and designer clothes. She repeated the tenets of each story back to herself, like she'd done when memorizing Marlowe at Sheffield, then neatly folded the paper so it looked untouched and tucked it back where she had found it.

After a slow round of golf that took up almost the entire day, Evelyn was starving by the time the group was supposed to leave for the party at Camp Sachem. Or the dinner at Camp Sachem—she couldn't figure out precisely what tonight's event was. Invitations at Lake James were always vaguely presented and executed. Sometimes "drinks" meant a glass of wine, and sometimes it meant a formal five-hour dinner crammed with toasts and stories of boarding-school exploits. She wondered if the hostesses of Lake James made their decisions on the spot, evaluating the hardiness of the various houseguests before they promoted them to a full-fledged meal.

Charlotte, who'd fit in a quick dip in the lake after golf, had dashed into the shower, leaving her sweaty golf clothes and wet bathing suit on the floor between the beds. Evelyn nudged them beneath Charlotte's bed with her toe and took a final look at herself in the mirror. She took off her headband, then, last minute, shimmied into the lime Lilly Pulitzer dress she'd brought.

From the laundry room across the hall, she heard Mrs. Hacking taking things out of the dryer. Evelyn walked to the laundry-room door, announcing her presence with a tap on the doorframe.

"Oh, hello, Evelyn!" Mrs. Hacking said, her arms full of sheets. "We were just getting ready to leave. I'm running behind." She wore a double-breasted blazer with brass buttons and white pants, a confidence-inspiring ship's captain.

"What can I do? Do you need me to take those sheets somewhere?" Evelyn said. The day so far had been expensive. Someone had to pay for the dinners and the outings and the drinks, and Evelyn worried it was becoming obvious that that someone was never Evelyn. Preston had paid for the greens fees, Char had covered the golf-club rentals, Scot lunch at the club, and Nick a round of drinks. Chrissie got a pass, as she was Bing's girlfriend. The bottle of Veuve Evelyn had brought up, which cost her $90, had been rendered pitiful when she saw the two cases of it in the Hackings' pantry. She reached for a sheet and began to fold it before Mrs. Hacking could protest. Evelyn would need to offer payment in work if she wasn't going to cover other costs. Evelyn knew her place: she would volunteer for the bad rooms and she would help with the laundry and she would wash the dishes, as she had last night.

When she'd finished the folding, she laid out a box of Parmesan straws from the pantry on a tray, at Mrs. Hacking's direction, and took them down to the dock. Several yards ahead of her, Nick and Preston, in sockless loafers and sunglasses, and Scot, in what appeared to be Tevas, were strolling down to the water over the shallow stone stairs. After the rest of the group gathered on the dock, the smell of gasoline strong, Mr. Hacking, following directions from Mrs. Hacking, shoved the Chris-Craft from the dock and sprang in. Bing was off with some friends of his from Tuck, and Pip had lobbied to stay at home, though she looked like she regretted this decision when Chrissie announced that she would babysit and they could play Scrabble.

Scot sat on the floor of the boat, his long legs jammed up against the motor covering in front of him, and Charlotte sat precariously on the gunwale. As Mrs. Hacking slowly backed out of the boathouse, and Mr. Hacking began to fill plastic tumblers with wine, Evelyn balanced herself next to Charlotte.

"So I'm totally on-plan, Char," Evelyn said.

"With PLU? What, have you signed up Mrs. Hacking?"

"Nope, but the camp we're going to, Sachem? It's Camilla Rutherford's camp and she's, like, target number one for PLU."

"She summahs in Lake James, how mahvelous," Charlotte said. "Who is she?"

"Camilla? Well, she has a bit of a complicated history. She went to St. Paul's—"

"Of course," Charlotte said, biting into her cheese straw. St. Paul's was as preppy as schools came, and Charlotte had become fascinated with it at Sheffield after she swam against them and noted the whole girls' swim team carried monogrammed towels.

"Your favorite. Then Trinity for college, but in her senior year her parents got divorced. You have to have heard of them. It was on Page Six basically constantly. Susan, Souse, is the mother. And her father is Fritz Rutherford."

"Wait, sorry, Rutherford like Rutherford Rutherford? As in, she probably owns founders' shares in J. P. Morgan?"

"Sssshh," said Evelyn, indicating her head toward the Hackings. "Yes."

"And our heroine couldn't even get through Camp Trin-Trin?"

Evelyn had dropped her voice to a whisper. "She ended up getting her degree in Hawaii or Ecuador or someplace. She fled town after the parents' divorce. I looked up the details—apparently it had to do with Fritz's refusal to support the Guggenheim."

"I can't hear you. What was the divorce about?" Charlotte seemed to be increasing her volume on purpose.

"Fritz's refusal to support the Guggenheim," Evelyn hissed, again casting a look over her shoulder to see if Mrs. Hacking had heard her.

"We all think we have our problems, but thank God we don't have husbands who don't support the Guggenheim."

"Charlotte, keep your voice down. She does events for *Vogue*. I think even the heads of PLU will be impressed if I get her."

"I'm not quite sure what to say, Beegan, but I like your moxie," Charlotte said.

Mrs. Hacking slowed the boat as they approached Sachem, which was on a private island in the middle of the lake. Scot and Charlotte began peppering Mr. Hacking with questions about how, exactly, provisions for a private island were supplied, but the wind carried their words past the bow of the boat and the American flag whose wake-wetted fabric slapped against Evelyn's head.

When Mrs. Hacking downshifted again and the boat made grunting leaps toward a dock, Preston sprang out and tied up the Chris-Craft with a few quick knots. The dock was less elegant than Evelyn was expecting, just a wooden roof making a V over a platform with some benches on it, and a long, thin dock bobbing next to it where a variety of motorboats and rowboats were tied up.

Evelyn had gotten out of the boat ahead of everyone else and, trying to look like she knew where she was going, started up a path to an A-frame structure that seemed to be made of giant Lincoln Logs. She heard a whistle from behind her.

"Wrong way, Ev," Preston said.

"Isn't that the house?"

"That's the teepee."

"That's a teepee?"

Mr. Hacking, who had overtaken Evelyn on the uphill path and was studying the house like it was a rare raptor, stepped in. "It's called the Typee. After Melville. Where the men would carouse. Far enough away from the main lodge that they could have their liquor and smoke cigars without the women knowing. The whole hill below it is, legend has it, covered in glass. Can you guess why?"

Evelyn, feeling like she had not done the reading for third-period history, shook her head.

"Liquor bottles," he said, enunciating. "They would throw bottles over the edge of the railing and shoot them."

"Oh." Evelyn looked back down toward the dock, but couldn't see another path; she looked higher up, and saw another house, about three hundred yards above the first one, looming red and large on the hill. "That's the main house, then? Up on the hill?"

"No," Mr. Hacking said, now pleased with his student, "though that's a good guess. That's known as the chalet. The Hennings were, of course, great rivals of the Bluestadts, of the barbed-wire fortune, and the Bluestadts had a place just east of this, on East Lake. From the Bluestadts' house, one could see the top of the hill at Sachem, which at the time held servants' quarters—the servants were on the hilltop because it was farthest from the water, of course. Well, the Hennings were infuriated that the Bluestadt guests would have a view of the servants' quarters, so they built a chalet façade for the servants' quarters just so the Bluestadt guests would not think badly of them."

Charlotte had caught up to them by now. "The egos of these guys. Jesus," she said. "A Potemkin village. Or, I guess, a Potemkin chalet."

"Very good," Mr. Hacking said happily.

"So the main house?" Charlotte asked.

"We came in through the servants' boathouse. Easier to find space there during parties. There's a path to the main house from just off of there. Quite well hidden, really," Mr. Hacking said.

"Yes, God forbid the servants be able to find their masters," Charlotte said.

The rest of the group had already taken off along the path. After a short walk through the woods, the path petered out, with hostas marking the edge of what looked to Evelyn like a fancy Girl Scout camp.

On the water's edge was a huge wooden lodgelike structure, three or four stories high, that was made out of the typical Adirondack-camp logs with bark peeling from them. Across a piece of bright green grass marked with croquet wickets was a similar building, this one smaller and squarer, with a sort of rotunda at one end looking out over the water. Behind that was a tennis court, then more structures— Evelyn counted six in all. The huge red door in the middle of the lodge was open, and there were a few dozen people streaming in and out, leaning over the porch, running down to the water. Children, adults, laughing, talking, moving with ease. She stood for a moment, her sandaled feet tickled by the grass on the side of the path. She had guessed wrong on the dress, as had her mother when Babs had pushed the Lilly. This wasn't Vineyard tennis club; this was Adirondack sensible. One woman was in a fisherman's sweater. Another in a skort. The women looked as rustic as the houses they had come from, in clothes that dirt and water would only ameliorate. Evelyn decided she'd need to rely on her instincts more.

Scot and Mr. Hacking had also paused, though for a different reason.

"It almost looks Swiss," Scot said, sotto voce, to Mr. Hacking as they studied the main lodge.

"Oh, yes, at the time, really the only idea Americans had of the wilderness was what the Swiss were constructing, and from the beams to the small peaked roof, you can see that influence," said Mr. Hacking. "You see this in our camp as well. Notice all of these rustic elements." Evelyn looked at the porch railings, made of branches arranged in pretty crossed patterns using their natural curves, and the planters of hollowed-out tree trunks that flanked the doors, and the peeling-bark logs stacked to make up the house.

"Letting the wild in," Scot said.

"Precisely. This was really a new idea at the time, you'll recall; while the Astors and Belmonts and Vanderbilts were building European-style houses in Newport, these hunting lodges promised something quite different. Inside, you'll see a real tour de force of architecture, with spruce beams made of a single tree supporting the great-room ceiling. And look at this exterior—this is white cedar. It's more than a hundred years old and it still looks fine. It's really expert craftsmanship." Mr. Hacking explained that the Rutherford house had been built in 1880, though it had burned down twice, as every house worth living in on the lake had, and that this version dated from "'aught-nine."

"Wow," Scot intoned. "And the croquet green?"

"That's a story. It would've been, let's see, the great-grandmother, I think, Frances Henning, of course the main heiress to the Beech-Nut fortune. She was the doyenne of the place until her death in 1950—what was it, 'fifty or 'fifty-one? She insisted her guests arrive by sleigh in winter, even after the other private islands were using cars to drive across the ice. She was a serious croquet player, as you can see. Of course, it's a terrible croquet green, but she knew all its bumps and proclivities and would handily beat anyone who dared to play against her."

Evelyn could see all of it in front of her—the croquet games, the sleighs with fur blankets atop, the era when everyone knew who they were supposed to be. She heard a shriek of laughter as a tall girl loped up from the water with a croquet mallet in hand, and Evelyn wondered for a moment whether the ghost of Frances Henning had decided to attend. As the girl got closer, though, Evelyn saw Nick approach and kiss her cheek, and Evelyn knew that she knew that long caramel hair, and she recognized that voice, sun-soaked and deep gold.

"Camilla," she said quietly, watching as the girl threw herself over a red Adirondack chair at the side of the croquet green.

"We have to check out this house," Charlotte said, starting to head for the door. "This is seriously historic-preservation status."

Evelyn's eyes were fixed on the croquet green. The light was strange, silvery and still, and the air smelled rich and wet, of cinnamon and dirt and leaves. Camilla was now playing croquet with Nick.

"They know each other?" Evelyn asked.

"Who? Nick? Oh, shit, that's your girl?"

"Camilla, yeah. Do you know how Nick knows her?"

"Ev, I barely know who this girl is. I definitely don't know how Nick knows her. I want to go to check out the inside. Mr. Hacking was saying it was awesome."

"Great," Evelyn said, watching Camilla lean on her mallet. It was not so much Camilla Rutherford's looks, which were pretty, or her body, which was toned and long limbed and moved elegantly. It was that Camilla Rutherford was eminently comfortable. She had not thought twice about what to wear or what to say, Evelyn could tell, unlike her.

Evelyn heard a rattle of ice cubes behind her. Preston was surveying the croquet with amusement. "Fine romance, eh?" he said.

"You mean Nick?" Evelyn said.

"Oui. Et Mademoiselle Rutherford."

"They're not . . ."

"They're doing the dance of love, et cetera."

"Nick and Camilla Rutherford? Really? How did they meet?"

"At a benefit. Kidney Cares, I think. Or Liver Cares. Whichever is the popular organ that all those girls are involved in."

"Is the liver an organ?"

"Do I look like an anatomist?"

"So they're hooking up? Or dating?"

"Good God, woman, I don't know. Do you think you should have The Talk with them?"

Evelyn took Preston's drink and sipped from it; then, when he cried out in protest, handed it back. She followed Preston indoors but kept glancing back at Camilla.

Inside, Evelyn understood what the lines and logs and decor of the Hacking camp were drawn from. Sachem's central room could legitimately be called a great room, versus the marketing-speak used to sell condos, wherein a "great room" meant a single living/dining room. It smelled of library-book pages and peaty smoke. Broad horizontal windows looked out over the lake, and all the coffee-table books and Navajo pillows and thick blankets looked so casually strewn about that Evelyn suspected they probably were, not carefully placed just before the party.

An antler chandelier hung from above, and a giant fireplace made up of flat, broad gray stones hulked over the side of the room. Mr. Hacking was squatting in front of it.

"Very good, isn't it? You see a lot of these fireplaces, but the masonry here is hard to match. Do you see why?" he said. Evelyn looked to Scot, the straight-A student, to answer, but Mr. Hacking beat him to it. "The mortar!" Mr. Hacking said. "It's very thin. It shows skilled work. Most fireplaces like this have mortar of a centimeter or more. This, no. Fine work."

Charlotte was eager to go see the dining room, in a separate building from the main house, and she, Scot, and Mr. Hacking hurried off. Evelyn turned toward the room. People were milling, talking. She heard one woman say that she would never touch turnip, and another say how much she hated Portland. It wasn't just Camilla who had that sense of belonging. All of these people did. Everyone knew what to do, what to drink, what to talk about. They knew what they liked and what they did not (Portland and turnip the beginning of a no-doubt long list). There were other things Evelyn couldn't see that were surely going on, she knew—alcoholism here, an affair there—but their rules protected them and kept everything running so smoothly.

Adjustable-rate mortgages? Why had Evelyn been reading about adjustable-rate mortgages? These people didn't care about that. She had no idea what she was supposed to say to any of them, and she was going to return to PLU a total failure because she couldn't manage to think of anything that would interest these people and she certainly couldn't sign them up. Evelyn felt as if there were a large neon arrow over the thin-mortared fireplace pointing down to her and blinking OUTCAST—OUTCAST—OUTCAST.

The warmth of fingertips on her elbow made Evelyn start. She snapped her head to see the woman she'd been watching minutes ago who'd been dissing turnips, a brunette in a gray pearl necklace. She looked familiar in that way that Evelyn found rich white women did; perhaps she'd seen her in one of Barbara's *Town & Country* back issues, or her doppelgänger had umpired at an Eastern Tennis Club match Evelyn had played in. "I always think the opening moments of a party are the hardest, before everyone has had enough to drink," the woman said.

Evelyn knew a life rope when she saw one and clutched on gratefully. "So true," she said. "Though I'm not sure we can safely say that everyone here has not had enough to drink."

The woman laughed, a rich, cigar-smoke sound. "I'm Margaret Faber," she said, extending her hand.

"Evelyn."

"It's nice to meet you, Evelyn. And how do you know the Rutherfords?"

"I'm staying with the Hackings, on West Lake. I went to Sheffield with Preston, one of their sons," Evelyn said, watching Margaret closely to monitor her response, and saw Margaret's mouth turn up.

"Sheffield," said Margaret. "Marvelous place."

Open sesame, thought Evelyn, and continued, "Everyone at camp is very excited for the Fruit Stripe. Mrs. Hacking is quite determined that we'll make a good showing."

"Knowing Jean Hacking, I can assure you that the camp had better make a very good showing. Are you racing?"

"Ah, no," Evelyn said. "I'll be spectating."

"Do you know, I think I will, too," Margaret said. "I don't have any interest in getting drenched at my age."

The woman's kindness had lifted Evelyn, and she felt like she might actually be able to handle this. Seeing Mr. Van Borgh coughing into a napkin, she excused herself to talk to him, persuading him to walk outside with her so Camilla might see her with a Lake James elder. After a conversation with Mr. Van Borgh and Maisie somebody and Wim somebody else, who were trying to sort out the best treatment for tartar on dachshunds, Evelyn turned toward the croquet game, which Camilla and Nick were just wandering away from.

She planted herself in Camilla and Nick's path, in front of a table filled with cheeses. She showed her back to Camilla first, so it wouldn't seem like she was trying to wedge her way in, and then reached for a cheese knife at the same time as Nick.

"Oh, excuse me," Evelyn said, and flicked her eyes up. "Oh! Nick! Sorry."

"NBD, Evelyn," Nick said. "Get down with your Roquefort."

"Thanks." Evelyn smeared a wedge of cheese on a hunk of bread, and then let her eyes go to Camilla. "Oh! Hello." She looked to Nick expectantly.

"You two know each other? Camilla Rutherford, Evelyn Beegan."

Evelyn let Camilla, as the higher-status person, extend her hand first, a Babsism she remembered. "Thank you so much for having us. We're staying with the Hackings. You know Preston Hacking, I'm sure? It's so nice to formally meet you."

"Nice to meet you," said Camilla. On her wrist, a gold charm bracelet, with what resembled tiny waffles hanging off it, jangled as she grasped a drink that looked to be a Dark and Stormy.

"I love your bracelet," Evelyn said, trying to hold on to the conversation before Camilla got distracted. "What are those?"

"Oh, Racquet Club championships. That my grandfather won. It was my grandmother's," Camilla said.

"Amazing," Evelyn said. She let the importance of the bracelet sink in; the Racquet Club, still, defiantly, men only, still elite, still so traditional it allowed members to swim nude. Of course, everyone in the know would know precisely what Camilla was wearing and precisely why it was so much more valuable than a bracelet of rubies or diamonds. Camilla gave it a musical shake.

"My grandfather was a serious court-tennis aficionado," Evelyn said, so fast that once the words were out, she didn't know how to explain them. She barely even knew what court tennis was, only that it had arcane rules and was extraordinarily preppy.

"Really? Where did he play?"

"Oh, in Baltimore, before it urbanized." In truth, her grandfather had been an accountant who hadn't gone to college and who'd left his family when her mother was a kid, and Evelyn doubted he'd even played regular tennis. She hoped desperately that Camilla wouldn't ask for specifics; luckily, Camilla, warming up, wanted to talk about her own foray into court tennis.

When Nick weighed in on the cork core of court-tennis balls, Evelyn took the opportunity to cast her eyes around the lake. Evelyn's eyes passed over one camp and then the next. When she was ready, she lifted her chin at Camilla's empty glass.

"I think Camilla could use another drink, Nick, my dear," Evelyn said.

"Oh, of course. Just a minute." Nick headed off toward the bar.

"It's so interesting about Camp Piemacum, isn't it?" Evelyn said, moving closer to Camilla and throwing out one of the camp names she had heard on the boat ride over.

Camilla narrowed her eyes. "What about Piemacum?"

"Are the owners here?"

"The Pratts? No, they're in Maine for their daughter's wedding."

"Ah." That made things easier. "I'd heard that the head of NBC, or was it the head of ABC, had made an unsolicited offer on the camp, but it was contingent on his building an Italian villa on the grounds."

"Really?" Camilla cut herself a corner of blue cheese, but was observing Evelyn as she picked it up. "Don't they have a conservation easement? I thought that limited what they could do with the land."

Evelyn fluttered her hands in the air; she needed to stay vague. "That might be right. I thought someone posted about it on People Like Us, but, honestly, I'm terrible with details. It may not even have been Camp Piemacum. Maybe it was something in Upper St. Regis?"

Camilla ate the cheese with tiny bites. She was absorbed in the party and didn't seem to be interested in what Evelyn was saying, and Evelyn was trying to think of another way in. Then Camilla said, "Posted about it where?"

Evelyn let out a tiny exhale. "People Like Us. It's a site for influencers to connect with one another. I work there, actually. It's cool. Travel tips, and where to buy certain hard-to-find things. People are able to track down their best friends from summer camp in Switzerland in 1992, that sort of thing. I thought someone posted about the transaction in the real-estate section, but I could be wrong."

"I haven't heard of it. The site," Camilla said. She cocked her head, considering.

"It's invitation-only for the moment, so it's quite small. They're focused on signing up just a few key influencers in each social circle. If you're interested, I'd be happy to pull a few strings. They'd love for you to weigh in on fashion."

Camilla took her time before she said, "I also know a lot about the arts."

"Absolutely. The arts. People would love to read what you have to say."

"People Like Us, you said?"

"Here." Evelyn pulled a card from her clutch, happy that she had sprung for the heavy card stock. "I'll have my staff set up your whole profile. You won't have to do a thing, except, of course, let people know what your take is on fashion shows. Or, better, art shows."

When Nick returned with the Dark and Stormy and pulled Camilla away, Evelyn chewed her lip for a moment, then got another gin and tonic, which she drank fast enough to get hiccups. Through the rest of the party, she kept track of where Camilla was as though the girl were a potential beau: talking to a younger blond girl, who must be her sister, Phoebe; hooking arms with Nick.

Later, while a Chubby Checker record played, Evelyn tracked down Preston, who set down his gin-and-something, leapt into the air with the grace of a crane, and offered his hand to Evelyn. As they did their rote prep-school swing dance, she appraised the other dancers on the lawn. They would all go home tonight to imposing houses, and over breakfast tomorrow discuss the evening, remembering the glasses of champagne and gin that caught the twinkling lights, and feel secure in who and where they were. They had been nice to her, that was the surprising thing. She thought they'd be cutting, and they were kind. Welcoming.

Evelyn, spinning as Preston increased the pressure of his hand against her upper back to turn her, saw Scot's gawky figure outlined before the black Adirondack lake. Preston spun her again so her eyes settled not on Scot but on Camilla, now standing on the sidelines, taking a delicate bite from a radish.

CHAPTER FIVE

A Bottle of T

Wearing two coats unearthed from a Shuh-shuh-gah closet, Evelyn sat vibrating with cold in the motorboat as the Fruit Stripe got under way. Bing was racing with a neighbor boy, despite pleas from Pip to race with her (the neighbor boy weighed less, and thus Bing's boat would move faster), which left Pip paired with Chrissie. Mrs. Hacking had stopped by Camp Jumping Rock, where the Fruit Stripe reception was being held, to load up on drinks before heading out to the course, and Nick, Scot, Charlotte, and Mr. Hacking had stayed at Jumping Rock to help with sending off the boats.

Evelyn had volunteered to go with Preston and Mrs. Hacking, mostly because Scot, at the party last night, had cornered Evelyn and asked for her phone number and then had been unable to talk to her in the boat back or at breakfast this morning, and Evelyn wanted to avoid more stiff encounters. However, now, stuck with Mrs. Hacking in the motorboat, Evelyn saw the wisdom in remaining on land.

Mrs. Hacking, wearing a wide-brimmed maroon rain hat and a Dole-Kemp sweatshirt, scanned the sails for the ones from her camp, all marked with blue stripes. It was a chilly Adirondack day, and the race participants wore heavy foul-weather gear but for Chrissie, who had unwisely worn a silk scarf on her head as though she was starring in the "True Love" scene of *High Society*. The one time Evelyn had watched the race before—the time of the badly rigged boat that she would apparently never live down—she had assumed that the Fruit Stripe was a serious race. Now she knew the drill better. The day before the race, all the older teenagers and twentysomethings on the lake would go to the host's house to help mix drinks. They would pour into paint buckets one bottle after another of lemonade, cranberry juice, or white-grape juice with a dump of green food coloring. Varying amounts of vodka were added, mixed, and then poured back into the juice bottles, now evoking the colors of Fruit Stripe gum packages, with a mark on them of *V* for "virgin," *S* for "strong," and *T* for "toxic." The drinks were stored in an ice-filled canoe onshore during the race, and last time, Evelyn had spent the awards ceremony hurling into the shrubbery at Camp Georgia after selecting a bobbing bottle marked *T* from the canoe and thinking it meant "tame."

Most of the racers took the Fruit Stripe lightly, taking a bottle of T with them and, when the wind was too weak, using a paddle to move around the course and happily disqualifying themselves. However, Mrs. Hacking had a Yankee reverence for outdoor sport, and expected Shuh-shuh-gah's residents and guests to win, place, or come in last. First place meant possession of the Lake James Yacht Club trophy for a year, second meant she got to hang the Fruit Stripe banner from her boathouse, and last meant the racers got all the leftover drinks. A boat from her camp coming in second to last, which showed the racers had neither skill nor wit, made Mrs. Hacking turn red with fury.

In the back of the pack, in a dead spot on the lake, Evelyn saw the blue-striped sail that belonged to Chrissie and Pip. Mrs. Hacking gunned the motor, spraying freezing water onto Evelyn and Preston.

In under a minute, the motorboat was circling the sailboat. Though it was not long after the start, Chrissie's boat had taken on several inches of water already, and Chrissie was trying to bail out the boat with a travel coffee mug while Pip lay miserably on the bow of the Sunfish.

"Your line in the water is too low. Bail her out. Bail her out!" Mrs. Hacking said.

"I'm bailing!" Chrissie shouted. "We got off course!"

"Look to starboard, Chrissie. You're getting pushed into shore." The wake from the boat was rocking the Sunfish, and Pip wrapped her arms around the hull. Mrs. Hacking had procured a megaphone from somewhere inside the motorboat and now began booming into it. "Chrissie! The wind is coming from the west side of the lake. Come about. Come about!" With her other hand, Mrs. Hacking spun the steering wheel so she stayed nipping at the sailboat's side. "Pip, show Chrissie what to do!" she yelled.

Pip pushed the brim of her raincoat hood back. "I'm trying, Grandmother," she said, resigned.

"Come, Chrissie, look at the angle. Look at the angle. You'll never get out of it now! Grab the rudder—watch it—watch it—no, no, no, no! Good Lord! Watch it!" Mrs. Hacking shouted as the boom swung over and nearly cracked Chrissie in the head; Chrissie desperately shoved the rudder back and forth. "I thought Bing said she knew how to sail," Mrs. Hacking said to Preston, though she said it into the megaphone. Preston took a long drink of his cranberry juice, the T version. Evelyn reached for the bottle and took a swig in sympathy— with Chrissie, with Bing, with Pip, or with Preston, she wasn't sure— but she was trying not to move too abruptly, lest Mrs. Hacking turn the megaphone on her.

"It's luffing. It's luffing!" Mrs. Hacking shouted as a wave came up and hit Chrissie in the arm. "Everyone else is around the third buoy, Chrissie! You've got to get out of there! This is a dead spot. Get out of there!"

"Can I get back in the boat with you, Grandmother?" Pip called out.

"I wish you could, Pip, but you're going to have to finish the race."

A horn sounded from the other end of the lake. "That's first place!" Mrs. Hacking yelled. "We have to get back to the party! Get some wind, Chrissie. You're going to be out here for hours!" Pip, lying flat on her stomach in the front, waved a sad farewell.

Mrs. Hacking gunned the motor again, heading toward Jumping Rock, and the wake deposited a few more inches of water in the sailboat once the motorboat left. Evelyn looked back, watching Chrissie get smaller. Chrissie was overly anxious and had made her own mistake in forcing an invitation to the Hacking house, claiming sailing know-how, and generally trying too hard. And Chrissie's presence on the other side of the invisible behavior line let Evelyn stay cleanly on this side of it. Yet, looking at Chrissie dipping her cup into the freezing water that went up to her ankles, with the patrician girl in the front who was doubting her every effort, Evelyn wished a gust of wind would come and help them out.

"Simpsons are moving ahead! Tom Junior is behind you with Lally!" Mrs. Hacking cried as the motorboat skipped away.

At Jumping Rock, Evelyn jumped out of the boat and ran up to safer ground. Nick was about ten drinks in and had decided the path to the Jumping Rock guesthouse should be marked with cairns, and he enlisted Preston in gathering stones from the woods. Tired, Evelyn retreated to the boathouse deck with a bottle of S green punch, settling into a deep Adirondack chair. She was drunk enough forty minutes later that she could almost tamp the uneasiness she felt about the finish. Bing was lingering just to the side of the finish line in his boat, and when he saw Chrissie and his daughter finally coming toward the line, he made another loop so he could come in last, and his daughter and girlfriend would get the dreaded second to last. As Evelyn listened to the air horn marking Chrissie's place, then the second air horn marking Bing's, she exchanged the S for a T. Bing stood up in his boat to laughs and applause from the shore, bowing. Phoebe and Camilla flew down to give him hugs, and Mrs. Hacking, who'd brought her megaphone onto land, yelled her congratulations into it.

Evelyn looked for Chrissie and saw her trudging up the hill, her wet and wilted scarf still glopped around her head.

Evelyn scrambled to her feet and hurried to the boathouse bathroom, where she grabbed one of the stacked beach towels she'd noticed earlier. "Hey," she said when she'd caught up to Chrissie. "You must be cold. I thought you could use this."

Chrissie turned, soaked, as Evelyn held out a towel.

"That was so awful," Chrissie said, wiping her eyes. "So awful. So wet, and so long, and then Bing . . ." She trailed off.

Evelyn shook out the towel with one hand and draped it around Chrissie's shoulders, and Chrissie clutched at it. "Thank you," Chrissie said.

Evelyn had brought the bottle of T, and held it out to Chrissie with a sympathetic smile. "It's strong," she offered. "I can't promise your problems will go away, but at least you'll be drunk when you see everyone back at Shuh-shuh-gah."

Chrissie considered this, then poured the T down her throat. When she handed the bottle back to Evelyn, Evelyn took a long drink, too.

Sag Neck

It was the long July Fourth weekend, and Camilla's profile, created by Evelyn, had gone live on PLU two days prior. Evelyn had chosen a fabulous profile picture of Camilla and, via the overpaid PR consultant the site had hired, had parlayed that into a Page Six mention: "WE HEAR . . . that saucy socialite Camilla Rutherford has joined People Like Us, and other people like her are clamoring for the site's coveted invites." She had put up a page for Nick, too, and Bing, and had even managed to start a lively discussion about Adirondack real estate so that Camilla would have a harder time figuring out that she had been bluffing about Camp Piemacum. Evelyn was starting to get unsolicited bids for profiles and, in approving members one by one, she approved many but turned down a few without explanation, as the random rejections would make the acceptances all the more appealing.

Barbara had made it clear that she didn't want Evelyn coming home over the summer at all, really—it was the season to be hopping between summer spots and meeting a future husband. Their conversations had been stilted lately. Evelyn had called after Lake James, brimming with excitement over how well things had gone there and wanting to describe the parties and the dinners that she thought her mother would love hearing about. Her mother had instead responded that she had never been very interested in sales. Her father was no better, asking if she was still hanging around with socialites. "In my day, you didn't get paid for that," he said.

Evelyn hadn't called back since and was surprised to get a message from her mother summoning her home for the Fourth of July. It was Sally Channing's annual blowout for patriotism—Tommy Channing was a partner at her father's law firm, Leiberg Channing—and the family wanted Evelyn home for it. Evelyn briefly thought about disobeying and heading to Nick's house in the Hamptons instead. Yet this new world required a lot more money than Evelyn had; she needed a loan from her parents, and if she needed a loan she'd have to submit to their rules, at least briefly.

She got off the Amtrak at New Carrollton, Maryland, where the summer air hung heavy around her, and she felt like she was breathing cotton. She had called her father en route, both on his cell phone and at his office, but he hadn't responded. As the heat evaporated the train's air-conditioning sheen from her skin, she began to sweat. Lifting her bag to her shoulder, she circumnavigated the parking lot. When she passed a vaguely familiar tan Datsun, and saw a broad-shouldered woman standing next to it, Evelyn recognized the woman as Valeriya, the disapproving Russian woman who had taken over as Sag Neck housekeeper a few years ago.

"Hello! Eveline!" Valeriya called, raising her hand lethargically.

"Hi. Valeriya. My parents aren't here?"

"Please, put your bag in trunk, not in backseat. I think in backseat it will have too much dirt and I will have to clean again."

Evelyn complied and arranged her bag so it didn't quite touch the pair of Chinese slippers and grocery bag of vinyl gloves in the trunk. She hopped in the back and saw the outline of a man's head in the passenger seat.

"My husband, Alexei, he is here, too. He does not like me to drive alone in the night. There was a, what do you say, robbing of car with the lady in it on the highway last week."

Alexei, with short blond hair cut Hitler Youth–style and a leather jacket folded in his lap, raised a hand in a wordless greeting.

"Valeriya, thanks for driving me, but my father was supposed to pick me up. Is he working?"

Valeriya took a fast, screeching right turn out of the parking lot. "Your father, *pffft*. He comes home and they are having fight."

"Tonight? They were having a fight tonight?"

"Tonight, last night, every night. I tell Alexei that the American wives are very difficult with their husbands. In Russia, the women are not difficult like this. It makes for the fighting."

"Wait, it was last night? Or tonight? Wasn't he supposed to be in Wilmington until this afternoon?" Her father usually spent weekdays at his apartment in Wilmington, where his law firm was based.

"My first husband, in Russia, he always say that Russian women are most strong-headed of women. But I think this is not true. My first husband, he is easy at the house, and clean, clean like a woman, but he drinks. Vodka. What can you do? So I leave, and I am here." She lay a fist on the horn, startling a pedestrian who looked up in alarm and sprinted across the street.

"But, Valeriya, you said my dad came home already?" Evelyn asked.

"Your father, yes, he come already. Thursday. Wednesday."

"He's been there for two days? What has he been doing there?"

"I tell you that it is difficult. Your mother, she close the door to her room and she tell me, from side of door, she would not let me clean inside, which is difficult because she need help. She say, Valeriya, was a mistake to marry this man. This is what she say."

"What? Valeriya." Evelyn believed her mother had said that; she just didn't believe she'd said that to the housekeeper. Her mother observed distinct caste lines, and with "the help"—she actually called them "the help"—spoke slowly and with an exaggerated smile. "Sorry, so, my father has been home since Wednesday?"

"I tell you only what she say. I say to her, Mrs. Barbara, it is hard on the woman always. They argue over the charges. The charges this, the charges that," Valeriya said.

"Wait, the charges? That's what they've been arguing about?" Evelyn drummed her fingers against the window, then stopped when she saw Valeriya was glaring at the fingerprints she left. Her parents helped her out with money here and there, but the only charges she'd made on her parents' credit card in the last couple of weeks were ones she'd specifically cleared with them. She'd bought a ticket to a bene-fit for underprivileged kids on their card expecting she could ex-pense it, but Ann, the HR and administration person at PLU, had rejected her expense report, saying that Evelyn would have to pay for benefit tickets herself as they weren't a direct business expense. She'd had to buy a dress for the benefit, too, as her dowdy black dresses wouldn't work for a summer party, and had spent another $200 at Bloomingdale's on that. Her father had said that he didn't think they should cover these kinds of things, so she had promised to pay him back but couldn't quite afford to at the moment, as her PLU salary was so low. Valeriya's comments weren't a promising start given that she needed to extract even more money from her parents this week-end. "They're fighting about the charges, Valeriya? On their Master-Card?"

"The MasterCard? No, it was not this." Valeriya switched to rapid Russian, and Alexei was making soothing sounds of assent. Evelyn nestled up against the side of the Datsun. As words like "MasterCard" and "Bloomingdale's" and "benefit" softly started bumping into each other in her head, she closed her eyes and fell into a fitful, clammy car nap.

She was jostled awake as the car passed onto the Chesapeake Bay Bridge, and her droopy eyelids opened to see the vertical cables that marked the decreasing distance between herself and her hometown of Bibville. She drifted off again, and when she opened her eyes, Valeriya was rattling up the gravel drive to Sag Neck, Evelyn's house. Valeriya did not turn off her engine, and Evelyn had evidently made some faux pas, because Valeriya was curt when Evelyn said good-bye; Alexei, however, wished her a thick, "Good luck to you."

Sag Neck was a mansion, Evelyn had said when they moved there when she was in elementary school, until her mother told her not to use the word "mansion." It was a grand wooden house with lines of trees protecting it from its neighbors, with a gentle slope in the back down to Meetinghouse Creek. Downstairs was an imposing central hallway two stories high, marked by a chandelier and a thick wooden staircase. To the left was the living room, an underused library, and a formal dining room overlooking the grass and then the creek. To the right was the large piano room—Barbara called it a ballroom, but no ball had taken place there under their reign—that ran the length of the house. The kitchen was tucked into the back. It had been a massive upgrade from the house Evelyn had been born in, a split-level in the D.C. suburb of Silver Spring with brown walls and brown cabinets and brown grass, which they'd all happily left behind after her father started winning his big cases.

The door to Sag Neck was unlocked, and swollen with moisture, as it always was in summer. When Evelyn yanked the door open, the house was silent inside.

"Hello? Mom? Dad?"

"Evelyn, is that you?" Her mother's voice came from upstairs somewhere.

"What's going on? Why didn't Dad pick me up? I had the strangest ride with Valeriya and her husband."

"Yes, why didn't your father pick you up?"

Evelyn was tired and not in the mood to play her mother's word games. "Do you know where he is?"

"I don't know anything your father does, apparently." She heard a door shut, and a lock slide, and that was it for Evelyn's welcome home.

"Mom?" she tried once more, but there was no answer. Evelyn flipped on a row of light switches and headed back to the kitchen. Her head was inside a lower cupboard, where snacks could sometimes be found, when the sudden clatter of the back door sent Evelyn's head smashing against the cupboard's top. Dale Beegan burst through the door, sweating, panting, in alarmingly tight bike shorts, and almost tripped over his crouched-down daughter.

"Jesus H. Christ, Evie, what are you doing hiding out in the kitchen like a scurrying rat? Stand up and be seen!"

"Ow. I would have, if I'd known you were going to startle me like that," Evelyn said, touching the back of her head. "I think I have a lump."

Dale headed to the sink and gulped down a glass of water. He still had great hair, brown and thick and glossy, and the plump cheeks of a happy baby. His teeth were very white, as he put on his Crest Whitestrips every evening after dinner and wore them for the recommended thirty minutes without embarrassment. He was starting to look more like Barbara's son than her husband, a change Evelyn knew better than to ever hint at.

"What're you doing, scaring an old man like that?"

"I didn't expect you to be home, since you didn't pick me up and everything."

He filled the glass with more water. "I'm sure you'll be A-OK."

"Let's hope so. So Valeriya said you've been home for a few days?"

Dale plopped his used glass down on the counter. "How is that fine city of yours, Evie? The fancy people you work for giving you an easy time?"

"Actually, the work is somewhat challenging," she said sharply.

"Dealing with rich folks always is," he said. "I've always found it more satisfying to work with people who are struggling, myself."

But you fly first-class to do it, Evelyn thought, ripping open the cardboard top to a box of saltines. Her father had been born in North Carolina, in a textile-mill town, and both of his parents worked at the mill. His family's house was on the other side of the creek from the solid brick houses of the richer management families. Dale said he saw how the mill owners came down on people's lives, and that made him want to become an advocate for the people who couldn't get heard on their own, people like his parents. In his town, the stores downtown closed early, because they wanted to cater to the brick-house wives, who didn't work, rather than the mill-worker wives, who did. Though Dale went to school and church with the brick-house boys, in summers he was the one behind the ice-cream counter, and they were the ones in front of it. Dale determined he'd become a college graduate, and that he'd go into law, and that he'd show those stiff-collared rich boys that everyone deserved a shot.

He'd been in solo practice when Evelyn was younger, when they'd lived in Silver Spring, and became known for consumer lawsuits against big pharmaceutical companies. Leiberg Channing, a large plaintiffs' law firm out of Wilmington, soon offered him a job handling its pharmaceutical lawsuits.

She'd seen her father at various trials, and he was captivating. He didn't use notes, yet took down his opponents with one subtle point after another. He knew what to say to jurors, how to play to their emotions and get them to feel for him as well as his clients. He seemed to know exactly what to say to people everywhere except for the ones at home.

Though her father had made a lot of money on pharmaceutical lawsuits, he couldn't seem to decide whether he was now a big shot, or he still hated big shots the way he had as a mill-town kid. He was into gifts, flashy and meant to make onlookers ooh and ahh. At Sheffield, the monthly box of fruit galettes from Harry & David that he sent were the envy of her dorm, while the giant gold Rolex he'd given her for her Sheffield graduation was embarrassingly expensive and she'd buried it in a box with old yearbooks, then bought herself small pearl studs with saved-up allowance money as her own graduation gift. When and if he spent money, it was always on his terms; he was the moral arbiter, the one who decided what was worthy and what was not, the only one who understood the value of money.

In her postcollege life, her father expected her to support herself, to work in a field he considered worthy, and also to serve the greater good. Evelyn, well aware that social-services jobs would not cover her rent or be prestigious enough to meet with either parent's approval, instead tried, in her first months in New York, to volunteer for a girls' mentoring group. The group had told her that there was a yearlong waiting list for mentors, she would need three professional references, and they'd really prefer someone with more career experience.

She resisted saying any of this aloud; if her father was upset about the credit-card charges, and she needed more money still, she couldn't afford an argument. "So why are you home? Leiberg Channing is allowing teleconferenced trials?" she asked.

"You must be tired from the travel. Let's have a talk in the morning, all right?" he said. He started to leave the kitchen, his used glass still on the counter for someone else to put in the dishwasher.

"If it's the charges, Dad, we might as well talk now." She frowned at the saltines label, as they were the salt-free kind. "You specifically said it was okay to put certain things on your card. And that's a fraction of what New York costs. Honestly, lunch costs eleven dollars, and that's for, like, a salad in a plastic container. I'll pay you back. It's just, with the job and everything, things are a little intense right now."

"I think we'll save it all until the morning," he said. "Good night, honey. Is that a new shirt? It's a nice color on you." It was a new shirt, and as he left the kitchen and walked upstairs, Evelyn, nibbling around the perimeter of a saltless saltine, thought about how her father always managed to throw in something charming that made him impossible to hate.

The next morning, Evelyn decided to get a coffee in town to fortify herself for the argument with her parents. When she hopped off the final stair and onto the ground floor, she saw two figures to her right in the living room, her mother perusing the driveway from the front window, her father shuffling through a stack of papers.

"Evelyn." Her mother turned a few degrees from the window and uncrossed her arms, holding them out like Evita on the balcony of the Casa Rosada, which was her signal to Evelyn to approach for a hug. Evelyn obeyed, and mother and daughter embraced by touching forearms and bobbing heads.

"Hi, Mom. You look pretty," Evelyn said. Her mother, in a gray sweater that was far too heavy for July and a pair of white pants, in fact looked like she had put on weight, and Evelyn was still frustrated with her over the People Like Us slights. After the meandering conversation last night with her father, though, Evelyn figured she would need an ally.

Evelyn waited for instructions, but both her parents were silent. She looked from one to the other. "Well, I was just going to head into town," she began.

"No, Evelyn, your father"—her mother made the noun heavy with sarcasm—"has something to tell you. Sit down."

Her father was in one of his preternaturally relaxed poses, draped across a scratchy wool-upholstered armchair, his right ankle balanced on his left thigh. Evelyn tried to get a glimpse of the papers he was looking at so she could be prepared, but her father stacked them and turned them over, setting them on the coffee table. Evelyn sat on a hard wooden chair near the door.

"Well, glad to see you, Evie," he said, stretching his lips wide. "There's something we need to discuss."

"Something?" Barbara spat from her post at the window.

"You know about my work, and you know that I care about that work, as do my fellow lawyers." He pronounced the first syllable of "lawyer" to rhyme with "raw."

"Our job is to fight on behalf"—and Evelyn could finish the sentence in her head, from the countless times she'd heard her father say it at awards dinners, at parties, to people he had just met—"of people who are too poor or disempowered to have a voice. We've been doing that the best way we know how."

"Is this about my job?" Evelyn said. "Listen, I know—these people do have a voice, I'm not saying they don't. They're really not as bad as you think. They're—well, Mom knows. They can be really nice. It's not sales, anyway. It's membership, which is a different thing. Membership is more coming in at their level. And it was just four hundred and fifty dollars, which, I know it's not great, but it's—"

"Honey, honey," Dale interrupted. He looked at Barbara, but Barbara didn't turn. "It's not about your job. It's about my job. When you fight for people, you make life harder for the people in charge, and guess what, the people in charge then try to go after you. The Republicans are out to show plaintiffs' lawyers how much power they have, and the government found someone who's telling them that we've done some illegal things, that we've made some illegal, ah, illegal offers.

"Now, you have sat in the courtroom as I've argued case after case. You have listened to the witnesses, the expert witnesses. You have listened to the judge. You know how the whole process goes. Why did I bring up expert witnesses? Well, we need those witnesses—often doctors—to explain to the jury the effects that some of the drugs can have on our clients."

"Right," said Evelyn, wary.

"Do you remember the Oney case, Peg Oney out of Cresheim? Remember her, the Wallen Pharma case?"

"Yes," Evelyn said. She had been in middle school then, and she and Barbara had traveled to Pennsylvania to watch her father give opening arguments in the case. The lawsuit was over Wallen knowing but not disclosing side effects for one of its drugs. The case was complicated, full of chemistry and drug-development procedures, but her father made it simple. He had started by describing how Peg lost feeling in her fingertips as a result of taking the drug. "Now, fingertips mightn't seem like much," he said in his thick Carolina accent. "It's not a leg. Not an arm. Not even a hand. But when Peg holds her hand in front of a candle, she doesn't feel warmth. When she goes to pat her dog Scout, she can't feel his fur. When she touches her one-year-old baby's cheek, she doesn't feel his soft skin. Fingertips are just the tips, but fingertips are also the world." He had made every juror feel just what it was like to be Peg, and then he left the podium, walking close enough to the jury box that the jurors in front could touch him. "Right here, in this courtroom, you people of Pennsylvania get to say today to this huge conglomerate, 'We've had enough. You don't get to take our senses from us. You don't get to tell us we can't feel warmth, we can't pat our dog, we can't touch our baby. We've been misled enough, we've been fooled enough, we've been lied to enough. It stops here. It stops today.'" It took jurors fewer than three hours to award Peg Oney an enormous sum.

"Peg's injuries, the effect on her body, were complicated," Dale was saying now as he neatened his stack of papers. "To hold Wallen responsible, we had to have experts tracing exactly what Wallen had tested, exactly what they knew, exactly what the effects were on Peg and the other plaintiffs. You've got to have good experts and we searched high and low for the right ones, a doctor and a chemist, who offered very compelling trial testimony. The award in that case, Evie, was significant for the Oneys. Very significant."

And for us, Evelyn thought; she remembered overhearing her parents discussing the millions her father had won as his portion in that case, and her mother had hired an interior designer to revamp Sag Neck, from wallpaper to chandeliers, just after that. "So what's the issue?" she said.

"Peg's husband, ex-husband by then, later asked us to look into another pharmaceutical case. I don't think he saw much of the verdict money, and he was angry. He was hurt. He, I now believe, was seeking revenge on Peg, and he chose us for his revenge. He told us at the time that he was doing some pharmaceutical investments and uncovered what he thought were questionable quality-control policies at one of the big firms and came to us with the hopes that we could make a case out of it. We looked into it and filed a case, and it ended up settling fast. The ex-husband apparently was not satisfied, though we'd done our damnedest to help him and his family and his town. When the government came knocking he said that we, that Leiberg Channing, were bribing these experts to give the testimony they gave. The Wallen Pharma case didn't fall within the statute of limitations, but he alleged that these payoffs occurred in his second case.

I think he had little more than a single e-mail where we'd talked about paying these experts, which of course is perfectly legal." Dale leaned back in his chair, as carefree as if he were out tanning on spring break.

"But the government can't make a case out of that," Evelyn said.

Dale directed a smile toward her mother's back that dropped like an unreturned serve. "That's right. I knew you'd get it. There isn't"— he pronounced it "idn't"—"anything there. The pharmaceutical companies are major donors to the Bush administration, and all these Bush prosecutors with their Ivy League schools want to go after the small fry like me who are helping everyday Americans. But the joke's on them, honey. All they've been able to produce after their big investigation is a single ex-husband of an old client who says that we did something illegal years ago. The Bush administration and the Republicans want nothing more than—"

A thwack of a hand against glass. Barbara, at the window: "Will you stop blaming your problems on a Republican conspiracy?"

Dale flipped his palms up to signal that he was being open. "Barbara, we can argue about this all over hell and half of Georgia, but when federal prosecutors can subpoena whatever they like and whoever they like to investigate a firm that is notably hated by their major Republican donors, the connection is not hard to make."

Evelyn looked to her mother, but Barbara was staring down a squirrel outside. Evelyn turned her head back to her father, who was wearing a bright green polo shirt made of a too-thin jersey material that emphasized his ribby midsection.

"So what's going to happen?" Evelyn said.

Dale propped a leg on the coffee table. "They haven't charged the firm or any of the partners, because the evidence—or what they think passes for evidence—is thin grits and they know they can't get anywhere with it. I—your mother, mostly—thought you should hear about this from us, though."

"Then why don't you tell her what's actually happening?" Barbara said, spitting out the words. "Or tell her what to say when she's ignored at the Channings' party today. That's right, you didn't mention that part, did you? Why don't you tell your daughter all about how these Republican prosecutors seem to be focusing on you? Not Tommy Channing, not Larry Leiberg? Or tell her what the government's really looking into—that your firm was doing large-scale bribes, giving the experts a cut of the jury verdict or the settlement, so that maybe, just maybe, they might overemphasize what happened to poor Peg Oney, or poor whomever you're representing?" She was talking so fast that her words slammed together, and when she was done, she leaned against the window frame, looking exhausted.

Dale blinked, the pleasant smile on his face not changing. After a minute, he picked up the conversation again. "Well, secret's out, I guess. Because I was the lawyer handling these cases, from what we can put together, it looks like some of the focus may be on me. Let me be clear, the three of us—Larry, Tommy, and myself—all worked together on all the cases."

"The charges," Evelyn said quickly, shaking her head. "Valeriya. Valeriya said you've been home since Wednesday. That's not normal for you. God. She meant legal charges. What are they?"

"There's a grand jury. Your father is being investigated by a grand jury," Barbara said.

Evelyn stood up so fast that the chair's wooden legs shrieked over the floor. "A grand jury? How long have you known about this?"

"Well, this is an ongoing investigation," Dale said.

"Yes, I understand that. But how long have you known about the grand jury?"

"Months," Barbara said.

"Barbara, many grand jury investigations go on for months," Dale said, his voice sharp. "It doesn't mean it's going to go anywhere."

Evelyn gripped the chair's back. "This doesn't make sense."

"It doesn't," Dale said. He'd modulated his voice now, and it was all brown sugar. "I'm sorry we're just springing it on you now, honey. We didn't think it would go anywhere, and we still don't, but the government's been leaking things to the press, and it was bound to get out."

Barbara turned from the window. "This shouldn't have happened," she said. Her hand was shaking, but her body was still. "This shouldn't have happened."

"Well, it did happen. It is happening." Evelyn was trying to keep her voice even, but it kept modulating unpredictably as though someone else were controlling the volume knob. "It happens that Dale Beegan is being investigated by a grand jury. It happens that maybe you should mention that to your child before several months have gone by. Maybe that would be a good idea."

"We didn't think it was necessary—" Dale said.

"Well, it was. It was necessary."

"Evie, don't get all worked up. The investigation seems stalled in its tracks except for this one unemployed fellow making false claims. We thought we'd talk to you about it in person because we knew you were coming down for the party—"

"And what a lovely party it will be!" Barbara cried, ridding herself of the slight Baltimore accent that she sometimes sank into when tired or angry, and plowing into her Sag Neck chatelaine voice, long Katharine Hepburn vowels mixed with the nasality of Ethel Merman. "Now, Evelyn, what do you say, shall we go to the Channings' party in our Fourth dresses and pretend as though nobody knows your father is being investigated for—what would it be? Money laundering? Bribery? Doesn't that sound like a lark? I'm sure Sally Channing will be just delighted to see us there, this trio of Dale Beegan and his wife and daughter, and give us a warm welcome. Sally's friends will be delighted to see us, too, after reading the fascinating newspaper accounts of how the United States government says you've been breaking the law."

"Barbara. That's enough. I told you, if you want to skip the party, you can," Dale said.

There was something especially troubling in what they had said, swirling above the upside-down idea that her father was being investigated by a grand jury, above the tension in the room, above the dreadful day that was ahead where Evelyn would either be forced to go to this party or forced to stay home with her furious parents. That was it. Newspaper accounts. If this was getting coverage, all her friends could potentially know about it already. They could've been e-mailing it around in the days since Lake James; she could practically see Nick's message: "Looks like someone's life is less perfect than she's pretending." Camilla, too, might be a newspaper reader, and even if she wasn't, with the way everything went online and spread quickly these days, there was no controlling or predicting what would be read by whom. Evelyn would be laughed at. "This is in the papers?" she said in a small voice.

Her mother let out a high-pitched "Ha!"

Her father ran his tongue over his front teeth. "That's what papers do, Evelyn. They try to make something out of nothing."

"In New York? New York papers aren't writing about this, right?"

"I haven't followed it that closely, honey."

"Oh. No." Evelyn backed a few steps away from him and from her mother, moving back toward the thick wooden door to the foyer. "Dad, you're not serious, right? This has been written about? With your name in it?"

"The newspapers are writing about pure speculation. Pure speculation."

"Is your name in it? In the pieces?"

He squinted at her with a big grin, the one he used in summations that she had long ago termed the Bedazzler. "I don't recall whether the papers said my name or the firm's name. It doesn't matter. We all know the truth."

"Do we?" said Barbara as Evelyn backed up a few more steps; she figured if she could just get to the door frame, she could leave without their noticing. She wanted to Google it; she didn't want to Google it. Someone would have said something to her if they'd heard about it in New York. Preston or Charlotte would've mentioned it, and Nick and

Scot probably read only about finance. Definitely only finance. Camilla couldn't be a newspaper reader. Camilla probably didn't even know Evelyn's last name. New York blogs wouldn't care about a Maryland lawyer. It was all right. It would be fine.

"The truth," Barbara was saying loudly, "is that every single person in Bibville knows about what your father has done. Leiberg Channing, champion of the tort cases, darling of the Democratic Party, finally brought to its knees by the Republican government it so hates. Or, let me be specific, not Leiberg, not Channing, but Dale Beegan, who never could manage to get his name on the plaque at 422 North Market."

This stilled the room. Barbara was staring at her husband with eyes that had lost their light. Dale had stopped his fidgeting and was studying his locked-together hands. Evelyn felt the energy draining from her, and the orange-wax smell that Valeriya must have put on the wooden floors seemed like it was getting stronger.

It was her father who finally broke the silence by clearing his throat. He patted his knees. "Well, I'd best be returning to preparing for this deposition. Got any other questions?"

Evelyn shook her head no and raised her eyes toward her mother, who was now looking lost and distracted in the living room. Evelyn tiptoed backward and turned off the lights as she exited.

CHAPTER SEVEN

Social History

Upstairs, Evelyn sat cross-legged in the window seat of her childhood bedroom, looking out toward the creek and the bay grass, watching the neighbors' affenpinscher tussle with a branch just outside of a clump of trees.

Peg Oney's case. That was when her father's career was starting to take off. He came home on weekends sometimes, but just as often he stayed in Beaumont, Texas, or Caddo, Arkansas, or Tallahassee, Florida, places Evelyn looked up in the giant atlas in the piano room. She still thought her father was glamorous then, that his double-breasted suits were fancy and his styled hair made him look like Howard Keel, not that the suits were tacky and the hair was overdone. Sometimes she wished she could still see him like that, like when she was a little girl and she'd slip into his study and pat his smooth leather briefcase as he'd pass her a butterscotch with a wink. She would stay there for a long time sometimes, quietly braiding the fringe of his rug as she listened to him scribble on his yellow pad.

Her parents had met in her mother's sophomore fall at Hollins, a small, horsey college in Virginia. Barbara Topfer had been born in

Baltimore but her family left Peabody Heights for the suburbs in the 1950s. Her father ran off with a young secretary at his shipping company when Barbara was a teenager. He sent enough money that Barbara and her mother were comfortable, but Barbara saw his absence as a shame and a judgment. Stranded with her mother in Towson, Barbara watched movies, and Barbara read books, and Barbara was pretty, and Barbara decided her destiny was greater than to stay where she was. She applied to Hollins College, and by the time she got there, she had her story all worked out: she was from old shipping money, and her father hadn't run off with a secretary but had died young, leaving Barbara a great fortune. (Evelyn had been startled to hear this version of events from a friend of her mother's from Hollins.)

Barbara's sophomore fall, she'd gone to a University of North Carolina homecoming and met Dale Beegan. Dale, who'd gotten a scholarship to NC State for college and had near-perfect grades there, had made it to UNC for law school, where he was a star. Barbara's date for the weekend was one of the preppy classmates Dale couldn't stand, so he took great pleasure in wooing her away. Barbara was easily wooed; she thought his ambition, charm, and blue-collar roots made for a political cocktail. She once told Evelyn that she'd believed Dale was on his way to becoming an ambassador or a senator or even president. Barbara had ambition, too, raw ambition that she as a girl wasn't allowed to admit to. In Hollins in the 1960s, that ambition was allowed to go precisely one place: wifehood. If Barbara couldn't drive the car, she wanted to sit in the passenger seat. They married after Dale's law-school graduation; Barbara never finished college.

It wasn't until Evelyn was at Sheffield that Evelyn deduced that something must have happened to explain the twelve-year gap between her parents' wedding and her birth, when Barbara was an ancient-for-Hollins-girls thirty-three. She found out what that was one afternoon on summer break from Sheffield, when Barbara, deep into a bottle of white wine, called her to the terrace to warn her that women's fertility does not last long.

Barbara had trouble getting pregnant once she and Dale decided to try, she told Evelyn, who winced and turned toward the creek. The weeks stretched to an unbelievable length as she followed her doctor's advice of carefully prescribed intercourse ("Mom!" Evelyn said, but that did not stop Barbara's speech), waited, and wondered if she felt especially tired, then felt the regular cramps and disappointment return. It took a year until Barbara was finally pregnant.

When Barbara told Dale, after a doctor's appointment, that the baby was now the size of a pea, Dale took to calling the baby Li'l Pea. As Barbara relayed this anecdote to Evelyn, Evelyn heard her mother's voice catch.

Barbara was three months pregnant and blotting white paint for a sheep's fleece onto a mural in the baby's room when she started bleeding. There were cramps and dried blood in her underwear, Barbara said—and here Evelyn again tried to make her stop, but Barbara, who had barely acknowledged the existence of bodily functions in her life, seemed insistent on giving Evelyn every detail of the miscarriage without betraying any emotion about it. She drove herself to the hospital, as Dale was trying a case in California, and was given sedatives. When she awoke, the doctor told her that she had lost the baby—that *she* had lost the baby.

The bleeding went on for more than two weeks, when Barbara would awake after a restless tossing sleep in the middle of the night to more cramps, more expulsion, waiting for her body and her baby to disintegrate. Each new cramp mocked her body's inhospitableness, her inability to do this one simple and basic thing that women all over the world could do and she could not. At Dale's urging, she went to church after the miscarriage, but left when the priest asked the congregation to pray for the people who have died, and she didn't know whether the church thought that the collection of cells inside her had been a person who had died.

Then your father, Barbara said, her face grim. Your father. He did nothing but work for weeks after. He sent his secretary to check in during the day—his *secretary*, she said. Ten weeks after the miscarriage, Dale arrived home early. "He told me that he'd looked at everything—my medical records, my medications—without my permission—and found that there was a cause for it. That a drug I was taking, pentathilinate, was problematic, and that there were other cases where women had miscarried while taking the drug. He found a doctor in Kentucky who refused to let pregnant patients near the stuff."

Evelyn remembered reading about the case. Her father had shown her a *Washington Post* article about it. Thanks to his case and others like it, now women had to sign something promising they wouldn't get pregnant if they were taking pentathilinate. Dale had cemented his reputation with the case. He'd asked the jury and onlookers to imagine what the little pea—the phrase her father used, she remembered with a wisp of nausea—would be feeling, saying, "'Let me live. Let me hold on,' right as she could feel that drug working against her." The *Post* had said his speaking in the voice of the unborn baby had made some jurors sob, especially as he described the life the girl could be living now, toddling around and grabbing everything in sight and growing shocks of silken hair. Dale Beegan had to stop at that point, the paper said, to gather himself at the podium; the reporter could see his shoulders shaking.

"He wanted me to testify," Barbara had said. "He thought I'd be just the ideal witness, up there serving up my past to perfect strangers so they could judge me. I didn't know, Evelyn. I would never have taken the drug if I'd known. It was for skin, just for clear skin, and I never would've."

"It's okay," said Evelyn, lifting her gaze from the creek to her mother.

"We didn't know then—"

"It's okay," Evelyn said again.

"It wasn't his," her mother said, anger piercing the words.

"The baby?" Evelyn said, too loudly.

"Of course the baby was his, Evelyn. What on earth gets into your mind? It just, it wasn't his to take. To exploit. I'm the one who lost the baby."

Evelyn guessed her parents started sleeping in separate rooms starting then.

With Dale working, Evelyn's youth had been mostly her and Barbara, a table for two at the Eastern Tennis Club. As a kid, on Monday mornings, Evelyn would wait until she heard the crunch of her father's shoes on the gravel, then would slip out to the piano room and sit under the itchy navy blanket on the couch. She tried to keep her eyes open until her mother joined her minutes later, but was often dozing when she felt the cool hand stroke her hair, and then Evelyn would open her eyes, and her mother would open the piano and begin to play. Barbara started with scales, light and fluid, and then moved to "Oh, What a Beautiful Mornin'" or "Bill." Sometimes she'd ask Evelyn what she wanted to hear. Evelyn, who'd always been thinking about this question for several days, would tell her. If her mother and father had been angry with each other, Evelyn would ask for "Waitin' for My Dearie" or "If I Loved You," thinking that no one could play those songs and not be in love. If her mother had been having a moody few days, Evelyn would ask for a funny song, like "Sister Suffragette." Sometimes, when her mother had been happy for a day or two, and was making plans with friends or for Evelyn, Evelyn knew she could ask for what she really wanted: "Somewhere," from *West Side Story*. There's a place for us, she'd sing to her stuffed animals at night.

Evelyn started to play when she was five, and her large-note Clementi and Mozart workbooks were still stacked in the built-in cupboards on the side of the Sag Neck piano room, along with Irving Berlin and George Gershwin and Frank Loesser from when she improved. She was surprised by how much better her pieces sounded when they moved in—the piano room was almost like a concert hall. No one bothered her in there when she was playing, but sometimes Evelyn could crane her neck over the piano and see her mother sitting outside on the patio, listening. Those were the best times, her mother there but facing away from her and watching Meetinghouse Creek list by, a window offering a firm divide between them, Evelyn's fingers creating songs.

Evelyn used to wait up on Fridays for her father to come home from Wilmington for the weekend. That had changed after the Peg Oney case. After opening arguments, her family went out to dinner with the plaintiffs at an Italian place with plastic menus on the side of the highway, and everyone in town had come up to her father to thank him for the work he was doing. "Your father's such a special man . . ." "He's been real good to us . . ." "You're so lucky . . ." Her father was so busy taking in adulation that he barely spoke to her and her mother, even after their long trip.

Barbara hauled Dale away from the adoring crowd, and Evelyn wanted to hide under the table when she saw her mother pull from her purse a handmade pink-paper valentine that Evelyn had brought home from school the week before which said "Dad" in her scrapey handwriting on the front, and shove it at Dale's chest. It felt like that was her own pink heart beating on that rough paper as her father stared at it and then his mouth turned into a line and neither he nor her mother said anything to her about it and she couldn't sleep well that night, imagining the valentine on top of a pile of old linguine in the restaurant's Dumpster. Barbara and Evelyn left Cresheim three days ahead of schedule.

That was when Barbara began making Evelyn her confidante and coconspirator, which was thrilling sometimes and sometimes hugely uncomfortable. Barbara explained that Dale was free with his own purchases when he felt like it, but stingy with Barbara. So she would send Evelyn into his study to ask him if they could please have new tennis rackets or a landscaper, and he would sometimes acquiesce. As Evelyn grew older, she started to feel wringing inside when she did this, seeing his eyes lift from the page once again to see his daughter, now taller in the study's door frame, now asking for things she wanted: money so she could travel around Europe during her term in Sarennes, the additional fee for a single room at Davidson.

As Barbara drove Evelyn to school, or the Eastern Tennis Club, Evelyn heard a steady sound track. Your father's never here. Your father's canceled again. Your father's the reason I didn't get on that committee. Your father's a social liability. If your father hadn't been a plaintiffs' lawyer. If your father hadn't been a lawyer. Then, Evelyn, then we really could have made it.

The affenpinscher was now springing around with a sparrow-sized bird in his mouth. Evelyn wondered if he had killed it first or if the poor bird was dying of fright as she watched. The idea that a grand jury was investigating her father was massive, pulsing, scary. It was so careless of him to put himself in this position. Her father gave her a hard time for her People Like Us job, but he had done something questionable enough to have federal investigators looking at it? She had to come begging for $450, but investigators thought he had bribed experts to get multimillion-dollar verdicts?

"Evelyn!" she heard her mother shout from down the hall, then footsteps.

"Evelyn?" Her mother opened the door without knocking. "You're not changed."

"Changed?"

"For the party. We're leaving in thirty minutes."

"You're still going to the Channings' party?"

"We are still going, yes. I have no interest in not going and letting that be the talk of the party. Get dressed," Barbara said.

Evelyn continued looking out the window.

"Evelyn, I mean it. Get dressed. You have five minutes."

Evelyn shifted around on the window seat and looked at her mother. Barbara had clearly put effort into her outfit. She had a scarf wrapped around her neck and wore her largest pearl necklace, a navy linen shift, and beige Ferragamo pumps. She was also wearing her upgraded diamond ring that she'd selected for her and Dale's twentieth anniversary.

"I don't want to," Evelyn said.

To her surprise, Barbara was silent. To her greater surprise, Barbara crossed to the bed and sat down on it and picked at the corner of a bolster pillow. Evelyn tried to categorize this behavior—she had only seen her mother sit on her bed perhaps twice in her life, when Evelyn had been sick. Barbara plucked loose a thread from the pillow and was slowly unraveling it. Evelyn slipped over to the bed and quietly took the pillow away from her mother. Evelyn felt strange standing above her.

"This is not good, Evelyn." Barbara was staring at where the pillow had been.

"Maybe it's okay. We don't know." Evelyn awkwardly proffered the bolster back, but Barbara didn't seem to see it.

"This is not good."

Overhead, the fan whirred and moved the thick summer heat around the room but didn't provide any relief.

"He thought—I thought—it would be easier. Background seemed like it wouldn't matter; it was the sixties. I wasn't a hippie, but it seemed to be all changing. Something for a new generation. And it just—he just—it all fell away. Those early years were so hard. Your father just worked, and I was alone, trying to make linoleum seem like something good." She paused, smoothing her hand over the covers. "You think it doesn't matter how money is made. It's always there, though. Always around, underneath it, is how he made it. A trial lawyer. Suing the people who are actually working and inventing."

Evelyn squeezed the pillow hard. She did know, too well, that it mattered how money got made, or, more important, when. She'd seen it at Sheffield, where the girls with terrific middle names that signified old family money had sailed into and out of whatever circles they wanted to, confident they would be accepted, and she saw it now with Camilla. You couldn't cover up the smell of new money, sharp and plastic as a vinyl shower curtain just out of its box. You could try, layering over it with old houses, old furniture, and manners that mimicked those of people who'd been living this life for centuries. But unless your fortune was generations old, too, it—you—would never count in the same way.

She loosened her grip on the bolster. The issue with her father was awful, but maybe it was allowing a new Barbara to come forward. A

Barbara who was accessible, vulnerable even. A Barbara who sat on her daughter's bed.

Barbara stood up then and brushed her hands together. "Evelyn. This mess with your father is going to hit, and it's going to hit soon. If they charge him, if this ends up in a trial or a plea bargain, it could mean money, too. Us paying the government money. You have to cement where you are in New York before then. Do you understand what I'm telling you? Your position. Your reputation. I think your website job may be good for you, after all. You're friendly with Camilla Rutherford now, and you're reviving your friendship with Preston. You've got to keep on it. You need something solid underneath you before this all—" She let her hands drop. "Do you understand?"

Evelyn carefully replaced the pillow on the bed and tucked the loose thread behind it. "I understand."

"Those friendships could be very, very important." Barbara looked searchingly at her daughter. "I'd like you to come to the Channings'."

Evelyn nodded slowly and gave her mother what she hoped was a reassuring smile. "I'll come."

When Evelyn went downstairs in her dress, her mother's shoulders were back and her eyes were fierce, and on the car ride over Barbara talked about how Sally's garden had become infested with aphids this year. Somewhere between Evelyn's room and the front door, her mother had heard a cue, and she had remembered her lines and taken the stage. Their conversation would be left in the wings; it had nothing to do with their assigned parts.

CHAPTER EIGHT

New York, New York

Evelyn leaned toward the Amtrak window, searching for the TRENTON MAKES, THE WORLD TAKES sign, which she always looked for on the ride back to New York. She knew now that Trenton was a run-down Jersey city, but she remembered the first time she'd seen it, on her first trip to New York when she was ten. Everything on that train ride up had been magical, and she had cast Trenton as some kind of Santa's workshop after seeing that sign, a town that spun sugar candy and gossamer wings.

Even Penn Station was enchanting that first time, filled with more people than Evelyn had ever seen at once. Barbara had pulled her through the crowd and up to the street, then hailed a cab that smelled of Porta Potty fluid and had a fir-tree-shaped cardboard air freshener dangling from the window that Evelyn had to ask her mother to explain.

They were staying at the Plaza Hotel and, immediately after arrival, went to tea. At afternoon tea—never call it high tea, Barbara had said—Evelyn showed off what she and Barbara had been practicing at home. Her brow was furrowed throughout with concentration, as she didn't want to ruin her mother's happy mood. Napkin in lap as soon as you sit. Napkin on seat if you leave. Cream in English breakfast, fine; cream in Earl Grey, never. Cream goes in after tea. (When Evelyn asked why, Barbara could only tell her to stop asking so many questions. Later, on a Sheffield trip to Bath, Evelyn found out that the English middle class used to try to stop their teacups from staining by pouring in the milk first. The upper class either never had to get the stains out themselves or had enough backup teacups that it wasn't a problem.) Cucumber sandwiches in elegant bites. Dab at the mouth with your napkin; don't wipe.

When her mother went to the bathroom, Evelyn popped one of the edible flowers on the table in her mouth, chewing it with gusto; she was sure that was not on the list of appropriate behaviors.

The next morning, Barbara declared that she was going to show her daughter Barbara Topfer's New York. A few of her Hollins friends had lived here, and Barbara had spent happy long weekends in the city. At the Frick, after they had spent an hour looking at the art, Barbara disappeared for some time, then returned waving a shiny booklet.

"Do you like New York, Evelyn?" Barbara said, sitting next to her daughter on a cold marble bench. "I think we ought to spend more time here, don't you?"

Evelyn, who had seen a billboard for *Cats*, said she did and asked if they could go to the show. Her mother responded that Times Square was full of sexual deviants.

The next morning, Barbara woke Evelyn early, telling her that they had salon appointments and then were going for lunch with a close friend of Barbara's from Hollins. Her friend Push, as her Hollins friends had known her, had not only married into the Van Rensselaer family, but was a Pierrepont on her father's side and a Phipps on her mother's.

Push? Evelyn had asked.

Don't be rude, Barbara had replied.

Evelyn imagined a woman layered in folds of fat who knocked over china whenever she turned.

Barbara had her hair washed and set at the salon at the Plaza and

had Evelyn's hair curled into long ringlets that were already drooping
by the time they left the salon. On the elevator back up, Barbara told
Evelyn more about the mysteriously named Push, that Push was supposed to have attended Barbara's wedding but had canceled at the last
minute, and of course Push had other engagements in New York and
would have come except that she wasn't feeling well and it was such a
long trip to Durham. Push was a well-known debutante whose coming out was covered in *Life*, though it wasn't Push's fault—Push
hadn't allowed public photographers at her debut, yet that pushy press
corps had fought over getting a picture of her.

Even at ten, Evelyn didn't quite buy her mother's tale. All of a
sudden her mother was very close friends with a Van-Something-or-
Other who was a Something else on her mother's side? Also, her mother
was now an expert on debutantes, whatever those were? A question
flew around Evelyn's mind like a mosquito, and she tried to bat it
away, yet her ringlets were brushing annoyingly against her shoulders, and she wanted to see the Alice in Wonderland statue in Central Park instead of having to wear some itchy dress, so she let it out.

"Did you have fun at her wedding, Mommy?"

Barbara waited for the elevator doors to open and turned right
quickly. "Oh, I couldn't go. New York was really a very long trip at
that point, and I had my own social life to tend to."

The mosquito was buzzing louder, looking for flesh to chomp on.

"Was Push sad that you couldn't come?"

"Oh," said Barbara, jabbing to try to fit the key in the lock, "I'm
sure she was sad that any of her friends didn't make it."

"Did you keep the invitation? It would be neat to see it."

"Evelyn, you should change your clothes. That dress makes your
stomach look big."

Evelyn shimmied out of her dress. The mosquito wanted blood.
"It must have been sad to miss such a huge society event."

"Watch it, Evelyn. I don't want to hear a word about it when we
meet her. Are we clear?"

Push had grown up at Sixty-sixth and Park, and in the intervening decades had moved two blocks up and two blocks over, to Sixty-eighth and Fifth. Barbara did not want to walk there from the Plaza, as she was worried about grime from the city soiling their clothes, and had ordered a special long black car to take them there. Barbara wore a pink suit with golden buttons down the front and had Evelyn wear a seafoam flowered Laura Ashley dress with a lace bib at the front that Evelyn thought made her look like a Puritan.

The first thing Evelyn saw when they got out of the elevator was a painting of a young military drummer with bright red cheeks, hung over a gilded table with pink flowers on it. A maid led them past room after room, until they reached a room with windows on two sides, where the ceilings appeared almost as high as in the Plaza lobby, and there was a big chandelier and more vases of fresh flowers. She knew that fresh flowers were very expensive because her parents were always fighting over whether they were necessary or not.

Evelyn went to the window and watched taxis below, until her mother said, "Evelyn!" and inclined her head toward a chair, and Evelyn buried herself in a big green armchair where her feet did not meet the floor.

Then, announced by a tinkle from her bracelets, in came Push. Evelyn knew it was Push right away by the hurried worry of a servant behind her, and because she wore a kind of blouse Evelyn had never seen, all swooshy around the neck. Her hair was pulled back into something that looked like a cinnamon bun, held in place by will and a chopstick. Push wore red lipstick, which Evelyn's mother had once told her was only worn by call girls, and though Evelyn didn't totally know what those were, she was pretty sure that Push was not one of them and her mother might be wrong on that.

"Barbara, so lovely to see you again, you haven't aged a day," cried Push as she approached the couch that Barbara had jumped up from. Evelyn half stood, then sat again, completely forgetting whether she was supposed to be upright or seated when she shook an adult's hand. She was confident in her handshake, though; her mother had had her refine her handshake two years ago, because to have a weak hand-shake is to invite disrespect.

Then the grown-ups were talking, and it was a while before Push noticed Evelyn, hovering in a squat over the chair in case she was called upon to either sit or stand.

"Well! This must be your daughter!" Push said. "Hello, I'm Mrs. Van Rensselaer," she said, extending a hand to Evelyn, and Evelyn shook it with purpose, and responded, "I'm Evelyn. It's a pleasure to meet you."

"Are you going to be a Hollins girl, too?" Push said.

"I hope to be," Evelyn said, in an accent she thought sounded close to the Baroness Schraeder's from *The Sound of Music*.

"Well! How lovely," said Push. She turned to Barbara with a smile. "I have a daughter, too, though she's just a toddler. We'll see if we can sign her up for Hollins someday, too."

The adults continued chatting, then Push signaled to someone, and a tray of tea was placed on the table, and Evelyn figured out what she and her mother had been practicing for at the Plaza.

Push poured a cup for Barbara, then one for Evelyn, who lifted it by the handle. She watched to see if Push would put in cream with her tea. She did, after the tea, so Evelyn deduced it was English break-fast, and Evelyn reached for the cream, too. Then Push put in lemon, which Evelyn had thought was a no-no, and Evelyn, lost, looked to her mother, but her mother was not paying attention.

"Well, it's so nice to see old friends," Barbara began. "And just wonderful to be back in New York. The city has so much verve."

"It's a wonderful place to live," agreed Push.

"One thing we're sorely lacking in Bibville is the sort of cultural life you have here," Barbara said. "I took Evelyn to the Frick yester-day and she was just transported."

This was not true; Evelyn had liked the water pool, but the art was boring.

"Bibville," Push said vaguely.

"A lovely spot on the Eastern Shore, heavy with politicians come summertime."

"The Eastern Shore."

"Maryland."

"Of course."

"The Frick is doing fascinating work," Barbara continued. "You're on the board there, I think I remember."

Push furrowed her brow. "Just recently, yes."

"It's such a worthy institution."

"Yes."

Evelyn's mother curled her pinkie around the teacup's handle. "I'm hoping to spend more time in New York now that Evie's nearly out of the house," she said.

"Is she really almost out of the house? How old are you, Evelyn?"

"Ten," Evelyn said.

"Almost eleven," her mother said, "and we're seriously considering boarding school."

This was the first Evelyn had heard about it but, being an enthusiastic reader of *Pen Pals*, a teen-novel series about girls named Palmer and Shanon who attended boarding school, she was into it.

"Well, my boys are at Sheffield and they just adore it. I was a Porter's girl. So you'll hear only good things from me."

"I'll hate to lose my darling, but you know how it goes. Regarding New York. I so loved it when we came here in college. I was thinking, I'd love to get more involved in the Frick."

Push lifted the teapot, and placed it back down again, glancing toward the door, but the servant had gone. Barbara continued, "Its collection is so strong. It is, of course, such a center of social life here."

"Thank you. It is a remarkable institution. I can't imagine where Rosa has gone. Wouldn't you like some shortbread?"

"Thank you, no. Regarding the Frick, though, I'd very much like to be more involved there. If you remember, I was a huge art enthusiast at Hollins."

Evelyn was sitting very still.

"Well." Push adjusted her napkin. "There are docent programs, though I would think they're better suited for people who live here. The schedules can be surprisingly demanding."

"I was really more interested in a board position, should one open up."

"A board position? Barbara, I think that's—that's really up to the other directors and the executives and the development office. I'm nothing more than a glorified party planner on that board, really. I have very little influence."

Barbara smoothed her skirt. "Well, my husband's firm is always looking for corporate sponsorships."

At this, Push looked up. "What firm?"

"Leiberg Channing."

Push didn't look like she'd ever heard of it. "Mmm."

"They're out of Wilmington, and they are very influential. Very influential."

"I'm sure they are," Push said. "We really don't deal with other cities very much; we really are a New York institution. I so appreciate your interest, but I'm really not the one to handle this. Certainly there are some galleries in Bib-Bib—in Maryland that would be thrilled to have your help."

Barbara pulled her lips in toward her teeth.

Push raised a finger, and this time Rosa materialized, responding to the three-inch change in Push's finger altitude. Rosa whisked the half-full teacup and saucer Evelyn had been holding from her lap, and then the whole tea tray was gone. "Well, I'm so glad you liked the Frick. I'll be sure to tell the curator that it pleased the discerning eye of a Hollins girl," Push said pleasantly. "All those funny art classes we were forced to take. Ah, that reminds me of why we're here. I'm so glad you told me you were visiting New York, because I can't stand doing this sort of thing over the telephone—it's so impersonal, I think. Now, I hate to be so direct, but this is a reunion year, and we were hoping you might increase your level of support."

Evelyn saw her mother had turned her head toward the window, faking rapt interest in the rabbit-colored sky and building tops. Evelyn glanced at Push, who was looking expectantly at Barbara, but Evelyn knew this game and knew it would go nowhere. Evelyn waited until the silence got so extended she wanted to scream and tried to will her mother to say something, but Barbara didn't. Then Evelyn gave Push a hesitant smile.

"My mother really loved Hollins. She talks about it all the time."

Push's gaze moved to the left, then down, as though she were looking through binoculars to locate an especially small amphibian.

"Oh! Isn't that lovely!" she said.

Evelyn tapped her ankles against themselves, and pressed her knees together. "It sounds like it was such a fun experience. Tinker Day especially sounded so fun."

"Oh, my dear, Tinker Day was such a wonderful Hollins tradition, wasn't it, Barbara?"

Barbara turned her head slightly back with a disconnected smile, as though Push and her daughter were on a television screen, objects of mild interest but in which she had no emotional stake.

Push didn't seem fazed. "That's right, and Tinker Day meant classes were canceled for the day, and everyone would tromp up Tinker Mountain," she said. "Some of the girls got quite physical on that hike. What savages we were!"

"Didn't you have good picnics once you got there?" Evelyn asked.

"The picnics, oh, yes, of course! Oh!" Push clapped her hands very loudly. Rosa hurried in, but then hurried back out when she saw that Push was just being enthusiastic, not giving orders. "I think I have something you'll like very much! Come, come." In an instant Push had sprung from her chair and was charging toward a swinging side door. Evelyn rose, too, then looked back to her mother. Barbara was looking straight at Evelyn, and the skin around her lips had gone slack. An acid claw started scraping against the side of Evelyn's stomach, but she was out of her chair already, and Push was waiting expectantly. Evelyn turned and followed Push through several small rooms to a library, with wooden cases of books sitting upon more cases, and a ladder on wheels that attached at the upper wall.

"Now, it's in here somewhere," Push was saying, gliding on the ladder and pushing it with one leg, like a scooter, around the room. "I haven't looked at this in years, but I suspect—come here!" Push said. Evelyn did. Push was now flinging ribbons and cards about from a small box, then picked out a wide pink-and-green ribbon. "Here it is! This is what I wore my sophomore-year Tinker Day, as a headband, you see. We all wore such strange things, and it was marvelous to wear something that an alumna had worn. Now, if you're going to be a Hollins girl, I think you ought to have it."

Evelyn looked up at the older woman uncertainly.

"Go on, take it!"

The ribbon was made of rough grosgrain, knotted at the ends and faded. Evelyn took it as though it were an injured swallow, placing it gently in her cupped hand.

"Thank you very much," she said.

"It's my pleasure. It's wonderful when the next generation gets involved with Hollins. Now. We'd better get back to your mother, shouldn't we?"

"Yes, Mrs. Van Rensselaer," Evelyn said.

When they reentered the living room, Barbara was standing with her shoulders back. "Thank you for the tea," Barbara said in a low voice.

"Of course, Barbara. Do think about the donation. Really, if your husband's firm is interested in philanthropy, I can't think of a better place for it to focus than Hollins. Some of the scholarship programs are really—"

"I see," Barbara said, and began to walk back toward the elevator without glancing at Evelyn. She was half a room away by the time Evelyn figured she had better follow her.

"Now," said Push gaily, shouting from the sitting room, "I've put you and your husband down for five thousand. He might expect a call from the development office. I'm so glad Hollins can count on you!

Esse quam videri, as the school taught us! Good-bye, lovely to see you
again! Enjoy Bibbington!"

Evelyn barely made it into the elevator before the doors closed,
and her stomach increased its tumult when Barbara did not speak as
the elevator dropped, nor as the black car with its motor running
swallowed them. Evelyn fingered the fraying material of the ribbon,
still tucked in her hand, which felt like a cat's soothingly rough tongue.
Each minute that passed in furious silence piled up the pressure and
made it more impossible to fix the situation.

It was not until they were in the Plaza elevator that Barbara spoke.

"Well. That was quite a performance." Her voice was like a lid on
a pot of boiling water.

The claw in Evelyn's stomach scraped again, harder this time. She
made her voice soft, hoping it sounded vulnerable. "What do you mean?"

Barbara's mouth warped into an awful pout, and she wrinkled her
nose. "Oh, my mother just loves Tinker Day," she said, in a voice an
octave too high. "Oh, I'm just so excited to be a Hollins girl." The claw's
scrapes were turning to hot liquid now. "What on earth did she want
to show you?"

"What?" Evelyn asked, stalling.

"When she took you back. What was it she wanted to show you?"
Barbara jammed the key into the hotel room door and nearly kicked
it open.

"Just some stuff from the school. A yearbook."

"A yearbook?" Barbara squinted at Evelyn. "Did she give you something?"

"No," said Evelyn, tightening her fist around the now-damp piece
of ribbon.

"You're lying." Her mother's voice went lower. "You're terrible at it.
Let's see it." Barbara held out her hand. Evelyn tightened hers.

"Now," Barbara said.

Evelyn backed toward the wall, toward a large chest of drawers,
where she thought she could quietly hide the ribbon. Her mother

grabbed her wrists before she could get there, and uncurled her fist and pulled out the memento.

"What is this? Hollins colors—something to do with Tinker Day? Did you ask for this?"

"No—no. Mrs. Van Rensselaer gave it to me."

"Like hell she did. After you were hustling in there like a goddamn traveling salesman. You never had any sense of pride. Just like your father."

Evelyn flinched with each word, trying to back away farther, but there was nowhere to go.

"I'll tell you what you can do with this goddamn Tinker Day souvenir," Barbara said. She whirled and walked toward a wastebasket, then paused, doing an about-face to the bathroom, brushing by Evelyn so hard that their elbows collided. Evelyn stood still with her eyes shut, trying not to breathe too aggressively. She heard a flush, then water from the sink, and then the bathroom door close. Evelyn wondered how still she could make her body. She was afraid that if she made too much of a sound, it would make her mother exit the bathroom before the anger had blown over. So she stood, hands at her sides, listening only to the whir of the air conditioner go on and then off in even pauses as it tried to keep the room a constant temperature. She found that if she breathed just a half amount of the normal air through her nostrils, her chest would not even rise. She could even very nearly float out of her body, and look at the top of her head from the ceiling.

CHAPTER NINE

Wall Street Blues

The Amtrak deposited Evelyn at Penn Station, and she followed the crowd up the escalators and into the waiting room, still fogged with the New York of sixteen years ago. She got a cab in seconds, as the long July Fourth weekend had rendered the city empty on a Sunday. Her family had gotten through the Channings' party, as Evelyn knew they would, Barbara forced and gay, Dale discussing a motion, Evelyn hanging back by the crab cakes and deviled eggs. No one, inside the family or out, had mentioned the grand jury investigation again. Still, Evelyn was drained from the weekend, and she tapped her finger against the cab's window, wondering if it was too late to cancel her second date with Scot that night. He'd chosen a French bistro on Sixty-ninth, and the thought of watching Scot dither over steak tartare versus steak au poivre sounded deadly. After the cab dropped her at her apartment, though, the investigation was taking over her thoughts, and she decided she needed to get outside and interact with someone. She would pay for her half of the meal, she reasoned, and let Scot know at the end of it that while she had enjoyed meeting him, this—them—wasn't quite working.

Evelyn had reluctantly agreed to a first date with Scot when he'd called after the Lake James weekend. She had come to the date armed with four or five conversational topics but hurtled through these before the waiter even put down the bread basket. She was pulling the conversation, and the yoke was heavy. They traded sentences about themselves: he grew up in California, but moved to Arizona after his mother got remarried, and had always felt like he wasn't an Arizona guy, but hadn't really felt at home until getting his MBA at Harvard. She said that she grew up in a Chesapeake Bay town, and the water and the shore were beautiful. He talked about his college thesis on the overlap between Adam Smith and Friedrich Hayek, and she tried to stifle a yawn. So he changed the subject, or thought he was changing the subject, to talk about the capital-gains tax rate, but that led to an argument with himself over the inheritance tax. He was sweet, a nice guy, and when he kissed her after the first date and she rather obviously wiped the saliva from her mouth, she felt like a jerk. She also couldn't nail down a good reason not to go out with him again.

Evelyn prepared for dates like she was cramming for a test in a class she'd barely attended. For Harris Reardon, a dull McKinsey consultant she'd dated straight out of college, Evelyn had studied fantasy baseball until she had strong opinions on B. J. Upton's RBIs. For Jack Lynch, a friend of a friend of Charlotte's who was a research analyst at Bear Stearns, she'd tried to learn enough about wine that she could talk of the nose and the bouquet as pretentiously as he did. This was how she approached all men, figuring out which version of herself to present in order to get a guy interested in her.

Evelyn couldn't quite put her finger on why her dating life had never taken off. It had been slow from the start, in Bibville. The boy she had a crush on in middle school, Josh Meisel, had shown a brief and surprising interest in her in sixth grade, when he would call her on her private line during *Quantum Leap* to ask about the math homework, but at school Evelyn was too nervous to talk to him and, during their rare conversations, stared into the middle distance with an expression she thought looked European. It did not entrance him.

The world always said to just be yourself, but it turned out when Evelyn was herself, no guys were at all interested, so she was left with games of make-believe, expressing enthusiasm for whatever the men wanted to do, be it rock climbing or going to a cheese-beer pairing or a Knicks game.

As she walked west on Seventy-fourth, trying to keep thoughts of her father's case out of her head, she managed until a woman in a gray suit who had the sharp angles of a prosecutor gave her an unsettling second glance. Evelyn turned south. At Seventy-second, she started to wonder what papers the case had been covered in. By Seventieth, she worried that her father would go to jail. By Sixty-ninth, when she turned west, she thought that all her friends and her bosses at PLU might know already and were just snickering behind her back about it. When she finally stopped outside Le Charlot, her whole life was careening away.

She thought she had composed herself when she walked inside and saw Scot at a table sipping water. She walked over, and meant to open her mouth and say something light and happy, and instead she found that she was standing with an open mouth and with no sound coming out, and then she was crying.

Scot wriggled out of his seat and, to Evelyn's surprise, didn't hesitate, just pulled her into an enveloping hug. His chest was hard and warm, and his arms long enough to wrap her right up, and his cotton sweater was soft, and he smelled like Christmas, and for once he said the right thing by saying nothing.

"Do you want to walk?" he said, after a few minutes during which she soaked his shirt with tears. She nodded, and tried to dab at the dark spot she'd left on his sky-blue cotton, but he just said, "Shhh," and guided her through the blurry restaurant. As he turned her onto Sixty-ninth Street, Evelyn started blurting out one-word attempts at explaining herself. Scot didn't force anything, just left his big, warm hand on her back and walked slowly with her down the block, across the street, down another block, across another street, occasionally circling his hand around her back, but otherwise just letting her cry. Finally, she sank onto a bench outside an optometrist's office and tried to subtly wipe away what must be pooling mascara from under her eyes as Scot sat down beside her.

"Sorry," she said. "It's just family stuff."

"Okay," he said. She couldn't remember being so relieved at a word. No questions. No prying. Just okay.

"Okay?" she repeated.

"Okay." He stroked her hair, and she felt that delicious soothing tingle she'd felt the few times she was invited to middle-school sleepovers and the girls braided one another's hair. "Do you still feel like eating?" he asked softly.

She shook her head.

"Do you want me to take you home?"

She shook it again.

"Should we just sit here for a while?"

She looked up and saw, through her tears, someone across the street who looked like a Sheffield classmate. It wasn't, but it was close enough that she just wanted to leave the area. "Why don't we go to your neighborhood?" she said.

"Wall Street on a Sunday? It's going to be quiet."

"Quiet sounds good," said Evelyn, sniffling. "Quiet sounds very good."

Scot squeezed her closer to him, then rose and hailed a cab.

His apartment was in a giant tower on Gold Street, where all the buildings loomed over narrow colonial-era streets, making them feel dark and dank even on this early summer night. He guided her past the clanging and drilling from construction, the profiteers selling tacky postcards promising we would never forget, the tourists trying to figure out which one was Fulton. The building itself was typical Wall Street bachelor, with a pool in the basement and a giant lobby of black-and-white tiles and couches that no one ever sat in.

Scot's apartment, number 5G, was similarly huge and bare. The living room contained an enormous and hard-looking gray couch, a flat-screen TV, a sound system with giant silver speakers, and two stools lined up at a pass-through window to the small kitchen.

When Evelyn followed Scot into his bedroom, he turned on classical music, "In the Hall of the Mountain King," and then sat on his bed. Evelyn wasn't going to have sex with him so early, but wanted more of that warmth she'd felt on the street. They began kissing, and she finally unbuttoned a few buttons on her shirt when it became clear that he wasn't going to. He responded by standing up, taking off his shirt, folding it, placing it neatly on a chair, then returning and waiting for her to proceed. She gave him a hand job while he rubbed at her, and though he grunted appreciatively the whole time, she had the feeling it was just as lame for him as it was for her. Afterward, though, when she made noises about leaving, he said, simply, "Stay." And she did. She brushed her teeth with toothpaste and her index finger, washed her face with his Irish Spring, and wore one of his T-shirts that fell to her knees to go to bed. He wrapped his big arms around her and tucked his legs in behind her, and Evelyn stiffened at first, but then, there on that unfamiliar bed, Evelyn felt protected, and ran her thumb over his nice thick forearm and fell asleep to the strains of Grieg.

The next day, an e-mail from Nick: "So, I heard you held each other. Hot."

CHAPTER TEN

South of the Highway

Evelyn was so absorbed in Nancy Mitford that, when the Long Island Railroad train pulled into Bridgehampton, she nearly missed the two-minute window for unloading. August was high season in the Hamptons, and the train was more packed than a subway car, with girls sitting and standing in the aisles for much of the three-and-a-half-hour ride. Evelyn had gotten a seat, and with the help of her books, the ride had gone by fast. She had decided that she needed to study if she wanted to continue her People Like Us success, and she'd been reading like a fiend: old Emily Post from the 1920s, before the etiquette adviser got too mass-market; Paul Fussell's *Class*; Mitford's "The English Aristocracy," where the aristocrat laid out "U and non-U" speech. Evelyn had just learned that the frank "die" and "rich" should be used rather than the florid "pass on" and "wealthy." She shouldn't say "cheers." She was annoyed to find that monogrammed stationery was to be engraved, not printed; she'd just spent $300 on correspondence cards but they were printed, and now she'd have to reorder them. Camilla would absolutely know the difference.

Evelyn had been to the Hamptons twice before, an embarrassingly low count: once for a pool party hosted by her old boss in Westhampton, which didn't rank. Then last weekend for a People Like Us–hosted wine tasting she'd organized in East Hampton, where Evelyn had felt worker-bee wearing her laminated name tag when Preston and Nick had dropped by to say hi. She'd signed up fifteen new members out of it, which she thought was a good result, though Jin-ho felt like the few-thousand-dollar price tag on the tasting hadn't been worth it. Evelyn argued that just being the kind of site that hosted East Hampton wine tastings was good for the brand; you couldn't do a strict cost-benefit analysis on all of this.

"Ev! Look alive!" Charlotte was leaning out the window of her red rental in the parking lot.

Charlotte, to Evelyn's relief, didn't seem to know anything about her father. Evelyn didn't plan on telling any of her friends about those problems and regretted having broken down in front of Scot; weakness gave everyone else the advantage.

Evelyn got into the car, and Charlotte sped the short distance to Nick's house. Nick's place was south of the highway, though just barely, and as they drove, Evelyn saw why everyone made the south-of-the-highway, north-of-the-highway distinction in the Hamptons. One side was estates, hedges, money, privilege. The other was lacking.

Charlotte spun into the driveway and Evelyn was surprised by how attractive Nick's house was—she knew from Preston that it had cost $900,000 and was expecting something that was glass and chrome, not a sweet weather-beaten shingled house with white trim. That Nick owned a house at twenty-six was, as he would term it, NBD. Nick must have had more money than she thought; while banking paid well, an associate's salary wasn't enough to fund a starter summer house, and Preston said that Nick's parents hadn't helped him out with the place. It made her wonder if all her friends had some secret store of money.

Inside, in the living room, it was clear that a bachelor had bought the place—there was an overstuffed couch against one wall, a bar table against another, and a dining table against a third, with everything as close to the walls as possible. The place had just the mix of money, manhood, and a latent promise of domesticity to give every Jenna and Jenny and Sara-pronounced-Sahrah that Nick brought home from clubs a feeling that she could tame the house, and tame Nick; there was a steady parade of them, Evelyn knew from Preston. None made it back a second time.

Charlotte was three steps into the house when she announced to Evelyn that she was going to squeeze in a run, as she had to work that night. Nick was in town picking up charcoal, and Scot and Preston were taking an evening Luxury Liner. "Are we supposed to just claim a random room?" Evelyn said.

"I think so. I did. Not Nick's room, obviously, but there aren't that many people coming this weekend, right? So we don't have to worry about it."

"I guess." Evelyn took her bag upstairs to a narrow hallway that was flanked with bedrooms. Each bed was neatly made with linen-colored, linen-material linens. The one at the end was marked as Nick's from the gigantic wooden sleigh bed there and two oil paintings of the forest; the rest had no wall decor. Evelyn ducked into one on her right, with twin beds, nice tall windows looking out on the lawn, and its own bathroom. It was too early to share a bed with Scot—she didn't want to deal with the comments from Preston and Nick, and the hooking up had not improved much—so the twins were a happy find.

The next morning, a cacophony of laughter and a high-pitched "Niiiiiiiick!"

The group had gone to the Jeroboam the night before after everyone finally arrived, a club that had sprung up on the edge of the Montauk Highway in a former run-down hotel and had instantly become the center of banker nightlife in the Hamptons. Nick had pulled some strings to get them all in, "even Scot," as she had heard him telling Preston, which made Evelyn twitch. Scot's sweetness was appealing when they were alone, but in groups like this, his cloddishness made Evelyn so self-conscious that she couldn't enjoy herself, as she was gauging how harshly everyone else was judging her for being with him.

The Jero, as it was known, was basically a Twenty-seventh Street club deposited in the Hamptons. The club was hot and red inside, thumping and dark like an artery. Evelyn had followed Nick through a crowd, getting knocked by the hips of shaggy-haired men in button-down shirts. They'd waited for drinks in a line five deep and seven across, emerging with $15 Grey Goose and sodas quite a bit later. The drinks were small, and gone in a matter of sips. Charlotte was in hell—Evelyn knew this because Charlotte kept saying, with a clenched-tooth grin, "I'm in hell!" Evelyn didn't have the luxury of that point of view, though, so she decided she was going to like the Jeroboam. She downed two drinks very quickly and joined Nick and Preston on the dance floor, where a machine was spritzing something into the crowd. "Pheremones," yelled Nick, pointing, as droplets misted over them, and Evelyn just wiped sweat from her forehead and kept on shimmying to "I'm N Luv (Wit a Stripper)."

At some point later on in the evening, when the group had acquired a table and a group of random girls was dancing on it, Evelyn remembered blotting out cranberry juice from her skirt, and also an image of a bottle of Grey Goose in a bucket of ice; she had a bad feeling about the Grey Goose but couldn't say why.

Charlotte, still in her pajamas, wandered into the kitchen, where Evelyn was opening cupboards, looking for a coffee filter.

"Did Nick take someone home?" Charlotte said, waving at the screeching from upstairs.

"I think so. Nick and Pres had a bet: whoever could pick up a girl with an opening line about something—what was it called—the litter or something? Some interest-rate thing?" Evelyn said.

"The LIBOR?"

"That was it."

"Jesus. These poor girls. When we were out in NYC a couple of weeks ago they did the same thing with whether America should stay on the gold standard or not," Charlotte said.

"Who won that one?"

"I think Pres, though he left the gold-standard girl at the bar."

"Naturally."

"Nick was a little, ah, energetic last night, wasn't he?" Charlotte said.

"How so?"

"Like he was riding the white horse, dummy. One of the Morgan Stanley saleswomen is basically a cocaine trafficker for her clients. I think she routes surplus to Nick."

"Not that I'm shocked that Nick is doing coke, but someone's distributing it in her official capacity as a Morgan Stanley saleswoman?" Evelyn asked.

Charlotte opened the fridge. "Client services. Some guys want champagne, some want uppers, some want downers. She also has to take them to strip clubs and pretend she's into it. It's sick, but that's how business gets done. I would like to see her expense report, though."

"Seriously. Do the Colombians give receipts?"

"Seriously. How late did you stay?"

"Two or so."

"I can't believe you're not more zonked. Do you remember springing for that ridiculous vodka?"

The Grey Goose. "Ridiculous how?"

"Um, did you see the price list?"

"What did it cost?"

"Three-fifty. Four hundred."

"For a bottle of vodka?" Evelyn opened a cupboard that contained only a jar of spice rub. That was what was bothering her. She could've easily gotten away with letting Preston or Nick pay for the vodka, but it had felt good, for once, to step up and offer to get something that expensive. The boys had cheered her purchase, and she had gallantly poured hefty amounts of vodka into each of their glasses while they roared their approval. "Well," she said, "I'm a guest here, and it's done, so whatever."

"It was the guys who wanted table service. It wasn't like you had to pony up."

"You got a round."

"But Ev, I work in banking. I know what you make at PLU, and, look, you don't have to feel like—"

"Charlotte. Enough. I wanted to do something nice. You don't have to dissect it."

"Whatever you say." Charlotte turned into the living room and flopped on the couch.

Evelyn finally found the filters in a drawer with grill tools and was scooping ground beans into the coffee machine when she heard heavy footsteps on the staircase. Neatly pressed, but with his voice half an octave lower than usual, Preston materialized in the doorway. "Coffee," he said pleadingly.

"It's not quite ready," Evelyn said.

"Now," moaned Preston. "Why can't you be a good secretary and do as I say? File! Take my dictation!"

"Good morning, Mr. Hacking," Evelyn said. "Thank you, Mr. Hacking."

"Do you remember the coffee in Sarennes? I believe it was a solid, not a liquid," Preston said as he opened the fridge, took out a jar of mustard, and contemplated it as if trying to discern its meaning before gently placing it in an empty wooden bowl on the counter.

"God, yes," Evelyn said, pouring the first of the coffee into a mug and handing it to Preston. "I love that we were high schoolers on a term abroad and yet we became such serious coffee drinkers."

"We were in France. Of course we did." Preston took a sip. "Not that I liked the Sarennes jet-fuel coffee much, but good God, woman. Is there even caffeine in here? This is basically hot water." The machine was still clicking away, and he swung the filter arm out, dumped in more ground beans, then moved the pot and put his cup directly under the stream.

"So who did Nick bring home last night?" Evelyn asked.

"Who does Nick ever bring home? A girl. She's rather beat. Thirty-five or something," Preston said.

"Isn't he still hooking up or whatever with Camilla?" Evelyn said, trying to sound casual.

Preston sucked at his coffee. "Kind of, though I don't think Camilla wants anything serious."

They heard a clatter on the stairs and peered into the living room. Nick was trying to usher the girl, her eyes dark with mascara stains, out the door before anyone saw her. "Hi, I'm—" the girl started to say as Nick said, "We're just going to do a quick drop-off, then I'll be back with muffins, okay?" Evelyn saw a look in the girl's eye, a desire for possession, and knew that Nick wouldn't be returning her calls.

Nick came back fifteen minutes later with a Golden Pear bag, after Scot had joined everyone downstairs. "All right, campers. Here's your food," Nick said, tossing brown waxed-paper sacks to everyone. "Did my CIM come?" he asked Scot.

"Yeah," Scot said, pointing toward the door, where a FedEx box sat. "That's yours there, Nick."

"CIM?" asked Evelyn.

"Confidential information memorandum," Nick said. "For deals."

"Wow, you're such a big shot," Charlotte said.

"What, Hillary? You're peeved because you're not important enough to get a CIM on a weekend?" Nick said.

"Bite me. I get about five of them a week. My boss dropped one off for me last night. Door-to-door service," Charlotte replied.

"Where's his house?"

"Southampton. Meadow Lane."

Nick was fixated on Charlotte. "When did he buy it? Which one is it?"

"The huge gray one with the gables you can see from the road. Like two down from Calvin Klein's."

"That was on the market for so long."

"Yeah, he bought it maybe eighteen months ago."

"For what, thirty bucks?"

"More. It was in the *Post*."

"Goddammit. He's living my life. Isn't he the one with that hot wife, too?"

"She," Charlotte said, smiling, "is absurd. She'll call his VP, who's, I don't know, thirty-six and fabulous, and ask for financial advice. As if, (a) the wife has any control over the family finances and (b) this VP, who makes a good million a year, has time to direct her day trades. I think it's seriously, like, she sees something on CNBC while at the gym. And, in her leotard—I picture her wearing a leotard— she calls this woman, all 'The ticker on the screen said the forint was losing value, and I was just wondering what that meant for my portfo-portfo—oh, what's that silly thing that makes all the money!'"

Breakfast over, Nick dispatched Charlotte to get towels for the beach and Evelyn to get snacks. Evelyn retrieved two bags of Terra Chips and a bag of Twizzlers from the pantry. Up in the bedroom she and Scot were sharing, she threw on her new Tory Burch caftan, which Nick had seen at Lake James and referred to as the erection killer, and then tossed Scot's items in her beach bag: research reports, annual reports, a pair of sunglasses, his asthma medication, a biography of Nathanael Greene, two *Economist*s, SPF 55, and a bottle of aloe vera for when he inevitably got sunburned.

The beach outing was cut short by afternoon clouds, which were threatening rain by the time Evelyn and Charlotte got back to the house after a stop at the UPS Store, where Charlotte had to mail some paperwork. Evelyn got out of Charlotte's rental car, salt encrusted inside and out from the sea and the Terra Chips she'd been eating, and rubbed her hands over her bare arms; the air had dropped from warm to cold. Charlotte was typing on her BlackBerry in the car, and Nick's car was in the driveway, as was an additional one, a blue Jaguar with the license plate BIGDEAL, making creaking noises that indicated it had just been used. Nick's boss, maybe, over for drinks?

"Hello?" Evelyn called out as she dropped her tote by the door. "Nick? Are you here? Scot? Pres?" She hurried upstairs. If she ran the bathwater right away, she could be submerged in that good-looking tub by the beginning of the storm.

She was startled by a pile of laundry sitting in the hall, lumped over Nick's Oriental runner. Then the pile took shape into specifics. That was her brown bikini with the tortoiseshell clasp. The white dress she'd hung in the bathroom, crumpled beneath the clay-covered sole of a Jack Rogers sandal. Her makeup case, open, with a tampon poking out indiscreetly. Her turquoise travel toothbrush, wet and splaying its bristles against the hallway floor. Was somebody doing laundry and had accidentally gathered Evelyn's stuff? The toothbrush and makeup case, though? Had Scot—but he wouldn't put her stuff outside, and certainly not without folding it. She approached the pile and saw that everything she had so carefully chosen for the weekend had been jumbled together in a furious mess. Scot's suitcase—which he had not unpacked, and was still neat and intact—was behind the pile. Was Nick mad? What had she done wrong?

She peered into the bedroom she had claimed a day ago, looking for a clue. On the bench at the end of the bed, where her bag had been, was a tote with the pink initials CHR. She decoded them immediately.

"No, keep it in the C corp," Evelyn heard from behind Nick's door. "What? Because if we structure it this way we can use the tax loss carryforward. The tax loss carryforward," he said again, with conviction. "Rich, get your act together, okay? We'll talk again in a couple of hours and I want those numbers done."

The door at the end of the hall opened. "Evelyn," said Nick, holding his phone and looking at the mess. "I take it all that finery is yours."

Evelyn realized she was not only squatting, but fingering the wayward tampon. She angled her arm to try to block Nick's view of the tampon, and with her foot, pushed the cup of a bra away.

Nick gave her a strange smile. "Camilla decided to come out for a couple days. I guess she wanted the room you guys were in. Sorry about that."

Evelyn blinked fast. "No, I'm sure it's my fault. I didn't know Camilla was coming. I shouldn't have claimed a room." As she said it, she thought it sounded absurd; should she have napped quietly at the base of the stairs last night?

Nick's smile relaxed. "Yeah. Camilla came up last weekend and really liked the view from that room or something. Sorry."

"Last weekend?" Evelyn had been at the PLU wine tasting and hadn't heard a thing about Camilla coming up last weekend. She was already excluded, apparently.

"Yeah. If the rest of the rooms are taken, you and Scot can bunk in the den on the fold-out couch. Sheets are in the closet next to the kitchen."

The den on the fold-out couch. Great. Camilla would probably be standing over her in the morning, pointing at the saliva crust that formed around Evelyn's open mouth when she slept. "Will do. I just need my bag. It doesn't seem to be here."

Nick kicked at a neighboring bedroom door with his foot and located the duffel wedged behind the door. "Camilla has a good throwing arm, but her aim is a little off," he said grimly, handing Evelyn the open duffel and loping toward the stairs. Evelyn shook out a shirt and began refolding her clothing slowly. When she heard Nick's footsteps downstairs, she jammed everything into the bag. She clapped the Jack Rogers together with an unsatisfying thwack, and hurled the toothbrush down the hall so it bounced off the wall. If Nick had seen her stuff in the hallway, so had Preston, and Camilla had gone through all of it. The bloodstained period underwear that a thousand washings had made mud brown that she'd thrown in at the last minute. Her toothbrush on the germy hallway floor. All dumped in the hallway for everyone to see. What rule had she forgotten to study? What had Nancy Mitford forgotten to forewarn about American social mores in 2006? She took her bag downstairs to the small, dark den and sat on the couch as the sky outside got grayer. She kicked the bag. She knew what Nancy Mitford would've said: Evelyn shouldn't have claimed the second-best room, certainly not in Nick's house, where she was at best the fourth-ranked guest. She kicked it again.

"Fuck!" She heard Charlotte walking by the den, typing on her BlackBerry. "Why didn't this fucking file attach?"

"Language," Preston said from somewhere outside. Evelyn skulked into the hallway and looked out the glass doors to the backyard and pool. Camilla was indeed there, lounging in—Evelyn squinted—a fisherman's sweater, bikini bottoms, and worn-down Top-Siders. Evelyn retreated to the den. She had to smooth over this thing with Camilla. Show her it hadn't fazed her. She wriggled out of her caftan, leaving her bikini on, then faced the obvious question: Did Camilla have a bikini top under the sweater, or did that take away from the whole thrown-on effect? She buttoned up a thin green cardigan but it looked bizarre. She tried the bottoms with an anorak, but then she looked like a seafaring prostitute. Evelyn pulled on a long-sleeved T-shirt over her bikini, and hoped that was close enough.

Everyone was in conversation when she approached the door. Evelyn looked around the kitchen for, literally, something to bring to the party. There was an open bottle of red wine in the kitchen, but Evelyn vaguely recalled a rule about not drinking red before four o'clock. She saw some dark rum on Nick's bar cart, and grabbed it, remembering seeing ginger beer in the fridge. She poured one Dark and Stormy, tasted it, wiped away her lip marks from the glass, added a lime, and then poured a second.

She walked outside, the ice in the glasses clinking. "Anyone want a Dark and Stormy?" she asked.

"Yes!" hooted Camilla from her chair. "Please." She waved her hand at Evelyn, who promptly felt, clutching these slippery drinks, that her own swimsuit look was entirely off. "Evelyn! I didn't know you were coming. I love my People Like Us page. Yesterday I posted a question about Gorsuch and got an answer in, like, three minutes."

"Amazing." Evelyn giggled, making a mental note to find out what Gorsuch was. "How funny. You're a Dark and Stormy girl, too? There aren't many of us. So good, right?"

"Mmm-hmm," Camilla said. "You guys, this is too funny." She

had the weekend *Journal* spread out in front of her. The shade of Nick's body fell over the newspaper.

"Private planes story," Nick said. "Little do you know I forwarded that story around at ten A.M."

"Little do you know I forwarded it at nine-thirty," said Charlotte, clonking down her BlackBerry on the wooden picnic table. "Wireless Internet, gotta love it."

"And that's why you're not married, Hillary," said Nick.

"What's the story?" Evelyn asked.

"It's people refurbishing planes for their personal use," Charlotte said. "Entire passenger planes. One hedge-fund guy uses his plane to transport his horses."

"The weirder part is the lawyer who has the 737," Nick said. "It doesn't add up—the lawyer kicking the tires of this plane? What kind of lawyer has a plane? On, what, one-eighty bucks a year, he's buying a 737?"

"If it's a plaintiffs' lawyer, they're making a lot more than one-eighty bucks a year—a Big Tobacco case or something?" Preston tapped a pack of cigarettes on a side table. "Basically, our Parliament dollars are paying for this guy's ride."

"Pres," Charlotte said sharply, nodding her head toward Evelyn.

"Oh, shoot. Sorry, Ev. I forgot about your dad."

Evelyn smiled wanly and sat down at the picnic table.

"What about her dad?" Nick said.

"Dale Beegan, plaintiffs' lawyer," Preston said.

"You joke," Nick said. "What firm?"

"Leiberg Channing, out of Wilmington. You haven't heard of it," Evelyn said. "It's pharma cases, mostly. Where the companies didn't do enough testing on a drug, that sort of thing."

"Leiberg Channing," said Camilla, of all people. "It's a big firm?"

"Medium," Evelyn said, willing the topic to die a quiet death.

"Nick, can I borrow your BlackBerry for a minute?" Camilla said.

Nick handed it to her as he said, "Pharma. I swear I didn't know that. Wait, is that the one—"

"I can't believe people still smoke," said Charlotte loudly.

Preston stretched his lean body out in his chair and ran a hand over his curls. "This reminds me, fellows. We can't sustain this train situation any longer."

"You don't like the feeling of being a Jersey commuter with the LI double-R?" Charlotte said. "Wait, didn't you guys take the Luxury Liner yesterday?"

"The Luxury Liner, my dear, is still a bus. Anything with four wheels and a tin toilet—not to mention anything that christens itself 'luxury'—has nothing to do with the real thing. What we need to do, group, is upgrade altogether. I think we ought to take a helicopter out here next time."

"So pretentious!" said Charlotte, laughing.

"Dude. Preston has forty g's on his wrist and we're sitting around a Bridgehampton pool—I think we passed pretentious some time ago," Nick said, lifting his chin at Preston's Patek Philippe watch. "I'm in for the heli. We'd get out here in half an hour. The helipad is about two minutes from my office."

"Why must you say 'dude,' Nick? Your work trips to L.A. should not give you license to talk as if you were from California. Sorry, Scot," Preston said.

"I'm from Arizona."

"I don't recognize Arizona."

"What, like as a state?" Charlotte said.

"No, from a diplomatic perspective. Trade, reparations, that sort of thing. At any rate, the thing to do is not to rent a helicopter. Renting . . ." Preston smiled indulgently at the notion.

"We don't want a helicopter," Nick said. "My boss has a great twelve-seater. Keeps it in the private airport at JFK. Heliport to JFK, plane to the East Hampton airstrip. Half an hour, tops. When we get our bonuses."

Camilla looked up from Nick's BlackBerry. "Must you be so crass?" she asked him.

"It's not crass when it's achievable, darling C," Preston said.

"You guys are idiots. I like my bus." Charlotte shifted her weight on the picnic-table bench.

"What about you, Scot? Where do you stand on this divisive issue of air travel to Bridgehampton?" Preston asked.

Scot, who was wearing blue swim trunks which needed to be so long to cover his thighs that they looked to Evelyn about the length of her inseam, cleared his throat. "Well," he said, and Evelyn peeled a splinter of wood from the table, "mass transit is actually incredibly efficient, and air travel relies on fossil fuels and obviously gives off heavy carbon emissions. Beyond that, I'm not sure—" He looked at Evelyn, who was examining the splinter. "Sorry, am I being boring?"

"Not at all," Nick said. "Please. The floor is yours."

"Well, I guess you have to think about the issue of materialism. I think our generation is obsessed with too much. We keep wanting to trade up, and if you think about Schopenhauer, the futility of striving and the ultimate emptiness of human desires . . ." Evelyn looked at the group: Charlotte looking sleepy, Preston studying his watch, Nick evaluating the sky like a satisfied cat looking for a snack of birds, Camilla tapping on Nick's BlackBerry. Evelyn had thought the weekend in the Hamptons, at Nick's house that he owned and didn't rent, with her friends who had gone to Sheffield and Enfield and St. Paul's, Harvard and Dartmouth and Tufts and HBS, was enough. Yet she had taken the train when she was supposed to take the bus, and the bus wasn't good enough so they were discussing a helicopter, and then the helicopter would be subordinate to a plane, and there was never enough, and nothing was ever good enough. Always, the more danced around, taunting her.

"Sorry. Um. I guess that's heavy for the beach," Scot concluded.

"I love Schopenhauer at the beach," Charlotte mumbled, her eyes closed. The others were silent.

"Scot," said Evelyn briskly. "Would you mind getting me some water?"

"Sure." He jumped up, accidentally kicking the chair, which squealed loudly over the bricks and skittered to a halt. "Oh. Ha." He strode inside with the focus of a man carrying out an important mission.

"Your boyfriend is a blast," Preston said after Scot had shut the door. "I look forward to his evening lecture on geology."

"Seriously, what the fuck was that?" Nick said.

Camilla was looking at the door that Scot had gone into. "I think he's very smart," she said simply, and handed Nick's BlackBerry back to him. With that, the meanness evaporated and the mood was kind again, and Evelyn wondered if she'd underestimated Camilla.

"Can we work on dinner plans?" Camilla said. "I'd like steak. Grilled and with chimichurri. Nick, will you make me chimichurri?"

"I'll make you anything you desire," Nick said, his voice soft, pleasant.

"Ooh, let's have tiny lobster-salad rolls to start! Isn't that fun and beachy?"

"You got it."

"We'll go get supplies," Camilla said, and then looked at Evelyn, who jumped up from the picnic table when she saw that Camilla was including her in the "we." "I suppose I have to put on pants. I'll meet you at the door in five minutes, Evelyn." Camilla walked inside, handing Evelyn her empty glass as she passed her.

"So," Nick was saying as Evelyn headed in, "I now have a Best Buy credit card because of this zero percent APR offer they were running when I bought the flat-screen. I'm thinking, time value of money, it's a year of interest-free financing, I'll take it. But it's so bush league, having a Best Buy credit card in my wallet."

Evelyn hurried to wash and dry the glasses, go to the bathroom, pull on some pants herself, and be waiting by the door within five minutes, as Camilla had instructed.

A few minutes later, Camilla knocked on the den door and walked in without waiting for a response. "Hi—oh. That was your stuff?" Camilla looked amused as she scanned Evelyn's things, spilling out of the duffel.

Evelyn quickly slammed her hand down over the tampon. "Mine? Oh, yeah. It is."

"I threw it out of the upstairs room."

"Oh, that was you?" Evelyn said, she thought unconvincingly. "I figured it was just in the way, or something."

"Oh, my God," Camilla said, starting to laugh. "I saw that, like, spangly turquoise bathing suit and thought whoever Nick slept with last night must have left her stuff there. Nick and I hooked up the last time I was here, and Preston said there was some girl here last night, and I just saw those dresses hanging in the bathroom and I thought—well."

Evelyn hadn't thought the turquoise bathing suit was overdone at all and wondered what was offensive about the dresses—her clothes looked like they belonged to the random girl that Nick brought home? She had bought half of that stuff at Calypso, when that girl was probably shopping at Rampage. "Seriously, the den's really cozy," Evelyn said. "It's fine."

Camilla leaned against the door frame. "We're hooking up. Nick and I. It's truly, like, the least interesting thing. But FYI. My palmist says that I need to work on being more open, so I'm telling you. I'm just bored and need someone to mess around with."

"Completely. Completely. I think that's great. Nick's a good guy, and—"

"I wasn't actually looking for your opinion. I just wanted to be open and honest, and being open and honest is a practice rather than a quality, the palmist says. So that's all." Camilla seemed to be waiting for something. "Oh, I Googled your father."

"My dad? Just now?"

"On Nick's BlackBerry. I found some very interesting things."

Was Camilla actually coming in here to haze her, like this was *Dazed and Confused* and she was a freshman piggy? Evelyn was trying her hardest with this girl, but this was getting ridiculous. She plopped on the edge of the fold-out bed, facing away from Camilla. "Look. It was a guy from years ago who's bitter, basically, that started all this. They're not going to find anything."

"What guy?"

"The grand jury, Camilla. If you're coming in here to let me know that you know that my father is being investigated, very good. Go tell it on the mountain."

Camilla walked around the bed and tilted her head. "Your father's being investigated by a grand jury?"

Evelyn looked at Camilla, unsure how to answer.

"You're not worried, are you?" Camilla said.

"Camilla, it's a federal investigation."

She heard Camilla laugh, and it was a kind, tinkling laugh, not a cruel one. "Oh, my dear," Camilla said. "It is so not a big deal."

"What?"

"Darling, everyone who's anyone is being investigated by grand juries these days. You're not taking enough risks in your business if you're not, truly. Two of the girls in my St. Paul's class have had their fathers indicted in the last two months." Camilla was nodding confidently. "First of all, no one ever goes to jail, and if they do, they go to, basically, camp for a couple of months. The wives love it; they get a break from their husbands. My mother just planned a trip with one of her best friends whose husband is going away for three months. The Amalfi Coast." Camilla clapped. "I'm serious. You cannot be worried about it. It is not even an issue. By the way, I brought up your father because he sounds very real," she concluded.

Evelyn, despite herself, laughed.

"I think it's so important to stay connected to real people," Camilla said. "Like, I'll bet your father's clients are people who are in real poverty."

"His clients?" Evelyn said. His own family had been. She had visited the town where he had grown up only twice. Once when his parents were still alive, and Evelyn could only remember a dark house with dentures floating in a smudged glass, and everything smelling like wet wood. Later, in high school, Dale had made a great fuss about a father-daughter weekend they'd have together, but instead of going golfing like he'd initially proposed, he had taken her to his hometown, now mostly abandoned and somewhat frightening.

Whatever it was he had wanted to tell her, he hadn't been able to find the words, and they'd ended up silently eating greasy burger patties at the one operating restaurant and then spending the night in Charlotte. If Camilla had already read about her father, Evelyn wasn't going to be able to paste over that background, but she could still shape Camilla's impression of her mother's lineage. "The clients are definitely real people. As is my father. I mean, he and my mother are such a funny pair. She's from this old Baltimore family, shipping—shipping fleets—and they'd been in Baltimore for generations, and her parents nearly lost it when she brought home this North Carolina mill-town boy."

"That's so romantic."

"Very."

"I love that. That's so amazing. I want you to introduce me."

"To my parents?"

"To your father." Camilla folded her arms, looking quite pleased with herself. "I want an introduction." She turned toward the door and, walking out, tossed Evelyn a set of car keys. "Can you drive? I'm a little woo-woo."

"On it," said Evelyn, a bit befuddled as to what had just taken place.

Camilla's car was the blue one, tiny and sleek.

"I love your license plate," Evelyn said as she opened the drivers'-side door.

"What do you mean?" said Camilla.

"'BIGDEAL'? It's so funny."

"Oh my God," Camilla said. "That is not my license plate. This is my mother's boyfriend's car. I decided I needed it for the summer. He could not be tackier. That license plate gives me conniptions."

"Right," Evelyn said quietly and put the key in the ignition; at least she had learned to drive stick in Sarennes.

When they pulled up to a stoplight, Evelyn saw that Camilla was wearing the same racket bracelet she'd worn at Sachem. Camilla directed her to go to Southampton, which, she said, had better shopping than Bridge. Evelyn obeyed and, improbably, found a parking spot on Main Street once they arrived. "So, do you want to get the steaks and the lobster salad? I'm just going to pop into the drugstore," Camilla said. "Johnson's is a block that way."

Camilla hopped out of the car and crossed the street between a Volvo and a Vespa, both seafoam green, both stopping in the middle of the street for her. A pug in the basket of the Vespa was wearing goggles. "Thanks! You're a doll!" shouted Camilla from the other side of the street. "Ooh, and some wine! A cab or something!"

Evelyn thought about the Grey Goose she'd bought last night, and then thought that not getting wine when Camilla had requested it was a bad idea. She made the liquor store her first stop. In the store, nothing over $150 was displayed within arm's reach, partly to discourage the petty thieves of Southampton, partly so those who wanted to buy a Ducru-Beaucaillou could announce those intentions loudly to the crowd. Evelyn walked directly to the Bordeaux section, so anyone watching would seem to think she knew what she was doing, and picked up bottles until she found one that cost $125; even if it wasn't cabernet, it was expensive enough that no one would complain, and she got two for good measure.

She found Johnson's after she'd passed by it three times. It was an old-fashioned butcher shop. Long and slim, Johnson's was not made for crowds, and as a result was always very crowded, with everyone wishing everyone else would go back to Manhattan so they could enjoy the authentic Johnson's. After twenty minutes, she ordered. "I need some steaks?" she said. "Um, six, I guess? Or eight, if people are hungry?"

"You call ahead?" said the butcher.

"I didn't, actually."

"Porterhouse, flank, filet, strip, whaddaya want?"

"Uh, filet mignon, I guess?"

"Whole filet, or center cut?"

She was guessing like it was an eye exam. "Center cut?"

"How big? About a pound each?"

Evelyn checked the display case for a price, but she was in front of the pork section, not beef. "Sure."

"Six filet mignon, center cut, pound each!" the butcher shouted.

"Eight, just in case."

"Eight!"

"Some lobster salad, too? I guess, how much would you need for six people?"

"Six people, two pounds and a half for sandwiches."

"Okay, that sounds fine."

She got her packages and struggled to the front, plunking down the heavy, chilly parcel of beef and the vat full of lobster salad on the counter. The woman ringing her up was chewing gum and busied herself blowing a giant pink bubble before she said, "Five forty."

Figuring the woman spoke Nick-ese, in which five bucks meant, variously, five thousand, five hundred thousand, or five million, Evelyn deduced the woman meant $50.40, and handed her three twenties.

The woman chawed her gum and stared. "What's this?"

"It's for fifty-forty. Sorry, I don't have forty cents."

"Ha!" She laughed, spitting berry-colored saliva over the cash register. "Bill! Get a load a this! Fifty dollars for all this crap!" She waved her hand over the packages. "You just made my day. No, it's five forty. Five hundred forty."

"What? Dollars?"

"No, lire. Whaddaya think, dollars."

"What? It's just some beef and lobster salad."

"Filet mignon," the woman said loudly, holding it up, "thirty-four a pound, eight pounds. Lobster salad, ninety a pound, two and a half pounds. Plus sales tax. That's five hundred forty. We take Visa or MasterCard, no AmEx."

"The lobster salad is how much?" Evelyn started to say, but then noticed a pair of sockless loafers and frayed cuffs behind her, and knew an impatient Southhamptonite was waiting his turn, judging whether she was really that naive or really that low on funds. "I'm so sorry," she said to the clerk, while smiling at the man behind her and handing over her debit card. She weighed whether to tell Camilla the story. On the one hand, it showed she was insouciant about money. On the other, shouldn't she already know that lobster salad in the Hamptons cost $90 a pound?

"My wife's the same way," the frayed-cuff man said, and Evelyn gave him a who-me? shrug and laughed.

"Aren't they all," the clerk muttered, and ran the card through.

"That's what you get when you send civilians to do the job, I guess," Evelyn said, and met the guy's eyes as he laughed. "My cook usually does all the shopping here," she added. "Have a great afternoon."

CHAPTER ELEVEN

Alumni Affairs

Evelyn had been hesitant to invite Scot to the Sheffield alumni reception, which her parents would also be attending. She liked being alone with him: he had recently taken her to *The African Queen* at the Film Forum in the Village, and had smuggled in Good & Plentys, and the fact of being on a date with this sweet and thoughtful man had been reassuring. Their forearms touched on the shared armrest like they were shy teenagers, albeit from a teenage phase Evelyn had never experienced. Afterward, making their way through the drooping August city, they'd gone to Scot's favorite bookstore and then drank cold white wine at a tiny dark-wood-and-candles bar. She felt like a happy part of the Ella Fitzgerald "Manhattan" song on the summer weekend, a young couple ducking into places bohemian and smart.

Her mother's judgment would come down eventually, though. Barbara's questions about Scot were getting increasingly pointed, and Evelyn in some way wanted her mother's opinion. Evelyn did like Scot, sometimes a lot, but needed outside confirmation that he was a good boyfriend, someone who reflected well on her and could keep up with her pace, which was getting faster by the second. She'd received invitations to two fashion shows, even though the assigned seat for each of them was a few rows back. She had gone to Shuh-shuh-gah again and Nick's twice more, Camilla had invited her up to Sachem in the fall, and everyone was talking about a ski trip to Jackson in the winter.

With the sky still light at seven, and drizzle falling, Evelyn tried to get to and through Times Square without body-checking anyone. She pulled her trench coat tight as she walked past button stores and trim stores and other remnants of industry that had clung on despite the city changing around them. She was squished, slammed, and sandwiched between tourists who stopped three across on the Seventh Avenue sidewalk so as to block any linear traffic flow. She was approached by someone sampling PowerBars, someone sampling toilet paper, and someone sampling what looked like chunks of white chocolate in fluted cups, which she was about to pop into her mouth when the promoter cautioned her it was artisanal soap. Twice, her stiletto heel sank into the gummy mortar between sidewalk panes, and she had to yank it out while trying to look elegant and unflappable.

Barbara was dissatisfied with this alumni event in advance. She had lobbied for this dinner to take place at the Harvard Club, but as neither she, Dale, nor Evelyn had actually gone to Harvard, she held little sway there. When Evelyn met her mother outside the Marriott Marquis in Times Square, she was huddling under an awning as though it were pouring and dramatically ignoring a comedy-show busker who kept asking her if she liked to laugh. Not your demographic, Evelyn wanted to tell him.

"Evie. Is that the dress I bought you?" Barbara held her at arm's length, appraising her as she gripped her shoulder.

"Yes." The Marquis Theatre was playing a swingy tune from its loudspeakers, and Evelyn, twitching her knees imperceptibly in rhythm, looked longingly at the musical poster the theater displayed, for *The Drowsy Chaperone*.

"It works well. I'm surprised. Beige is a color most women can't wear. Your father is not here, as usual. Did he tell you where he is?"

"I'll check. I wish you would get a cell phone." Evelyn flipped open her phone and listened to a voice mail from Aimee, his secretary. "He'll be late."

"Of course he will be," Barbara said. "I didn't think he should come at all, but he says it's important not to act like a guilty man when he's not. I'm not sure Delaware prosecutors are monitoring Sheffield alumni events, however."

"I don't think he's been to a Sheffield event since I graduated," Evelyn said. It was maddening that her father was choosing now to attend her events, when it apparently mattered for public perception, rather than when she had wanted him there. It put her in an awkward spot; she had decided that, big deal or not a big deal, it was better not to say anything about the investigation to her friends, and as far as she could tell, no one but Camilla knew about it.

"No. I don't think he has," Barbara said. "So. Where is this friend of yours?"

"You can say 'boyfriend,' Mom. I told Scot to meet us inside."

"Should we go in?"

As the two women entered the lobby, they saw several men waiting. Unfortunately, Evelyn saw, her mother's face brightened when she spied a man with strong shoulders in a sharp gray suit who emanated confidence. Not Scot. Evelyn gave a lame wave to the actual Scot, who was standing storklike on a single foot.

"That tall one? That's Scot?" Barbara said.

"That's Scot."

Barbara considered this.

"He reminds me of that handyman we had. Large features and that darkness."

"He's a banker, Mom." The handyman. Christ.

The two women had the same stiff stride as they approached Scot. Evelyn had been hoping Scot would be relaxed and boyish, as he had become with her, but he fumbled with his BlackBerry, almost dropping it before he managed to replace it in his pocket. "Hi," he said, and bent over from the waist to greet Evelyn, then raised both arms toward Barbara. Evelyn, alarmed, stepped between them before he could hug her mother and tried to subtly press one arm down so he could only perform a handshake.

The strange modernity of the Marquis, with its extra-long escalators and its semicircle of elevators without elevator buttons, was an odd fit for Sheffield. Evelyn was glad to see the alumni association second-in-command there outside of the coat check, as her mother immediately went to quiz him about why Sheffield was sponsoring an alumni cruise on the Yangtze. Across the room, Evelyn saw Charlotte and Preston, huddled by the bar, and headed toward them with Scot.

"Well, well, well," Preston said. "We were just talking about you. Scot, good to see you."

"She does exist," said Charlotte to Preston. "We were debating whether you were a figment of my imagination. Hi, Scot."

"I saw you, like—" Evelyn said.

"The Hamptons in July," Charlotte said.

"Oh," Evelyn said.

"Solo sightings are getting increasingly rare," Preston said, adjusting his glasses. "Though one just has to look for Camilla and Evelyn will be near."

"Oh, come on, Pres," Evelyn said.

"Camilla," muttered Charlotte. "Scot, how's your chess coming along?"

Scot lit up at this and began describing a game he'd played recently in a Lower East Side park with some Russian men, as Preston sidled to Evelyn and slung his arm around her waist.

"Bringing Scot to a Sheffield event. Bold. To meet the formidable Babs. Does Scot know what he's in for?" Preston said.

"He just met Babs."

"He's still standing? Wasn't shot on sight? That's something. I remember the first time I met your mother, she plied me with liquor, but then I was a favorite son."

"She did not give you liquor. You were sixteen."

"Oh, Miss Beegan, I beg to differ. I remember it well. Babs took us into Portsmouth for dinner and I swear to you I ordered a chocolate martini. It was right after we got back from Sarennes."

All of a sudden Evelyn could recall with perfect clarity the martini glass with the milky liquid sitting on the white tablecloth, and the feeling of success she had as she watched her mother chat with Preston Hacking.

Her attendance at Sheffield and friendship with Preston there were by no means preordained. One Sunday morning when Evelyn was twelve, she woke to the sounds of Barbara's piano playing and was about to get up when the playing stopped. Barbara knocked on her door and told her she could stay in bed for another hour. Then, Barbara gave her a stack of reading material: a book called *Preparing for Power: America's Elite Boarding Schools*, a J.Crew catalogue, an SSAT study guide, and a Sheffield admissions catalogue. Barbara said that Gibby Hodge's daughter had gone to Sheffield and there had met, and eventually married, a Cabot from the Massachusetts line. Evelyn knew that Gibby Hodge had nothing to do with it, and it was because Push Van Rensselaer's boys had gone there that she was being sent there. Happily, her grades were good enough that she got in without a problem, and Dale could easily cover the tuition.

Preston was a year above Evelyn, and she had known his name before she had found out what he looked like. That was in part due to her mother. After finding out that Preston's mother was a Winthrop, and that he was from Beacon Hill, Barbara had suggested that Evelyn get him to ask her to the Lower Social. This idea was so laughable that Evelyn did not even know how to explain to her mother what would happen if she, an unknown and pudgy prep, were even to speak to Preston Hacking. Or she knew what would happen: she would likely end up writing an English paper on his behalf instead of going with him to a dance.

He wrote a humor column, "Perched on the Ivory Tower," for the school newspaper. It was initially supposed to come out every week, but Preston didn't believe in deadlines, so it earned the subhead "An Approximately Fortnightly Column" after its debut. Preston played club squash, not varsity, because he found bus travel to weekend tournaments uncivilized, and was the nominal vice president of the Young Republicans, largely because his great-grandfather had been the secretary of state under Teddy Roosevelt.

Knowing all this, Evelyn was startled to discover what Preston Hacking actually looked like. It was the Alumni Appreciation Day assembly, and the headmaster had asked Preston to say a few words about being fourth generation at Sheffield. Rather than the dark-haired and dashing guy she had come to imagine him as (his directory photo was blurry, and taken from a strange angle, allowing Evelyn to add all sorts of dramatic flourishes), she realized he was the tall, skinny fellow with wavy blond hair and alabaster skin that she'd seen lounging about on campus benches dressed in sweaters with elbow patches. He was of the cool kids, absolutely, but also seemed eccentric in a way that Evelyn envied.

Evelyn herself was neither eccentric, nor cool, nor anything at Sheffield. That was clear on her second day there, Tryout Day: the Key Association in the library, the Ben Jonson Players in the experimental theater, the Federalist Society in the Academy Building, the Indian dance troupe Aananda in the JV squash courts. Evelyn, with her piano background, had long had hopes of being in the theater. One bad morning in Bibville, though, Barbara had said that she was singing flat, and Evelyn had stopped singing. She went from chorus roles in Bibville middle-school musicals to painting the backdrops, thinking maybe she could direct or something someday. Before eighth grade, she'd tried once more, as she'd wanted to attend music camp in Virginia, but her mother took one look at the brochure's cover, showing a plump girl singing, and said that these theater people needed to spend some time getting exercise outdoors. Babs enrolled Evelyn in tennis camp again that summer instead.

Evelyn worked up the nerve on that second day of Sheffield to go to the arts center and hear about the upcoming theater season, but when her hand was on the auditorium door, she heard a girl talking about how she had played Young Cosette in the touring production of *Les Miz* over the summer. She almost ran back to her dorm. It was clear to Evelyn by the end of the tryouts that a handful of students was already picked for stardom. A freshman in Wyckoff had done an amazing job as a soccer forward that morning and was going to be a three-sport prep. The Cosette girl, a prep in McGeorge, was favored for Sarah in the fall production of *Guys and Dolls*. Evelyn sensed she had been cast in her Sheffield role without attending a single tryout: Girl in Background #4.

Barbara had somehow procured her own copy of the Sheffield student directory, and in addition to asking about Preston, she would quiz Evelyn about James Scripps Robinson or Sarah Monaghan Lowell. "The Scrippses started the art museum in Detroit," she would say. Or, "We had a Lowell girl at Hollins a year or two ahead of me. I think she went on to marry a de Puy." Preparing for her mother's inquiries, Evelyn learned the signs—the Tuxedo Park addresses, the old-money family names even for towns like Cleveland—that worked as a decoder ring for this world. Sometimes, on scraps of paper she'd tear and throw away immediately afterward, she'd try out her name with some of the more august surnames: Evelyn Beegan Cushing, Mrs. James Cady Robinson (Evelyn). But she mostly sat in front of *Reality Bites* or *Four Weddings and a Funeral* or whatever the dorm head had gotten from the video store that week and listened to the knots of girls in the common room next door singing Lisa Loeb.

It was Sarennes that changed Evelyn's social fate at Sheffield. Barbara observed Evelyn over the summer break after her prep year, Evelyn's nose in a book and fingers on the piano keys, and determined that her daughter was, if anything, even less social than she had been prior to Sheffield. Barbara decided immersion therapy would work best, tracked down Mrs. Germont, who headed the fall term-abroad program in Sarennes, France, in Alsace, and petitioned for Evelyn to be a last-minute addition to the program. The idea almost paralyzed Evelyn when her mother told her about it, as she knew who was going on the term, namely Preston Hacking and his pals.

Evelyn was placed with a baker's family above the small town bakery, with a stern matriarch who would get up at 4:00 A.M. and acted as though Evelyn was her paid assistant. The matriarch spoke French initially, apparently in order to get the fees for a boarder, but it was all Alsatian once the Sheffield faculty had gone, and Evelyn could barely understand anything the woman was saying. Evelyn's first day with them was a Sunday, when the bakery was closed and, despite being dragged to a long and boring Lutheran service, Evelyn didn't have to do much. On the second day, the woman woke Evelyn at five o'clock so Evelyn could stand guard downstairs and accept the pots of stew from the ladies of the town. The baker then covered them in rounds of raw dough, and the ladies would return after doing their washing and chores for their baeckeoffe, and Evelyn, smelling of fatty meat and flour, wondered how quickly she could get out of this.

On her third morning as an indentured Alsatian servant, Evelyn decided she would sneak into town and use the phone at the restaurants to find out about flights home. The street at dawn looked empty, but then she saw Preston Hacking loosely leaning on a broom handle in front of a door frame down the street. Evelyn's instinct was to turn and go toward town in the other direction, so she wouldn't have to embarrass herself with a strangled hello. But that would add several minutes to her trip, and she had to be back before Madame returned from her morning errands. So she pushed herself forward, waved her hand inelegantly from across the narrow cobblestone street, and, in a voice that sounded false and high to her, shouted, "Hello!"

They had not spoken so far on the trip, Preston hobnobbing with his own group of friends, but he looked up with something like interest.

"What a place," he said, in his lockjaw dialect. "What on earth am I doing with a broom in my hand this early in the morning?"

She had to fight her urge to give a flat smile and jog away. She sucked in the cool air. "Manual labor?"

"Manual labor. That is correct. We're paying these Frenchmen to let us stay here, and they not only don't appreciate the money, they wake me at the crack of dawn and put this item in my hand. Do I look like a street sweeper?"

"A well-dressed one." Evelyn waited for Preston to ignore her comment, but instead Preston smiled and kept the conversation going.

"There is no such thing. No such man. Certainly not I. What are you doing at this ungodly hour? Off to wring the neck of a chicken?"

"I was actually going to go to the restaurant."

"The food's that bad in your homestay?"

She giggled nervously and took a few halting steps across the street toward him. "To use the phone, actually."

"Calling Mumsy to bail you out?"

"Well, no, actually. I was going to call the travel agent."

He slapped the broom handle. "I dig it. Going straight to the source to break free from this prison camp. Won't your parents be alarmed when you show up at home unannounced?"

"I hadn't really thought it through. Maybe they'll be happy?"

"After what this forced-labor program cost? Doubtful."

"Well, maybe I'll have the agent send me to Paris for a while, then."

Preston laughed, and Evelyn felt her cheeks redden and the flush spread throughout her body. She couldn't believe she had made someone like Preston laugh. She was here, talking to one of the most popular uppers—and, seemingly, keeping him entertained—when she had spent a whole year barely talking to boys at all. She wished someone were filming it, so she'd have evidence of social success that she could look back on during those long nights in her dorm.

"I like it. Escape to Paris, fully funded by the 'rents. They'll never be the wiser. Evelyn, right?"

"Right."

"Evelyn what?"

"Beegan."

"Beegan. What is that, Irish?"

Evelyn shifted her weight to her back foot. "Korean. Russian. African."

Preston smiled and released the broom handle, balancing it carefully against the doorframe. "Multiethnic. How modern. I'm going with you. I want to see if escape is indeed possible." He stepped over a small puddle, and his loafers shone even in the low light as he joined Evelyn in the street.

At the bar, he'd bought both of them thick, almost chewable coffees, as she—having forgotten about the time difference—left a message for the travel agent in Easton who'd arranged her flights.

She ended up not needing the flight out. That night, Evelyn heard hoots from below her window, and she dropped to the floor, crawling over so she could see who was there and why they were making fun of her. It was Preston with Charlotte Macmillan, an international-set girl from Evelyn's dorm who was rumored to have gotten restrictions for sneaking into James Ying's room after hours. They were with a few other "coolies," as they were known at Sheffield, and they didn't seem to be jeering at her. Preston was actually calling for her to come out with them. She stood up, waved, and joined them.

As the term went on, she found it surprising and comforting to finally have friends, a group, people who didn't mind her and maybe even liked her. She sent pictures to her mother of her with actual humans. There were other kids in the Sarennes program who were odd and said weird things and wandered by themselves among the Loire Valley châteaus on weekend trips, and she wasn't one of them. She was part of something. She constantly monitored herself to make sure she wasn't being annoyingly overbearing or too dull and played her role well as the easygoing straight man to the antics of Preston and the others.

When she returned to Sheffield, she wasn't quite popular, but she had a place. One of the Sarennes girls said she would be perfect for lightweight crew and took her down to the boathouse on the first day of spring term, and the coach said she should be a natural with her build. Then she had another new group of friends to sit with and make inside jokes with and fling Ammonoosuc water at and sing with on the bus to weekend races at Groton and Kent. Now Charlotte was flopping down next to her in the dorm common room and asking her if she wanted to order Delvecchio's chicken-finger subs. Charlotte asked Evelyn to room with her for upper and senior years so they could get the "hot-doub," the fourth-floor double with a balcony and a hidden back closet where Charlotte could smoke cigarettes. Evelyn now had a reference tag on her, friends-with-Preston, that made her stand out among the masses at Sheffield.

Her mother came up for Easter weekend Evelyn's lower spring and insisted she invite a friend to dinner. "Mommy, what do you think about taking out a whole group?" Evelyn suggested.

"What group?" Barbara asked.

And Evelyn let each name drop like a hard candy into an eager mouth: Preston Hacking, Charlotte Macmillan, Nick Geary—Preston's best friend from middle school who was visiting from Enfield that weekend.

Barbara decided to make a night of it and hired a car to drive the teenagers and herself to Portsmouth, signing each of their faxed permission slips with a flourish and taking them to a riverside restaurant. Nick, hearing that the Saturday-night plan was to go to Portsmouth with someone's mother, found a pot dealer he knew from Brookline and got high before the drive but charmed Barbara nevertheless. Preston did have that chocolate martini, and Evelyn remembered her mother ordering wine for the rest of them. The fact that Evelyn had managed to gather together a group from Brookline and Beacon Hill (Barbara was not as impressed with Charlotte, who wore the albatrossian pigtails that night) made Evelyn feel like she was going to explode with achievement. To suddenly have friends, and to have your mother seeing you have friends, when all your life you'd been a social fumbler—Evelyn wanted that evening outing to last for hours.

"I do remember that martini, actually," Evelyn said. "I wouldn't think Babs would slip liquor to underage students, but there you go."

"I am quite looking forward to seeing her again," Preston said.

"You're getting a triple scoop of Beegan tonight. My father's also coming."

"Charlotte," Preston said, "did you hear that we will see the Yeti-like Mr. Beegan tonight?"

Charlotte looked oddly pale. "I didn't know your dad was in town, Ev."

"He's decided late in life to be a Sheffield alumni supporter. What can I say?" Evelyn said.

"His legal practice—" Scot began to say in his trumpetlike voice, but Charlotte quickly cut him off.

"So the old Muscovite opened with pawn to where?" she said.

Dale bustled in a few minutes later, accompanied by the assistant director of alumni affairs, whom he had never met but who was nevertheless laughing her head off at something he was saying. Especially among New York males, who resembled a school of darting silver fish, all in sensibly understated gray suits, Dale stood out. Today, he wore a suit that looked like it was made of denim with a bright pink pocket square; he should have had an antique stopwatch dangling from his neck. Even at home, his look was ostentatious, and Evelyn wondered how he managed to draw attention to himself in New York, where people wearing leg warmers or Druid robes barely merited a second glance. He saw Evelyn and bade farewell to the assistant director with, evidently, one more hilarious joke.

"Well, hi, there, honey. This city of yours is as hot as Hades, isn't it?" he said. He hit the "idn't" particularly hard.

"Dad, you remember Charlotte and Preston? And this is Scot," Evelyn said.

Dale, who hadn't seen Charlotte and Preston since Evelyn's

Sheffield graduation, and who, to Evelyn's recollection, hadn't once asked about them, didn't pause. He looked each of them in the eye as he shook hands. "Charlotte, you're looking pretty as ever. Preston, thanks for looking out for my little girl in the big city. Scot, it sure is a pleasure."

Charlotte was shifting her weight. "Nice to see you, Mr. Beegan. I'm just going to go grab some food. Does anyone want anything? No? Okay," she said, and she darted off.

"Well," Dale said, looking around the room. "This looks like quite an event. What's that you're reading there, Scot?" A white volume was sticking out of Scot's messenger bag.

"An economic journal. An article about Nouriel Roubini," Scot said, as Preston, behind him, feigned narcolepsy.

"What did Mr. Roubini have to say?" Dale asked.

"He thinks America's about to go over a cliff. Housing, bank failures."

"The prophet of dooooom," Preston said in a Scooby voice.

"Well, it would be nice to see Wall Street taken to task," Dale said.

"Dad, let's leave Wall Street alone, okay?" Evelyn said.

Dale looked around, then perked up. "Ah! Look, that's Jim Weisz over there. I tried a case against him in SDNY last year. I'll just go say hello." He strode off as quickly as he had arrived.

"SDNY?" said Preston.

"The Southern District of New York. Federal court," Scot explained.

"Oh, good. I was afraid it was a state school," Preston said, pushing aside the straw in his drink to drain his glass. "Another round?"

As Preston went to get drinks, Evelyn joined Charlotte at the appetizer table; caviar was just toppling off Charlotte's piled-up plate.

"God, isn't this all a bit much? How much do you think this event cost?" Charlotte said.

Evelyn picked up a plate, surprised that Charlotte, who always seemed to be staying afloat with her salary, would have noticed cost.

"Don't you ever—" Charlotte said. "I mean, all of it, all this prep-school stuff and everything that surrounds it, the weekend trips and the wines and the dinners. Like, when we were at Nick's in the Hamptons, everyone was just sort of congratulating themselves on being part of the WASP hegemony, when it's not really meaningful anymore."

Evelyn picked up a smoked salmon crepe. "I don't know, Char. It has its appeal," she said.

"How?"

"I guess it's in the tradition of it. The way of life, the code of manners. Treating people well, and serving a greater good. The people—Char, not to be all PLU propaganda, but I thought the people would be awful and they're nice. They're great, in fact."

"But"—Charlotte swept her hand over the meeting room—"who in that crowd, or here, for that matter, is achieving a greater good? It's a bunch of self-involved kids who have jobs supplied for them by their parents."

"That's not true, Charlotte. You're saying that because everyone's young, and no one's really had a chance to shine yet, but Camilla's going to run the New York social scene and, you laugh, but it is pretty important charitable work. Nick's grandfather was a Massachusetts governor, and he'll probably go into politics."

"That's crazy talk. Nick can't even get a promotion to VP and has a long history of cocaine use that would waylay any attempt to run for office. You think any journalist covering him isn't going to turn up the, like, thirty women a year he slept with and never called back before he marries whatever proper wife he ends up marrying? Also, in order to be in politics, shouldn't he be doing something other than banking right now?"

"He's not going to be a banker forever. He was talking last weekend about moving back to Brookline and running for selectman. The banking background gives him some real-world experience."

"I don't think it works like that anymore. Look at the kids out there who actually are trying to do politics as a career. About half of the kids I went to Harvard with were dead set on being president. They were scary as hell, but that's a side note. They were presidents of their high-school classes, and they joined the Institute of Politics the first week on campus, and by the time we graduated they were interning in D.C. and organizing conferences with Henry Kissinger. A banker with family connections can't just sail in and get elected anymore."

"Look at the Bushes. There's something about family connections that people trust."

"The Bushes! Okay, except for an incident where Daddy buys you out of trouble and gets you the presidency—"

"Charlotte, please, I don't really need your lecture on this. The Kennedys, if you want an example of a Democrat."

"I'm just saying that money is made in so many more interesting ways now."

"Well, but doesn't that make the tradition more important? If anyone can make money, isn't it desirable to have, I don't know, breeding, or tradition—"

"Say it. Class."

"Charlotte."

"Class. Class class class class class."

"Whatever. I'm just saying that as all these colleges and clubs and whatnot open up to literally anyone who can buy their way in, and even to people who get in on their own merits, then maybe people still want somewhere where family and tradition and—"

"Insularity and aristocracy still reign? Keep the rabble out, right, Ev? Look, the WASPs used to be in charge of everything because there was no one else there. Now there is. We live in a meritocratic society, or at least what's supposed to be a meritocratic society, so you have people with actual ability who are gaining power. I mean, the manners of the WASPs are still good, yes, but there's nothing else to look up to. Nobody cares about the WASPs except the WASPs themselves."

"I just don't think that's true. Look at, I don't know, fashion.

Michael Kors's fall collection is all *Gatsby* and *Love Story*. Rugby stripes everywhere."

"You care about fashion now?"

"You don't need to be so dismissive, Charlotte."

"Okay. It's a cultural reference still, I'll give you that," Charlotte said.

"Look, the other paradigm for someone with money is, like, Phil Giamatti or your dreadful boss with his house on Meadow Lane. I'm not sure that's something to aspire to, either."

Charlotte snorted. "Did I tell you my boss named his new yacht the *Never Satisfied II*?" she said.

Evelyn laughed. "The *Never Satisfied I* should've been a clue."

When the parental Beegans joined them at dinner, Charlotte abruptly got up from the table, claiming she had promised to sit with her old swimming coach. That meant Barbara seated herself next to Scot, where her conversation grew seemingly more and more random, though Evelyn knew precisely what Barbara's aim was as she brought up tennis to see if Scot played, then talked about great Baltimore families that Scot couldn't have known, then asked where he prepped. When he said he had gone to high school in Arizona, Barbara inquired if it was a public school, and when he gave an affirmative, she asked if it was on an Indian reservation.

Evelyn was eager for the break when the speaker, an alumnus who was now ambassador to China, spoke. She drifted away during the boring thrum of his speech, but snapped back during the question-and-answer session when she saw Scot's hand raised high. Her mother inclined her head, and Evelyn put one hand on his knee. "It's not really that sort of an event," she whispered with a light smile.

"They just asked for questions."

"I know, but people don't really ask questions at these dinners," she said.

"I think it's fine to ask questions," Dale, sitting on Evelyn's other side, said loudly. "Fire away. Good to hold people in power responsible."

From across the room, an old alumnus croaked out a question about the Yangtze cruise accommodations, and Scot gave Evelyn a quizzical look, raising his hand higher.

"Yes," Scot said when someone brought the microphone to him. "I was curious about whether there's any movement on the notion that President Bush should pressure Hu Jintao on the artificially low value of the yuan, and how you're thinking about the effect of that on American manufacturing versus the effect a freely traded yuan could have on U.S. interest rates."

Preston, sitting across the table, made spirit fingers at Evelyn, Barbara gripped her napkin, and Dale grinned, entertained. The ambassador answered the question, and Scot then indicated he wanted the microphone back, but Evelyn waved off the microphone holder. "That's good, Scot. That's enough," Evelyn whispered.

"I thought—"

"That's good," she said, with an eye on her mother's knuckles.

"I like his spunk," Dale said.

As they got up from their seats, Barbara clutched Evelyn's shoulder. "This is a Sheffield alumni event, not a news conference," Barbara hissed. "I presume the ambassador thought he was speaking to friends, not interrogators."

Evelyn rearranged her napkin on the table. "Well!" she said to the napkin. "Should we get going?"

"So. He's from Nevada," Barbara said, as she steered Evelyn toward the coat check.

"Arizona."

"His family is still in Arizona?"

"His mother is."

"A widow?"

"No, she's divorced."

"Divorced." Barbara pursed her lips. "I'll tell you something, Evelyn. The Topfer women may not have been happy, but we have never resorted to divorce."

This was true; even after Barbara's father had fled with the secretary, Barbara's mother, who spent most of her time smoking cigarettes and cutting coupons, never filed for divorce. Evelyn pulled two singles from her wallet for the coat-check girl.

"I told you to start wearing suntan lotion on your hands," Barbara said. "You have to be careful about wrinkles. The hands are the first to go, Evelyn. The hands and the knees. Have you been wearing suntan lotion on your knees?"

"I don't know."

"They're a dead giveaway for age. You're already almost twenty-seven. Is this really the best way to be spending your time? With this Arizonian?"

"Twenty-six. Most people my age aren't married."

"A lot are. Palling about with an Arizona boy is fine when you're just out of college, but at this age—"

"Mom, he's, like, he's really smart. Charlotte says he's one of the smartest people at Morgan Stanley. He was recruited there by David Greenbaum, who's a hotshot, and he's one of the youngest VPs there, which is a position even higher than Nick has. It's not like he's a subway musician."

"I'm sure he's perfectly qualified for his work. I thought your website job would take you into new circles, however. Lead you to meet new people."

"It has."

"It's just with the investigation—" Barbara guided Evelyn to the end of the hallway, where no one was listening.

"Everyone's father is getting investigated these days," Evelyn said. She had been trying to convince herself of this ever since Camilla had said it, and the mantra sometimes helped tamp down her anxiety about the investigation, but it rang false when she said it aloud.

"Oh, are they?" Barbara's tone was sarcastic. "How nice to know New York has become so accepting. In Bibville, they do care, as it happens." Barbara extracted a mauve lipstick from her bag and applied it precisely. "To tell you the truth, all of my friends at the Eastern have been asking me about you, and saying they just don't know why someone hasn't snapped you up yet. Because deep down, people think something is wrong with you when you aren't married or engaged at twenty-seven. It starts to be strange."

"Why don't you tell them I'm dating someone?"

"I don't want you to make the same mistake as I did. Marrying someone on the fringes of the circle just puts you on the fringes of the circle, don't you see? The life you're conscripted to, of constant social adjustments because your husband doesn't bother with what he thinks are silly social niceties, isn't a pleasant one. Rules are rules for a reason. Scot doesn't even play tennis. Do you really want to spend your life with someone who can't play tennis?"

"Mom, that's so old-fashioned," Evelyn said. Yet Evelyn had felt disappointment when Scot sat on the sidelines during the tennis games at Nick's, lost in his history book, not caring that he couldn't play, while Evelyn had to partner with Nick's fat friend from Enfield who flung sweat all over the court.

"I wanted to talk to you about Jaime Cardenas. He's on all the junior benefits committees, and went to Harvard and Stanford business school. Fernando Cardenas's son. Do you know him yet?" Barbara said.

Evelyn was often amazed by her mother, who managed to track young New York social circles almost as closely as Evelyn now had to, despite Barbara's barely knowing how to use the Internet. Evelyn didn't know Jaime, but she knew of Jaime; she had Googled Jaime several times after seeing him in some pictures with Camilla. The family fortune started with a Venezuelan bottling plant a few generations ago, and then Jaime's grandfather had built up a conglomerate of consumer products, retail and banking businesses. Jaime was now a vice president at the family business and had hit the New York social scene with some force, including an unheard-of election to the Met Museum's board of trustees at the age of twenty-eight. He was one of her eventual targets for People Like Us, but she hadn't yet run into him to give him the pitch. "It's pronounced 'Haime,' Mom, and 'de Carden-yaz.' Or 'de Carden-yas.' Jaime de Cardenas. Scot went to Harvard, too."

"The business school isn't the same thing as the college. Jaime de Cardenas." Her mother said it slowly and as if there were olives stuffed in her mouth; Evelyn wondered if it was the only Spanish she'd ever spoken apart from "Rioja." "Good. So you do know him."

"Not really."

"Now, normally I'm not sure how I'd feel about someone, you know, Chicano," Barbara was saying.

"I don't think people say 'Chicano' anymore."

"The fact is, the world is changing."

"I'm sure Jaime will be delighted to hear that."

"Stop that sarcasm. It's unbecoming. I think you should consider dating him."

It was Sheffield all over again. Her mother thought a simple directive was sufficient to make Evelyn achieve social glory. Just make friends with so-and-so from Watch Hill. Just date a Venezuelan billionaire. Yet her mother had never made it at that level, Evelyn thought, and had been trying to make up for it ever since.

"I have a boyfriend," Evelyn said.

"Call it what you will. Evelyn, I hate to say it, but your looks will start to fade, and your body will start to sag. It's been happening to me for the last thirty years, and it's just dreadful. When I think about what I could have done at twenty-six—well. Jaime de Cardenas is linked to Spanish nobility. That is something you just can't argue with. Susie—you remember Susie, her daughter is in Washington— was saying he's heading the Save Venice ball this year."

Save Venice, and the young friends of the Frick, and the Apollo Circle at the Met Opera, yes, yes, Evelyn knew.

"You ought to keep an eye out for him. He sounds like the last of the eligible bachelors," Barbara said.

Evelyn saw Scot, at the other end of the hallway, waiting for her and doing an awkward arm stretch. Her mother's verdict was in; Evelyn was silent for a while, pressing her thumb over the top joint of her pinkie.

"That's all I wanted to say," Barbara finally said. "Can you please help me with my coat?"

CHAPTER TWELVE

Summer in the City

Camilla had deemed one of the final summer weekends an "urban incursion," ignoring Scot's correction that an "incursion" was a sudden invasion and not the opposite of "excursion." "It'll be fabulous," Camilla had said to Evelyn. "All of the restaurants will be practically empty, and we can go anywhere we like, and do Pilates, and don't have to wait for appointments at Exhale."

"You never have to wait for appointments at Exhale," Evelyn had said.

Camilla had just smiled.

Evelyn snuck out of PLU at noon that Friday, after an intense and tiring argument with Arun and Jin-ho. The Habsburg founder was unhappy with the membership numbers, and Arun and Jin-ho called her into one of the conference rooms to discuss it. They wanted more traditional marketing, they said; Evelyn should do whatever it took to get the numbers up.

"Like what?" she'd asked. "You want me to buy mailing lists from real-estate records in tony neighborhoods? Do you know how expensive those are, and how much unsolicited mail those people get? The point of this site is that it's selective. If you want mass, you can go to MySpace, and even Facebook isn't restrictive about colleges anymore. We don't need to copy what they're doing."

"We need something else," Arun had said. "The one-off events you've held have been expensive and haven't resulted in big yields."

"It's a long-term strategy. At this point we shouldn't be doing huge events with huge numbers. If you want to spend on a real launch party, terrific. I'll happily get behind that. But that's going to be in the hundreds of thousands of dollars and I don't think we have the budget for it. The smaller events are relatively cheap and are building buzz: we've been on Page Six, we've been in Styles, and the members we have are purely A-list: Bridie Harley, Caperton Ripp, Camilla Rutherford, Preston and Bing Hacking, to name a few. That's precisely where we want to be."

"Ulrich feels the numbers should be higher by now," Arun had said.

"Ulrich is Swiss and, with respect, in his seventies. We're going after American twentysomethings. He's going to have to trust us."

"One of my buddies works in the Rangers front office," Jin-ho had said. "You should talk to him once hockey season gets going. They're pros at comarketing."

"The Rangers? Are you kidding?" Evelyn said. "I don't think providing foam fingers as men knock out each other's teeth screams elite. We're trying to prove that this is a site for the highest social strata. If we do something off-brand now, we lose them. They can smell error. They can smell weakness."

Arun had twisted his lips, then smiled; he was nicer than Jin-ho. "Okay, Evelyn, but like it or not, we all work for Ulrich, and if he says we get the numbers up, then we get the numbers up. It doesn't have to be a Rangers game, but you've got to figure something out."

Evelyn had folded her arms, not wanting to commit to anything. When she'd seen Arun and Jin-ho leave the building at noon, headed for some Vegas bachelor party, she'd strode out onto the street, hitting the pavement so hard she made dents in her heels, to meet Camilla at Takashimaya, a Japanese department store on Fifth.

It was quiet as a library in there when Evelyn found Camilla on the second floor, examining a travel nail-care kit encased in crocodile. "This is cute, don't you think?" Camilla said when Evelyn arrived. Evelyn felt like her head was emitting clouds of steam.

"What?" asked Camilla.

"Work," Evelyn groaned. "They won't listen to a thing I have to say."

"Who won't?"

"The co-CEOs. Arun and Jin-ho."

"Whoosie and whatsit? Who are they?"

"Stanford grads. Random Stanford grads, I might add. Jin-ho buttons his top button, and Arun unbuttons to, like, three or four buttons, so we can all share in his chest hair. Yet they think they know more than I do about what to do for the site."

"That's cray-cray. Ignore it!" Camilla said gaily. "My acupuncturist says we have to dismiss all negative energy in our lives. I want leather sandals."

As though Camilla had summoned a genie, a white-haired man approached. Evelyn let her eyes slide over him, mimicking the frostiness with which Barbara had always treated salespeople, and expecting Camilla to do the same. Instead, Camilla leaned in.

"Hello!" said Camilla, as if the man were a favorite uncle. "How are you? Isn't it beautiful outside today? I love your tie pin. I'm hoping for some sandals. Size seven."

The man gave her a gap-toothed grin that made him look sweet and alive, not like a laid-off office worker who could only find a job selling ladies' shoes. This was the magic of Camilla. "Sandals," the man repeated, and headed into the back. He returned with three large boxes and squatted below Camilla.

"You're too funny," Camilla said, as he fastened one pair on her feet.

"I'm sorry," Evelyn said. "I'm still thinking about this work thing. They actually mentioned doing a marketing event at a Rangers game today."

"Ew. I don't want my profile on there if there are going to be sports people on it."

"No, no no no no. They're not actually going to do it. I'm not going to let them. I will preserve the site, I promise." Evelyn couldn't lose Camilla as a member, and she quickly formed a new idea. "Members should come from people like us, per the site name. I was thinking they should do something with, say, the new crop of debs."

She watched; it worked; Camilla bit. "Ooh, that would be good. I could totally see the deb set using it," she said.

Evelyn turned her head, trying to keep the smile from spreading over her face. She had been studying debutantes lately for her PLU work, reading about them at the New York Public Library. In microfilm and microfiche, she had learned—with some difficulty, as part of the code of being a deb was you didn't speak or write about being a deb—about New York debbing.

She had first gotten wind of the New York debutante scene at Sheffield, where Preston had been an escort at some of the balls. "The season," to the degree that it was still a season, was an approximation of the London Court parties that inspired the American debutante tradition.

The Bal Français was the first of the balls, held in June, just as the seniors were graduated from high school. With the prestigious balls occurring over the holidays, the Bal served as a training ground. The Junior League, at Thanksgiving, was a bit new-money, though considered a fun party. At Christmastime, the Infirmary was the big social event, with girls from old Greenwich and Boston and D.C. families in addition to New Yorkers; since the debs could invite friends, it was a popular party for the young set. The Junior Assembly was the real deal, a small, old-school ball limited to debs, family, and escorts, where it still raised eyebrows if a girl was Catholic. The International, held close to New Year's, completed the season, but it was for new-money arrivistes, the daughters of Russian oligarchs and Southern chicken-parts kings.

Evelyn had read, too, about the sociology of debutante balls, about why this seemingly archaic tradition still occurred in cities all over the country—from Dallas to Seattle to Boston—and why they kept going even as eighteen-year-old girls were clearly no longer being introduced to society for the first time at them. "Rite of passage marked with social status symbolism," she had scribbled in her notebook. "Effort at social stratification." "Way to pass on class markers/place in society to children b/c Americans have no Brit-like titles—same fxn as Social Register." "Cultural capital." "Invitation-only means elite get to decide invitees. Distinguish elite from not-so-elite."

"Right," Evelyn said. If Camilla was talking about debutantes with her, she must assume that Evelyn had debbed, too; that was the code. "Absolutely. I'd think it would be a big draw for the site. Even just the content around the balls—where should I look for my dress, where should we postparty, et cetera."

"I could see it," Camilla said.

"I had such issues with my dress, because I was fitted for it in the summer and then went off to school and gained eight pounds, and the dressmaker was so angry with me." The words tumbled out, and Evelyn didn't even want to stop them. She wanted to see where this would lead.

"Where did you deb?" Camilla asked, pointing at the sandals.

"The Bachelors' Cotillion," Evelyn said casually. She hadn't spent all that time with microfiche for nothing.

"The Bachelors' Cotillion," Camilla repeated.

"In Baltimore." Evelyn quickly added to her pitch. "It's so funny and old school. When my grandmother did it, they all had to wear long-sleeve dresses, and there was complete chaos when one of the girls wore a strapless dress. We used to see that woman at the tennis club, and by this time she was seventy, wearing caftans, and my grandmother still considered her so risqué." She was fascinated by how the words sprinted out faster than her brain seemed to form them.

Camilla just smiled. "Hilarious." Then she leapt up, handing the man her AmEx Platinum. "Can you just wrap these up for me? Thanks so much. Evelyn: we have to talk."

Evelyn started to backtrack on the debutante story, but before she could, Camilla continued, "You know my mother's forcing me to be the junior-committee host for the Luminaries, right?"

"Sure," Evelyn said. It was the key fund-raiser for the New-York Signet Society, a charity that supported artistic and literary events around the city.

"I was thinking, your father would be a great Luminary."

"My father? He's not a New Yorker."

Camilla winked. "Sometimes we can make exceptions. Particularly if the Luminaries are supportive of the group."

"Milla, he's not a literary guy."

"I was thinking he should come in at the Luminary Patrons level. There's a fabulous dinner that he'd love. He sounds so fun, Evelyn. We never get people from the South and he would spice it up."

"I'm sure he'd love to, but honestly, I don't think it's his kind of thing."

"Evelyn, you support my things, I support your things," Camilla said in a low voice, narrowing her eyes. Evelyn half expected a "Capisce?" from her.

"I'll definitely ask, but—"

"So the Patrons level. He'll really enjoy it. I'll put together the information for him. Let him know I'm counting on him for a Patrons donation. It's twenty-five thousand, so."

"Twenty-five thousand." Evelyn licked her lips. "Right, the thing is, though—"

The man returned with a triangular shopping bag, and Camilla took it as she continued, "He will have a great time. I don't want to hear another word about it. Now, lunch." She started to walk away, leaving Evelyn a little stunned.

———————

Evelyn had pictured the whole New York weekend being just her and Camilla, shopping and ordering drinks and brunching, but when she joined Camilla that evening at Sant Ambroeus, Camilla had ordered Aperol spritzes for seven.

"Who else is coming?" Evelyn said, taking a sip of the fluorescent-orange drink.

"Nick, Brooke Birch, Will Brodzik, Pres, and I think Pres is bringing your friend Carrie," Camilla said.

"Charlotte?" Evelyn said.

"Isn't it Carrie?" Camilla asked.

Brooke had gone to St. Paul's and Trinity with Camilla, Evelyn had discovered when Googling her after an earlier mention. Her plump boyfriend Will had played water polo at Enfield but was squarely middle class; he had been an Enfield day student, practically a townie, Camilla had once explained. Brooke and Will had been uncompetitive sorts who moved to San Francisco after college, electing a life of triathlons and second-tier markets instead of the elbow throwing of New York. Brooke had worked for two years doing fund-raising at the San Francisco Museum of Modern Art. She had quit not long ago, and talked vaguely about opening a boutique in Pacific Heights, but her mother's second marriage had been good enough that she would inherit plenty and didn't have to work. Indeed, the marriage, to a ski-resort developer, was also good for Will, who worked for Brooke's stepfather's firm.

Brooke arrived when Camilla was in the bathroom and, when the maître d' took her over to the table, flat-out glared at Evelyn before sitting.

"I'm Evelyn Beegan. It's so nice to finally meet you. I've heard so much about you," Evelyn said, scooting out from her chair to offer her hand. "So you know Camilla from St. Paul's?"

"We're very old friends," said Brooke, who had thin blond hair and pointy ears, emphasizing the "very." "I thought it was just me, her, Will, and Preston tonight, actually."

"Nope," said Evelyn.

"You met through a website?"

Brooke was being jealous, and thus bitchy, and Evelyn took her time sitting back down before she responded. "We met in Lake James. But yes, I work for a website. People Like Us? There was a Styles feature about it last week."

"It's online dating or something?"

"No. Not at all, actually. It's a social network. We have a few clusters of members. In New York, of course, but also Dubai, London, Geneva. Aspen," she said pointedly, given that she remembered Brooke's stepfather had a giant place in Vail so Brooke probably had an inferiority complex about Aspen.

"Well," said Brooke.

Nick, Preston, Will, and Charlotte tumbled in en masse, midconversation about an acquaintance.

"He went to Wharton, though," Charlotte was saying.

"He went to Wharton because his father gets everyone else important into Wharton," Nick said. "His dad fucked up the Federated LBO."

"His father didn't get you into Wharton," Charlotte said.

"Get over yourself, Hillary. The point is, he's an idiot but his CDO group at Lehman made billions last year. Billions. Enough profits for the whole firm. They package these bullshit mortgages for, what's the term, Pres?"

"Subprime."

"No, the other one."

"Oh, NINJA."

"Right. No income, no job, no assets."

"CDO is collateralized debt . . . ," Charlotte said.

"Obligation," Nick finished. "Banks selling packages of mortgages made to the losers in Nevada and California."

"First of all, it's not the fault of the people getting the loans, it's the banks' fault for making the loans. Second of all, the housing market isn't that hot anymore," Charlotte said.

"German banks are buying this shit like it's candy, so it's a no-lose," Nick said. "I just can't believe this Lehman dude gets that kind of bonus."

"I'm bored," Camilla said, sauntering back to the table. "Enough business. Do we all know one another?"

"I'm surprised to see you here," Evelyn said quietly to Charlotte as Camilla handled introductions.

"I'm surprised to see me here, too," Charlotte said. "Pres called me and I was done with work early, and I figured it was worth braving Ms. Rutherford to have a real dinner out and see you two. Nobody's been in the city all summer."

"So. Are we all thrilled about our urban weekend?" Camilla said, speaking over Charlotte.

"I thought we were going to get out of the city," Brooke said. "We didn't fly in so we could spend the weekend in Manhattan."

"Well, I thought a weekend here would be fun," Camilla said coolly. "So you're welcome to make your own plans if you disagree. For those of us who actually want to have a good time, we'll have drinks at my place after dinner."

Brooke exchanged a look with Will that Evelyn couldn't decipher. "That sounds good," Brooke said weakly.

"Good," Camilla said. "Anyway, I told you the Realtor wants to get his beasts into the École, right? So guess who's been recruited as a debutante supervisor for the Bal?"

Camilla should travel with a translator, Evelyn thought. "The Realtor," aka Ari, was Souse Rutherford's boyfriend, he of the BIG-DEAL license plate. His company, AF Holdings, owned much of the important real estate in New York—the Pierre Hotel, the Lord & Taylor building. Camilla didn't like him, hence "the Realtor." Ari lived in a giant floor-through apartment on Fifth Avenue, having swooped in and gotten a lowball price of $21.5 million when a higher bid by a Bahraini prince was rejected by the co-op board over concerns that his diplomatic immunity would lead to weapons caching in their building. The "beasts" were Ari's two small children, who were

something like four and six, and "the École" was the École Interna-
tionale, a French-language school on East End Avenue that was notably hard to get into. And "the Bal"—Evelyn felt like she was
completing a timed quiz—was the Bal Français, the debutante ball
whose hostesses were largely École parents and board members.

"You as an example to young minds? What on earth are you going
to do, lead waltzing lessons and slip them some whip-its?" Preston
asked.

"And do the danse d'honneur," Camilla said with a bow. "Where
they have the deb from ages past skip around with the ambassador?"

"It's so important," said Brooke, with wide eyes. "Bill Cunning-
ham always puts a photo of the danse d'honneur in his column, and
Marchesa lent a dress last year to Sophie Gerond for it. Milla. That's
amazing."

Camilla set a spoon spinning on the tablecloth. "Phoebe's doing
the Assembly and Infirmary, obviously, but my mother has signed her
up for the Bal Français in June because Ari thinks it'll help with his
children getting into the École. Who knows?" Camilla said.

The Bal Français, Evelyn knew, ranked near the bottom of the New
York balls, but was still important—those who succeeded at the Bal
often got invitations for the wintertime balls that were the true society
gatherings. However, being a deb at the Bal without following with the
Assembly or the Infirmary was like being a Staten Island Yankee.

A waiter put down a bread basket. Charlotte was the only girl to
reach for it.

"Does Ari even speak French?" Nick said.

"Ari speaks dollars," Camilla said. She stood the spoon on its end,
and Evelyn watched the light bounce off the metal. "Anyway, darling,
it's not about speaking French. It's about the school. The École had,
like, eleven kids accepted to Yale early this year. I'm sure the Realtor
wouldn't care if they were instructed in Tunisian with that acceptance rate."

"Tunisian's not a language," said Charlotte. "They speak Arabic.
And French."

"Exactly," said Camilla.

Brooke made a happy moan. "How fun for Phoebe. I did the International in college. I loved it."

Camilla nodded. "You're right. The Bal is at least oodles better than the International. Phoebe will have fun," she said, so quickly that Evelyn wondered if Brooke had even sensed she'd been slighted. "Evelyn, when you debbed, was it a big party or a small one? I don't even know how it's done outside of the real cities."

Evelyn glanced at Charlotte, who had a fat glob of butter on the side of her lip. Evelyn didn't give her the dab-it-away signal; if Charlotte wanted to do her whole intellectually superior thing with "Tunisian's not a language," Evelyn wasn't going to help her out.

"It's a party in Baltimore," Evelyn said. "Medium sized."

Charlotte pushed her tongue at the spot of butter, but missed it. "You were a debutante, Ev? Why don't I remember that?"

"Well, who's going to brag about it, right?" Evelyn gave a high laugh.

"What the what? Why didn't I get an invitation?" Preston said, adjusting his eyeglasses. "I was the best escort. At one of the balls, I got so smashed that a mother took me outside the Plaza in a snowstorm to try to sober me up. I think I tried to make out with her. I think, in confidence, she slipped me the tongue."

"Ew!" Evelyn laughed.

"I smuggled in pot when I was an escort," Nick said. "Trust me, that made the midnight breakfast really tasty."

Camilla narrowed her eyes at Will. "And you, Will?"

"Oh, I didn't do that stuff," he said.

"Oh?" Camilla let the silence fall, waiting a few beats. "So, Birchie," she continued. "Will may think this all rather puzzling, I suppose, and old-fashioned. For the Bal, you'll help me, right? My mother has signed me up for the hostess committee—they like a young person to corral the debs—and I can't handle all those teenagers by myself so she said I could pick someone to do it with me."

"Oh, my gosh, yes. Of course, Milla."

"That's great. It's not a lot of work, honestly. Just a few meetings and then the ball itself in June."

"In June?" Brooke shot a glance at Will. "Well, I'd love to, though the thing is, in June I might be busy. Sweetie?"

Will stood up and clinked his spoon against his water glass, an entirely unnecessary motion, as the restaurant was quiet other than their table. "We have an announcement," he said, leaning too heavily on the "we." He looked to Brooke, who thrust out her hand, her ring finger erect. It had a diamond ring on it, which she must have slipped on in her pocket, as she hadn't been wearing it a moment ago. "We're engaged!" she squealed.

Preston and Nick were instantly on their feet, clapping Will on the back and kissing Brooke on the cheek, and Charlotte got up, too, proffering masculine handshakes to them both, but Evelyn stayed seated when she noticed Camilla, across the table, also seated and carefully folding pleats into her napkin. "Wow, congrats, kids," Camilla said.

Brooke rushed around the table. "Do you want to see the ring?"

"Yes, definitely," Camilla said, batting away Brooke's hand. "It's so round."

Evelyn stood up and awkwardly patted Brooke on the back. "That's great," she said to Brooke. "So pretty."

The waiter then appeared with a bottle of champagne and several glasses. "To celebrate!" Will called out, and the group accepted their flutes and Nick called out a toast to the couple.

Camilla drank fast, finishing her champagne in a few sips and holding the glass out for the waiter to refill, then sloshing a bit over the side. "Oops. My cup runneth over," she said, raising the glass in the direction of the betrothed.

After dinner, Evelyn and Camilla walked straight to Camilla's apartment; Nick insisted on stopping at the wine store with Preston, arguing that the last time Preston had gotten a Burgundy it was so thin it tasted like it was from Long Island, and Charlotte, who was drunk and arguing with Nick over the 1986 Red Sox lineup, went with them. Brooke, complaining that her heels were too high, said she and

Will would take a cab. As Evelyn and Camilla peeled off, they heard Brooke, almost in tears, saying to Will that this was not how her engagement announcement was supposed to go.

Camilla was walking down Madison so quickly that Evelyn had to jog to keep up. "So. What just happened? The engagement theater? I'm surprised there wasn't a floor show," Camilla said.

Evelyn measured what she knew: that Camilla and Brooke had been best friends at St. Paul's, that the wedding was interrupting Camilla's plans for the Bal, and that Camilla disliked Will. She went with a neutral statement. "They certainly wanted a celebration."

This worked as she had hoped, eliciting more from Camilla so Evelyn could figure out where to head next. "First of all, they had to have gotten engaged a while ago, and they were just keeping it from us to make us celebrate their fabulous choice. I mean, the viewing of the ring? The ordering of your own celebratory champagne? There are no words. I should've ordered my own bottle of champagne and had everyone toast to me."

"Camilla, for her latest string of successes . . . ," Evelyn said.

"Right? Why not?" They paused at a red light, a motorcycle zooming past. "You don't know Brooke, obviously, but back, before, she was the most fun. A total original. And now? Will? Will Brodzik? Evelyn, his parents own a car dealership. A car dealership, Evelyn. And he gets to marry Brooke? Really? I'll bet that she'll pull the goalie on the wedding night, and Brooke will be pregnant within a month. Then what? They'll move to some San Francisco suburb, Will will go to his absurd job and pretend he cares about his career, and that's it. We were in the same house at St. Paul's, and senior year she was always talking about living in Italy and designing her own clothing line, and now she's basically going to be a suburban wife. I mean, what's the point?" They passed a closed shoe store, the shoes uplit like jewelry. "I'll bet their first child will be named Will. Their second child will be named Birch. That's about the level of imagination we're dealing with. It kills me."

"Brooke Birch Brodzik?" Evelyn said with a chortle.

"Oh, my God, I hadn't even thought of that. Brooke Birch Brodzik. Evelyn, there's so little greatness in our society today, so little actual greatness, and so much—this sounds terrible, but you understand—focus on work and drudgery," Camilla went on. "Can you keep a secret?"

"Like a cat." This wasn't quite the comparison Evelyn was looking for.

"I'm going to quit," Camilla said.

"Quit work?"

"Let's be honest—it's pointless, isn't it? I don't know what me learning about Microsoft Outlook is going to do for the world. It's not good for the skin, or for the body, to sit inside an office all day. I think I'd be so much more useful and helpful to society if I became more involved in real work now, rather than pretending like I care about coordinating the waiters' outfits for another event."

"I hadn't thought of it like that," Evelyn said.

"Will Brodzik! When people our age are actually doing things. Like Jaime de Cardenas, and yet there's boring Will." She swung her arms like an ape.

"Jaime? Completely," Evelyn said carefully.

"You know him?"

"I know—I think I've met him at the Harvard Club," Evelyn said.

"I think he's going to be a great man. A great man. Are you going to marry Scot?"

"I've only been dating him for a couple of months."

"I see." Camilla frowned, though lightly; she was always careful not to frown in a way that would increase wrinkles. "It's so hard to imagine Scot at Harvard, isn't it?" She turned onto Seventy-first. "Scot's a good match for you, anyway."

Message received, thought Evelyn, trying not to roll her eyes at Camilla's undercutting.

At Camilla's apartment, a classic six on Fifth that looked over the

Central Park Zoo, the group reassembled. By the fourth bottle of wine, Brooke had brought the conversation back to her engagement.

"I wanted to do Asscher cut, though I had always thought of myself as a princess-cut girl, so that's what we ended up going with," Brooke was saying.

"Wow," said Camilla, looking at the ring with a big smile. "It's so beautiful, Birchie. Just what you always wanted. So you're thinking June?"

"I think so. It's so much planning. My mom is helping me, of course, and she thinks June flowers will be just right, with the roses and the lilies."

Evelyn poured herself a big glass of wine, wondering what Camilla, her attitude completely changed from hours earlier, was up to; she was now asking Brooke about her preferred bridal-gown silhouettes. It was only when the rest of the group had come to attention that Camilla stopped, letting a Brooke statement about necklines hang in the air.

"Birchie," said Camilla, though she was addressing the room, "it sounds like the wedding will be an absolute ton of work. I don't want to take you away from that, so I'll be a good friend and let you out of the Bal." Before Brooke had swallowed her sip of wine, Camilla tossed her hair and turned toward Evelyn. "Evelyn, you can do it, right? You'll have time?"

Evelyn looked up from her glass. Everyone but Will had frozen midsip.

"Evelyn? You were a deb, so you know the whole thing," Camilla said.

"I do. I do. I'd love to. I mean, if Brooke—"

"Brooke's a bride-to-be now. She has flowers and guest lists and becoming Mrs. Brodzik to deal with. Right, Birchie? Ev," Camilla said, thrillingly shortening her name for the first time Evelyn could remember, "you are going to love it. I think it's one of the best parties in New York."

"That's fine," said Brooke, her eyes bright. "That's fine. I will be busy in June, Camilla, you're right."

"That'll be great," said Evelyn. "That'll be fabulous."

Will, oblivious, finished his glass with a slurp. "Anyone up for golf tomorrow?" he said.

"It is a city weekend, Will. You can golf back in San Francisco," said Camilla, who had turned to look out the window.

Later, when Evelyn stepped over a supine Preston to go to the bathroom, he tapped her ankle with the Cohiba he was smoking. "The Bal. That's all right," he said.

Part Two

CHAPTER THIRTEEN

Rich and Happy

When Evelyn had seen the e-mail with the subject line "FW: Bal tea and planning meeting," she had made herself wait to open it, just to savor its deliciousness. She half expected Camilla to forget about her offer, or to reinstate Brooke on the committee, but there in bright black and white was the information: "hi Ev see below excited xx." To her delight, she saw it was at Margaret Faber's apartment, the woman who had been so friendly at Sachem, and then she saw Margaret Faber lived at one of the best addresses in all of New York.

She wasn't sure what her mother's reaction to the debutante-committee invitation would be, but her mother had been thrilled. Warm, even. "I'm so happy for you, dear," Barbara had said. "It's supposed to be a really wonderful party. I'm so glad you're finally doing all this. I've been telling you for years how interesting these people are." Barbara even called back later, to ask about party details, and sounded genuinely happy. For once, Evelyn had made her mother that happy.

Evelyn felt success at the Bal was vital. If she was a smash here, that could lead to not only more credibility at PLU but more invitations on her own merits. She could be a guest at the Junior League and the Infirmary in the winter, and maybe even join the committees once her children were old enough.

As she arrived at Margaret Faber's apartment on Park, a man in a Hermès tie hurried around Evelyn, and the doormen rumbled, "Good day, Mr. Shuder." Rob Shuder, Hollywood producer, Evelyn thought: new purchaser, a half floor, and a *New York Post*–chronicled fight with neighbors over what constituted public space when his interior decorator added brass studs to the shared hallway.

Evelyn followed him. "Hello," she said. "Evelyn Beegan, for Margaret Faber."

The doorman—or should she call him a concierge?—on the right smiled. "Yes, Miss Beegan, Mrs. Faber is expecting you," he said, without consulting a list. "Please, follow me." His footsteps barely made a sound as he walked across the marble floor, while hers, embarrassingly, squeaked. He called the elevator, and yet another attendant was inside there. "Miss Beegan for Mrs. Faber," he told the attendant. The attendant put his key into the panel and turned it, pressed 12, and with his arms straight at his side and his eyes high, rode up with Evelyn.

"Thank you, Miss Beegan," the attendant said as the elevator swallowed him again, the doors whooshing shut. Evelyn took an uncertain step forward toward a room with rows of chairs and looked—for what? a maid? a butler?—when she saw Margaret Faber, in a waist-nipping blue suit (bouclé like hers, Evelyn noted with relief) sprint into the hallway.

"The cheeses are practically frozen!" Margaret said.

Evelyn pulled herself tall; she hoped she had not been mistaken for a caterer. "I'm sorry to hear it," she said. She looked to her left, down the hallway, where she saw the hostesses, their husbands, the debs-to-be, and the girls' parents mingling in a large living room with built-in bookshelves. The windows overlooked Park, with heavy-looking rose and taupe brocade curtains framing them. Something about the couch looked familiar; Evelyn wondered if she had seen it in *Architectural Digest* before. In an adjoining room, Evelyn could see a camera's flash.

"I'm Camilla Rutherford's friend, Evelyn," she said. The woman's pleasantly expectant smile didn't change. "We met at Sachem? I'm helping out with the debs?"

"Ah, yes. Of course. I didn't realize you were one of Camilla's friends when we met at Sachem. Souse and I have been friends for years, and I've known Camilla since she was a tiny thing. Souse! Souse!" Her voice was booming and loud, and she had no compunction about hollering through the museumlike foyer.

A blond woman came running from the room of minglers—Souse Rutherford, bristling with even more energy than her friend, with a golden tan and beautifully toned arms that were bared in a wool shift dress, also bouclé. "The macarons are coming!" Souse shouted, like an epicurean Paul Revere.

"Camilla's friend is here! Evelyn!" shouted back Margaret.

"Evelyn? Evelyn!" Souse leaned in to inspect her, and Evelyn smelled a mix of perfumed face powder and Chanel No. 5. "Well! I've heard so much about you, and Camilla has been keeping you from me all this time! Look at her. Just adorable. Look at that jacket. That's fabulous. Isn't that fabulous?"

"That is fabulous. It is vintage?" Margaret said.

"Yes, I got it from my mother," Evelyn said. She had gotten it from a consignment store, but the two women's smiles widened, as she hoped they would.

"I wish my daughter would wear my old things." Margaret frowned. "I have a few old Balmains that are just turning into colonies of moths."

"Camilla is, predictably, late, but you ought to come in and meet everyone. The tea's being served in the living room, and the girls are getting their photographs taken in the library, but we have to have a business meeting first with the committee members, just in the anteroom," Souse said.

"We're starting that in five minutes, though half of the women are always late, and unless we rectify this cheese situation—the cheeses are really so hard . . ." Margaret trailed off, looking quite disturbed.

"I can do it. Handle it. The cheese situation. If you just point me in the direction of the kitchen? Just a few seconds in the microwave, I know it's terrible, but it will make them soften." Evelyn could hear her mother's voice: Everyone appreciates a helpful guest. And her own: Sing for your supper, Evelyn.

"Yes!" Margaret clapped. "How clever! Rosa does not know what to do with cheeses, and they are blocks of ice, practically. A cheese needs to breathe! It wants to be out in the world! You don't have to go. I'll call her in here and tell her. Wonderful. Wonderful!"

Evelyn was looking behind Margaret, trying to figure out why the rosy-cheeked drummer boy in the painting seemed so familiar, when she heard Souse say, "Push, should I wait in the lobby, so they don't give the macaron fellow a hard time?"

The round O of Evelyn's mouth matched that of the drummer boy. The apartment appeared to lift up and start spinning around her, and she saw that vase, that table, that rug from years ago. Her hand closed and dampened, as though it were still wrapped around that wadded Tinker Day ribbon, as though it, too, remembered the pressure her ten-year-old self felt to try to hide everything, to try to fix everything, to plaster over her mother's silences and inappropriate grasping and make New York what she and her mother both hoped it could be. But no, Evelyn thought. No. She was not that girl anymore. She would not let herself be unmoored by some old memory, by some past weakness. She had changed. She could show she belonged. She just had to show she belonged.

She tried not to stare at Push, now with darker hair and in a different apartment but otherwise the same woman as all those years ago. As a third woman who had joined them discussed finishing school in Lausanne, Evelyn unclenched her hand and forced her heart rate to slow.

"Such a shame that the girls these days insist on finishing schooling in New York," the woman said, and Evelyn shook her head in sympathetic solidarity.

"This is why we must put them through this debutante season, isn't it? The training is so lacking," said Push.

"All of us are, to a degree, insecure, so anything that gives us confidence can't hurt," said the Lausanne woman, whose calves were thick with muscle.

"Well, American schools used to be different," Push said. "At Hollins, we were required to wear gloves to dinner, if you can believe it, and take flower-arranging classes. Of course, it was a hundred years ago."

"Hollins?" said Camilla, stepping off of the elevator at just the wrong time. "Hi, Mom. Hi, Push. Hi, Mrs. Egstrom. Sorry I'm late. Didn't your mother go to Hollins, Evelyn?"

"Oh? What's her name?" Push and Souse said together.

"She's so much older than you, I'm sure you didn't meet," Evelyn said. "She was"—she did some subtraction quickly, trying to find a big enough age gap that the women wouldn't inquire further—"class of 'fifty-three."

"My!" said Push with a frown.

Realizing she had just cast her mother as somewhere north of seventy, Evelyn let out a Tinker Bell laugh. "I was a late-in-life baby," she said.

"I have one of those, too," said Push with a wink. "Wythe's probably setting fire to the tartlets as we speak."

Wythe, Evelyn thought. She remembered Push having a small child, back when Push was a Van Rensselaer.

In the anteroom—Evelyn was happy she now knew what an anteroom was—the hostess committee gathered for a brief meeting. The ball's chairwoman, Agathe, with wispy white hair and the thin frame of a twentysomething, tallied the debs for this year—three Spence, two Brearley, four École, and one Chapin—then admonished the members. "We did an outing, as you are aware, to the children's center in Harlem in September. It was the only site visit of the year, and the number of people who came could be counted on less than two hands. We must decide whether we ought to continue combining the ball with a charity component when clearly our members have only lukewarm interest in that."

"I think the ball is focus enough—we have so many other fundraisers," said an old and watery-voiced woman in the back, either turning her hearing aid on or off; Evelyn couldn't tell. "I think it's lovely to see the young girls learn how to dance and how to behave. Perhaps the site visits and all of that ought to be secondary."

"I went to finishing school in Lausanne," boomed the stout brunette, "and there we learned how to speak, how to carry ourselves in society, which the girls are learning as debutantes. I, too, think that's a marvelous element."

"Yes, but I point to the trouble of finding the debs. Yes, our daughters will do it, but we have the Assembly, the Infirmary, which really are taking the top tier of New York girls," protested Agathe. "There's a feeling among the younger girls that these parties aren't quite democratic."

"What is more democratic than helping children?" the Lausanne woman said.

"We are inconsistent to tell our daughters and their friends to participate for charitable reasons when our group cannot go to a children's center for one afternoon to see a program we are supporting," Agathe said.

The women looked at their shoes and out the window.

"Well, we have two young women here. What do you think of the tradition?" Agathe said, squinting at Evelyn.

Evelyn looked at Camilla, trying to hand off the question, but Camilla reached into her bag to fiddle with her phone and Evelyn saw she had to respond.

"Being a debutante," Evelyn said, stalling. "I think it's a wonderful way to connect with history. To connect with what our mothers and grandmothers did, to learn about proper social behavior."

The faces were still looking at her expectantly, and she saw she needed to establish her bona fides, even if they weren't very bona, or fide.

"I was a debutante in Maryland, where my family is from," she said.

She saw nodding heads of sleek silver and pale yellow. This was the right track, then. "In a world where anyone can be anything, and everyone can go everywhere, and so few people know how to behave, isn't it nice to have a tradition that says that someone is really someone?"

"Also," said Camilla, looking up from her phone, "it's basically champagne and pretty dresses, which teenagers like."

Souse looked like she might clap.

"We have to go to so many tedious events—we all do, Louise, don't look at me like that—where it's white wine and broiled fish and the speaker going on about the Abercrombie and Kent safari at the silent auction," Margaret Faber said. "I mean, terrible. So this is a big party with a group of people you know. Having the debutantes makes it younger, fresher, and I think it's a lovely family event. Many, most, of us here were debs and remember it fondly, and given that our daughters are on their phones and computers constantly, isn't it nice to give them a flavor of tradition and the world that we grew up in?"

Mrs. Faber's defense silenced the naysayers, even Agathe.

The issue apparently decided on, Agathe dismissed the meeting, and the group wandered in to the tea. Each of the debs was having her photograph taken, and each wore a fussy sweater and lacy skirt, with carefully styled and curled hair.

Then there was a clatter, and Phoebe, Camilla's younger sister, jumped into the room, followed by a girl who looked just like Margaret Faber: her daughter, Wythe Van Rensselaer. Phoebe stomped her foot and threw up her arms in a forties-movie-star pose. Her top was a wrinkled white oxford, and she wore ripped jeans and Keds, one with pink laces, one with chartreuse.

"Do the Phoebe, man, that's what they say on the runways," said Wythe, and Phoebe popped her hip to the side and strutted toward Camilla.

"Mom's finally free?" Phoebe asked loudly. "I feel like this is her thing and I'm just standing there looking pretty. And, Milla, the other girl from Spence who's getting her picture taken now is, like, a sub-zero loser. Jennifer. Ugh. I have no idea what she's doing here."

Camilla tapped her sister's wrist. "Hello. You're not standing there looking pretty. Pull your shoulders back. You look like a hunchback."

Camilla herself was in a particularly odd outfit given that this was an afternoon tea, wearing a dress made of tweed and black leather, and spiked boots with a distinctly dominatrix air about them. Evelyn, though, was glad she had gone with bouclé: the CEO can swear and have affairs, but the aspirational junior executive has to show up to meetings on time and be polite.

"They're total randos, Milla. I don't know why Mom is making me do this with all these girls," Phoebe said.

"Because Ari wants you to. Evelyn! Come meet my pest of a sister and her BFF. Phoebe, Wythe, this is my friend Evelyn."

After Evelyn shook the girls' hands, the Lausanne woman cast a worried look toward the library, where Jennifer was sitting for her photograph, and tapped Evelyn on the shoulder. "It is Evelyn, yes? Can you please go make sure these photographs are going all right, the girls are appropriate?"

Evelyn walked into the other room, where Jennifer's mother, a brunette with thyroid-bulged eyes and curling-iron ringlets that matched her daughter's, was trying to wrest the camera from the photographer to review the photos. "She has to get her dress made because she's too petite," the mother said.

"I'm a double zero," the girl agreed.

The photographer seized the camera back and aimed it at the girl. "So it's Jennifer? Tell me about what you like to do when you're not at Spence."

"I hardly have time not to be at school," Jennifer said. "I'm taking four APs and doing fencing."

"She just won a painting prize, the Courbet Award. Her teacher said she'd never heard of anyone actually winning the prize in all the years she'd been submitting Spence girls," her mother said.

"Okay. Relax the lips. You must be off to college, right?" the photographer asked.

Her mother fielded this one, too. "Whitman. In Washington. It's essentially the Williams of Washington."

"Have you always known you'd be a deb?" the photographer asked, moving her tripod over a few inches.

"I—"

"When she was asked, which was just after she sent in her Whitman acceptance, in December, Jennifer said to me, 'Do women still do debuts? It's so old-fashioned.' I said to her, 'It tells people who you are. If you do it, for the rest of your life, you can always say, 'I was a debutante.' It was her decision, entirely," her mother said.

"You were one, too?" the photographer asked.

"I could have been." The mother took notice of Evelyn at this point, and Evelyn evaluated her quickly. Just behind her was another painting Evelyn remembered from before, an abstract in angry daubs of black and blue, tinged with malice. No, this mother could not have been. This mother was a product of a suburb in New Jersey, who had probably not known that debutantes still existed until she made it into the city and pushed her stage-managed daughter to add one more credit to her social résumé. Jennifer's very presence here cheapened the whole ball, made it something that the Infirmary and Assembly attendees could frown upon.

"Some people feel, maybe, put off by it, but that's just because they're not part of it," Jennifer said. "It kind of represents being accepted into society. My dress—it's so funny, everyone thinks it's a wedding dress, and I'm, like, I'm seventeen—is just classic. Sweetheart neckline with a full skirt. Mom, can you touch up my lipstick, please?"

"It's in my purse in the other room. I'll be right back," said the mother, hurrying past Evelyn.

"I'll take a break, too," the photographer said, and headed out another door.

Jennifer pinched her cheeks.

"Mom, can you touch up my lipstick, please?" Evelyn heard in a mocking voice—Phoebe—so expertly calibrated that even Evelyn could hardly hear it, though Phoebe was just inches away from her.

Phoebe picked up a fake pearl necklace from a pile of accessories that sat next to the photographer and threw it at Wythe, who caught it with one hand. "Wythe! Style me," Phoebe commanded, and Wythe looped the necklace three times around Phoebe's neck.

The other debs crowded in behind them, wanting to figure out the rules of engagement.

"Well? Jennifer? How's your photograph going?" Phoebe said.

"Good," said Jennifer, lifting her nose.

"I don't know. I think you need something. A beehive. With some glasses, maybe," Wythe said.

"A beehive," Phoebe mused. "Very fifties housewife. I think it would look great, Jenny–Jen–Jenno."

"My mom did my hair," Jennifer said.

"Oh, your mom did your hair? I didn't know. Wythe, her mom did her hair."

"Well, then," Wythe said. "Even more reason to change it."

Jennifer, still in the chair, smiled hesitantly and tugged at one of her ringlets. She glanced at Evelyn, and Evelyn could hear the breathing of the other debs around her, watching to see how far this would go. Evelyn was supposed to be the adult here. She should step in.

"Evelyn! Will you tell Jennifer she needs a hair makeover?" Phoebe said.

As Evelyn looked at the girl with her overdone curls, her over-done Jersey mother waiting somewhere, she felt a tremolo of power rise and vibrate, and then her hand shot out and grabbed a comb from the accessories table. "I think a beehive would look great," Evelyn said, surprised by how tart and good the words felt on her tongue.

Wythe shouted "Hooray!" as Phoebe chanted "Go, Jennifer! Beehive! Beehive!"

Evelyn took a step closer to Jennifer, wielding the comb like a knife. She wanted to not just comb out the curls but to yank the comb through the girl's hair, to see how it felt to be the high-school queen that everyone feared.

"Beehive! Beehive!" Wythe chanted as Phoebe tossed faux pearls into the air in ecstasy.

Evelyn was just reaching out to ensnare Jennifer's limp, sad curls when the Lausanne woman, passing by the room, caught part of the exchange. "What's happening, girls? Jennifer, you should not fuss with your hair. And put all those necklaces back. Really, can't you girls follow simple instructions? Did I not tell you to listen to Evelyn?" She gave Evelyn a sympathetic smile.

Jennifer shook her head mutely and dashed out of the room, her curls shaking. Evelyn watched her go and now the comb in her hand felt ridiculous—what was she doing, harassing a teenager? Then she felt a squeeze on her arm from Phoebe, and looked back to see the other debs staring at her with awe.

"Love Evelyn," Phoebe said to Camilla, who had just cut a path through the crowd of debs to join them. "But I don't even want to do this ball. My dress is kind of fan-fucking-tastic, though. I got it at a vintage shop for twenty dollars. I think it was originally a slip."

"Jennifer's," Evelyn said, mimicking the girl's mincing voice, "has a sweetheart neckline with a full skirt." Phoebe and Wythe laughed, and the debs in the background did, too. Even Camilla smirked.

"Ugh. I'm going to ask the band to play 'Hot Legs' when I do my curtsy," Phoebe said.

Camilla let out a lengthy sigh. "Can you and Wythe stop this alt-whatever-it-is you're doing? Please? Just get normal dresses and invite normal escorts and we can all get through this in one piece. Evelyn?"

"Camilla's right," Evelyn said. "At my deb ball there was a girl in Doc Martens, and it just made her look nuts."

The younger girls hooted. "Doc Martens! How old are you?"

"Doc Martens. Oh, my God, the grunge era just kept going," said Camilla.

"Her mother almost fainted when she lifted her dress to curtsy." The strange thing was, Evelyn could picture this almost as if she did remember it.

"Where did you deb?" Phoebe asked.

"Oh, in Maryland, where I'm from. The Bachelors' Cotillion."

"Bachelors'," Camilla repeated. "I can't believe that about the Doc Martens."

"Lucky it wasn't flannel."

Wythe leaned in, examining Evelyn's gray pearl-drop earrings; Evelyn had put the molarlike pearl studs in a box a month earlier and hadn't brought them out since. "Those are fierce," Wythe said, snapping her fingers in a Z formation. "Phoebs, do you have a cig?"

Phoebe and Wythe were barreling toward the door, though the tea was still in full swing, when Souse finally resurfaced. "Oh, *Mother*, thanks for giving me the opportunity to become a debutante and fulfill your every wish," Evelyn heard Phoebe saying to Souse in a singsong tone.

"Oh, *Phoebe*," Souse said back. "Do you have money for a cab?"

Phoebe, now needy, smiled sheepishly. Souse delivered $20, then, after Phoebe raised her eyebrows, another $20 into her hand.

As the girls left, Souse turned to Evelyn and motioned a waiter for two champagnes.

"Hello, again. I'm exhausted. Come, sit. My two minutes with my daughter, isn't it modern? Phoebe's upset her father, Fritz, is not coming. What am I supposed to do, dance with two men at once? Ari gave quite a bit of money to the organization, so he staked his claim to this. Fritz will do the Assembly. We must take turns. Now, sit, Evelyn." Souse plucked a crustless sandwich from a tray. "One of the most civilized things I do is have teatime daily, so this is my indulgence for this afternoon. How badly can a day go when you have a finger sandwich in the middle of it?"

"Our housekeeper always made really good cucumber ones, with just the littlest bit of butter," Evelyn said. They hadn't hired Valeriya until a few years ago, and the only food Evelyn had seen her produce was the hard rolls she brought from home and occasionally forgot in the Beegans' cupboard.

The demonstration of caste solidarity seemed to work, though, as Souse said, "So I understand you're from Baltimore."

"My mother's family is, yes."

"Have they been there a long time?"

This was a line of questioning that would have unnerved Evelyn just a few months earlier. Evelyn, however, had been reading, and she had been practicing. The mistruths skipped off her tongue. She told of the shipping business, the side-by-side Tudors for her maiden great-aunts in Roland Park, the tales she grew up with of Baltimore before automobiles, the family connection to Johns Hopkins, the summer place on the Eastern Shore that they decided to make their full-time residence—everything, she thought, that Souse would need to pinpoint her as old money.

"How lovely. I barely know Baltimore, but it's so nice that it has such tradition," Souse said when she was finished. "And Camilla tells me you have a boyfriend."

"I do, yes. Scot."

"Who is he?"

"Ah, he works in finance. Morgan Stanley's media group. He works with David Greenbaum."

"Finance. You girls these days are such traditionalists. My generation, we were all rebels, and the girls these days, well, it's the Eisenhower fifties, isn't it? Then there's Ari. Real estate. Truly. I met Ari on a rainy day on Madison, isn't that terrible? At a bar, if you can believe that. He got drunk quite fast, because, as it turns out, he only has one kidney. He's really very good to the girls."

"I'd imagine. I can tell Camilla has a lot of respect for him."

"Can you? I wouldn't know it. Tell me, Evelyn, because Camilla certainly won't, is she bringing anyone to the ball? A date, I mean?"

"She was thinking of bringing Nick Geary, just as a friend, though. I think Camilla's happy being on her own right now, to be honest. It's not for lack of interest on the men's part."

"Oh, I know, I know. Shouldn't she be dating, though? I don't know. I don't understand how the young people do it these days. Everyone's so busy. Like Jaime de Cardenas, do you know him?"

Evelyn sat up. "We've met once or twice. He seems like a terrific fellow."

"He is. And a marvelous shot."

"Game?"

"Ducks, primarily. It's really something. He comes up to Sachem when he can, and it's fun for everyone. Though it's been ages. Young people these days. Everyone's overtaxed. I meant to tell you, Camilla's so glad to have your father as her guest at the Luminaries dinner."

The Luminaries dinner, with its $25,000 price tag, which Evelyn hoped Camilla had forgotten about. She was about to equivocate when she realized that if Souse was glad to have her father attend the dinner, Camilla must not have told Souse about the grand jury investigation, and that really didn't matter, not as long as everyone believed in Evelyn's august lineage.

"My father is just thrilled to be going," Evelyn said.

"His gift is quite generous. Truly. Oh, dear, Push is flapping her wings at me. I still haven't found silent auction items and must go atone. I'm glad we got to talk. Why hadn't we met before?"

The implied meaning that Evelyn was in, or near to, Souse's circle made a tingle run up Evelyn's neck, even if she was getting into a deeper hole with her stories. "Oh, I'd been busy with work and just got to know Camilla better. This event has been delightful. It's always a hoot to revisit deb days."

"It is, you're right. Keeps us young. Or keeps me young. You, you don't have to worry about that, do you?" Souse flitted off, and Evelyn, who did feel young in this crowd, wandered over to the platters of food, quiche, tabbouleh, and raspberry-lemon tartlets. Evelyn filled a small plate and tried to subtly suck out the tabbouleh's parsley from her teeth as she listened to the women talk. "Ani is in early to Princeton, but Michael only to Oberlin . . ." "I have known several people who have gone to Oberlin, and they came out just fine . . ." "We bought near Stockbridge . . ." "Chicken is all people seem to eat or serve anymore . . ." "The touring choir auditions . . ." "Americans ask always about Marie Antoinette and think it's interesting that we beheaded a queen."

CHAPTER FOURTEEN

A Selection of Jamón

Evelyn watched her father through the glass of Bar Jamón. He was ringing with energy, pointing at one ham hock after another and then throwing his arms up into the air as he laughed at whatever he was saying. With no indictment yet, he and Leiberg Channing thought it would be best for everyone to proceed as normal. He was in New York for a settlement meeting and it must have gone well: his khakis were practically ballooning with pride.

He was standing at the marble bar, and the counter guy was waiting for him to order, but Dale was too busy delivering his monologue about the ham hanging overhead. Evelyn had selected their meeting spot, Bar Jamón, from *Zagat*, which said it was "Iberian chic" with an "insider's vibe"; it was close to where his meeting had been. She hoped it would be quiet, as her father got distracted so easily, and she needed to ask him for money. The last time she'd attempted this, in Bibville, news of the indictment had knocked her off track.

"Dad," she said upon entering.

Dale turned and grinned. "I'm just looking at all this food. Now, we have ham where I'm from, but it's not ham that looks quite like this!" He examined the droopy-eyed counter guy, and Evelyn could tell he was looking for the jury-box response, the twitch of a smile and the slight creasing around the eye that indicated Dale had him, but it wasn't there yet. "So. What about ham, son?" Dale chuckled.

The young man lifted his heavy eyes and mumbled, "Jamón serrano, jamón ibérico de bellota, jamón ibérico de cebo," pointing at the hocks of cured pig.

"No good old Virginia ham?" Dale asked.

The man looked devastated. "No."

Dale laughed again, so heartily it practically bounced off the walls. "Well, Evie, your tastes certainly are getting sophisticated. Now, my good man, can I just have a plain black coffee?"

The counter guy set about making an Americano with grief-stricken movements as Evelyn and Dale sat down at one of the high tables, a candle flickering between them though it was light outside.

"Well, New York is not the town for me, but in the fall it's not too bad," Dale said.

"Autumn in New York," Evelyn half sang.

"What's that?" He signaled the man to bring over the coffee.

"It's counter service, I think," Evelyn said.

"Right over here," Dale said. To Evelyn's frustration, the guy brought over the coffee to their table. "Nothing a big tip can't fix," Dale said loudly.

Evelyn made a face at the tabletop. She couldn't become annoyed with him; she was here as a supplicant, making a pitch for money. It was a ridiculous position to be in. She had tried so hard to support herself and had done a great job of it until recently, and now, as her father was being investigated by the government for bribery, she still had to come beg and allow him to pass judgment on her once again. Even the parental MasterCard had been canceled without explanation, so there was no backup source of funds.

The simple fact was she needed more money. She'd been able to somewhat keep up with her new social set so far, but the pace was quickening. In the past few weeks, Camilla had been pressing her to come to various events that were $500 or $750 apiece, and it wasn't like she could ask Scot or Preston to pick up the tab. The clothes, too; she couldn't believe how silly it sounded, but it was true. She had to have a whole slew of cocktail dresses, since wearing the same thing to events where she saw the same people was as weird as wearing the same jeans to work two days in a row. Those dresses were, even on a good sale, $600 each. Evelyn had ransacked the 401(k) from her textbook job, which helped for a while but disappeared fast. One key way to afford all this was to be able to afford it, like Camilla, in which case all the invitations were comped because the party organizers wanted Camilla on the step-and-repeat, and designers sent her dresses because they wanted the free publicity.

Everyone else had funds galore, if not from a job—and it rarely was from a job, except for the bankers—then from trust funds, parental subsidies, or other mythic sources. Evelyn wondered why, when she'd tried to be responsible her whole life, her parents didn't find her worthy of such support. Actually, to be precise, she knew exactly why: because her father claimed to believe in the value of frugality, even as he was busy buying the dreadful and no doubt expensive maroon blazer he was wearing. He appeared to be especially shiny and salesmanlike today just to test her.

"So how are you, honey?" Dale said.

"Fine, Dad. Tired today; I was at a benefit with Preston and Camilla last night that went until two."

"I thought your boyfriend's name was Tate."

"No. It's not Tate. It's Scot. Preston is one of my oldest friends. From Sheffield? You saw him at the Sheffield event."

"Preston, that's right. He's that thin one. What does he do for work?"

What did any of these people do for work? Preston's ill-defined investment work meant, as far as Evelyn could tell, he played golf and took lunches. Camilla had quit her *Vogue* job, as she'd said she would; the final straw had been when, as the special-events staff started work on the next year's Costume Institute gala at the Met, Camilla had seen that Jessica Simpson was on the celebrity-invitee wish list and had thrown a fit.

Camilla's friends had part-time jobs that gave them plenty of time to do the benefit scene—global ambassador for a jewelry brand, or marketing consultant to Citarella, the gourmet store on the Upper East Side and in the Hamptons. Nick, who did work, was constantly late to parties, if he didn't miss them altogether, and Camilla had been getting increasingly furious with him. There wasn't a way to hold a job and do all of this, and in fact, the holding of a job seemed to disqualify you from ever really belonging in this group.

"Preston does investing stuff. But he's a Hacking on his father's side and a Winthrop on his mother's, so it's not like he really has to work," Evelyn said. Yet money flowed his way still, thanks to his connections; Charlotte had been dumbfounded when she'd heard he'd made a bundle on a tech IPO that everyone in the market wanted in on.

"While I worked my way through law school I was a dishwasher, at a gritty old diner in downtown Chapel Hill."

"I know, I know, Dad. I'm not sure Preston's entertaining a career in dishwashing, though. Most of my friends don't have full-time jobs."

"That doesn't follow."

"I think it's really hard to keep up with modern life and work all the time. It's sort of one or the other."

"That can't be true, Evelyn. Your friends all say no thanks to work?"

"Not all my friends. Just, well. I work," she said, shifting her weight on the stool and giving him what she hoped was a winning grin. It had been a relief, since she graduated from college, to have her own paycheck so she didn't have to do this song and dance, but that paycheck barely covered anything in her life anymore. "So, Dad," she said. "I was hoping I might get a check from you, just as a cushion."

"You're a grown-up. And you, I'm pleased to say, do have a job." His eyes were looking behind her, at the menu written above the bar

on a black chalkboard. "What about that. Pickled pigeon. Do you
think they're getting the pigeons from the sidewalk? My man?" he
hollered, apparently about to ask that question, but Evelyn waved the
counter guy away.

"Dad, forget about the pigeon. What I was saying is, most people
in New York get help from their parents, and on my salary, it's not
exactly easy to keep up."

"You're not most people. You were raised with some standards."

"But Dad. I know it sounds dumb, but these benefits are really expensive."

"Benefits, Evelyn? If you want to go to parties, you can pay for
those parties." He waved his hand at the counterman. "I think I just
might have to try some of that special ham."

Evelyn twisted around again, but the man was busy with another
customer. She turned back to her father. "The benefits are part of my
work, and I'm just asking for the smallest bit of help."

Dale moved his lips to one side as Evelyn caught sight of her mother
walking into the restaurant. Barbara wore the giant sunglasses that
she had lately started to wear from first light until dusk. She carried a
lilac Bergdorf's bag, though Evelyn could see a larger Duane Reade
one crammed into it.

"Mom, Dad and I were just talking about whether I could get
some extra money going forward. All of these benefits and dinners
and trips add up," Evelyn said.

"I was telling Evelyn that I do not want to step in to fund a social
life," Dale said. "If it were true living needs, that might be another
matter, but I don't think a party dress qualifies as a necessity."

"Your pocket square cost two hundred dollars!" Evelyn spat.

"I made my money and can spend it as I want, just as you can
spend the money you make as you want."

"Right. Silly me."

"I've had this argument with your father for decades, Evelyn. He has
no idea what it costs to maintain a semblance of a social life," Barbara

said. She still hadn't taken off her sunglasses. "Are we supposed to sit at this communal table?"

"Mom," Evelyn said. "Just sit. It's supposed to be like Spain."

Barbara grudgingly balanced herself on a stool. "Dale, Evelyn is having the time of her life, and that doesn't come for free."

"Then she can pay for it. Simple as that," Dale said.

They were all fuming and all looking at different walls. The counter guy approached, evaluated them, and retreated.

Finally, Barbara said, "Your father's right, dear. Budgeting is important."

"Mom." Evelyn was exasperated.

"How's the apartment search going?" Barbara said.

"What?"

"Evie was planning on moving," Barbara said, to Evelyn's surprise; she wasn't. "Her apartment now is rather dangerous. The location, that is. We'd been talking about her moving west of Lexington, where it's less seedy." Barbara shot Evelyn a conspiratorial smile. "Wasn't there an incident outside your apartment recently, Evelyn? A safety incident? That's why we'd been talking about the move."

"Right," said Evelyn, getting the hint. "Right. The apartment I'm looking at is quite a bit more expensive, though. Because it has twenty-four-hour security, which is important these days, because of the crime. It also has an alarm system."

"I didn't think your neighborhood was high crime," Dale said.

"It's becoming so, with the projects; there are lots of muggings, and where I am just doesn't feel that safe at night," Evelyn said. High crime in that occasionally a teenager from Brearley stole some nail polish from Duane Reade, but she didn't need to specify that. "The new building isn't that much more money. It's just a few hundred more a month. I think that's invaluable in terms of me feeling secure." She felt bad as she watched her father consider this, but also remembered what her mother always said: that because he was insistent on controlling the money, he was the one who forced them to act this way.

"Where's the new apartment?" he said.

"It's, um, Sixty-eighth. East Sixty-eighth. Just off Park."

"It's a few hundred more a month?"

"Right."

"I guess that's reasonable," he said. "I want you to get some Mace, too."

"Of course." She and her mother smiled at each other. Evelyn would stay at the Petit Trianon, easy enough to conceal from her father since he never visited, but the difference in "rent" would mean $400 more a month straight to her. After just a few months of that, she calculated, she could afford the Chanel cap-toe ballet flats she'd been coveting. Budgeting wasn't so hard.

"New York is full of crime."

"I know, Dad."

Her phone rang and she looked down. She had promised to meet Camilla for a pedicure in the Village and needed to leave momentarily. She picked it up and told Camilla that she was at Bar Jamón, trying to wrap up with her parents, and she'd hurry to Jin Soon afterward.

Mission accomplished on the money, Evelyn was asking her father questions about the Tar Heels' football season ten minutes later, when a gust of cold air and pavement smell announced the arrival of someone from the street. Evelyn turned around and saw with a start that Camilla was cantering toward them. Evelyn just had time to turn back to her parents and whisper, "That's Camilla Rutherford. Don't—"

"Hello!" Camilla called out merrily. "Mr. Beegan. Mrs. Beegan. It's such a pleasure. I'm Camilla Rutherford. I'm so sorry to interrupt, but I was nearby and Evelyn said you were here. I couldn't pass up the chance to meet you."

"Camilla!" said Evelyn. Why had her father chosen today to wear that ridiculous maroon jacket? "What a surprise. These are my parents, but I guess that's obvious."

"It is so nice to meet you," said Camilla earnestly, shaking Barbara's hand and submitting to Dale's grasp-and-pump. Evelyn noticed that the cuffs of his shirt were too short and that he was wearing a yellow LIVESTRONG wristband.

"Mom, Dad, we're actually late for a pedicure appointment, so we should probably be going," Evelyn said. "Mom, can we figure out the check situation tomorrow morning? I can come by your hotel."

"No, no," said Camilla, "don't be silly. We can get a pedicure anytime, but it's not every day the Beegans are in town."

"We have six o'clock appointments." Evelyn had to cut this off, or who knows what her parents would say? Her mother would say something to give herself—and thus Evelyn—away as solidly middle class, and her father would be all oozy Southerner.

Camilla waved her hand. "Evelyn, don't worry about it. Jin Soon can take us anytime. This is such a pleasure for me."

"I made the Jin Soon appointment three weeks ago," Evelyn protested.

"Well, why don't you sit down, Camilla?" Dale said. "I'm having this fancy ham, and I've got to say, it's pretty good."

"No, we're really in a hurry. It's just jamón serrano, Dad. It's not that rare. They have it everywhere in New York," Evelyn said.

"The new gourmet store in Easton has plenty of it, Dale," Barbara said. "Really, it's not like we live in a backwater."

"I'd love to join you," Camilla said. "What kind of coffee are you having, Mr. Beegan? That looks delicious. I'll have one of those. And some of the jamón, too, why not?"

"We don't have time to stay. We really have to go," Evelyn said.

"Camilla, I understand you're very involved in visual arts philanthropy," Barbara said, "as am I. Evelyn sent photos of you at the MoMA event and I thought your dress was just stunning."

"No! I didn't send photos," Evelyn said. She had. "You're thinking of—I think you saw the paper the next day. I didn't send photos. Honestly. So weird. So it's a black coffee, Camilla?"

"An Americano, they call it here," Dale said, signaling to the counterman. "Yo soy Americano."

"Dale learned Spanish to talk to some of his lower-class clients," Barbara offered.

"The coffee?" Evelyn almost yelled. "Another Americano? Please?"

"Now, Camilla, I hear you're rising through the banking world as fast as a jackrabbit," Dale said.

"Dad, that's Charlotte, and it's private equity. Charlotte's my Sheffield roommate? Who you've known for, like, ten years? Camilla doesn't work in banking."

"It's so easy to mix up, Mr. Beegan," Camilla said, and Evelyn got the unnerving feeling that Camilla was flirting with her father. "All of these New York girls and our jobs. But, no, I worked in event planning and community relations until recently."

"Community relations, that's wonderful. I always tell Evelyn that you have to consider the wider world in your work, but I'm not sure she listens."

"For *Vogue*," Evelyn said, digging her nails into her wrist. "*Vogue* magazine? The fashion magazine?"

"This is delicious," Camilla said, smelling her coffee like it was wine. "Excellent recommendation, Mr. Beegan."

"Isn't it tasty?" Dale asked, the "idn't" ringing in Evelyn's ears at the same time that Barbara said, too familiarly, "Camilla, how is your mother?" as though she and Souse had met.

Camilla looked from one of them to the other, and apparently chose Dale. "Mr. Beegan," she said, leaning close to him, "I hope I'm not being too aggressive, but I wanted to talk to you in person about the Luminaries support."

"Oh, Camilla, I haven't had a chance to talk to him about it," Evelyn said, her heartbeat increasing.

"That's why I dropped by," said Camilla, putting her hand on Dale's arm; both Evelyn and Barbara looked at the hand with suspicion. "I thought we should talk about it one-on-one. The Luminaries, Mr. Beegan, is such a marvelous event. It's thought leaders from business, the arts, philanthropy, and, of course, law"—she squeezed his arm—

"coming together to talk about ideas. I would be honored if you would be my guest, and a Luminary Patron."

"Your guest? Surely you can find someone younger and more lively than me."

"Not at all, Mr. Beegan. You would be perfect for it. It's a really nice event. It's at Georgette Scharffenberg's apartment, Constellation Capital, and it has the feel of a private dinner, so it's not too formal," Camilla said.

"Constellation Capital," Dale said. "The private-equity firm? I don't think they'd be too happy to see me. They backed a company I recently won a settlement against."

"We have all sorts of interesting financial firms in Bibville these days," Barbara interrupted.

"Mom," said Evelyn. Barbara was not acting like a shipping heiress in the slightest.

"Oh, no, it's not like that," Camilla purred, ignoring both the women. "It's purely a social event. Honestly, David Boies came last year and everyone loved him, even though the people hosting last year basically single-handedly funded the Bush side of Bush v. Gore."

The thought of her father circulating around a party talking about his mill-town childhood to Georgette Scharffenberg made Evelyn cringe. Why did Camilla want him, anyway? Souse could help Camilla line up whomever she wanted—and then Evelyn felt hot. Of course. A double whammy. This way, Camilla got the $25,000 donation, which would help her overall social power, but bringing an under-investigation Southern plaintiffs' lawyer to the party would be a giant fuck-you to Souse and would lend Camilla some rebellious notoriety.

Evelyn pushed a knife across the table to get her mother's attention, and, when Barbara looked up, Evelyn gave her a hard look and mouthed, *Grand jury*. Her mother could put a stop to this, and would at least want to protect the family's, if not Dale's, reputation in New York. "I'm not sure the time is quite right," Barbara said, taking the cue. "Dale is trying to focus just on his work these days and not on public appearances. Aren't you, Dale?"

"Well, this doesn't sound too public," Dale said.

"There's also a donation involved, right, Camilla? A donation. A required donation," Evelyn said. She was almost shouting.

"The Patrons support the event, but almost all the money goes to literary programs for underprivileged youths, like library makeovers in public schools. It's really a terrific cause," Camilla said.

"I'd be proud to support a cause like that," Dale said.

"It's just, in terms of your money—attention—time—time—maybe it's not a great time," Evelyn stuttered, standing up from the table.

"Are you trying to stop him from going?" Camilla said. Her voice was innocent, but her eyes were flaring.

"No! No. Of course not. It sounds lovely. Just, Dad can overcommit himself so easily. Can't you, Dad?"

Dale grinned at Camilla. "I do overcommit myself, but this sounds like such a nice invitation that I may have to say yes."

"I think it'll be fantastic, Mr. Beegan. So fun. I read your guest lecture at UNC on how Wall Street is working against the American public, and I know the other attendees would love to hear about that."

"I can't imagine that anyone wants to hear about that," Barbara said, not very quietly.

"Camilla," Evelyn said, almost pleading. Her father looked so buoyed. Evelyn wanted to protect him; Evelyn wanted to sacrifice him. Evelyn mostly just wanted to get the hell out of there. She started edging toward the door as though she could magnetically pull Camilla with her.

"I'd be honored," Dale said, beaming.

"I'll put you down as a Luminary Patron," Camilla said. "Thank you so much, Mr. Beegan."

Evelyn stayed standing, tapping her foot and willing Camilla to get up and leave; Camilla finally did, following Evelyn outside and hissing, "What was that? You're supposed to help me."

"I was. I was! He's honestly really busy."

"Too busy for me, I guess?"

"No, that's not it. At all. There's just a lot going on."

Fifteen minutes later, and thirty minutes late for their appointments, Evelyn and Camilla descended into Jin Soon on Jones Street. Camilla picked up a gray-brown polish from the rack of polishes. "Make sure he can go. All right?"

Evelyn shook her head no, but said, "Okay. Okay."

Camilla handed Evelyn the nail-polish bottle. "This would look good on your toes," she said. It was the color of dried mud.

CHAPTER FIFTEEN

Appointment Book

Fall whirled by, orange-tinted afternoons and thick white envelopes holding party invitations. There was the Tuesday evening when Camilla invited Evelyn to dinner at the Colony Club, the old-money women's club on the Upper East Side that Evelyn had walked by many times but never been inside before. Camilla, as she led Evelyn through the lobby, mentioned she always had her birthday dinner at the Colony on her exact birthday, July 13, and that she would've invited Evelyn to her most recent birthday party a few months earlier had she only known Evelyn better then. Evelyn was happy to be in the Colony at all, especially for a dinner à deux with Camilla, though she was surprised by how shabby parts of it were, with the lumpy old couches that would've been relegated to the cat in any new-money house but here were a marker of WASP thrift. The food was sub-country-club level, broiled fish and Waldorf salads served in a coral dining room. Evelyn saw women talking to the open air and realized they were used to addressing expectant servants.

There was the Thursday afternoon when Camilla insisted that Evelyn join her for the Met's Louis Comfort Tiffany exhibit (for which,

Evelyn noticed when reading one of the introductory wall plaques, Camilla's grandparents' family foundation had provided generous funding). Evelyn called in sick to People Like Us for the day to do it. Afterward, they went to E.A.T. for salads. Camilla, not wanting to use the bathroom there, insisted on going to Evelyn's apartment instead. With each block east, Evelyn felt her dread rise; she couldn't remember whether she had just hinted to Camilla that she lived just off Madison, or whether she'd said so definitively. As Camilla started to make jokes about the Orient, Evelyn grappled to explain how she had gotten stuck so far east: her father's secretary had found the apartment and signed her up for a long-term lease. Evelyn ran into the apartment ahead of Camilla and, while Camilla was in the bathroom, sprinted around picking up the Mitford and Post and Fussell as if they were porn, shoving them under her bed, and throwing a blanket over her stack of twee Rodgers and Hammerstein CDs. Camilla found her in the bedroom, took one look at Evelyn's floral-patterned bedspread, and said that Scot must feel like he was sleeping in a dollhouse.

Evelyn got highlights that made her a blonde for the first time and signed up for three-times-a-week blowouts with Camilla's stylist so her hair could approach Camilla's level of shiny perfection. The price struck her as high at first, but she found that, freeingly, the more she spent, the less she cared. Her mother had come up with a secret check from somewhere, giving Evelyn an extra $10,000 and telling her to spend it wisely, along with the difference in rent money for the "new apartment." Evelyn understood that spending it wisely meant spending it on establishing herself in this scene. She bought a high-powered T3 hair dryer so her hair was always straight and voluminous, though she couldn't use it at the same time as her window air conditioner without blowing a fuse. She navigated the main floors at Barneys and Bergdorf's and Saks, picking up just the right toiletries: she bought the $23 hand soap from Molton Brown, scented with white mulberry and bay leaves. She bought the boar brush from Mason Pearson. She bought Perles de Lalique, in large part because Camilla liked the bottle, even though the perfume smelled weirdly of black pepper; she hoped she would become one of those women known for her classic scent, so when she stepped into the room people would say, "Ah. Evelyn." At an antiques dealer in Soho, she bought an Art Deco sideboard for her living room to house the full set of silverware her mother had recently sent; Babs had enclosed a note saying Evelyn would need to start entertaining soon and might find it useful. After spending an irritating seven minutes with a jar of silver polish, Evelyn loaded the silverware into a tote bag and took it to the Indian restaurant three doors down, offering a Bangladeshi busboy $100 if he would wash and polish it. He agreed, and Evelyn now found it quite chic to breeze by on the way home and pick up her glimmering silver and some papadum.

The disconnect between her work and evening life was increasing. The more involved she became in the social scene, and the more she learned about what these people wanted, the less Arun and Jin-ho listened to her. They were pushing for huge growth, to the point that Jin-ho suggested Evelyn stop approving or denying members one by one and allow open registration. Evelyn maintained that that would wash away any market position they had. Meanwhile, she was regularly fighting with the ad side, like after they recently placed a giant Uggs ad in the center of the homepage, and the content side, which had started soliciting reviews of drugstore beauty products.

People Like Us still hadn't gotten her an actual desk, and they'd hired some coder named Clarence to sit next to her at the long linoleum table. There were only a few unregulated inches between her and Clarence, and whenever Evelyn's eyes shifted a tiny fraction from her computer screen, they'd land on his bulging white calf, broken up by thick, sparsely planted dark hairs. He had worn shorts to work every day since he started in August. Clarence sat typing with his tiny arms stretched all the way forward, his fat lower lip hanging down, breathing through his mouth. He sucked in air regularly, and his lip, shiny with spit, would bounce when he did. His feet, encased in thick black high-top tennis shoes, barely reached the floor. He would occasionally receive phone calls—one was about how insurance wouldn't cover his Propecia prescription—and he'd continue typing as he talked, as if he were some all-important executive who couldn't be distracted. Evelyn always felt like she was inside his bodily functions, his chest-shaking coughs that spewed forward onto his computer screens, his reverberating five-syllable yawns. She planted her iPod buds in her ear and turned up the *Annie* sound track as loudly as she could stand to try to drown out Clarence's mouth sounds. "And maybe real nearby," Annie sang in the hopes that her perfect life was out there. Meanwhile, Evelyn would get e-mails from Camilla—"spa day can you join?" or "heading to Q let know if you can go," about her godmother's place in Quogue—that made Evelyn's work life seem even more drab.

Evelyn particularly hated using the work bathroom to change for a night out. The fluorescent lights made her eye whites look jaundiced and made it impossible to distinguish whether she was showing a dewy glow or just an oily T-zone. It was also degrading changing into her pretty evening dresses while she listened to the rip of a tampon wrapper from one stall over, and the stifled moans and plops broadcasting the digestive-tract issues of Ann, the HR woman, who was always in the bathroom at 5:00 P.M. How workaday Evelyn felt in that steel-and-linoleum bathroom with its pink liquid antibacterial soap; how much she felt like a tired secretary from some 1950s film who should be pulling off soiled stockings before taking the El to Astoria.

Generally, Evelyn would wait in a stall until she heard Ann heave herself off the toilet and out the door, and then would gingerly step out of her work clothes, balancing in the toe part of her Givenchy heels. Trying to keep everything from touching the floor, she'd end up with her toiletry bag squeezed between her elbow and her ribs, a pair of trousers slung around her neck, and a sweater clasped between her knees as she wriggled into her dress. Her shoes would already hurt; they were meant to be accessorized with a car and driver.

Evelyn would emerge from the stall to follow her prescribed freshening-up routine: a spritz of rosewater on her face, Touche Éclat on her inner eyes, a blotting paper on her nose, shimmery beige shadow for her eyelids, classic Chanel pink for her lips, topped by ChapStick, a spritz of Perles de Lalique over the scent of Ann's Perles de Bowel. All that didn't erase the workday, though. She knew it was etched into her face as surely as coal dust would have been after a day of mining. There was no way to get the refreshed, rested, yoga-ed, blown-out look of the women who came from their Upper East Side apartments and with whom Evelyn had to compete at the evening events.

The worst part was carrying the toiletry bag to and from the bathroom, so all these losers could smile at her in solidarity. She wasn't some *Redbook*-reading working girl who thought adding a scarf and punching up her look with some jewelry would accomplish a day-into-night transformation. She knew better. Since people at the events would know she was coming from the office, she always changed into clothes that she could plausibly have been wearing at work. She didn't want them to think she'd actually changed in a work bathroom stall.

But at night, once she left PLU, it was like she stepped into an enchanted world. She knew the codes now; she could step up to a bar and order a Cockburn's port and pronounce it "Coburn's," and get an impressed look from the bartender. She said "cottages" for Maine and "cabins" for Jackson Hole (which was just "Jackson") and "camps" for the Adirondacks. She met Preston for Met premieres and went to dinners at the Knickerbocker Club, where she gave clever toasts celebrating the birthday boy or the newly engaged couple. She ducked into La Goulue, where the maître d' now knew her and sat her at almost the best table. She swanned into parties and laid a polite and appropriately intimate hand on hostesses' arms. She was part of the group she used to wonder about, one of those being ushered upstairs or downstairs into restricted parts of already-restrictive clubs and restaurants, nodding respectfully when she saw the older versions of herself, who nodded back politely, for they had been young and privileged not so long ago. Evelyn was twenty-six, and for the first time in her life, she was seen. Recognized. It wasn't that heads were turning—she wouldn't ask that much—but just for a moment, one man would hold her gaze a little longer than he should. Or a woman's eyes would flick over her dress with jealousy. She could now be a missed connection on Craigslist, a fragment in a song lyric, the inspiration for a girl in a musical. She was walking down grand staircases, made to feature women at their best, and looking down at a crowd looking up at her. Her mother was approving for the first time in her life. She was invited to Newport for the weekend; Newport! Stepping into history with those marble sinks, those copper fixtures, those beds with their high posts, that town that had been society's center. The stresses of modern life—the dirty streets, the trash, the expenses—melted away into her stage set. She felt like she practically had a chorus line behind her, kicking up and shimmying as they cheered her on.

"Miss Evelyn, you are getting so much in the mail these days. The mailman left all this for you because he could not fit it into your box." The weekend doorman—Randy? Andy?—handed Evelyn a bundle of letters with a large rubber band straining to hold them together. She saw right away that there were enough thick square envelopes and textured black ones, standing out from the rectangular bills, that this was an excellent invitation haul.

To open her mail, Evelyn dimmed the lights in the living room, put on Judy Holliday singing "The Party's Over," and poured herself a glass of wine. She placed a round silver tray on her coffee table to hold the invitations, opened her red Smythson, and took out her favorite chiseled brown Sharpie, writing down the title of each invitation, followed by its sponsor. The pages of the Smythson daily diary were starting to droop with the weight of the multiple inscriptions each week:

Dinner New York Antiques Show—MAYBE? (See if Pres
    going)
Chanel documentary premiere, Paris Theater, afterparty,
    Bergdorf's—YES—CHR dinner before

Pediatrics dinner New York–Presbyterian—√ red Ungaro
Annual fund-raiser lunch Sloan Kettering—√ white Milly
  jacket
J. Mendel shopping benefit, New Yorkers Fight Lupus—NO
Ivari (Jessa Winter's jewelry line) launch party Barneys—
  (maybe? Conflict w/Chanel docu)
ArtBall @ Studio Five, Chelsea—YES—CHR table—
  confirm Scot can go?

As usual, she separated the good stuff from the bills. She went through those as quickly as she could, edging them out of their envelopes and looking only for the monthly minimum and not the full amount due. She scrawled out checks, then shoved the bills together and deposited them at the back of her silverware drawer, where their accusatory statements belonged.

Then she could relax again. She turned up Judy Holliday with her remote control and reviewed the invitations once more. This was the best part of the whole thing, the anticipation. Getting these invitations meant that someone had sought her out and tracked down her address. Someone had wanted her.

CHAPTER SIXTEEN

Silent Night

Evelyn opened the door to Sag Neck, a decaf skinny gingerbread latte in one hand, noticing her parents hadn't even put a wreath up this year. Usually, Barbara Beegan's forced holiday march started with a Christmas Eve service, Christmas Eve dinner (turkey with oyster stuffing and a side of fried oysters), Christmas-morning coffee cake and stocking opening, followed by presents, then carols, then a late lunch of roast beef, then pie and more carols. Evelyn liked all of it, even the ribbon-wrapped Mason jar of pickled peanuts—slime in brine, as her father called them—that Sally Channing left at their front door every year.

She and Scot had celebrated the night before she left New York. It was just the two of them, and he took her hints and booked a dinner at Daniel and got her the triple-gold Cartier ring she wanted. Throughout the fall, she'd been trying to change the Scot that was into the Scot that could be. She'd sent him to get a bespoke suit, the precise hand stitching visible on the lapel, and made him switch his outlet Polo shirts for Lacoste. He seemed eager for her compliments, and would always wear the selected clothing when they went out, which made her feel weirdly guilty. She worked on his manners, too, trying to lightheartedly correct his knife placement and his revolving-door etiquette. When they were alone, she liked him, liked his slight nerdiness and his sweetness, but when they were in a group, all she could do was note that his shirt still looked off the rack and his laugh was too loud.

When one November Sunday morning Evelyn was leaving 5G and she heard Scot whisper, "I love you," she pretended she hadn't heard and kept walking toward the elevator. How, she wondered, were you supposed to know when something was right and when it wasn't?

It was Camilla's number that she put at the top of her phone's favorites list.

The Cartier ring was perfect, though, substantial in its three types of gold, and Evelyn wore it on her middle finger and angled it to catch the light for about half the train ride home. She pulled out Scot's card every now and then, too: "Dear Evelyn, you have made this year wonderful. Merry Christmas. Love, Scot." The handwritten card gave her the feeling that a middle-school mash note from a real live boy did: Someone likes me.

She had left at her apartment the gag gift that her friends had given her at the hot-toddy-fueled Christmas party they'd held at Camilla's. Preston had picked it out: a plastic tiara, as, he said, Evelyn was now queen of New York. By the end of the evening, Camilla was wearing the thing.

At Sag Neck, not only was there no wreath, but there was no tree. (Cleaning up all those pine needles for one day of celebration wasn't worth the hassle, her mother said.) Her parents no longer hung woolen stockings from the wooden rods of the banister. For Christmas Day, her mother had made a reservation at the Eastern Tennis Club to use up part of their mandatory monthly food minimum, and the Christmas Eve plan was cold sandwiches. There were no Sally Channing pickled peanuts deposited at the door this year. That part, at least, wasn't a surprise to Evelyn.

Her father was upstairs in his study, and her mother was sitting at the piano, though Barbara was not playing, her hands suspended over the keys as though she were waiting for a marionettist to pull the strings.

Evelyn tossed down her purse in the hallway and walked upstairs, pushing open the door to her father's office as she knocked. He was sitting at his desk with a glass of bourbon, a thick book open in front of him, excavating dirt from under his nails with a file.

The study had been largely decorated by Barbara, meaning wooden oars and wooden skis and a letter to the secretary of the navy signed by William McKinley and addressed to "My dear Pots." (Evelyn had long ago deduced that this had nothing to do with her mother's family at all.) To this Dale had added his own ephemera: a UNC pennant, books on epidemiology and chemistry and biology, and *Inside the Jury*. One shelf was filled with crystal pyramids and metal paperweights testifying that Dale Beegan was BOARD MEMBER EMERITUS, ATTORNEYS AND AID and TAR HEEL DISTINGUISHED ALUMNUS, 1999, and VICE PRESIDENT, DELMARVA TRIAL LAWYERS, 1995.

He put down his nail file and gestured for Evelyn to have a seat.

"No, that's okay, Dad. I just wondered if we couldn't figure out something for a Christmas Eve dinner. The cold sandwiches Mom got are depressing."

"They're from a new sandwich shop in Easton. I don't think they're too bad."

"That's what Mom said. The point is that I don't want to eat a cold sandwich on Christmas Eve. I mean, you guys aren't doing stockings, you're not doing a tree, and we're not cooking anything. It's not very festive."

"If you want a tree, go get a tree."

"That's not the point."

"Bourbon?"

"What?"

"Do you want some bourbon? You like it, don't you?"

"Not particularly." She held up her coffee cup.

Her father splashed bourbon into a glass for her anyway, as the voice from his record player crooned, "Goodnight, Irene, goodnight, Irene."

"I've got something to tell you," he said.

"Is it bad?"

Her father didn't answer and waited until Evelyn had put down her coffee and stuck her tongue into the bourbon. She made a face and switched it for coffee. "How much have you been reading about this whole thing?" he asked.

"Nothing. I thought it was best to stay away from it. You said there hasn't been much written."

He refilled his glass and carefully wedged the top back on the bottle. "Did I? Well. That's right. There hasn't been, much. Well. It's going to be a pretty long Christmas vacation for me, as it turns out. I decided to take a leave of absence from the firm."

"You barely take vacations."

"I think it'll help clear up some of the issues and help calm down the government."

"Dad, doesn't that kind of implicate you? If you're leaving the firm in the middle of this big investigation?"

"I'm not leaving the firm. I'm just taking a leave."

"Nothing's happened, right? The grand jury hasn't found anything?"

Dale tapped the nail file against the desk. "Not to my knowledge, no."

"So isn't this asking for it? Shouldn't you just carry on as if nothing's wrong?"

"My lawyer and I think it's best."

"Dad, grand jury investigations are not that big of a deal. It's how you handle it that matters. Taking a leave will make people talk. I'm serious. Taking a leave will make people wonder if you did something wrong. You should just go on and pretend like everything's fine."

"Why don't we entertain the notion that I know more about the law than you do?" Dale said. He tapped the file against the desk several times, then placed his hand on a thin beige volume that was open to a page of black-and-white photos. "Do you know what this is?" he said.

"No."

"Take a look." He stood up and walked the book, yellowed around its edges, to her. His hair was speckled with gray now. Evelyn tried to remember when it hadn't been, when he had last had a full head of brown hair, but she couldn't. When does the body start to bend forward, the tics become strange old-man habits? Dale cleared his throat as if to answer her, and the clearing turned into a heavy, phlegm-filled hack.

"Scipio High," Dale said. "I was on the baseball team. The Raiders. All of the mill towns had them then. Older folks' leagues, too. They'd hire a foreman just because he was a great shortstop." He looked at her, searching for something he did not locate, then flipped the yearbook to a page that the book easily opened to. It was a photo of her father, with knee socks and a self-assured grin and a flattop haircut, leading a group of swaggering boys across a field. His eyes were trained on the camera even as he shouted something to the pack with sly parted lips.

"I was the baseball captain. I was pretty good. That's Jimmy Happabee there behind me. He was a hell of a catcher. We used to drive around town like a couple of crazy men in his dad's truck on Saturday night. That was the one night we didn't have to work." He pulled the book back, then closed it. "Another world, I guess. The old folks said it then, and damned if I haven't turned into one of them." He looked at her. "You're happy, aren't you? You liked Sheffield and Davidson?"

"Yeah, Dad, I did."

"You've got good friends. You've got money. Plenty of money."

She took a sip of coffee. Was that why he'd done this, if he'd done it? To provide for his family? Or was it to provide for himself? Whatever it was, it wasn't enough. She didn't know exactly how much money her family had, but estimated it was at least several million, given the big sums her father had won balanced against the often excessive way her parents spent. Her father probably thought those millions were enough to gain instant entry into New York society, when several million was what a mediocre hedge-fund manager made in a single year.

"I'm doing fine, Dad," she said.

His hand trembled as he replaced the book on his desk. "That's good. That's good to hear. I'll put this back. It'll just be on the shelf over there. You can look at it if you like."

"Yeah."

"I want you to know, Evelyn, that even if the grand jury finds something, all right, that the law means everything to me, and I would never have, never did, cross it."

She didn't quite believe him. Her father had always managed to line up ambition and the law, and this was an instance where it was ambition versus the law. She was pretty sure what side he would have chosen. You never think you're going to get caught, she thought, until you get caught. "Okay," she finally said. "Dad, if you're on leave, what about the Luminaries?"

"The what?" He shook his head. "Oh, your friend's dinner. You'd best cancel."

"I'd best cancel? I was the one who told you not to do it in the first place."

"What does it matter, Evelyn? It's one dinner."

"She's signed you up. She's going to kill me if you drop out. And what about the money?"

"What money?"

"The donation? That you have to give? She signed you up for twenty-five thousand."

"You never mentioned a twenty-five-thousand-dollar donation."

"I'm positive I did." She knew she hadn't.

"You said there was *a* donation, Evelyn, not one that's more than the yearly salary of many Americans. Promising that I'll give twenty-five thousand dollars to a cause of your friend's? What were you thinking?" He stared at her, unblinking.

"I didn't make the promise. You were the one that wanted to go."

"Evelyn, I do not think anything will happen with the investigation, but if it does, and frankly, even if it doesn't, do you know how unseemly it would be for me to be giving such a large donation to one of your friends right now?"

"What am I supposed to tell her?"

He smiled and picked up the yearbook again. "Lord, Evelyn, tell her I can't go."

"It's not as easy as that."

He wasn't listening anymore, though. He had again opened the yearbook again, to the same page. He was tracing his finger over the caption; Evelyn could only read the first part, "BASEBALL BOYS' BREAK TIME, captain D. Beegan . . ."

He did not look up when Evelyn slid her unfinished bourbon toward him and left.

CHAPTER SEVENTEEN

Security Questions

The sharp ring of the Petit Trianon apartment phone startled Evelyn awake. What was it? Where was she supposed to go? It was dark; was it today or tomorrow?

Another ring and she lifted herself off the couch. "Hello? Yes?"

"Miss Evelyn, Miss Charlotte is coming up."

"What—what time is it?"

"Eight oh-five, miss."

It took Evelyn a couple of seconds to place herself in the evening. She'd left PLU early to go to Equinox for a vinyasa class, trying to quiet her mind, reverberating with worry about her father and her money situation and the Luminaries dinner, but it didn't work. In the locker room after class, Evelyn got dressed again, not wanting the other girls putting on heels and skirts and makeup in preparation for nights out to think she had no plans for the evening. She joined a blonde blow-drying her hair in front of the long primping mirror and gave her a knowing smile as Evelyn smoothed her own hair. Evelyn's look lasted long enough to take in the ring pressed against the girl's hair dryer: princess cut, platinum, the ring a banker would bestow.

She was pretty sure, lately, that if she dropped enough hints, she could get a ring like that from Scot. Wedding rings were everywhere, and Evelyn didn't want to be the pitied single girl forever. But what was the point in extracting a ring from Scot? If you were going to marry and not feel much for your husband, that husband should at least give you the life you wanted. Sarah Leitch, whose husband was squat and boring but had made $20 million last year, was redecorating her Napa winery right now.

Standing at the mirror, Evelyn, too, had blown her hair dry, patted concealer around her eyes, stroked mascara onto her eyelashes, added lip balm, and put on her Jimmy Choos. She'd then twisted a gold-set ruby ring on backward on the fourth finger of her left hand so it resembled a wedding band. She'd walked to the lobby of the gym looking the very picture of a married girl off to a social event, for anyone who was looking.

"Can you tell her I'm not here?" she said to the doorman.

"I'm sorry, Miss Evelyn, she is a regular guest so I let her up already. It is policy." She had not seen Charlotte much lately. Charlotte was always going to museums with names like the American-Jewish Museum of the West African Diaspora and making a point of how much she learned there and how much more instructive it was than what Evelyn was doing with her time. Evelyn knew that her life sounded ridiculous to Charlotte—Charlotte had said that much directly. What Charlotte couldn't know was how addictive it was.

There was a knock on the door. Evelyn switched the ring to her right hand and tried to sound surprised: "Yes? Who is it?"

"Charlotte."

"Oh! Char! Coming! Sorry, they didn't call up."

She opened the door to a tired-looking Charlotte wearing a smart gray suit, pulled together, no doubt, by the Saks personal shopper she'd hired who specialized in lady bankers. On her feet were L.L. Bean duck boots, slushy from the outside world.

"Do you have any beer? I could use some."

"What are you doing in the neighborhood? And out of work at eight?"

"I'm not staffed on a deal for the first time in ages. Also, sorry, you're asking me what I'm doing here? When you're the one that's basically dropped off the face of the earth? Seriously, do you have a beer?"

"Just wine."

"You always have beer."

"Just wine, Char."

Charlotte plopped on the couch and took the wineglass Evelyn offered. "You look dressed up. Are you heading out?"

"No, I had an event. After work," Evelyn said. Yoga could sort of be counted as an event. "So what are you doing up here?"

Charlotte made a weird air sound with her cheeks. "Date. Bad one. I feel like I just scream 'lesbian' to everyone I meet."

"Did you wear the duck boots?"

"Evelyn—" Charlotte started to get up.

"I'm sorry. I'm sorry!" Evelyn held her hands up.

"No, I didn't wear the duck boots. Thanks for asking."

"I just meant—" Evelyn poured wine into Charlotte's glass. "I'm sorry about the date. You're such a catch. Look at you. You're going to be running Graystone sooner or later."

"In my duck boots?"

"Honest opinion? Not in the duck boots."

Charlotte let out an angry laugh. "Graystone. Yeah, I'm a woman. That's not going to happen. I just can't play the New York game. If I get out of work at a reasonable hour, by the time I go to the gym and get home it's time to go to bed. Rinse, repeat for seven days straight. When, exactly, am I supposed to meet someone? Then I meet this guy, at a freaking work event, by the way, and he tells me I'm too intense for him because of my job?"

"Char, Char. It's crazy. He's crazy." Evelyn sat down next to her friend and awkwardly patted her knee.

"Oh, look, Evelyn Beegan's offering physical solace. It must be bad."

Evelyn smiled.

"I remember the two times at Sheffield you hugged me," Charlotte continued. "Graduation and when my uncle John died."

"It seemed called for."

"The Babs still has never hugged me, after all these years. A firm handshake is all I get. You were trained by the best."

With her finger Evelyn stopped a trickle of red wine that was escaping from the bottle. "You could say that."

"How's work?"

"It's so annoying, Char. They're all about boosting membership numbers. I get that, but that's not the site's brand. The world doesn't need an also-ran MySpace. The high-end idea makes sense, and we're getting members and creating influence, and they basically want to throw that away to show big membership growth."

"That does seem strange. I think the brand works. I mean, it's not my bag, but advertisers must love having access to the Camilla Rutherfords of the world."

"Exactly. But the site has essentially shunted me and that strategy off to the side. One of the co-CEOs, Jin-ho, has taken over some of the membership and marketing and he has no idea how to appeal to these people. It's cray-cray."

"You say 'cray-cray' now?"

"I've always said it."

"Okay, Camilla. So do you want to tell me where you've been these last few months, if you haven't been throwing yourself into work? Did you and Camilla get a domestic-partnership license and go on your Fiji honeymoon?"

"I haven't been anywhere. I've been in New York, mostly. Aspen, too, Bridgehampton, obvs. Oh, Newport. Quogue, which is beautiful in winter."

"You can stop there. Who would've thought the girl who wore pleated khakis in the Sheffield senior photo would become such a social butterfly?"

"They weren't pleated."

"They were so pleated."

Evelyn was giggling now, settling back into the couch.

"Ev," Charlotte said softly. "The stuff with your father—"

"What stuff?" Evelyn sat up, on guard.

"The stuff with his firm." Charlotte groped for the words. "If you want to talk—"

"I don't want to talk. I don't know how you know about it, but it's not your business. It's not a big deal, nothing's going to happen, and I'd appreciate it if you didn't mention it to anyone," Evelyn said, hitting the consonants hard.

"God forbid Camilla finds out?"

"Camilla knows, in fact, Charlotte."

"Of course she does. Number one confidante." After a few moments, Charlotte breathed out heavily. "What about Pres? Have you seen much of him?"

"Pres? Sure. We were supposed to have dinner last week but ended up going to the River Club with Camilla instead. On Sutton Place? There's the most fun club downstairs. You wouldn't believe who I saw."

"About Pres," Charlotte said pointedly. "I went out with him on Tuesday to get drinks, which, in my mind, was like a drink or two, and he ended up blacked out. He texted me at one A.M. from the King Cole Bar, and then wandered over to Eleventh Avenue. I'm surprised he wasn't mugged."

"So funny. I was at King Cole on Tuesday but I didn't see him. It was earlier, because Nick and Camilla and Bridie Harley wanted to meet after—"

"Evelyn. Pay attention. Preston. I'm worried about him. He's drinking a lot more than usual."

"Sorry. Sorry. I haven't noticed it. I suppose I'm not that worried. It's winter and it's bleak outside so everyone's drinking more than usual, and Pres has such a high tolerance. He's coming to my birthday dinner at the Colony in a week and I promise I will watch him. I'm so sorry you'll be in Indianapolis for it. Did I tell you Camilla's doing a tropical theme? It sounds wild."

Charlotte looked upset. "Yeah, I'm sure it will be. Oh, right. He gave this to me to give to you. I guess he thought I'd see you before he did, which, obviously not. That's why I came by tonight. I've been carrying this around for weeks." Charlotte pulled something out of her bag. "Your Whiffenpoofs CD."

"The Poofs! I've been waiting for its safe return for months. Will you play it? My computer's on."

"Yeah." Charlotte walked to the sideboard, where Evelyn's desktop sat tethered to the Internet at an awkward height, flanked on each side by an upright Slim Aarons photography book. Charlotte shoved over one of the books and placed the CD in the drive. As it whirred and the Yale men sang "Rainbow Connection," she picked up Evelyn's checkbook lying face down on the sideboard. "Evelyn Beegan, don't tell me you still use checks."

Evelyn had no idea how long the checkbook had been there. Weeks? When was the last bill she had paid?

"You don't do online banking?" Charlotte asked.

"It's too complicated. Do you want some water? I'm parched," said Evelyn, trying to get Charlotte off the subject.

"Yeah."

As Evelyn filled up two glasses from her Brita, she could hear the fast clack of computer keys from the living room. "Char, what are you doing?" she asked.

"Just checking something online," Charlotte replied. Evelyn remembered that Charlotte had bought herself Mavis Beacon Teaches Typing and learned touch-typing during a summer Evelyn spent at tennis camp, a skill that was apparently still in full effect.

Evelyn returned with the water, and Charlotte, standing over the ancient IBM, was nearly beaming. "Look, I'm so helpful that I'm setting you up now. Your account number was on the check. You just need a username. What should we use, 'EvBeeg'?"

"Charlotte, I don't want online banking, okay? Can you back off?"

"Easy, Ev. I promise, it will save you time. Here. Just choose a username and a password."

Evelyn set Charlotte's water glass down hard and slid it over to her, watching the water marks it left on the sideboard and not bothering to wipe them up. "Do you have to bring all your, like, workday hustle to my apartment, Charlotte? I have zero interest in this."

"Yeah, yeah, yeah. Remember at Sheffield when you refused to get a debit card? You were still writing checks at the Seven-Eleven and waiting for your mom to send cash via U.S. mail. Look. It's super easy. Here."

If only her mother would send cash via U.S. mail, Evelyn thought, taking a tiny sip of water. It tasted tinned, and she returned to the couch, exchanging it for her wine. She knew she had to get hold of her money stuff. Maybe Charlotte could help. Maybe it wasn't as bad as she thought. All those letters from Con Ed and Time Warner Cable and her credit-card companies were sitting, silently threatening, in her silverware drawer, and she had so not wanted to face them that she had been using plastic takeout utensils lately when her Thai or her sushi was delivered, so she didn't ever have to open the drawer except to wedge more envelopes in.

Evelyn poured herself another glass of wine and stood up. "Okay. 'Evie98,'" she said, using her Sheffield graduation year. She leaned over Charlotte's shoulder and entered her standard password, "maybefaraway," from *Annie*.

"Good. Okay. Security questions," Charlotte said.

Evelyn scrolled through the dropdown menu: What was the make of your first car? Who was your childhood best friend? Who is your hero? Where did you meet your spouse? The cursor stood blinking at her, needling her for an answer. She couldn't pass this test. She had never had a car, being at boarding school when other people were getting their licenses. Her childhood best friend was, more or less, her mother, but she wasn't going to put that down. And who had a hero in this era? Who did this bank think it was, trying to fit Evelyn Beegan into the neat segments that defined its mass-market customers?

"Ev?"

"This is a stupid exercise, Charlotte."

"You're being impossible. I'll answer it for you. Hero: Brooke Astor."

"Very funny."

Charlotte typed in the socialite's name and began rifling through the mail on Evelyn's silver tray, but it was invitations and appeals for charity donations. "Where are your bills, Ev?"

Evelyn pulled at her hair, trying to think of the answer that would freak Charlotte out the least. "Dunno."

"Evelyn! I'm basically being your very highly paid data-entry assistant, courtesy of Graystone Partners, at the moment, all right? Can you not be a two-year-old?"

Evelyn remembered that her checking-account statement had arrived that week and had not yet been sequestered in the drawer, and shouldn't cause too much of a reaction from Charlotte; there wasn't a huge amount in the account, but at least she didn't owe anything on it. Evelyn pulled the statement from under a Gorsuch catalogue on the hallway table and handed it over.

"You mind if I open it?" Charlotte said, already ripping it unevenly. Evelyn, not wanting to watch, turned around and took a vase of long-dead flowers to the sink, pouring out the old water, which smelled completely unorganic, bacteria and slime and acid. She squirted Caldrea over the sink to try to cover up the smell with Mandarin Vetiver.

"This isn't a credit card, Ev. I need something that you pay actual bills to."

"Hmm? I don't know." Charlotte could be so harsh, so firm, that Evelyn felt she had made an error in giving her an opening.

"Where do you put your savings, by the way? It's good not to have too much in a checking account, but we should transfer some money in to cover your expenses. Where are you, Vanguard? Schwab?"

"Okay. Okay." Evelyn turned on the water to give herself a moment to think. She hadn't thought the checking account was in such bad shape, but Charlotte's reaction made it sound like there was next to nothing in it. The assumption that she had some secret savings or investment account somewhere to save her—this was another part of the world nobody had told her how to handle.

"We can even set up an automatic transfer monthly from your investment account, so we're not eating into the principal of your investments." Charlotte looked at her expectantly.

Evelyn managed to force out some words. "Not right now. I'm good for now," she said. Did everyone have separate investment accounts that funneled money to them monthly? How had she missed all of this?

"No biggie. So let's go back to online banking. We'll set up the recurring payments. It's, what, rent, cable, do you pay Internet separately? Cell phone. And credit cards, right? What do you have for credit cards? An AmEx, right?"

Evelyn let the water soak through a slightly soiled yellow sponge. Maybe Charlotte would know what to do. Maybe, if she was really in trouble, Charlotte would offer to lend her money. Evelyn would object unconvincingly, then accept graciously, and then she could pay the bills, or part of the bills, and everything would be fine. She wiped up the water around the vase. "Some others, too," she said in a small voice.

"Like?"

"A Visa, and Barneys, and Scoop."

"Scoop has a credit card, first of all? What's the APR on all of these?"

Evelyn's hands traced pretty windshield-wiper patterns with the sponge, so lightly she was spreading water drops over the counter rather than cleaning them up. "Not sure."

"Well, I need the statements."

"The statements."

"The statements."

Evelyn seized a second bottle of wine and took it over to the couch, where she plopped down and smiled. "Come sit, Char."

"No, I don't want the session to time out."

"Listen, grab the wine opener and we'll have another glass. Okay?"

"It won't take long."

"Really. It's time for wine."

Charlotte pushed herself away from the computer, then walked into the kitchen. "I don't see it," Charlotte said.

"The wine opener? Should be in the top drawer."

Evelyn heard a squeak of hardware, then silence. "You find it?" she said. Charlotte didn't respond. Evelyn hoisted herself out of the couch, then walked to the kitchen, where she saw, it hitting her almost in slow motion, that Charlotte had tugged open her silverware drawer. When Charlotte turned around, Evelyn saw she was holding the telltale light-blue paper from American Express. Its empty envelope was teetering on the counter's edge.

They stared at each other for a minute. "Put it down. Charlotte. Put that down," Evelyn finally said.

They were locked in place. Neither moved. Neither spoke. A pigeon brushed against the window, clacking in terror.

"Do you know what you owe?" Charlotte said. "Do you know what you owe?"

Evelyn pressed her hands against the frame of the kitchen entry. "Put the bill down, Charlotte. You have no right to go through my stuff. No right."

"That's neither here nor there, Evelyn. You need some help. Your credit card—and that's just one—"

"It's fine. All right, Charlotte? It's fine."

"No, it's not. It's not fine. It's not fine." Charlotte waved the papers. "I thought this was your rewards points, but you owe sixty-five thousand on your AmEx. Do you know what you're—no, it's okay, we'll figure this out. We'll sit down and figure out all the minimums you owe and transfer the balances—"

"I've been paying the minimums," she said loudly, though seeing Charlotte's panic at just this bill, which was only one of several, sent a sharp knife of fear through Evelyn. This problem was huge. A loan from Charlotte wouldn't fix it. Nothing would fix it.

"No. No. You're—do you see this? You've been late on your minimums, so the APR on this is up to twenty-two percent. That means you're paying, you're paying thousands of dollars just on fees on this one alone." Charlotte grabbed a stack of unopened bills from the drawer, new bills that Evelyn hadn't paid even the minimums on. The ripping sound as she opened them made Evelyn shudder. "Look, Barneys—and, Jesus, Visa—you can't have all these credit cards that you haven't paid off, Ev. This is going to massacre your credit rating." Charlotte was frantically reshuffling the bills like she was hoping for a better hand.

Evelyn looked at the ugly, unkempt sight of Charlotte, hysterical and judgmental over these papers, promising to help and instead making Evelyn feel worse. Charlotte's nose was oily and porous, her hair erupting out of her ponytail. The pressure in Evelyn's stomach was starting to rise, but she wouldn't allow Charlotte to see she'd affected her. "A credit card gives you credit." Evelyn spoke slowly, enunciating each word. "I am going to ask you to leave."

"No, Evelyn. Four thousand dollars from Gucci? Nine hundred from Saks?"

"Get out of my stuff."

"Ev, your parents—they can help—"

"You seem to have read all about my father, so you know that in fact they can't. Please put those papers back now, Charlotte. Now." Evelyn crossed to her and tore the envelopes from her hand, stuffing them back in the drawer and closing it with some difficulty against the bulging stack at the back. Charlotte opened her mouth but closed it, and took a step back, almost tripping on the threshold at the kitchen's edge. Evelyn didn't move, keeping her eyes trained on the drawer, as if constant vigil could keep the contents from filtering into her life. She eventually heard Charlotte pick up her things and then heard the door shut, but she stayed, watching, shaking with the effort it took to keep everything contained.

CHAPTER EIGHTEEN

People Like Us

"This is a bad joke," Evelyn said in a clipped tone to the wall, which was dark wood and covered with framed sports jerseys. Jin-ho had called in a favor with his front-office friend at the Rangers, and that had somehow, hideously, resulted in this People Like Us–sponsored Rangers-Devils game at a Midtown East bar on a Saturday afternoon in April. The beautiful, restrained People Like Us font and logo—a stylized fleur-de-lis that Evelyn had helped pick, meant to evoke a connection to European aristocracy—was now displayed on posterboards above two hockey helmets.

Evelyn sighed as loudly as she could, though she was too far away from the other people there—the busty girls Jin-ho had hired from some event-marketing firm, and the staff setting up chairs and pitchers of beer—for anyone to notice.

Evelyn turned toward the dirty glass door, where chilly air was coming in from outside, and dialed Camilla.

"You're psychic," Camilla said by way of greeting. "We're just about to go to lunch at—where is this place? I don't know, somewhere in Chinatown, where we'll eat soup dumplings and get totally drunk on cheap wine. Come join us. No, the snakeskin, please," she said to someone at the other end of the line.

"I'm at, get this, a sports bar in Midtown East. It's the worst."

"Whatever for?"

"People Like Us is having a membership event here."

"Yawn. Phoebe says this is the best Chinese food in town. A total dive. Then we're going to find a Chinese herbalist that will keep us forever young. I told you about the fleece flower root, right? Do I want a pair of green snakeskin pumps?"

"It's so dreary, Camilla."

"These are a really pretty shade of green."

"No. This PLU event. I'm seriously about to lose it."

"Then get out of there. Come join. We'll get that foot-acupuncture thing afterward. It's the first not-freezing day in about a century."

"I can't. I'm supposed to be doing recruitment at this event, but it is so massively wrong for PLU, I can't even tell you."

A girl from the event-planning firm, who was wearing a shrunken T-shirt that proclaimed PEOPLE LIKE US! in magenta cursive over her large breasts, grabbed Evelyn by the elbow. "Excuse me. People Like Us, right?"

"I'm on the phone," Evelyn replied.

"We need you to help with some collateral."

"I'll work on it once I'm off the phone."

"We need you to work on it now; the guests are arriving in ten minutes."

"Hold on." Evelyn spoke back into the phone: "Milla? Sorry, some girl in a baby tee is pestering me for something. I'll call you when I'm leaving, okay? Maybe we can meet at Bar Sixty-eight?"

"I'll probably be napping, but call."

"Thanks for the compliment on my T-shirt," the woman said in a sickly sweet voice as Evelyn pressed end.

"Anytime," Evelyn said in a matching tone. "What was it you wanted?"

"I was told you were going to help with some of the marketing flyers."

"People Like Us doesn't have marketing flyers. That's part of the point."

"There are flyers, and your bosses wanted them distributed in person to the guests."

"Flyers? Who made the flyers?"

"Our firm did, at People Like Us's request."

"This is absurd. I didn't even know about this and I'm the head of membership."

"Maybe you should try on one of our baby tees and see where it gets you," the woman said. "See Simon at the back of the room for the brochures."

Evelyn stalked back to where someone who had a HELLO, MY NAME IS . . . SIMON name tag stood. He was holding a stack of flyers, and Evelyn snatched one from the middle of the stack, sending several of the rest to the floor. As Simon scurried to pick them up, Evelyn got as far as "People Like Us, a new social network to connect with other fans of * sports * music * television shows" when she heard Jin-ho's voice behind her and whirled around.

"What the hell is this?" she said, pinching the brochure like it was a used Kleenex. "Connecting with music and TV fans? I thought this beer-hall outing was bad enough in itself, but really? This?"

Jin-ho was irritatingly calm, taking the flyer from her and placing it neatly on the table. "We asked for membership growth, and we didn't get it, so we're trying something else," he said.

"Without consulting me?"

"We asked you over and over to revamp the strategy, and your response was that your social friends wouldn't like it."

"That was not what I was saying, and you know that perfectly well. I was saying that we had to differentiate the site from the dozens of other sites out there. And pardon me if I don't think a televised hockey game and some stock-photo flyers are the way to do it. I'm sorry, but this is absurd. There is beer on the floor, there is sawdust, the bathrooms are a gigantic health-code violation, and soon we'll have commuters coming to get loaded before they take the four-fifteen to Paramus. These are not, by definition, people like us."

Evelyn watched as Jin-ho's ears turned pink. "I'm frankly not surprised at your response, Evelyn. Your attitude has been terrible for weeks, if not months, and you're not doing what we ask you to."

"I brought you guys the best members possible. Excuse me, Camilla Rutherford? Bridie Harley, who gets a front-row seat at Oscar and Carolina Herrera and she's only twenty-eight? Caperton Ripp, whose family basically created Charleston?"

"That was when you started. What have you done in the last three months, Evelyn? Really? Point to one thing."

"I've pitched one idea after another and heard nothing but no."

"Your ideas aren't particularly suited for our site."

"Oh, I'm sorry. I was under the impression that People Like Us members, I don't know, were well educated. Or well traveled. Or interested in the arts. In part because that's who you told me you wanted for the site, and that, Jin-ho, is who I got. So forgive me for thinking that this hockey game you've arranged with your Rangers friend is massively off-brand."

"Yes, Evelyn, you're quite familiar with this group, as you never cease to remind us. You haven't been doing what we've been asking you to do, however, which is increasing the membership to the levels Ulrich wants."

"It will cheapen what People Like Us does," Evelyn said. Jin-ho was just standing there, and she stared at him, waiting for him to admit he was wrong.

Jin-ho was looking behind her; Simon had vanished, and the busty girls were squeezing by to get supplies from the bar's kitchen. "This isn't working out," Jin-ho said. "We're going to have to let you go."

"You're firing me?" she said.

"Yes. Ann will call you Monday re the paperwork."

"You're firing me at a bar? Outside the bathroom in a bar?"

"I'm sorry if it doesn't suit your high standards." Jin-ho's ears were now a deep red, though his face had little color in it at all. "Your performance has been subpar for some time, Evelyn, and if you can't be bothered to participate in a membership event that we think is key to the site's future, that tells us everything we need to know."

"I want to talk to Arun."

"Arun agrees with me. We were going to do it when you were back in the office, but why drag this out?"

"Look, I can do this job. My ideas were really good. If you're that serious about these sports events, fine. I'll get on board with sports events, though I want to be on record saying they're a mistake."

"We're a small staff and we need people who are team players, frankly, not socialites playing at a day job." He looked at his watch. "I need to get things ready for this event. Good luck." He walked behind her to the kitchen.

Evelyn stood for only a couple of seconds before she got shoulder-checked by a baby-tee girl. She whirled around, grabbed her purse, and walked through the bar and out into the treeless section of Madison, blinking hard at the mirthless April sunlight. Half of her thought she should go plead her case to Arun, always the more sympathetic of the two co-CEOs. But then what? She'd keep marching to that dingy office while her friends bloomed and grew in their soft-lit lives? The M2 bus pulled up to the curb, stopped, and wheezed its dirty exhaust at her. The brown ad on the side of the bus was for Cellino and Barnes, injury attorneys. The M2's doors opened and started beeping, pressing her for a decision. They thought she was a socialite? They dismissed her very good ideas because of that? Fine. She'd be a socialite.

Evelyn started stalking uptown. Madison was so dreadful here, loaded with dentists' offices, kaiser-roll sandwich shops, and would-be luxury retailers that couldn't afford the rent farther up, that after two blocks she walked west instead of heading east toward her apartment. Fifth Avenue opened up, broad and proud, Central Park in the background, the trees beginning to push out green leaves and closed buds. She crossed the street, feeling tourists' eyes on her: Who is that? Is that someone? Yes, she told them in her head and, to show them that she was, pushed the door open at Bergdorf's.

She tamped down the mincing thought that she shouldn't be spending money. When things were rotten, you had clearance to do whatever you needed to do to get by, she was fairly sure Camilla had said once: throw money at the problem. She would get stock options from People Like Us, and probably some kind of severance or exit bonus. She was only going to get lunch, only going to create a glimmer of niceness in this day.

Up on the seventh floor, Evelyn ordered a Gotham salad and a chenin blanc. This was where she was supposed to be, up here off the dirty streets, with people who were actually like her, not People Like Us. Evelyn was feeling back to herself by the time she ordered an espresso with a twist of lemon and laid down her pretty silver Visa.

A few minutes later, as she glanced away from the Central Park view, she noticed the waiter hovering at her shoulder, mustache quivering.

"Yes?" she said coldly.

"I'm sorry, ma'am, do you have another credit card we could try?"

The "ma'am" distracted her, as it made her feel old, and it took her a moment to process what he was saying. "Pardon? What?" she said, making a Mitford fix.

"The credit card was declined."

It sounded like he had raised his voice on purpose, and she frantically scanned the tables of chignoned blondes around her to see if they heard.

"That can't be right," Evelyn said. "Please try it again." She had brought only the silver Visa with her because she knew she'd paid the minimum on that one, at least. Hadn't she? Visa couldn't stop letting her use it when the minimum was maybe one or two months late, could they? Wouldn't they have sent her a letter? Had they sent her a letter? Wasn't the point of a credit card to have credit? The silver card winked at her, taunted her, and she was glad when he took it away.

A piano played something insistent and Russian sounding, and Evelyn blinked. A young girl bumped into her chair, whining to her mother that they were already late for spinning, and Evelyn saw the girl was wearing a current-season Marni jacket. If the bills were as bad as Charlotte had thought they were—but no, they must not be—yet just on Thursday, she'd received a letter saying her April rent was past due and needed immediate payment. She tried to do what the Equinox yoga instructor said to do and thank each thought for coming, then let it float away, but the thoughts were not floating away and she couldn't force them away, not even here, where she was supposed to be able to escape.

Evelyn clenched and unclenched her jaw. The waiter came back and, before Evelyn could even sit up straight, handed her the card, on a silver tray. There was no receipt.

"I'm sorry, ma'am," he said.

"Excuse me, please, while I sort this out," Evelyn said.

He took a step back but remained at the table. "I said excuse me," Evelyn said. "I'll need a few minutes." He turned on his heel and walked off.

She gingerly picked up the card and examined it. On the back was an 800 number, and she turned toward the window and discreetly punched the number into her cell phone. "Customer service," she said quietly when prompted. "Customer service. Customer service. Customer service. Customer service!" On the other end of the line, someone with an unplaceable accent greeted her.

"Hi, my credit card isn't working? I just need you to clear this up so I can charge my lunch," she said.

"Thank you, ma'am," the woman on the line said. This "ma'am" sounded warm and inviting, not at all the judgment she was expecting. "While I bring up your account, I'll be glad to tell you about special offers and services customized for you. Ma'am, yes, ma'am, you have a past-due minimum-payment balance, and until that balance is paid, we've been instructed to withhold authorization. Would you like to pay that balance now?"

Evelyn scooted her chair closer to the window and leaned into the phone. "The thing is, I need to pay for lunch, and they're declining the card. Can we fix that?"

"Well, ma'am, our records show that a payment on this card has not been made since February and the outstanding balance is—"

"I didn't know it was that long. Honestly, I have a lot going on right now. I've been meaning to pay it."

"I see, ma'am. We are always glad to help our valued clients. I am authorized to create a payment plan for you at this time."

"Listen, the thing is, I'm at lunch right now and I just switched wallets so I only have this one card with me today. I had to go to this dreadful thing at a sports bar earlier, you see, so I kind of have to pay for lunch with this card. Isn't there something you can do?"

"Yes, ma'am, please hold, and let me see which offers we can bring you today." After a couple of minutes of Hall & Oates, the woman was back on the line. "I can authorize further charges at this time with a transfer of your balance to our Pewter Card, which is a new card specially created for credit-challenged consumers like you. Now, with this offer does come a higher APR and annual fee. Would you like to hear the details of this offer?"

"No, I mean, that sounds fine. So I can use my card now, right?"

"Yes, ma'am, you would be free to use your card at this time, and you will be able to continue using your new Visa Pewter Card once it arrives in the mail. I will need a verbal 'yes' at this time to activate the new member agreement."

"Okay. Yes. Great."

"Is there anything else?"

"No. Thank you. Thanks very much." Evelyn hung up and looked at herself in the window, smoothed her hair, then put up one hand in what she hoped was a lackadaisical fashion to attract the waiter again. "A snafu with the bank," she said when he arrived, and couldn't help smirking at him. "You can go ahead and charge this."

Ann called the next day and told her that since she hadn't been at the company a full year, she didn't qualify for stock options, and at any rate People Like Us was not close to being sold, so there wouldn't have been a way to make them liquid. The company didn't offer severance, which apparently was a benefit and not a right, and certainly wouldn't apply to her being terminated for poor performance, and when Evelyn asked about an exit bonus Ann actually laughed.

On Monday, after ignoring a call and voice mail from Sag Neck—there was no one she wanted to talk to less than her parents right now—she met Camilla for lunch at Café Sabarsky to get assurances that losing her job would be fine. Camilla was certain: this was the best thing that could've happened, and everything would work out. "Darling," Camilla said, "you can now focus on real life. You wanted to get more involved in charity work, and now you actually will, rather than spending time on that dreadful commute. You'll absolutely love it. And you'll finally be available for me during the day." Camilla gave her that life-is-golden smile, and Evelyn felt instantly better. Camilla was right. There were the bills, of course, but her paltry paycheck barely made a difference in those anyway. She had a tiny bit in her 401(k) that she could use until something, someone, stepped in to give her the life she deserved. Camilla never paid for anything, and Evelyn was almost at that level. Scot could take care of dinners and things like that for now, and if all else failed, she could always marry him, or marry well, in any case.

She would have time now to start focusing on benefit committees, like Camilla said, and going to the gym more regularly. She could get more involved in the Bal, too, as the midday planning meetings would be easy to attend. All those Manhattan things that were impossible with a job were now possible. She thought of the embarrassment of having to call her dermatologist from work while Clarence snuffled next to her and overheard all about her occasional eczema flare-ups. How the dry cleaner was always closed when she came home, and how the tiles in her bathroom walls had started coming off weeks ago, but because she had to be at work when the super was available, she didn't have time to handle any of it. She'd meant to learn to cook, but those classes all started at five, and she wanted to study

Italian, but the classes were only Tuesdays and Thursdays midday. There was simply no way to work and do everything else she was supposed to do. Like Camilla always said, it was all for the best and it would all work out.

CHAPTER NINETEEN

Scottish Fling

Day four of not working, and it was second nature. Evelyn had woken when she wanted to, when the sun in her window gently nudged her awake rather than her insistent alarm, and gone to a late-morning Equinox yoga class, then strolled in the park and looked at the cherry blossom buds before returning home to shower, change, and head out for the hair appointment that she had been able to book just the night before because her time was now so flexible.

Afterward, she stopped for tea and a macaron at Payard, settled into a seat under the amber chandelier, and pulled out her phone. There was another voice mail from her parents, but she didn't listen to it. She switched to the text-message function. She'd been putting it off, but she was seeing Scot tonight and texting seemed easier than a real conversation. She tapped out, "Guess what?" then erased it, then tried, "So update," before deleting and writing, and finally sending, "I have big news . . ."

Scot's response came seconds later: "?"

"Will tell u tnt," Evelyn replied.

"Wd like 2 know now."

Evelyn typed out, "So I was let go," then, "So I was fired," and finally settled on, "PLU had layoffs. Me. DONT worry. For the best."

"You were fired? RU okay?"

"Laid off. Y. Is good."

"What will u do?"

Evelyn took a tiny bite of chocolate macaron, the gold leaf melting on her tongue. Not knowing how to answer, she decided to pretend like she hadn't seen the question.

"See u Sothebys tnt?" she wrote.

"U ok?"

"Great. Bye!"

For once, Evelyn didn't care that she would have to arrive solo to the event, a Scottish Society fund-raiser at Sotheby's where she and Camilla were walking in a runway show. She could go from home, rested and refreshed, in an unwrinkled dress, with newly applied makeup. She was finally on equal footing with all the other girls.

When she walked into the benefit through a phalanx of bagpipers, she immediately spotted Preston, who looked like he was already several drinks in, gazing at a fern. "I need steak," he groaned when Evelyn approached. Evelyn wondered briefly if she should be worried, given Charlotte's concern about his drinking; she'd meant to observe him at her birthday party but had gotten totally sidelined.

"Darling P," she said. "You made it."

"Darling E," he replied. "The newly minted twenty-seven-year-old. I don't think I've seen you since your birthday dinner."

"Wasn't it the most fun? Bridie Harley's toast was just amazing, wasn't it?"

"Something like that," Preston said, pushing up his glasses.

"I was so honored that she took the time to come. She had a Central Park Conservancy dinner that night and she still stopped by my party."

"I'm glad her priorities are in the right place," Preston said.

"I couldn't believe that Camilla got the Colony to do a tropical theme. Didn't you love the palm trees?"

"A bit of Polynesia in this drear season. 'Whan that Aprille with his shoures soote.'"

"'The droghte of Marche hath perced to the roote.' Have I really not seen you since then?"

"Well, my dear, whenever I try to set up a dinner with you, we end up at a large-group outing," he said.

"Yet the Scottish Society could lure you?"

"I couldn't pass up the opportunity to not wear anything under my kilt," he said. He was wearing a suit.

"I'm glad I got you alone, actually."

"Well, well, well. Aren't we a forward little thing." He bared his teeth at her.

"You look like an angry wolf when you do that."

"Grrr," he said, surprisingly loudly, rolling his shoulders forward and extending one hand in imitation of a paw, but by the time several people turned to look at where the noise had come from he was innocently looking around, too.

"Be quiet, Preston! People are looking at you," Evelyn said. Two of the slightly older society girls, Alix Forrester Landau, whose father was said to have the private number of the investor Bernie Madoff, and Gemma Lavallee, whose mother had started a cosmetics line that included crushed pearls in all of the foundations, were craning their heads, looking for the source of the growl.

"I didn't know you embarrassed so easily," Preston said.

"Gemma and Alix are practically staring."

"Why do you care about Gemma and Alix?" he said.

"I care about elegance and grace."

"I repeat, why do you care about Gemma and Alix?" he said.

Evelyn sighed. "Oh, I meant to ask you something. I wondered if your mother could help me out with Sloan Kettering's associate committee. Since your mom's on the board of Dana Farber, she must know the key people at Sloan Kettering, right?"

Preston poked at the fern, and took a minute before answering. "You should ask your pals Gemma and Alix to help you."

"No, I know the people on the committee. That's not the issue. It would just be a stronger endorsement if someone like your mother were to—were to indicate that I would be a good board member."

"I don't think my mother is involved in Sloan Kettering."

"I know that, but these circles are small. I'm just asking her to mention me."

"My mother barely . . ." He trailed off, evidently engrossed by an ice cube he was trying to push to the bottom of his drink with his straw. "I'll try to talk to her," he said finally, his eyes still on his glass. "I just need another drink."

Evelyn reached for the glass. "I will do it for you, as thanks for your services," she said, expecting Preston to laugh, but he pulled the glass away. "I've got it," he said, and headed for the bar.

Nick and Scot arrived together at seven-fifteen, just as Camilla floated in. Camilla had severed her hookups with Nick a few weeks prior, explaining to Evelyn that she was trying to simplify and purify her life on the advice of a Reiki master she had gone to. Nick was determined to show how little the breakup, if one could call it that, had affected him; Camilla, on the other hand, appeared to genuinely not be thinking about it as she leaned in for a kiss. In return, Nick gave her a longing head-to-toe appraisal.

"Hi, Milla. Hi, boys," Evelyn said, mentally picturing how she looked holding her champagne glass as she talked to Camilla. Moments later, the Patrick McMullan photographer snapped the very photo she was hoping he would, and she leaned forward to speak into his handheld recorder like a pro, "Beegan, B-E-E-G-A-N."

Camilla just gave the photographer a wave; she didn't need to identify herself.

"Good day in the markets," Nick said. "Dow thirteen thousand, what-what?"

"It's as I said: the trend is your friend," Preston said. He had bounced back from whatever had been bothering him earlier, Evelyn thought. "Did you hear Monsieur Paulson last week? All this sub-prime nonsense is contained and he believes housing is about to go back up. What say we, should we buy some subdivisions?"

"Paulson should never've left Goldman," Nick said. "Dude left so much money on the table. Deal flow right now is intense."

"Is the subprime stuff really contained?" Scot asked. "The mortgage market is getting loopy. I offered to guarantee my mom's mortgage—she was buying a new house and had some bad credit history. The bank in Arizona said I shouldn't bother with the guarantee as the paperwork was a headache, and they were just going to bundle the mortgage and sell it off to another bank. They also tried to push her to borrow more money, which she didn't need and, frankly, shouldn't have qualified for. That just strikes me as untenable. I'm not sure the CDO crisis can be contained if banks are doing that."

"Way to be a downer, man," Nick said. "Why don't you just enjoy the ride?"

"It sets off an alarm bell for me, Nick. So the banks are creating and selling CDOs, hedge funds are doing credit arbitrage with them, the mortgage lenders continue to lend, and no one has any idea what's at the core of these holdings, right? The thing with my mom's mortgage drove it home."

"Who has a mortgage, anyway?" Camilla said. "If we are forced to talk about business, I would like to talk about how the pound is now absurdly high. Céline had to special-order a clutch from its London store for Evelyn and she had to pay in pounds. It was at least twice what it cost here."

Evelyn was both surprised that Camilla had noticed the price and flattered by the callout; she shifted the clutch, which was gorgeous, in front of her.

"Well, it looks sharp. I must say, Evelyn, you look good. Unemployment agrees with you," Nick said.

Scot, who was turning his large head around the room—Evelyn supposed he saw the unusual view of tops of heads, cowlicks, and thinning spots, given his height—snapped it back. "You told Nick?"

"It was a secret? Oopsies," said Preston, covering his mouth with his hand.

"You didn't know your girl here has joined Camilla in the ranks of the unsalaried?" Nick said.

Scot's mouth set in a line that Evelyn hadn't seen before, and he said in her ear, "So you told everyone but me?"

"I told you, too," Evelyn said, looking beyond him and opening her mouth in mock surprise as she waved at Bridie Harley, who had just walked in. "What time is it? I have to get backstage for the runway."

"Evelyn." He turned her so she was facing him straight on. "When were you laid off?"

"The weekend?" she said, biting her lip in a way she'd seen Camilla do with Nick.

"It's Wednesday. You just told me now?"

"I told you a few hours ago."

"Days after it happened?"

"We're time-stamping everything now?"

"Everyone else seems to have known for a while."

"Rumors travel fast," she said as Camilla glided over and said, "Evelyn, my dear, we have to go backstage immediately."

"Where are you going to work?" Scot said.

"Isn't it fantastic? Evelyn was never meant to work at that place anyway," Camilla said gaily.

"Where are you going to work?" Scot repeated.

Evelyn hoped Camilla would jump in to answer the question, but Camilla was looking at her expectantly. "I'm . . . not."

"What?" Scot said.

"It's just impossible to keep up my life and work at the same time."

"We'll see you on the runway, Scootles!" Camilla trilled, grabbing Evelyn's right elbow while Scot held tight to her left one.

"How are you going to support yourself?" Scot said.

Camilla released Evelyn's arm and rolled her eyes. "So practical," she whispered to Evelyn. Then, more loudly, "See you backstage!"

Scot was still staring at her.

"What?"

"How are you going to support yourself?"

"I don't know. How does Camilla support herself?"

"Are you being serious?"

"I suppose so."

"Camilla has somewhere north of twenty million dollars managed for her right now, and she'll come into about quadruple that when her parents pass away."

Evelyn blinked. "I—I have family money, too." Her parents would eventually loosen their grip on their money; they had to. Though her mother hadn't sent the faux rent money in a month or two, Evelyn remembered; she should track that down.

Scot dug his hands into the roots of his hair and tugged at it, waiting for her to say more, but she didn't. "I'm late," Evelyn finally said, ignoring his "Wait. Wait."

She turned, hurrying alongside the makeshift runway, and moved the curtain at the end of it back.

Camilla was sitting in a chair as an intensely angled woman applied eyebrow powder to her. "I knew Scot wouldn't understand," she said as a man with swooped-forward hair like Prince's pushed Evelyn into a chair next to Camilla's and began smearing foundation over her cheeks.

"Well, you were right. He seemed baffled."

"A man whose life ambition is dealing with media companies can't be expected to understand, can he? Scot's very sweet, but honestly. He's never been taught the virtues of charity work or anything like that."

"You don't think he's meant for greatness."

Camilla smiled at Evelyn sympathetically. "I really don't."

Evelyn looked at herself in the dark mirror, surrounded by Broadway-like bulbs. The Prince man, whose breath smelled of raisins, dipped a brush in a pot of eyeliner and began applying a thick stripe along Evelyn's lashline. "Scot's dressing better. Have you noticed?" Evelyn asked.

"He absolutely is, darling, but clothes only do so much."

"A pink shirt does not make the man," Evelyn said.

"I meant to ask you about your father's donation," Camilla said, shutting her eyes for eye shadow. "We have him down in the program as a Luminary Patron, so we do need the check before the event."

"Ouch!" said Evelyn, though the Prince man's eyeliner brush was in the pot of liquid. "Sorry, I just got something in my eye. Can I just—I need to just go get it out."

"Five minutes," the Prince man said, tapping his watch. "Go fast. There's a restroom at the end of the back hallway there."

Through a side door, Evelyn walked down an empty service hallway, one eye wet with liner, the other bare, rattled by Scot's reaction, Camilla's assessment that he still wasn't good enough, and the looming fact of that donation. She saw a water fountain and stopped to cool down and breathe. When she stood up, she saw, surprisingly, Charlotte, who she didn't think had been invited. Evelyn noticed with annoyance that Charlotte hadn't done anything to her hair besides stick a bobby pin in it so she looked like a ten-year-old, and her boring black cocktail dress had a milk stain on it, sloppy in a new mother and inexplicable in a twenty-six-year-old single banker.

The day before, Evelyn, feeling guilty that she hadn't spent much time with Charlotte lately, had made the mistake of e-mailing her to see if she wanted to have lunch, even offering to go to Midtown East to meet her. Predictably, Charlotte responded by explaining how busy she was and how she couldn't even leave for coffee, much less lunch, and then asked Evelyn why she was arranging a Tuesday lunch downtown. Evelyn e-mailed back that she had decided to depart People Like Us to focus on things other than her job.

Charlotte called less than a minute later. Evelyn didn't pick up. An e-mail arrived a few minutes after that, with a lot of caps and a lot of judgment, and the release Evelyn had been feeling since she had been fired was quickly stolen by Charlotte. She had put up with Charlotte when Charlotte was awkward and odd, and had never called her on her holier-than-thou behavior around Camilla, yet her friend couldn't seem to extend the same leeway to her. Now Evelyn needed two minutes, just two minutes, to collect herself, and apparently she wasn't allowed even that.

She edged behind the water fountain, but Charlotte looked down the hallway and started pounding across the linoleum toward her. "Evelyn," she said.

"Char. I didn't know you were coming to this. I'm surprised you got off of work."

"Well, I handed off some of the modeling to the junior associates. I figured you'd be here, and since you didn't return my calls—"

"Who talks on the phone anymore?"

"Or my e-mails."

Evelyn had typed out her anger at Charlotte's lack of support in a furious e-mail that she had never sent, opting instead to enjoy her workless weekday getting a facial and a hot-stone massage, which she thought showed not a small amount of emotional intelligence.

She drummed her hand on the water fountain. "Gosh, I barely check that account these days. I've actually got to dash. I'm in the runway show and I'm late."

"You e-mailed me from that account, so obviously you were check-ing it."

"Okay, girl detective. They've only done half my makeup. I'll see you after, okay?"

"Can you cool your jets for one minute? I actually have to talk to you."

"Char, I've got to—"

"Evelyn, I'm serious." Charlotte checked behind her back quickly. "Listen. The job thing. We need to talk about it."

"I am focusing my energies elsewhere," Evelyn said.

"You should be looking for another one," Charlotte replied.

"For your information, I got fired, Charlotte."

"It's a really bad idea," Charlotte said.

"Oh, I'm sorry, getting fired is a bad idea? Alert *New York* magazine. You've got a trend piece."

"Evelyn, you should be working."

"Charlotte, you've always liked your job, okay? I just realized that maybe getting fired is a great thing. Spending time staring at an old computer isn't really a useful way to spend my life. Think back to the classes at Sheffield where they talked about finding your passion. I've been basically ignoring that for the last almost five years, just jumping between things that aren't that fulfilling."

"Look, I like my job sometimes, but I've been doing basically data entry for the last three weeks, trying to figure out if the profitability trends at some random company will hold. It's not glamorous all the time. Or, really, ever. But every week, there's a paycheck. That's why they call it work."

Evelyn blew out a breath. "It's not the same, Char. First of all, I was getting paid nothing close to what I should be getting, given how much more qualified I was than the cray-cray guy who sat next to me, and given that my health is suffering because of it, which seems like a pretty big price to pay. My stress level is up to here, my skin is disastrous, and I hadn't been able to go to cardio sculpt in, like, a month, because of work. I've had essentially no time to myself or to get involved with any of the things I want to get involved in."

"Like cardio sculpt?"

"Forget it, Char." Evelyn's voice was hard. "I have to get ready for this show."

"Wait," Charlotte said. "The deal I'm working on. We're acquiring the pill-packaging division of a pharma company. Evelyn, it's a company that had been sued by Leiberg Channing."

Evelyn didn't move. Like a fear-of-flying airline passenger counting the seats to the exit row, she mentally measured how close to any eavesdropper they were. The drone of the overhead lights was the only immediate sound she could hear, the party muffled by the thick wall to her right.

"I know you said you didn't want to talk about it before, but the indictment against your dad came up in due diligence. Don't tell anyone I told you this—I'd get fired—but Evelyn, our lawyers say it doesn't look good for him."

"There's no indictment, Charlotte. There's a weak investigation, and that's all, and, as I said, it is absolutely none of your business."

"Technically, it is my business, since we came across it in due diligence," said Charlotte. "And Evelyn, there is an indictment. It's not just an investigation anymore. He was indicted on Monday."

Evelyn's laugh sounded cackling. "No, I don't think so."

"I know so, Evelyn."

"I don't . . . I don't . . ." Evelyn bent over the water fountain and took a long sip of water. She remembered the two or three missed calls from Sag Neck this week that she hadn't returned. When she stood up from the fountain, she felt pulled together again. An indictment wasn't that much worse than an investigation; it was just formal charges. It was better, even, because now it was clear what her father was dealing with, and his lawyer could respond properly. "Indictments happen all the time, Charlotte. I really have to get back." She began heading toward the door.

"Did you know the partners at Leiberg are planning to sue your father if he can't get the case dropped?"

"That's ridiculous. He *is* one of the partners at Leiberg." Evelyn had stopped walking and was staring down the empty hallway in front of her, which was too long and too gray all of a sudden.

"They're distancing themselves. Evelyn, that can be a lot of money. There's also restitution. I don't know how much your family has—"

Evelyn whirled back. Was everything fair game for Charlotte? Her job, her choices, her father, her family's money? "No, you don't, Charlotte. You're right, you could get fired for this, so I'm not sure you should talk about it anymore."

"Are you serious?"

"Are *you* serious? I have to go walk in this show and I'm about to cry from the stress of what was supposed to be a fun night, and I just wanted a single minute by myself, but apparently that's too much to ask."

Charlotte balled up her hand into a fist. "Fine, Evelyn. Fine. Go walk in your fashion show. Sorry that I tried to actually talk to you about something that's really fucking important. Sorry that I left work and changed into this ugly fucking dress, which is like Banana Republic 1995 and was the only thing in my office closet because I haven't had time to go shopping like you and Camilla seem to do every other day despite your massive—can we say massive? let's say massive—credit-card bills. Okay? You're right. Go take your minute to get your blush done or whatever the fuck you need to do and go do your fashion show. That's what's important."

Evelyn stepped back, then stepped back again. Her phone buzzed and she looked at it: a text from Camilla, "They nd u backstage NOW." Charlotte was pounding her fist against the water-fountain button, making water shoot on and off, and Evelyn left her, walking away so fast she was almost running. She rejoined Camilla behind the scrim. Ten minutes of makeup and ten minutes of hair later, she changed into her outfit, a kilt with a tight sequined sweater that was the more demure version of what Camilla was wearing. As she tugged on the kilt, Evelyn forced herself to ignore the uneasy feeling that lingered like bad breath from the conversation with Charlotte.

"You look good," said Camilla, sticking out her lower lip.

"You look better," Evelyn said, and got in line behind Camilla to strut along the runway. Evelyn indeed made the party photos at Patrick McMullan the next day. The photo caption read "Camilla Rutherford and friend."

CHAPTER TWENTY

Homeward Bound

The high-pitched trill of Evelyn's phone went off for what seemed like the fifteenth time this hour. Camilla had made the first call, wanting to know if Evelyn would be going to Sachem this weekend or not, and Evelyn put her off. She wanted to go, especially once Camilla mentioned that Jaime de Cardenas and some of Souse's friends were going. Yet there was also a fund-raiser for the Philharmonic on Saturday that some of the Sloan Kettering board members were supposed to attend, and Evelyn figured that if she had to choose, she was better off focusing on Sloan Kettering and meeting Jaime another time. She kept calling the Philharmonic development person to see who had RSVP'd, but hadn't heard back.

Everyone else that she didn't want to hear from kept on calling. Her rental management company called, telling her that her April and now her May payments had not been made, and she would need to get a check to them by the end of the week. "Tenant law is very strong in New York," Evelyn responded, repeating something her father had once said. She thought she had at least three or four months before she really got into trouble for skipping her rent, and she would have money sorted out by then, somehow. The woman on the phone said that tenant law wasn't that strong, and that further proceedings would be pursued. They're just trying to scare me, Evelyn thought, and Camilla would not let something like this bother her, and Evelyn resolved not to, either. Then a blocked number, a man who left a voice mail telling Evelyn that he was from a collection agency that had taken over her past-due Barneys account and to call back to work out a payment plan. She deleted that midway through the message. Plausible deniability, she thought.

After that, her father called and left a message, but Evelyn didn't listen to it. Once Charlotte told her about the indictment, Evelyn called home, and her mother confirmed that Dale had been indicted on bribery and other charges. Barbara was livid, and Evelyn was, too. That he could put the family in this precarious situation because of his own greed, his desire for maroon jackets and pocket squares and flashy cars was infuriating. Worse, she now thought he was stupid. He had been the only one at his firm to get indicted, and for someone who practices law to get so badly entangled in it meant he was careless and dumb. She had barely communicated with her father since. The one time he'd e-mailed her, it was to ask if she had a receipt for some dinner they'd had a year ago on a date prosecutors had been inquiring about. He didn't explain what had happened, or ask her how she was holding up, but pretended like everything was cheery and fine. She'd responded by asking him again what she was supposed to tell Camilla about the dinner, and he'd replied that it wasn't his problem.

The series of calls was capped off with her mother—a call Evelyn picked up, to see if she could get some money out of her so these other people would stop harassing her. Evelyn had to come home; it was an emergency, Barbara said.

"I've got a packed week, Mom. It can't be done."

"Evelyn, it's not optional."

"I'm either going to this big fund-raiser or to Sachem this weekend, and I have a lot to do before then."

"Tomorrow, if you can't today," her mother said. "You'll take the morning train and you can be back by the evening. We'll pay for it."

"Oh, thank you. Nice of you to pay when it's convenient to your ends," Evelyn said.

"Evelyn. You will be here tomorrow," Barbara said, and the line went dead.

Five minutes after Evelyn walked in the door at Bibville, the home phone began ringing. It rang four times, then five, then six, before Evelyn figured out that her mother must've turned the answering machine off. She was reaching for the receiver of the front-hallway phone when she felt a swift slap on her forearm.

"It's journalists," Barbara said. "Or other vultures calling to express their sympathy over your father. Really, they're so happy to see him taken down. Don't pick it up."

Evelyn withdrew her hand. "Ow. That hurt. Where did you come from? I didn't realize you were home. You wanted me here, so let's do whatever it is we're here to do. I have a ticket on the bus from Easton to New Carrollton in three hours, so unless someone wants to drive me to New Carrollton, I have to be on it."

The phone had stopped ringing, and Barbara took the receiver off the base. "Let them get a busy signal," she said. "You didn't see anyone in Easton, did you?"

"Just the taxi driver. We need to talk about money, too. This rent money you promised is nowhere to be found, and I need some for bills, too."

"Dale," Barbara hollered. "Dale! Your daughter is here!"

Evelyn heard the study door open and shut, and her father walked slowly down the stairs, clutching the banister.

"Hi," Evelyn said flatly.

"Hello," he said back.

Neither smiled.

Evelyn shrugged. "So what's the big mystery, parents?"

"We'll talk outside," her father said, and opened the front door. His shoes crunched on the gravel as he walked, and Evelyn craned her head to see where he was going, which was about thirty yards away, to a grove of pines that they'd planted when they moved in, which now were tall and elegant.

Her mother clomped after him, and Evelyn, with a bewildered look on her face for the benefit of anyone who was watching, followed them. Her parents were standing silently by the trees.

"Is now when we sacrifice a goat?" she said when she had joined them.

"Watch yourself," Dale said. He pulled a tiny branch off of the tree, and crushed the needles between his fingers. Off in the distance, a truck's horn left a smear of sound.

Her father studied the pine needles in his hand for a minute, then looked at her. "The federal investigators had a wiretap on our phone," he said. "I assume it's done with, but to be safe, we're talking out here."

"You think the house is bugged?"

Her father yanked at the bough, and her mother stood with arms folded looking toward the house.

"Guys," she said in an annoyed tone. "I hightailed it down here even though this is a massively busy week so that we could once again talk about this disaster. Are we going to sit around in silence or are you going to tell me whatever Dad's done now that's apparently so important that I have to drop everything?"

"Don't address your parents as 'guys,'" Barbara said sharply.

"Your attitude, Evelyn," Dale said, but he didn't complete the thought. He finished denuding the branch and then threw it on top of his car, which was parked on the gravel. "They've started to turn over discovery in the case, Evelyn. It's not as weak as we, I, thought. I'm not guilty of this. I want to be crystal clear on that. The wiretaps are challenging. An entirely innocent person, which I am, can sound suspect if a wiretapped conversation is taken out of context. The criminal-justice system in this country is so heavily stacked against anyone accused of anything, and white-collar crimes can get into huge suggested sentences, ten, fifteen years. I'm sixty-four. That's an effective life sentence."

"I thought your whole thing was there was no case," Evelyn said.

"I can't roll the dice at trial. I know how juries work and I've thought about it, I've discussed it with my lawyer, I've discussed it with your mother, and I, we, just can't take the chance."

"You've said all along you did nothing wrong."

"It's not worth the risk of trial. Rudy, my lawyer, is working with the government on a plea deal for obstruction of justice, which is a less serious offense than bribery, and if we can work something out, I think that's the best option."

"With no jail?"

"Prison," Barbara murmured.

"What?" Evelyn said.

Barbara pursed her lips. "It's prison. Jail is for short-term offenses, or so I've learned. We've already had to completely separate ourselves from anyone connected with the firm. I saw Sally the other day at the club and had to—"

"You'll avoid prison, right?" Evelyn asked her father.

Dale pressed his hands against his jaw. "We've asked for a probationary sentence, but there's a chance the judge will impose prison time," he said.

"Are you serious?"

"Yes."

Evelyn started shaking her head. "Hold on. Hold on. Juries are your thing. You're supposed to be able to convince juries of everything. That's what you always claimed, didn't you? Those newspaper articles and those awards? All those awards? Yet you don't think you can convince a jury of your own innocence? Really? Because I would think if you were really innocent, maybe you could use all your skills so you aren't leaving me and Mom and spending time in prison. I thought you were the guy who got to say what was right and what was wrong and whether my job and requests for money were worthy or not, not the guy who goes to prison because he can't handle the evidence the government has against him. Aren't you that guy, Dad? Or no, apparently, you aren't. Apparently, you, too, can do something wrong. Because guess what? Innocent people don't have to plead guilty.

Guess what else? They don't go after innocent people randomly. If you'd been more careful, like your partners apparently were, none of this would've happened. Rules aren't that hard to follow except, apparently, for you."

She heard a loud thump and jumped back, then connected it with her father's fist, which he'd slammed into the tree. His eyes were deep with anger.

"I do not know, Evelyn Beegan, when you became such a first-class brat," he said.

The moment did not end; he kept jamming his knuckles against the tree. Then he looked over his shoulder and the hurt Evelyn saw in his eyes made her feel unbalanced. He walked to the car, jumped in, revved the engine, and slammed the door shut as he sped off.

She turned to explain herself to her mother, but Barbara was already heading toward the house.

Evelyn touched her cell phone in her pocket, feeling lost, feeling like she needed someone to tell her she was okay, and, without considering it too carefully, dialed Scot.

"Ev? I'm just getting into a cab, sorry. How's home?"

"I'm fine. I'm good," Evelyn said.

"Everything's going okay?"

She stared at the house, beige dust in front from where her father had squealed off. Okay? Her father was going to prison and thought she was a wretch.

"He might plead," she said loudly. "My dad. My mom just told me."

"Lex and Forty-third," Scot said. "Your dad might what? Sorry, the connection's bad."

"Plead. Plead guilty. I don't know what you know, if you know, about the investigation. The indictment. But he's going to plead guilty. It might mean prison." Her voice was getting increasingly bitter. "My father in prison. Nice, right? The host committee of the Bal is going to be psyched about that one." For once, she wanted to talk about it. "Did everyone know? Does everyone know? I know Camilla says indictments are no big deal, but Scot, the idea of my dad in prison. He's not that tough, my dad, and prison, and my mom has never worked, and she's going to be alone, and it's going to be such a mess. And the money, Scot. I don't know what to do about the money."

"Ev?" Scot blurted.

"What?" She needed to hear that he loved her, that he would help her.

"Evelyn? Hello? Hello?"

"Scot. Scot?"

"There, I can hear you now. Sorry. I lost you there. So who did what?"

Evelyn's face constricted. "You didn't hear any of that."

"No, sorry. What's going on?"

Her eyes were still trained on her house; her mother hadn't bothered to shut the front door. "Never mind," she said, after an empty silence.

"No, I'm sorry, tell me."

"It was nothing. It is nothing."

"Something with your father?"

She walked to the front door and saw her mother sitting on the stairs. "No. Nothing. I have to go." Evelyn pressed end.

"Who was that?" Barbara asked.

"No one. Camilla," Evelyn said.

"Have you told her your father can't do her party?" Barbara said. "The party he was so flattered by?"

"God." Evelyn pressed her head against the cell phone and made it jam into her head "No, I know. I'm just—just give me a minute."

"So many phone calls to make, and things to do," Barbara said. "I remember that. Life. It used to be so short, Evie. Is that what yours is like? When I see the pictures of you, I think maybe it is. When the days went by in a whirl and the nights weren't long enough, and we were frantic with excitement for the next party. I can't grasp, now, how it all seemed like that. Can you imagine, wishing the next day would hurry and arrive? Now I wish it would hurry and pass. Life gets so long when you grow old."

"You're not old, Mom," Evelyn muttered without much conviction, still pressing her head into the phone.

"What's my obituary going to say, Evelyn?"

"What?"

"Don't say 'what'; you sound like a duck. I've spent all my life raising you and tending to your father, and what's my obituary going to say?"

"Mom, you're not dying."

"Mother and wife; that's a single line. Resident of Bibville; that's two."

Evelyn swallowed, watching her mother stare up at the ceiling. She wasn't wrong.

Dully, Evelyn turned and with heavy legs walked into the piano room. The one thing Evelyn could do over the muted roar in her head was play. If she could get her fingers to move over "Somewhere" she felt like she could get her mind away from this.

When she walked through the door this time, though, she saw the cabinets first, which should have been blocked by the piano. It took a moment for her to understand that the piano was gone. The only sign that it had ever been there was a rectangular patch on the floor where the rug had been.

"Mom? Mom?" Her voice was an octave higher than usual. She ran back to the foyer. "Mom, where's the piano?"

Her mother hadn't moved. "Evie," she said. "Along with a plea deal would be millions in restitution. The firm is suing him separately. And the legal bills are just astronomical. The Steinway dealer had an inquiry from an auction house."

"You sold it?"

"We didn't have a choice."

All those mornings of songs. All those late afternoon sunshine-drenched sessions. All the pieces she had mentally set aside as ones she would play with her own daughter, showing her the fingering and the pressure and imagining how patient she would be with the girl. Gone. She didn't get to play it one last time. Didn't get to tell it what it had meant to her. The smooth ivory and the shiny black keys and the heavy pedals and the cool wood, and the songs she could coax out of there and the times her mother had played and Evelyn had sat in the sunshine and been happy.

"It's not just the piano," Barbara said quietly. "It's the house. Sag Neck."

"The house?"

"We're going to have to sell it, Evie. The lawyer is working out some pittance for us to live on. We're not dealing with just the legal fees. If your father does go to prison, that's months without income, and of course he can't practice law again, so what we're left with we have to make last until death." She gave a bitter laugh. "You asked about rent money? Well, I've been looking at condos. Do you know what it feels like, having Jude Carea show me around a rental condo? How happy that trollop is that I've fallen so far?"

Evelyn's hand flew to her shoulder, where she began massaging it, pressing, pushing against the knots. This couldn't all be vanishing. She could do something. It wasn't too late yet. Any shot that her family had at survival, both social and financial, was now up to her. She was almost out of time.

The light was changing in the foyer, becoming cold and gray, when Evelyn turned to her mother with a clear, hard look in her eye. Her breathing was loud; she could hear it huffing out of her nose. "It's going to be all right," she said. "I have to get home. There are some things I need to do."

CHAPTER TWENTY-ONE

Trophy Hall

Camilla's erratic driving had gotten the foursome of Camilla, Nick, Scot, and Evelyn to Lake James with just one speeding ticket outside of Saratoga on the Northway; Camilla had been going ninety-three, she negotiated with the trooper to knock it down to eighty-seven, and Camilla said that by the time her family's upstate vehicular attorney contested it in traffic court, it would be dropped to a $200 fine and no points on her license.

Evelyn had called Camilla the moment she left Sag Neck to say that she'd love to come up for the weekend and sorry for being so flaky. She wondered whether Camilla would put both her and Jaime in rooms along the main hallway, which would make things easier. What did not make things easier was Scot being invited. When she'd met Camilla the previous night for drinks to float the idea of breaking up with Scot and see what the reaction would be, Nick had shown up at the bar with Scot at his side. The assumed inclusion annoyed Evelyn, and her digs at Scot that night got no cheering on from Camilla or Nick, which annoyed her further. Here, in the car, Scot was jabbing away at his BlackBerry and not partaking in the conversation at all. Barnacle Scot. Ubiquitous Scot.

In Bibville, after the cold thud she'd felt seeing the missing piano, she had identified Scot as being at the center of her problems. If she hadn't spent all this time dating him, she would be in a solid position. She would be engaged to someone more prominent, blithe about her family issues, confident and settled, with money to spare. She closed off her memories of the parts of Scot she liked and made the case to herself that Scot's sole function, the reason she'd put up with the wet kisses and the giant hands pawing at her, was to be supportive, to be the one person she could talk to about all her family problems, and he couldn't even get that right. Her father would be sent to prison, her mother would move into a condo, and she would be out of money and tethered to this oafish midtier banker who was unable to do anything about her situation.

Unless.

Camilla pulled the car up to the marina, and the four of them headed to the waiting motorboat. At Sachem, Evelyn was relieved, for once, that she hadn't gotten one of the best guest rooms; she and Scot had a twin-bed room, which meant she could get out of sex tonight easily.

While Evelyn read *Vogue* on one of the beds, Scot had gone out to do his "regimen," as he referred to his calisthenics that he had evidently lifted from a 1910 athletic-training booklet. He returned with sweat rolling down his face forty minutes later, and Evelyn hoped he'd had the sense to exercise where no one could see him. When he bounded over to her to peck her on the cheek, Evelyn drew back and wiped his lip sweat off.

"Did anyone call?" he said, picking up the BlackBerry, which he'd left on his bed.

"Not a one," she said, flipping the page of her *Vogue*. She was still in the thicket of advertisements before the masthead, as she'd spent the time he'd been working out trying to catalogue his faults and theorizing when and how Jaime might arrive. But nice memories of

Scot kept creeping in, and she'd think of how he brought her warm milk in a grainy homemade mug one night when she was unable to sleep, then she'd push herself to counter that with the Greenwich Country Club golf game where every shot of his went sideways, and she, Nick, and Preston had to spend about four hours over nine holes looking for his lost balls. "Workout good?" she asked.

"Sixty seconds on, thirty seconds off. Power intervals." He dropped the phone and reached for her hand, but, when she didn't respond, withdrew his. "I ran into Camilla's sister. Someone else is coming up later today, I guess. Another friend of Camilla's."

"Today?" she blurted, then tried to appear absorbed by the ugly knit tote for sale.

"Yeah, you knew other people were coming? I thought it was just this group."

"I—she mentioned something about it. I just thought it was later this weekend."

"Nope," Scot said, and wiped his forehead, flinging tiny beads of sweat onto Evelyn, whose whole body tensed. He headed toward the bathroom. "Today. The caretaker was just taking the boat over to pick them up."

Evelyn could see a narrow sliver of bathroom from her seat; Scot was folding his clothes and placing them, stacked, on the sink, so they wouldn't develop wrinkles during the five minutes he would spend in the shower. She heard him turn the water on, then groan as he stepped in. She couldn't pull this off with Scot here.

His BlackBerry began ringing. Evelyn slid backward against the bed, so Scot couldn't see her from the bathroom if he got out of the shower, then reached across to look at it. DAVID GREENBAUM WORK, the screen read. It took her only a moment to locate the phone icon on the BlackBerry.

"Scot Tannauer's line," she said pleasantly.

"What? I need Scot," said the gruff voice on the other end.

"I'm so sorry, he stepped out for a moment. Maybe I can help?

This is Evelyn Beegan, his girlfriend." She practically choked on the word.

"Yeah, I need to talk to Scot."

"Something's come up at work?"

"You could say that. I know he's up prancing around the Catskills, but tell him to call me, Greenbaum, right away."

"The Adirondacks. It sounds serious, Mr. Greenbaum. You're sure you just need him to call you? You don't need him in the office?"

"How is he supposed to get into the office when he seems to have gone away for the weekend with his girlfriend?"

"We're not far from the city, honestly. If he leaves now, he can be in the office by tonight."

"Good. Fine. Good. Have him come straight here."

"He'll be there."

A few minutes later, she heard the shower turn off. She didn't want to see Scot fresh from the shower, mussed and clean and hopeful, like a little boy. She stood with her back to the bathroom door and knocked on it. "David Greenbaum called," she said. "He kept calling, so I picked up, in case there was an emergency."

"What did he want?" Scot said, anxious.

"He needs you back in the city. ASAP."

"Darn it," Scot muttered. "I should call him."

"No, it's okay. He said just to head back. Not to call."

"Darn. I'm going to have to go. I'm really sorry."

"No, it's work, and it's okay. He sounded kind of mad."

"I should never have come."

"It's fine. I'll go figure out when the next train is. I think there's one around four and you'll be back in the city tonight."

"You're a lifesaver." He peeked out from the door and kissed her shoulder, and a look of pain flashed across her face.

After she got off of the Amtrak toll-free line, she relayed to Scot that there was a 4:05 train to Albany, and he could switch there for the city, then she arranged for a taxi to wait for him at the marina and told him to wait by the dock for the caretaker to take him back to town. She went down to find the cook to let him know that they would be one fewer for dinner and was walking back from the dining building when she heard the roar of the motorboat at the main boat-house, meaning the caretaker was back with Jaime. She ducked into a clutch of trees, the undergrowth plants tickling her ankles, and heard Scot talking in English-accented Spanish.

"So it's 'Es un placer—'"

"Placer," someone else said, correcting Scot's pronunciation, in a voice that sounded like it had been steeped in pine trees and to-bacco.

"Placer hacer negocios—"

"Negocios."

"Con ustedes."

"Sí. Perfecto."

"Placer hacer negocios," Scot repeated. "Thank you. I have to go to Mexico City in a couple of weeks for a meeting—encuentro, right?—with a . . . clientado?"

"Cliente," said the rich voice. "You'll do just fine."

"What the fuck, Scot? What is this, Spanish Immersion Day?" Evelyn heard Nick say. "Jaime, buddy."

"Oh," said Scot. "Oh, I just thought I would try out some of my Spanish."

"Nick, how are you?" said the voice, now in an alluringly deep British accent with a tinge of American. "It's not a problem at all, Scot. I'm glad you could practice. I have no doubt you'll do very well down there. Pleasure meeting you. Good luck getting back today."

"Thank you. Gracias. I just need to—have you seen Evelyn? I thought she was supposed to be here, but, I've got to—well."

Evelyn checked her watch. If the train was at 4:05, Scot would have to leave immediately. She stayed within the trees.

"Can you tell her I had to go?" Scot said.

"No problem," Nick said.

Evelyn waited, trying to slow down her breathing, until she heard the motorboat rev and a *thonk* that must be Scot's big foot getting into the boat. She smoothed her hair and stepped out from behind the trees.

She had been expecting someone quite tall, but Jaime de Cardenas was small, tan, and fit, with biceps neatly packed into each fatless arm. He looked as if he ran twelve miles several times a week, and was in the gym every other day doing weights and attracting looks from Equinox's boys and girls alike.

"I was just looking at the ducks down by the tennis court. There's the most fascinating group of—oh, hello! I don't think we've met. I'm Evelyn Beegan," she said.

A game of croquet was soon assembled, after Camilla skipped out and decreed it so. Evelyn was doing rather well—not, of course, beating Camilla, but holding her own.

Camilla tapped her mallet against Jaime's. "How's your room?" she said.

"It's great," Jaime said. "This place is amazing, CHR. I don't know why I haven't been up here in so long."

"Did you used to come up here a lot?" Evelyn said.

"Oh, God, for high-school summers, Sachem was the be-all, end-all," Jaime said. "All of us from St. George's would come up to see the girls of St. Paul's in their swimsuits. Remember, CHR? That one summer when you were going through that religious phase? She made us all parade to church every Sunday. She was in the choir at St. Paul's and was an awfully saucy choirgirl."

Camilla crinkled her eyes at Jaime in a way Evelyn hadn't seen before; she seemed softer, as though the top coat of nail polish had not been put on. "You make it sound like I was a backup singer, darling. I was a soloist."

"That's right. I remember your 'Ave Maria.' It was worth the forced sanctity."

This wasn't going in Evelyn's direction; Jaime had barely looked at her. She needed to establish herself, fast. "Isn't every boarding school essentially a forced churchgoing experience?" she said, shading her eyes. "At Sheffield, where I went, there was morning chapel every day. They would sort of nod at the Jews and the Muslims and pretend like it was nondenominational, but it was so clearly church."

Jaime turned to her and let his eyes rise and fall over her body, too slowly to be casual. "Sheffield," he repeated thoughtfully. Evelyn could feel an almost physical trail where his eyes had moved.

"Yes, Evelyn went to Sheffield from a funny town in Maryland. It must have been so foreign to you, Evelyn," Camilla said with a flip of her hair.

"I had grown up in London, so it was awfully foreign to me, too," Jaime said. His eyes flickered, but Evelyn couldn't read them.

"It would've been stranger for Evelyn." Camilla smacked her mallet and sent her ball hurtling over a bump, then it gently turned and dropped through a wicket. "Perfect," she said. "So I'm surprised, Evelyn, that you're playing getting-to-know-you with Jaime. Didn't you say you'd met him?"

Evelyn tried to look puzzled. "Did I? I don't think so."

"I do," Camilla said. "You said you ran into him at the Harvard Club. Maybe when you were there with your boyfriend?"

"It's possible," Evelyn said quickly. "Nick, it's your turn, isn't it?"

"The Harvard Club? Am I that ancient looking?" Jaime said with a laugh.

"I thought it sounded odd," Camilla said, gazing coolly at Evelyn. "Her boyfriend—"

"Do you know what I heard about the Harvard Club?" Evelyn interrupted. Her mind spun for something plausible. "When they tried to update the menu and take the old-school dishes, like beef Wellington and clams casino, off the menu, members lost their minds and threatened to quit the club en masse."

"I believe it," Jaime said. "I can't imagine members have the most adventurous palates."

"That's because they're so old their food is pureed. Shazam!" Nick said.

Evelyn smiled, ballooning with the weirdly good feeling of a lie well told, and tapped her ball with her mallet. Jaime put his mallet on the ground and turned to Nick. "I hate to break up the game, but, my friend, I have to go into town. If you want to come in with me, I could use the company."

"Stay here." Camilla pouted. "We can send the caretaker into town for whatever you need."

"No, I promised to drop this off to Jack myself. I'm in the same town; I can make the delivery."

"Well, don't take Nick, then. He promised me a game of tennis this afternoon."

"I have to go into town," Evelyn said. She could feel Camilla glaring at her. As Camilla started to say something, Jaime's deep voice got there first. "Great," he said.

"Evelyn," Camilla started to say, before Evelyn overrode it with an "Excuse me for a second," and tossed down her croquet mallet. She ran upstairs to her bathroom and, after a quick layer of lip stain and a combing of her eyelashes, started back down. But the door to Camilla's room was open, and lying on a dresser, just a few feet away, was Camilla's bracelet of Racquet Club victories.

Evelyn looked right and looked left, and didn't see or hear anyone. She took a light step forward, and paused again. She would just borrow it for the afternoon and put it right back. Friends borrowed each other's jewelry all the time. It was just sitting there. Glinting. If Jaime noticed it on her, he might believe that she, too, had Racquet Club lineage. She looked over her shoulder again, then dashed into the room and slipped it into her pocket.

Evelyn put on the bracelet during her made-up errand in town, telling Jaime she was supposed to pick up a wooden serving bowl with silver antlers for Preston's mother. At the counter, as she paid, she removed the bracelet from her pocket and fastened it onto her left wrist, so Jaime would see it from the driver's seat. It felt heavy and delicious and right.

She twirled her wrist back and forth as Jaime drove around the edge of James Pond, soothing herself with the pleasing clink of the rackets. She leaned in to adjust the radio's volume, making the bracelet hit the volume dial. "This bracelet is so clunky," she said. "My grandfather and great-grandfather were both serious Racquet Club members, and I think these were their most treasured possessions. They barely took care of their other heirlooms—our silver was so tarnished you could barely see that it was silver—but these were always polished and in perfect condition. Men love their victories, I guess."

He glanced over; she couldn't tell what he was thinking.

"Camilla has one, too," she said, as an insurance policy in case he'd noticed the bracelet before, "which is why we were instant friends. I'd had all the rackets for ages but had never thought of putting them into a bracelet." She reached for the sun visor.

"It's nice," he said loosely, then turned into a long lane. Evelyn looked at the sign and saw Jaime had driven them to the Lake James Club, a private men's club that, famously, only changed the rules banning tuberculars and Jews ten years ago.

"Do you mind? One of my father's colleagues is here and needed some documents," Jaime said.

"No, of course not," Evelyn said. "I'll just wait out here."

"You're going to sit in the car?"

She turned red—she had thought women weren't allowed in the club at all. She hated getting these things wrong. "No, no. I'd love to come in, if that's all right."

He smiled. "It's all right by me. It's hardly a confidential business deal."

She followed him as he hurried through the club. He greeted the guard and quickly scooped some peanuts from the bar into a tiny plastic cup, popping them into his mouth and sucking them in a way that made Evelyn's stomach light up. They passed indoor-tennis courts and a large library covered in Oriental carpets. He peered into that, then wheeled around, put a hot hand on her shoulder, and said, "Wait here." With the imprint of his hand feeling like a brand, Evelyn watched as he gave a folder to an older man, chatted, laughed, then shook the man's hand and rejoined her. "Finished," he said with a smile. "That wasn't so bad, was it?"

She was following him back toward the exit when he stopped, turned, and leaned in so closely that she could see the shine on his teeth and smell his scent of sweat and metal, and her lower abdomen went into spin cycle. "Do you want to see something?" he said.

She said yes.

He loped up two sets of stairs, and pushed open a door to a dim hallway with large windows on one side. It smelled of dust, and as her eyes focused, she saw it was filled with mounted dead animals' heads, deer and elk and foxes and bears and, at her feet, a snapping raccoon. Against the right wall were ducks, beautifully feathered and decorative and now dead. "Where are we?" she asked.

"The trophy hall," he said. His breath tickled her neck and she held perfectly still. "Whenever a member shoots something particularly worthy, it goes into here. I shot that one." He indicated a duck so gorgeous it looked hand-painted, with a handsome black mohawk and a lush patch of white next to its eye, its mounting plate balanced on a rickety chair.

"That one was beautiful," he said. "Flying with its mates over Saranac. I got three of them, but this was the cleanest shot."

She swallowed hard. "They're defenseless," she said.

"They're ducks, Evelyn."

"Isn't this a wildlife protection area?"

"All you need is a permit."

She tried to smile.

"Touch it," he said.

She didn't move.

"Go on, touch it." He put his hand on her lower back, and she started to tremble. "It's good luck," he said. "Touch it."

He was now inches from her, with his hand warm and firm on her back, and she was able to feel his body rise and fall through the conduit of his hand when he breathed. "You can make a wish if you touch it," he said. "You look like you want a good wish."

He pushed her forward. The duck was mounted on a board shaped like a shield, and she couldn't help thinking of its last moments, flying boldly over the still lake, thinking he was safe and free. "Just take your hand, like this," Jaime said. He'd now slid his right hand to her waist, and his left hand was on her left arm. With a sudden movement, he thrust her hand on the duck's head, pushing the rackets into her wrist, holding her hand there even when she reflexively tried to withdraw it from the duck's spiky feathers. He pressed harder, moving her hand to the duck's body and spreading it out. "Good girl, Evelyn," he said. His belt buckle pressed into her back, and she felt him straddle her legs. She was breathing heavily, too heavily, not ladylike, half terrified and half aroused. She pushed the thought of the duck aside and willed Jaime to press harder against her, here in this dirty upstairs hallway. She felt like there was a blinking red light emitting from their points of contact, his smooth, tan hand, his cold metal wristwatch, the buckle against her spine, his loafer pressing against her sandal. "Make your wish," he said in a low voice, and she did, then turned her face so her eyes would lock with his and he would just be able to see the fringes of her long eyelashes. "Like that, Jaime?" she said in her own low voice, looking up at him, trying to echo his tone.

He snapped his hand away and moved back, checking his watch. "We should get back," he said, and walked toward the door, leaving her heaving with her hand still pressed against the dead duck.

CHAPTER TWENTY-TWO

Typee

Dinner was served in the octagonal dining room at Sachem, along a long wooden table that, tonight, held seventeen. Souse had come up in the afternoon, and the crowd was more eclectic than at the Hackings': the couple who owned Camp Adekagagwaa, and a pensive man whom they described, apparently sincerely, as their "poet-in-residence" for the summer; a provost at Yale named Gardiner; a minister at Harvard who was also named Gardiner; a woman who had come in third at the golf U.S. Open in 1993; a wine importer named Chipp with two *p*'s, who always got the first crates of Beaujolais Nouveau in the States; the guitarist for Whitesnake and his twenty-year-old girlfriend; a stout older lady who had unsuccessfully pushed the Isabella Stewart Gardner Museum to do a pornography exhibit around the borrowed Madame X when she was on its board; a stout younger lady who said she worked at Cartier for years but "work just didn't take." Evelyn thought they were lively, and enjoyed showing off for Jaime as she asked about Block Island and Bar Harbor. She loved, too, that at Sachem, her hands wouldn't have to touch a dirty dish, as there was staff for that, and Evelyn's status was high enough that she no longer had to work as a houseguest-aide.

Preston arrived by boat just after dessert had been served. Having Preston there gave her social standing a boost, Evelyn thought, but it also made outright flirtation with Jaime that much more difficult—an old friend didn't let you get away with much.

"Weren't you supposed to be here for dinner? Where have you been?" Evelyn asked as she leaned in to kiss his cheek.

"Hither and yon," he said, opening his jacket to reveal a flask.

"What on earth, Pres? The Rutherfords have a fabulous wine cellar."

"I like a personal stash." Preston was half singing.

"Are you drunk?" Evelyn asked.

He leered toward her. "I don't touch the stuff. Where's your erstwhile boyfriend? Your man-about-town?"

"He had to leave. There was a crisis with work."

"Is there gin in this joint?"

"You seem like you've had plenty, frankly. Charlotte has me keeping an eye on you, you should know."

"Charlotte has you what? Are there G and Ts here?" Preston said.

"I meant to ask, did your mother get a chance to talk to anyone about Sloan Kettering?"

He drew his lips into a line. "If Fritz Rutherford were still here, there would be G and Ts everywhere."

"Preston, pay attention, would you? I thought your mother could mention that I'm helping with the Bal Français."

His eyes locked on to hers and Evelyn felt a surprising jolt of fear. "I am paying attention," was all he said, and then he turned to talk to the adults.

Souse excused herself soon after greeting Preston, saying she was pooped, and Camilla suggested the young people go to the Typee. Evelyn trailed them, letting a skipping Phoebe lead the way, listening to the others' shouts in the dark. Halfway up the hill, she paused, turning back to look at the camp, her feet on the springy ground, the cold night air and dark lake and bright stars enveloping her, her friends' voices receding.

She had lived for so long resisting her mother's version of what her life ought to be, thinking her mother didn't know much about life at all. When Evelyn was seventeen and taking her Intro to Psychology course at Sheffield, she had recognized her mother in descriptions of depression and repression. At one point, she suggested that her mother see a psychiatrist to figure out how to express how she was feeling. Barbara, scrubbing a metal pan with steel wool, had thrown the pan against the sink with a crash. "You want to know how I'm feeling, Evelyn?" she said. "Every day, I get up and say, 'Do the dishes, or overdose on pills?' That's how I'm feeling. Is that helpful?"

Barbara was wrong about life, Evelyn had thought at Davidson, where she'd purposely not joined the preppy eating house, making snide comments from afar as those girls smiled and chittered their way through college. Wrong, Evelyn had thought as she'd moved to New York, determined to make it on her own. Wrong, Evelyn had thought as she filled her summers with work and sweated on subway platforms while Preston and his friends went to fabulous, cool-aired vacation towns.

But Barbara was right.

Evelyn had fought her mother long and hard for a life that, prior to meeting Camilla, turned out to consist of TV and takeout. She was living in New York, but she wasn't *living* in New York. Then, just as the stable foundation of her parents and home in Bibville started to give way, Evelyn finally gave these people a chance and found that they accepted her. She had found her place. She was here.

"Ev! Did a bear get you?" Camilla shouted.

"'If you go out in the woods today, you're sure of a big surprise!'" Preston sang, Nick joining in.

Evelyn drifted up the path to the Typee and across its porch. The main room here was cozy and cabinlike, with everything done in Yale's colors: blue couch, white rug, blue blankets. Fritz Rutherford was long gone from Sachem, but his alma mater lived on.

Preston was largely avoiding her and everyone, as he took off his jacket and drunkenly nestled himself in an armchair with an old Archie comic book whose pages were wavy, wet and dried through many a rainstorm. When Jaime saw the book and asked Evelyn whether she was a Betty or a Veronica, she laid two fingers on his arm and said maybe she was a bit of both. She filled a tumbler with Scotch. It smelled like a Band-Aid, but she drank it down quickly, then drank down another.

She looked at Jaime, who was starting to get blurry, as he lit a cigar, and thought about the signals he had given her that afternoon. It was all working, and so easily. He would cover the donation for Camilla's Luminaries thing, absolutely; $25,000 was probably what he spent on a weekend out of town. What sort of form did wedding invitations with South Americans with three hundred middle names take? she wondered. Would it be covered in *Vogue*? Jaime was laughing, Nick was wiping his nose, she was drinking another glass of Scotch, and everyone was singing "Umbrella" and she and Jaime were dancing.

Then she was outside with Preston, the night air slicing through her. He was saying something but she didn't want to listen, so she leaned over the railing, looking below her for the broken bottles, but she couldn't see any of them. She leaned farther, fascinated by the lights reflected on the lake, then Preston yanked her collar. "What the hell are you doing?" he said.

"The lights are pretty," she said drunkenly, shifting her weight to one foot, then the other.

"I don't mean that, and you know it. You're in there doing the lambada with Jaime? What about Scot?"

"What about Scot? He's not here, last time I checked. Last time I checked, I didn't need permission to dance."

"I'm not talking about permission. Who are you trying to impress? You're twisting yourself into knots trying to fit in with this crowd. It isn't worth it, Evelyn. It is not worth it."

"Oh, that's rich, coming from you!" Evelyn teetered backward, and steadied herself with a hand on the rough wooden railing. "That's rich, Preston Hacking. Twisting in knots? Please. Practice what you preach. You're twenty-eight years old and you're all knotted up and phony yourself. What, are you jealous of me? Are you the one who wants to be in there rubbing up against Jaime?"

His face went slack, and he turned away from her, toward the lake.

"Oh, that's right. Keep on hiding, Pres. Nobody'll ever guess your little secret. Ssshhhh, don't say a word. But please, keep lecturing me about how I shouldn't knot myself up trying to fit in. Meanwhile, you can't seem to admit that you're gay when the entire world knows it. Like, come on out, Preston Hacking! Come on out!"

Her last word hung in the silent air, especially because Preston still wasn't moving. His thin silhouette was black against the blue sky, black as the trees and mountains and the lake. She felt like there was a cyclone in her head, whizzing around in a circle and about to pick her off the ground and take her with it.

"I never expected this from you," he said, in a voice low and clogged with anger. Then he ran. He clattered down the Typee steps and she heard his hard-soled shoes hit the packed ground of the path.

"Preston!" She ran down the stairs after him, and then her feet hit the hard dirt and caught on a root and she took a big, smacking fall, landing hard on her hands and getting the breath knocked out of her for a moment. She looked up; she couldn't see or hear Preston. She took two shaky, clattering breaths and hit the ground with her palms once, twice, again.

Then she stood up, dusted off her knees and hands, and went back upstairs to the party.

"To youth," Jaime was saying slurringly, sloshing a square bottle of something anise smelling into everyone's glasses. Evelyn downed one, then downed the one that Jaime had poured for Preston. Phoebe was stretched out in front of the fire, and Camilla and Nick were playing speed-Scrabble, and there was Preston's jacket that he'd left behind, and Evelyn drank another tumbler of Scotch so she didn't have to feel anything when she looked at it. Now Evelyn was sitting next to Jaime at last, her head bent with his over an old book about Adirondack guideboats.

Evelyn staggered to the bathroom, and saw her reflection looked ruddy, so she slapped her face to try to get the color evenly distributed on it. Returning, she looked blearily around the group in the living room. The beauty and perfect finish of the girls had given way to oily noses and puffing hair and red welts on their feet from their shoes. The boys, earlier fresh and shaved and smelling of soap, were now smelling of hormones and alcohol, their beards starting to push through their coarse skin, their mouths dry and hot with old Scotch. Where were her shoes? The gloss on her toes was like shiny blood. Preston had left, and Evelyn knew he was mad at her and knew it was important to remember why but she couldn't. Nick was saying something to her in the hallway, and then Nick and Camilla and Phoebe went running down the hill and Phoebe fell, laughing in the dark, and it reminded Evelyn of something but she couldn't concentrate on what. Just one lamp was on now, and Evelyn was sucking on Jaime's ear, and time mixed itself up. She couldn't taste the alcohol anymore, and added some Scotch to her Scotch because someone had given her nonalcoholic Scotch. Here was Jaime, grinning and singing, and now the lights were off, and everything was fine, spinning, fine.

Gray, swirls. Cold. She was cold. Her head, then her body, cold body. Quaking, naked, Evelyn came to on the Yale-blue couch, trying to warm herself under someone's scarf. She had the cloud of something bad having transpired around her, but woke and, even as she felt the chilled air and located herself in the strange room, did not know for maybe three seconds, four, what it was that had happened. She felt fine, was barely hungover. Then the coldness of her toes and fingers was replaced by another feeling, an awareness of stickiness between her legs. She sat up, her body heavy. Her stomach cramped.

She was shivering and naked on the couch, with wrinkled napkins and several smudged glasses and an empty bottle of Scotch on the chest in front of her. She had put on the Racquet Club bracelet at some point, and it had left deep red marks along her wrist. She winced as she separated her sticky self from the couch fabric, the fuzziness in her brain fighting with some physical urge that pushed her to put on her wadded-up dress, which she had to look around for, finally finding it in a sad heap on top of an old copy of *Treasure Island*. In her fuzz she could not find her underwear. Where was the underwear? She had a memory of Jaime pulling her hair, but pushed it away, and she sank to her knees to search with just her hands as though vision had deserted her altogether. Her hand came across her underwear, crusted into disgusting peaks, and she tried not to throw up as she put it on and felt the crust scratching against her. Her sandals, kicked to the side, were dark with the grease of her toe prints. It was all soiled, all used.

She stood up, shaking, the cold predawn light from the room's windows sucking the color from the room and from her body. She listened for the flush of a toilet or the shuffle of his feet, something to explain where Jaime had gone, but the room was too silent; she could hear only a few chirps from birds outside and the scratching of some rat or squirrel, but there were no footsteps, no sounds of motorboats, no signs of human presence.

She quivered, trying to keep her nausea from rising up, but couldn't, and ran to the bathroom. Here, too, a flash from last night: she had been in here giving him a blow job. Had she followed him into the bathroom? Her armpits smelled of earth and sex. The first heave came up and she remembered Jaime saying, "Are you sure I'm not taking you away from your friends?" She had kept forgetting his name and had avoided addressing him directly at all. Flash: Her sloshing "Can I cut in?" as she heaved herself from her chair when Jaime and Phoebe were dancing to "Hollaback Girl." Flash: Evelyn clutching his knee as she had discussed the importance of charity and $25,000 donations being such a building block. Flash: She had pushed him onto the couch. She had wrapped her legs around him. Flash: She tried to unbutton his jeans with her teeth before he pushed her head up with his hand and unbuttoned his jeans himself, one-handed. Flash: Some stupid idea she had read in *Cosmo* at the nail salon about using hair to titillate men during blow jobs. Jaime sitting there, arms folded behind his head, as Evelyn had swirled her blond hair back and forth over his prick, and erupted in what she hoped was a sexy moan. Flash: "No teeth—don't use your teeth." Flash: Evelyn crawling up to him after the blow job, hair a clumpy mess, him refusing to kiss her, her trying to be light and lively, saying, "Your turn," him saying, "Mmm, I don't think so." Flash: Evelyn pulling the racket bracelet along his body. They had had sex—she remembered him grunting on top of her, though not how they'd gotten there—and he hadn't even taken off his jeans fully; she remembered them chafing against her legs. Then he had gotten up, and she'd wondered if he'd wrap her in his arms like Scot did, and instead she listened as the water ran, and there was the *foom* of him pulling on his shirt and then she saw the scarf coming at her. A pashmina, light pink. "I'd like to see you in just this," said Jaime. It had settled on her face, and she did not know what to do, and then the room whirled around until she fell asleep.

Now, in the dark, kneeling in front of the toilet bowl, her eyes watered and dropped the tears straight into the bowl, and she heaved out yellow pools of the Scotch mixed with stomach acid. She was gripping the toilet seat, shaking with the cold, her stomach jetting out stream after stream of bile. Finally, stomach empty, Evelyn pushed herself up and limply threw her wrist against the light switch. In the clean mirror, she saw her clotted, oily hair, her smudged mascara and the dark purple shadows encircling her eyes, her colorless skin, the yellow puke outlining her mouth.

Moving as if through a thick custard, she turned on the cold water, cupping it against her face, but then her shoulders slumped forward and her head dropped into the sink, and the water subsumed her hair, capturing the blond strands in a rush of wet darkness, pouring down her back and arms and onto the floor, soaking her dress. Her feet stood in a puddle when she flung her head upright, red and gasping for breath. She used toilet paper to wipe the mascara from her face and clean off the counter, and flushed it all, flush after flush after flush. She'd have to get back to the main house, and get her hair washed, without anyone seeing her. Didn't she mention to Jaime that she went to Sheffield? That she had debbed and was from an old Baltimore family and was helping out at the Bal Français? He would've spent the night if he had just known her better, known that she was really somebody. Hadn't she signaled that?

Jaime hadn't bothered to shut the front door; anyone could have seen her as she lay there naked with her slutty scarf cover-up, she thought. She heard the ruffle of bird wings beat past the window, and a faraway squawk. She mushed her hands over her eyes and looked through the gaps in her fingers as if she expected a different scene to manifest itself, but it was only the dregs of last night. A fat black fly alighted on the oozing Camembert and began to suck at its pooling fat.

It wasn't until she looked at her knee, scratched and smeared with dirt, that she remembered falling, and remembered what had happened with Preston. She looked at the living room and saw his jacket was still there. He had fled. She had betrayed him, had made his deepest secret seem like a piece of gossip, and he had fled. She touched the jacket material, but didn't know what to do with it, so she left it on the armchair.

Evelyn staggered back to the main house in the gray light, getting up to her room without anyone seeing her. She was in bed. Asleep, awake, asleep. Then footsteps. A knock. A dream about her teeth falling out. Queasiness. Go to sleep. A dream about signing up for English at Sheffield and not going to a single class and it turned out she had never graduated. Sounds from downstairs. She was missing out already. Minutes, maybe hours, later, the word "omelet," which she shook off, receded into grayness, felt sick, rolled over.

Later, a sound. Evelyn pulled her encrusted eyes open. Daytime. Late daytime. It was a knock. "Evelyn?" Camilla. "Time to rise. It's ten. I think I want to get on the road early. So you can either take the train later or go with me now."

Jaime. Last night. Jaime. Scot. Camilla would kill her. Everyone would kill her. This was really bad. This was really bad. Evelyn shoved her wrist, still with the bracelet on, under the comforter. The rest of her stayed still, her heart racing from the sugar of the alcohol and the problem she had created. "Okay," she said back; her voice was cracked and dry. "How soon are you leaving?"

"An hour."

"Just let me shower."

On the way to the bathroom, she heard Jaime in the kitchen downstairs, saying something about making some toasted bread to go along with the eggs.

Of course he was making toast for her. Of course everything was fine. Jaime liked her, remember the seconds he'd let his hand sit on top of hers, the unbelievable attraction at the Lake James Club, and the way he had told her what a mischievously pretty—was that it, or just mischievous, she couldn't remember—girl she was, the way he'd hung around her after everyone left? She couldn't be some random girl he had slept with. She couldn't be that, some throwaway middle-class aspiring girl, another suitcase in another hall. This had to be the start of something serious. He had mentioned his mother—who talks about their mother unless they're serious? Meeting at Lake James was such a cute story, it practically vaulted them to the first slot in the *Times* wedding announcements. He would want to settle down soon, and Evelyn would be the perfect wife to accompany him to all his functions. She had gambled on this and she had to have won. It would be fine. It had to be fine.

But Scot. Put it away, she told herself. Don't think about it. Don't think of his big grin when he leaned on his elbow and looked at her on the Sunday two weeks ago when he woke up before her. There hadn't been another way, she told herself; she couldn't have broken up with Scot without knowing there was something definite with Jaime. People cheated. Kennedys and Paleys and Roosevelts cheated. She wasn't married, hadn't vowed to stay faithful. She was doing it for her family. She had done the right thing.

And Preston. Put that away, too. Friends said stupid things. Friends forgave. It was okay. It would be fine.

Evelyn got up out of bed, pressing a gold racket against the soft flesh of her palm. As she passed Camilla's room, she unhooked the bracelet's clasp and was about to deposit it on Camilla's dresser when a creak on the stairs made her jump. She refastened it and hurried into the bathroom. Turning the shower water as hot as it would go, she scrubbed and cleaned until her skin felt raw. The bracelet was wet when she stepped out, which meant she couldn't leave it on Camilla's bureau without raising questions, and, she reasoned, wouldn't Jaime wonder where it had gone when she saw him next? She picked up her duffel and tucked the bracelet into a side pocket.

Downstairs, she found Nick and Camilla downing coffee in the small family kitchen used for breakfast and snacks. "So you want to leave with us?" Camilla said.

"It's that or the train?"

"Yes."

"Is Jaime going later?"

Jaime then walked through the kitchen. "Hey," he said, tilting his head at Evelyn.

"Are you leaving later, Jaime? Could I get a ride?"

"I might leave soon. I'm not sure. I have to do some business on the way back, so you should really go with Camilla."

"So go get your stuff, Ev. We've got to move," Camilla said.

"I'm actually going to do a call now, so I'll see you back in New York, man," Jaime said, addressing this to Nick. To Camilla, he said, "Thank you so much for the lovely weekend. It was amazing." Camilla leaned in to kiss him twice on the cheek, and Evelyn stepped forward to do the same, but he had stepped back and was flipping through a catalogue on the table. "I'll see you all back in New York, sooner rather than later, I hope," he said.

This phrase reverberated through Evelyn's head as she brought her duffel downstairs, and by the time the Sachem boat pulled in, she wondered if it was meant especially for her. On the car ride, she analyzed it further. He knew her number. Didn't he know her number? She had a sudden still image of her sitting on the floor with her phone and asking for Jaime's number, and yes, there, at 3:02 A.M., was an outgoing text from her to a 917 number: "hi its ev come back soon." So she had texted him in the middle of the night. Way to play hard-to-get, but he would call soon. He had to. She left the phone in her lap, in case it buzzed, and watched the long stretches of green between Northway exits roll past out the car window.

Jamie would probably call tonight, so as not to look too eager. Or even tomorrow, once he was home and settled in. Definitely by tomorrow. She fiddled with the seat-belt buckle and tried to make time pass, but her head was throbbing and the dark self-loathing she had been trying to keep at bay since she woke up was hovering just around the edges of her consciousness. She checked the dashboard clock. It was twelve-fifteen. Her brain was a hungover muddle, first castigating her about Scot, switching to anxiety that that racket bracelet was still in her bag and she was now a thief in addition to a cheater and a liar, then zooming to worry that she was done and her family was done and it was all over. She was playing her last few cards. This had to have worked.

CHAPTER TWENTY-THREE

Le Bal Français

It had been six days since her return from Sachem. Six days without
hearing from Jaime. Six days of the rent people and the Barneys
people and her parents and—no, no, no, no, no, she wasn't going to
think about that today. Not today. Today was the day of the Bal. Nothing would ruin this day.

A voice mail from her father sat in her in-box, but Evelyn let it sit.
Nothing could ruin this day. Preston hadn't called. He had been supposed to attend the Bal after-party but Evelyn knew that was out
now. Evelyn had begun composing e-mail after e-mail to him, but
beyond the "I," she didn't know what to say, didn't know how to address the version of herself she'd been on that deck. She wouldn't
think about that today. Camilla, too, had been slow to get back to her,
and that could be—no, no, no, not today. Not today.

At five o'clock on the dot, Evelyn walked into the Plaza with her
Naeem Khan garment bag in hand. (She'd called Naeem Khan PR
and promised coverage of the ball, of herself, and of whom she was
wearing in both the *Times* and *Vanity Fair*, which, she reasoned,
wasn't entirely not going to happen.) The crying she'd allowed herself

after she got home from Sachem, the sodden tissues and the tear-stained shirt and red eyelids, were Visined and washed and eye-creamed out. Evelyn was in control now.

She checked the suite upstairs, where the debs were chattering about a guy from Princeton who had friend-requested three of them on Facebook. She almost banged heads with Jennifer as she rounded a corner, and the look in the girl's eye—pure loathing—was one that made Evelyn dig her fingernails into her palms. But this night was not about Jennifer, she reminded herself. She had not worked so hard to get here so some eighteen-year-old could make her feel bad. She headed to the ballroom to help with preparations.

Margaret/Push and Souse were already there, making tiny adjustments to items on the silent-auction table and giving sharp instructions to the servers about when to clear the salad course. Evelyn was starting to approach them when her phone rang. Seeing it was her father's cell phone, she silenced it and sent the call to voice mail.

"Mrs. Faber," Evelyn said, smiling.

"Evelyn, isn't it?"

"It is."

"You look lovely. What a pretty dress."

"Thank you. As do you. Wythe looks terrific, of course. I just saw her upstairs."

"She does? Good, good; getting her to wear a dress, you can imagine the challenge there. Let's hope she leaves her sneakers behind for the presentation."

"I'll make sure of it."

Souse came hurrying over from the other side of the room. "Evelyn! Hello, dear. Where's Camilla? Isn't she supposed to be with you?"

"I haven't heard from her, to be honest. I thought she was planning on coming at five, but I'm not sure where she is."

Souse threw up her hands. "Children," she said to Margaret. "This is her sister's ball and she's on the committee. You would think she could bother to show up when she said she would."

"At any rate, Phoebe looks lovely, and I was just telling Mrs. Faber that everything is running smoothly," Evelyn said.

"Well, at least you're on top of things, Evelyn, dear," Souse said. "What a terrific dress. Calvin?"

"Naeem Khan," Evelyn said.

"Of course. Girls these days are so hip, aren't they, Push? Well, you look lovely. I hope my prodigal daughter shows up. At this rate, she'll be late for the presentation. I thought this kind of behavior would cease in her twenties, but apparently not."

"It is too bad," Evelyn said. "I wish more people my age appreciated tradition. I'll hunt her down myself if I have to. Mrs. Faber, it was so nice to see you again, and I'm sure I'll see you later tonight. If you don't need my help here, I'd better get back upstairs and keep an eye on things. Phoebe and Wythe look wonderful, really. You'll be so proud of them when you see them."

At eight Evelyn went downstairs, where the guests were distributing double kisses, the preference of the Europeans. "I need to find the Swiss ambassador," one muttered to another. "Isn't he the man in the corner, with the red pocket square?"

"No, no, that's the Swiss consul," the other replied.

At the entrance to the ballroom, photographers were taking pictures. Margaret Faber did meant-to-look-candid poses with her husband, and Souse with Ari, and the photographers seemed to already know whom they wanted to shoot, and whom they didn't want. Evelyn didn't approach, in case she didn't make the cut.

Her phone buzzed. "Walking in," Camilla had texted, and when Evelyn looked over to the entrance, the photographers were snapping Camilla's photo.

The orchestra was swinging away to "Dites-Moi," and Evelyn watched Camilla finish getting her photo taken and come up to her. "Should we get our table assignment?" Camilla said.

As they walked to table ten, Camilla said, "Evelyn, I still haven't received the check from your father."

"Oh?" Evelyn said, opening her clutch and examining the contents.

"The invitations have gone out already," Camilla said. "It's in three weeks. If he has to give a gift of stock or something, that's fine, but his secretary has been weird whenever I've called."

"India," Evelyn said. "He's been on a long trip to India. Pharmaceutical development there."

"Wherever he is, I need the donation. I asked him months ago so I wouldn't need to deal with this last minute."

"I know. I know."

"The group reached a record level of donations this year thanks in part to him. There's a press release going out next week."

"I'm on it, Camilla." Evelyn grabbed one of the gilded chairs at table ten, which was already filled with A-list guests, including Ari and Souse. "I'm on it."

The girls slipped into their seats as the orchestra transitioned into an upbeat national anthem, and Souse held a finger up at her daughter, tsk-tsking her. Then the room darkened and a spotlight rose on a small boy, dressed like Little Lord Fauntleroy, singing "La Marseillaise." The crowd rose to their feet and sang along with him: "Aux armes, citoyens!"

Agathe, the Bal's chairwoman, took the stage, welcoming the guests with a wave as waiters served generous chunks of lobster over green beans with a sauce béarnaise. She introduced the evening's honoree, the head of the European studies department at Columbia. He was the third choice, Evelyn recalled from one of the planning meetings, after the first two selections had awkwardly declined, citing the professional difficulty of associating themselves with debutantes.

The lights went down as the presentation began, and the master of ceremonies, the head of fixed income at Whitcomb Partners, who was married to one of the hostesses, looked down at his first note card.

"Wythe Van Rensselaer is the director of a documentary film on street-graffiti artists in the style of the German Expressionists, a champion two-hundred-meter sprinter on varsity track, has had the pleasure of spending summers doing nonprofit work in Laos and Botswana, and likes playing poker. Her brothers John and Frederick were escorts at the ball in the past. She will be attending Yale in the fall." There were audible "oohs" from the crowd when Yale was mentioned. Wythe, decisively, came out on the arm of her escort, curtsied, and walked excruciatingly slowly toward the edge of the dance floor as Phoebe stepped forward.

"Phoebe Rutherford speaks fluent French, Latin, ancient Greek, Serbian, and Latvian. She especially enjoys archery and needlepoint."

Souse whipped her head to look at Camilla, who put her hand in front of her mouth.

"What?" Camilla whispered. "We thought it was funny. She could be into needlepoint and archery and all those languages."

"This is not a joke," Souse hissed.

"It is a joke," Camilla said.

"Do you know how hard I've worked on this? How hard all these women have worked on it?"

"Oh, Mother, honestly. It's a party."

"Evelyn got here at five o'clock today. You didn't even bother to show up until after the party started, and it isn't Evelyn's sister out there tonight. I don't demean your events."

"It was just a joke," Camilla said. "I thought it would be funny."

"Well, it isn't." Souse was tapping her fingers frantically.

Evelyn, on the other side of Souse, leaned toward her and said, in a voice low enough she hoped Camilla couldn't hear, "I'm so sorry. I would never have let her put that in the bio had I known."

"Thank you," said Souse, abruptly pushing her chair back from the table. She had disappeared by the time the MC said, "Jennifer Foster is a champion fencer, has released a CD of her own songs, and recently had her painting entitled *Empty Houses* as a finalist for the prestigious Courbet Award, the first girl from Spence to do so in two years. In the fall, she will be attending Whitman College, a small liberal-arts college considered the Williams of Washington."

Evelyn noticed Souse at the side of the stage, whispering something to Agathe, the chairwoman. Agathe gave their table a worried look, then she nodded.

The girls lined up with their escorts behind them, stiffly smiling as the photographer took pictures, then filed onto the dance floor for a jolting waltz.

The orchestra finished "Try to Remember," and Evelyn poked Camilla. "Is that a reference to how blacked out all the debs are going to get tonight?"

"If they're not already," Camilla said.

"Phoebe looked fantastic."

"She did, didn't she?"

The lights went back up onstage, shining on Agathe, who looked nervous and was saying something to the MC. "Very well," he boomed into the microphone, not realizing it was on. Agathe skittered to the side of the stage.

"Now, as is the tradition at the Bal Français, we have la danse d'honneur, in which we ask a former debutante to come forward and begin the second dance with our esteemed ambassador," the MC said. The spotlight swooped over to Evelyn's table, where Camilla sat up and gave a humble Oscar-nominee nod. "This year the hostesses of the Bal Français are pleased to ask Miss Evelyn Beegan to lead the dancing. Miss Beegan?"

Evelyn was squinting in the spotlight when she heard the applause, and looked to see Camilla smiling and looking straight ahead.

"Miss Beegan?" the MC said.

Evelyn stood up, her legs feeling awfully shaky. Her mother had enrolled her in a waltzing class at some strip-mall dance studio when she was a teenager, despite Evelyn's protests that she would never, ever need to know how to waltz. Well done, Mom, she thought. Evelyn looked once more at Camilla, who was staring at the MC, clapping, and dipped her head. It was all meant to be, wasn't it? The applause crescendoed, and it felt like it was washing around her in lovely warm waves. Then a more intense spotlight hit her, so bright that she couldn't see anything. A flashbulb went off from her left side. She could picture Jaime looking at the photograph later, realizing just who she was. She smiled, tentatively at first, then broad and confident as the applause and the light lifted her up. It was for her this time. At last, it was all for her.

The spotlight followed her as she walked to the center of the dance floor and held out her hand to the ambassador. "C'est un plaisir," she said in a mellifluous tone. She focused on his feet—if she was supposed to have debbed, she should know how to waltz perfectly—and matched his steps as the orchestra played "Que Sera, Sera." It had been one of her mother's favorite piano pieces, but it sounded so much lusher and realer here. Back-two-three, back-two-three, they whizzed around the room, covering the length and width of it as the ambassador turned her and spun her and they picked up speed, whirling and twirling and practically galloping. As the final notes played, the ambassador held her hand in an elegant arc as he gave a deep bow and she a modest curtsy. The ballroom lights came up, and a bright pop momentarily blinded Evelyn. Then the bulbs started flashing all around her, and she heard her name gather power like a wave: "Evelyn!" "Evelyn, over here!" "Evelyn, to the left!" "Evelyn, who are you wearing?" "Evelyn, straight ahead!" "Evelyn!" "Evelyn!" "Evelyn!" No more was she an and-guest, and-friend, the perennial second tierer. Everyone whom she'd ever met could see she was there, that she was worthy of attention. Joseph Rowley, who had audibly groaned when they were paired together at the Eastern Tennis Club's twelve-and-under mixed doubles round-robin. Margie Chow, her Sheffield prep-year roommate who hadn't wanted to room together after the first year. The people bothering her about rent and Barneys would find out who she was and that they shouldn't have been upsetting her. They would all shake their heads, rueful, regretful. Evelyn had that spark all along, didn't she? Wasn't she something? Weren't we stupid not to see it? Camilla, and Jaime, and Nick, and Charlotte. Preston, Preston would forgive her. And her mother, her mother! How happy Barbara would be. "Evelyn, over here!" "Evelyn!" The flashbulbs exploded, and everyone watching finally knew her name. They knew that she, Evelyn Beegan, belonged.

CHAPTER TWENTY-FOUR

After the Ball

On Sunday morning, Evelyn rose early and went to look at Appointment Book's new postings. She was pictured in a gliding waltz at the top of the page, with the caption "Dancing Dreams—Evelyn Beegan selected for the danse d'honneur at the Bal Français." She browsed through Patrick McMullan and saw herself in photo after photo. For kicks, she logged in to People Like Us and searched for her name. Someone in Istanbul had reposted a photo and written, "LOVE her Naeem."

She had sent Camilla an e-mail upon reading it, "Look at Appointment Book! Good picture of you," which was true, though Camilla was in a group photo and Evelyn was shot alone. Camilla didn't write back. A couple of hours later, she e-mailed Camilla again: "The dancing went soooo late. So tired :("

Still nothing. To try and mend things secondhand, Evelyn wrote Souse a particularly eloquent, or so she thought, thank-you note about the ball, assuming she would get some feedback about it from Camilla. Then she sent Nick some lighthearted texts about the coming weekend at Lake James and the Fruit Stripe, which Souse had decreed would be held then, to gauge whether Camilla had said something about her to him, but his responses were normal. She thought, frequently, of calling Preston, but how would she start the conversation?

Evelyn alternated between leaving her phone at full volume for when Jaime called—he'd have to have heard that she'd done the danse d'honneur by now—and turning it off so that she wouldn't be distracted by waiting for him to call back, but in either case she stared at the phone like it was a bomb. She turned it on, and off, and on, and off, and no new missed calls or voice mails came up. Not from Jaime. And not from Camilla.

To clear out her voice-mail box so there would be room if Jaime needed to leave a message, she eventually listened to the voice mail from her father from Friday. It was a single sentence: "I thought you'd want to know that my guilty plea was today, which you apparently forgot," he said in a quiet voice. An image of him, ashamed, in front of the judge, popped into her mind, then she rerouted herself. He had gotten himself into this, and it was all his doing. What did her parents expect from her? Comfort? Support? As though they were offering the same? They weren't doing anything to help the family's situation. She was. They'd have to get by on their own.

On Tuesday, a weird number began calling her; she answered the first time, hoping Jaime was calling from Venezuela. Instead, it was a different collection agency, this time for AmEx. Evelyn had said that they had the wrong number, then briefly quarantined the phone in her refrigerator.

By Wednesday morning, with no word from Camilla or Jaime, Evelyn deduced that something terrible must have happened to Jaime. His grandmother dying, maybe. Even if he hadn't liked her, he would've gotten in touch. She was a fellow houseguest at Camp Sachem and had done the danse d'honneur at the Bal Français, for God's sake. Unless Verizon had had some sort of outage when she'd sent the text with her phone number? Had Verizon had an outage? Where was Camilla? She needed people on her side.

These billiard-ball thoughts were angling around her head as

Evelyn hurried toward Central Park on the warm Wednesday afternoon. She had gotten nowhere with the Sloan Kettering associates committee, and certainly wasn't going to get Preston's help with his mother now, so she had signed up to volunteer for it with the hope that work on the ground would turn into a committee role. Evelyn had been assigned to help pass out water at a 5K run/walk to raise money for the children's hospital.

As Evelyn picked up tiny paper cups from the setup station, she practically collided with Brooke Birch, also wearing a VOLUNTEER badge, carrying an armful of energy-gel packets.

"Brooke?"

Brooke looked around quickly, but found no obvious exit route. "Evelyn," she said.

"What are you doing in town?"

"We're here through the wedding. At the end of June." Brooke was looking past Evelyn's head.

"That's fantastic. So nice of you to volunteer."

"Thanks for the encouragement," Brooke said.

"Hey," Evelyn said quickly. Her unanswered messages for Camilla and Jaime were nagging at her. If she was slipping, she needed more stability. More friends. The pictures in the social pages were good, a very good start. She wasn't quite secure yet, though. She needed allies. "Have you seen much of Camilla while you've been in town?"

"Honestly, Evelyn, I'm pretty sure you know we're not exactly on the best of terms. How was the Bal? Did you have fun as Camilla's assistant or whatever that was?"

"Look," Evelyn said softly as she stacked paper cups. "I don't really know what Camilla was doing with the Bal, but I didn't mean to—I didn't want to take your place."

"It's fine."

"It was kind of nuts, the way she cut you out of it. I wanted to say something at the time, but I wasn't sure what to do."

Brooke started to walk away. "We don't really need to talk about it, okay, Evelyn? You've known Camilla for, what, two minutes? Congratulations, you get to be her new best friend."

Evelyn walked after her, a calmness settling over her. She thought of her father, standing in his office and putting a paperweight on a stack of court documents. The secret to settlements, he had said, is to find out the essence of what's important to the other party and make sure they believe they're getting it.

"I love your ring, by the way. I didn't get a good look at it when we met," Evelyn said. "Did Will pick it out himself?"

Brooke halted her militant walk. "He did." She let one of the gel packs drop and didn't pick it up. "He actually got the idea for it from a ring my grandmother has that I've always loved."

"It's so beautiful on your hand. It catches the light so well. So you have your dress already? What does it look like?"

Brooke's frozen face relaxed a bit. "Oh, it's so pretty," she said, then paused, and Evelyn gave her an encouraging smile. "It's strapless, then fitted at the bodice, with a mermaid back and a train."

"In ivory?"

"True white." Brooke's voice almost trilled.

"Gorgeous. That will look great with your skin tone."

Brooke smiled, and Evelyn, who knew from fake smiles, thought it was a real one. Evelyn inquired about the bridesmaids' dresses, and Brooke, releasing the energy packs into a big bowl, began describing their grosgrain trim. Evelyn reached out and touched Brooke's hand. She knew what Brooke wanted to hear. Of course she did. "I just wanted to say that I'm sorry about Camilla. Well, not about Camilla, but about the Bal."

Brooke's voice was kinder now. "That's Camilla, right? I've thought about it so much, and it's just, like, she was so patently jealous that I was getting married and she wasn't. It's like, sorry I'm happy and not totally dependent on you."

"She seemed to be a little upset by the idea that you were engaged."

"I can't believe she said that to you."

Evelyn stayed quiet; that was another part of negotiations, her father had said. Letting other people talk leads them to reveal more than they think they are revealing.

"I guess I can believe it, I just—I've known Camilla since we were thirteen. We were prefects together at St. Paul's. I can't believe she's running around complaining that I have the nerve to get married. You think someone is your friend, and then *poof*. She's done it to everyone else; I don't know why I was surprised when she did it to me. At St. Paul's there was basically a Camilla castoff every year. One of them was truly odd. She had to wear sports goggles over her glasses for lacrosse games. Camilla gets her shiny new toy, plays with it, and then tosses it out. Now she's running around New York whining about how I'm getting married. Couldn't she just be happy for me? Like, for once, be on my side?" Brooke waved her hand, signaling a conversational change. "I saw on Appointment Book that you did the danse d'honneur."

"Yes," Evelyn said, wondering what had become of the goggles girl.

"Camilla must've been furious," Brooke said.

"She didn't seem angry," Evelyn said.

"She was planning on being chosen. I heard she even got a dress that would coordinate with the ambassador's military ribbons," Brooke said.

Evelyn thought back to it. Camilla's dress had had shades of red and gold, which would've matched the ambassador's lapel adornments. Her insides began to feel loose. She had taken a moment away from Camilla, which was a very dangerous thing to do. Evelyn was squeezing one of Brooke's gel packs so hard it was about to burst all over her arm.

"I'm surprised she's still talking to you after that," Brooke was saying.

"I think . . ." Evelyn began to make up some excuse to explain what had happened, but she stopped herself, perceiving that if she wanted Brooke's alliance, her best bet was to be frank that she, too, could be on the outs with Camilla. She began to laugh. "I've e-mailed her about eight times since then and I haven't heard a thing."

Brooke stared at her, alarmed, then started laughing, too. "Well, she was supposed to be a bridesmaid in my wedding."

The two started guffawing, Evelyn's eyes watering as she gasped for breath. "A coordinating dress for the danse d'honneur!" she shrieked. "She's going to have me shot!"

"She hasn't even sent her RSVP card yet!"

They were clasping each other's arms now, both bent over with laughter. "Don't you ever want to just tell her . . ." Brooke stood up, serious now.

"That she doesn't have total control over the social scene?" Evelyn said.

"Maybe it would be good for her to hear it. Everyone is always so scared of her."

"I think it would be good for her to hear it."

The two women looked at one another, nudging each other toward the edge of a cliff.

"That photo of you on Appointment Book must've given her a heart attack," Brooke said after a pause.

The laughter had felt so good that Evelyn wanted it back. "Like, how do you even know what the ambassador's ribbon colors are going to be?" she asked. They both started laughing again, and a whistle blew. Evelyn looked back; it was fifteen minutes to race time. "I've got to get to my station," she said. "Brooke, it was really good to see you. Maybe we'll run into each other again. Cancer or something else."

"Maybe so," said Brooke.

The giddy feeling evaporated as soon as Evelyn walked to her water station. By the time she met Scot for dinner that night at Le Bilboquet, a couple of blocks from Camilla's apartment, she was frantic and distracted, wondering if she'd said too much to Brooke. She tipped her chair back and forth as she waited for him, reading the menu over and over, Cajun chicken and endives aux Roquefort, Cajun chicken and endives aux Roquefort. . . .

"Hi," Scot said when he arrived. He was more nervous than usual and was practically hopping.

"Hi." She kissed him, counting out five seconds, then pulling away.

Sitting, he pulled at his napkin, tenting it into an odd shape before she reached over, shook it out, and placed it in his lap.

The waiter came to take their orders, and Evelyn saw that Scot had brought the napkin back up to the table and was twisting it into a rope. When the waiter left, she asked him about his day, but he didn't respond, just twisted the napkin into a rope in the other direction. Scot excused himself and walked toward the bathroom. When he returned, he was scratching his hairline, then tugging, hard, at tufts. He sat up straight and looked at Evelyn. Scot, despite his layers of social awkwardness, had been an excellent debate-team member in college, and Evelyn knew that when he had anything important to say, he practiced it carefully ahead of time and sounded fluid and confident, an effect he could never mimic in casual conversation.

"I need to talk to you about something, and it's been mounting," he said. "The timing isn't perfect on this, but timing is often imperfect."

She stayed very still, her hand spread out on the table. "Yes."

"I had heard something. I'm not a big believer in rumors, but I just need to hear from you that it's not true."

Evelyn's fingers gathered in a fist.

"It's about Jaime, at Lake James," he said.

Evelyn's breath was short, but she knew she could not show it, and she tried to keep her chest from rising. "Jaime?" she said, inflecting her voice to suggest she was trying to place the name.

Scot pressed on the tines of his salad fork, and it flipped up and tumbled over. "I heard some things that I don't believe, but I wanted to ask you directly about them."

"What could you have heard?" Her laugh, meant to sound light-hearted, was shrill.

"It's an ugly rumor, I'm sure. I'm sure it's not true, but what I heard was that something happened between you and Jaime. After I left Lake James."

Breathe in through the nose, breathe out through the mouth. "I don't know how to respond to that. It's patently absurd," she said. "When exactly would something have happened? And just after you left? Of course not. Of course not."

"I didn't think you would," he said, almost shyly.

"You know me better than that," she said. "Don't you?"

He exhaled a huge breath through his heavy lips. "I'm sorry. I'm sorry, Ev. I shouldn't have asked. I just—I was worried. Can you understand that?"

She pressed her wrist against the table to stop her hand from shaking and clasped her fingers around his. "Scot. I'm here with you. Please. Let's enjoy our dinner and forget about all of this, okay?" She squeezed his hand, but she couldn't tell if he was squeezing back or pulling away.

"Okay," he said. After a few moments, he started to talk about some banking thing he and Nick were thinking about working on, involving credit-default swaps and the CDO bubble, but Evelyn's head felt filled with cotton balls and she couldn't follow. She couldn't seem to bring her heart rate down during dinner or all through the night, even when she was supposed to be sleeping.

CHAPTER TWENTY-FIVE

10:15 Adirondack

There was just one train to Lake James on Fridays, the 10:15 Adirondack. Evelyn brought her duffel and, wanting to ingratiate herself with Camilla, two grocery bags packed with party supplies for the Fruit Stripe: cellophane bags, special-ordered from an online party supply store; bulk candy in yellow, green, and red, for which she'd had to make a trip to the Lower East Side; packs upon packs of Fruit Stripe gum. She also had her gear for the Fruit Stripe, which this year, Souse had decided, would be rowing, something Evelyn was actually decent at. She had called Camilla three times in the last day to see if there was anything else needed, but Camilla hadn't called back.

Evelyn hadn't slept at all after seeing Scot, and barely slept the next night, and was so tired that everything struck her as funny and terrible at once. When the conductor came through the train car, Evelyn started cry-laughing because she thought he looked like a robot, close to peeling off his face to reveal his alien visage. Visage, visage, she thought as the train scooted north and the Hudson widened, and the ground looked like it was lifting off and mixing with the sky. Her phone rang, the blocked number again, and she stuffed it into her duffel pocket, where her fingers ran against Camilla's racket bracelet. What was she doing? What had she done? The phone rang again, and this time it was the number for the AmEx collection agency. Why were they after her? Her gut began gurgling and panging as her heartbeat quickened and her throat felt tight and scratchy. Her breath was coming too fast yet never fast enough, and by the time the panic reached her brain she had lost any control over it. She sat in her train seat with widened eyes and shallow breath, reviewing everything she was trying to control. Her father, the case, Camilla, Preston, the calls from Barneys and AmEx—they were among so many bills, bills she hadn't even opened and didn't know the contents of. The rent, the $25,000 donation, Scot finding out about Jaime, how did Scot know about Jaime? Who else knew about Jaime? She tried to close her eyes at one point, but the sleep she found was too brief and dotted with unsettling dreams that left bare wisps when they were over. Wisps of failure, of reaching, of falling, and she woke up sweating, with an acid mouth, when she heard the conductor say, "Lake James, coming up."

"All passengers for Lake James," he repeated. Evelyn sat fixed in her seat, wondering what would happen if she stayed on the train north into Canada. But the conductor picked the punch card from her seat as the train slowed to a stop. "Your destination," he said, and cheerfully tugged her duffel to the aisle.

As Evelyn walked into the station house, she felt her phone buzz, and her heart shot up and then down. Of course everything was fine, and she was just being insane. She had handled things perfectly with Scot. She just needed some sleep, that was all. Just a little sleep. With a smile and a shake of her head, for the benefit of the station attendant reading *Buckmasters* magazine, she pulled the phone out of her bag, but there was no text, no new voice mail. She must have just jostled it.

She placed her duffel on a clean spot of floor and carefully sat on it. She waited for ten minutes, twenty, and then got up to pretend to examine a stack of brochures about various train destinations.

"Boston?" the man said abruptly.

"Excuse me?"

"The brochure you're looking at. Good city."

Evelyn looked down, and, indeed, she was holding a bent bro-chure, *Boston—the City on a Hill*, with a picture of a quiet-looking city at night, gentle yellow lights illuminating a brick church. It reminded her of her senior year at Sheffield, when she and Charlotte would visit Preston at Tufts, eating in Back Bay restaurants and getting served wine because Preston brought cigars to dinners and thus looked like he was about forty when he was nineteen and never got carded. She, they, were happy then. "It is a good city," she said.

The attendant ran his finger around the brim of his USS *Kearsarge* cap as he looked at Evelyn. "Sometimes it's good just to take a train somewhere else," he said.

There was a screech from the parking lot, and Evelyn looked out to see the navy Jaguar with the BIGDEAL license plate. She stuffed the brochure back into the display, and the attendant said something in response, but Evelyn was already out the door, not wanting to make Camilla wait. Evelyn opened the back door to place the bags of party supplies there when Camilla vaulted out of the driver's seat and put a hand out to stop Evelyn, like she was a little kid who needed to be prevented from wandering into the street.

"Evelyn, there's a problem," said Camilla. "Look, this is sort of awkward. I wish you had called or something before you got here. I don't think it's going to work."

Evelyn stood up. "What's not going to work? I did call."

"You, here, this weekend."

Evelyn gave a half laugh, hoping this was one of Camilla's jokes, but Camilla was standing steady, her sunglasses on.

"I'm already here," Evelyn said, dimly.

"Well, you should have double-checked before you got on the train."

"I texted you."

"Did you? I didn't get it, I guess." Camilla flipped the car-door handle a few times, letting it thunk against the glossy navy of the car. "Look, Evelyn, maybe you should watch what you do, okay? Prancing around the ball and Jaime de Cardenas, but I guess you already know his last name. It's probably in your file on him or something."

Evelyn pulled on her earlobe so hard she almost dislodged her earring. "Jaime," she said faintly. "How is he?"

At this Camilla took off the sunglasses and looked directly at Evelyn. "Yeah, I didn't really think you two had kept in touch after your whatever it was. Jaime's girlfriend is a great girl. A great girl. She was captain of the field-hockey team at Andover and played at Yale and has a Fulbright."

Evelyn stayed very still. An Andover-Yale field-hockey player? Jaime must have thought—she was just a joke all along—

"And, I have to say, Nick isn't exactly thrilled that you were throwing yourself at poor Jaime while you were dating Scot," Camilla said.

"How does Nick . . . Oh, God."

"What about you promising that your father would support my event basically just so you could embarrass me? You were never going to get him to give that check, were you? Your father's going to prison, so, um, I don't think it's going to happen. I don't know why you wanted to do that to someone who has never been anything but nice to you, and who gave you a hand and lifted you into this world. I've been working with my therapist on being direct, and he thought this would be a good experience for me to come here and tell you this myself. It's not easy for me." Camilla swished the sole of her flip-flop against a speck of gum ground into the parking lot. Evelyn looked down to the grimy gum, now almost as flat and gray as the asphalt with all the dirt and shoe mud it had absorbed. Back, forth, back, forth went Camilla's toe, unpainted and rather gnarly.

Back, forth. Jaime had a girlfriend. Camilla and Nick knew, and therefore they knew that Jaime had wanted nothing to do with her after their hookup, and the stuff with her father was coming out at last, too late for her to do anything, and her class was stamped on her as obviously as a tattoo. Maybe Scot; maybe she could still get to Scot before everyone else did.

"Nothing really happened with Jaime," she said finally.

"Look, Evelyn, I don't really need details, okay? It's just better if you go home."

"There's only one train back on Fridays and it was at noon. I have all this stuff."

Camilla looked it over. "I'll take the party stuff," she said.

"But—"

"I'm sure you've wormed your way into some other families up here. Surely one of them will take you in."

"Camilla, this is just a misunderstanding. Your mom wants me to race tomorrow."

"Evelyn, it's not a misunderstanding. And you're not racing. Back down. For once." With that, Camilla hopped in the car, shut the door with a firm click, and hit the gas. Evelyn realized then that Camilla hadn't even turned off the motor to talk to her.

Evelyn, glancing back to make sure the station attendant hadn't been watching, took her duffel and walked to the service road behind the strip mall next to the train station, so no one driving to or from town would see her on the main road. She walked by the unadorned backs of the grocery and the video-rental shop, both of their Dumpsters bursting. She walked by the touristy furniture stores and the motels and the boat-repair shops with their propped-up hulls. As town got closer, she walked by the ice-cream parlor, and the motel, and the hotel that was a step up from the motel, and the flower shop where all the summer brides ordered their bouquets. From this side, they were all the same, with giant garbage bins and cigarette butts and cars parked at odd angles in lonely lots.

Evelyn felt that if she could just keep moving, it would be all right and she could keep these things at bay. Camilla would backtrack; Jaime never mentioned a girlfriend, so something must have been amiss between him and this girl already; Scot didn't necessarily know for sure yet, and she could convince Nick and Camilla not to tell him;

she'd see Preston and he would see she was sorry; her father, her father, they couldn't all know about it, it wasn't possible. But it was possible.

After she had walked for three-quarters of an hour, a small hill demarcated the start of town from the strip-mall outlying parts. Evelyn pitched down it, hot and smelly, with a sore shoulder from where the stiff leather duffel strap had been digging in, looking for somewhere to land. After checking that no one she knew was in sight, Evelyn took a break next to the marina. So she had lied a couple of times. So she had violated Camilla's rules. She had worked hard to get here and deserved to be here and wasn't going to be defeated because Camilla decreed it so.

The marina was lively for that time of day on a Friday and, in preparation for the Fruit Stripe, was crowded with trailers holding single sculls, double sculls, fours, and eights. Some collegiate crews had shown up; a foursome carrying a boat down to the water for an evening row wore Yale jerseys. Evelyn remembered crew at Sheffield, the races on the Schuylkill and on Quinsigamond where they'd sleep in motels the night before and carbo-load. Two people were stringing up a banner: FRUIT STRIPE REGATTA 2007—HEAD OF THE FRUIT STRIPE. Evelyn was just under the Lake James Marina wooden arch when she saw Scot.

"Oh, my God," she said, tired, happy, relieved. She ran to throw her arms around him. "I'm so happy to see you. You don't even know." She shut her eyes and pressed her ear against Scot's beating heart, so glad he was there, so solid and warm, as if she'd summoned him, and it was three blissful seconds before she wondered why and how he was there.

"Jesus," someone said, and Evelyn looked behind Scot to see Nick, arms crossed.

"Nick?" she said.

"I think I can say with some confidence that Scot doesn't want to see you right now," Nick said, stepping out from behind Scot's shadow; Scot was gnawing at his thumb. "Camilla said you weren't coming."

Her stomach started to simmer and pop. "Scot's going with you? To Camilla's?"

"That's the plan." Nick began to steer Scot off toward the motorboat dock, until Evelyn grabbed Nick's shoulder.

"I'm sorry, Nick, but I'm allowed to talk to my boyfriend. You're not his bodyguard."

"No, Evelyn, I'm his friend. You need to go home."

She was a few inches shorter than Nick, but she managed to force him back and squeeze in between him and Scot, who looked like he had been teleported from apartment 5G. Nick moved toward her, but Evelyn put both hands on his shoulders and pushed him away. "I'm sorry. You understand."

"What the fuck?" Nick said as Evelyn guided Scot to a bench by a garbage can.

Scot sank onto the bench, still not making eye contact. She tiptoed to him, her hand hesitating until she rested it on his back. He flinched and moved his body away. He was not looking at her and had raised one hand to shield his eyes. She put her hand on his back again; it was warm. His hand now shot down from his face and chopped her arm away.

On the shore, she heard a cheer of "Bulldog! Bulldog! Bow, wow wow!"

"You should leave," he said. His voice was low, lifeless.

"I can't leave," began Evelyn, who was focusing on the dark line where the bench met the hedge behind it. The sentence hung there as the idiot Yalies on the shore shouted, "Eli, Yale!"

"I don't want to see you." His head was in his hands, and his voice sounded too low and too empty.

Evelyn wrapped her arms around herself when she heard him and asked a question she knew the answer to. "What's this about? Can you just tell me that?"

"It's about you sleeping with Jaime."

She pulled her arms tighter, digging her nails into her upper arms, and moved back from him. "Okay. Okay. We talked about that already. So you're just going to believe a rumor about me?"

"Don't." Now his voice was filled with fury. "Don't do that."

She felt like each word, if chosen wrong, could leave a lasting liability, and left long gaps between them. "I'm not . . . I . . ." She covered her mouth with her fingers, pinching her lips as though that would massage out a response. "It wasn't what it sounds like. I was . . . we were . . ."

"What? You were what?"

She couldn't find an end to this sentence, and the sun shone brighter and brighter.

"I was so drunk I didn't know what I was doing," she said finally.

"You're lying. I defended you, like a naive idiot. I nearly punched Nick." He pulled his knees in now; his huge body curled into a ball looked too vulnerable, and she had to look at the lake again, where someone was waving a Yale banner. "Why?"

"It was dumb. It was so dumb. Scot, things were, are, falling apart with my family, and I thought—" She put a tentative hand on his upper arm and he flung it off.

"Don't touch me."

The silence between them was now beating, threatening to grow, even as the cheering onshore intensified. "I just—I did something dumb, and I don't want to ruin things between us—"

She saw something fly; he had kicked off his shoe. "Get out of here."

"Scot. Please." Her voice was high now, pleading, like a child's. "Please. We can figure this out." She didn't know what to say next. "Scot, you're wonderful. You're so smart. And so kind. Please." She had to find something to say that would pull him out of this awful posture.

"So smart? You didn't even think I knew about your father, did you? You thought I was just that stupid? Such a rube? I knew, Evelyn. I was trying to give you time and space to tell me."

"I would've told you. I did. I tried. Camilla said that investigations, that indictments, that they weren't, that it wasn't—"

"Stop it. Stop. Leave. I was at Sachem. That morning. When
you . . ." He swallowed. The noise roared around her, the sound of a
conch shell at the ocean. She was desperate for him to crumble, for
him to hug her and let her wet his shirt with her tears.

"I made a mistake," she said. "A big mistake. I'll fix it. Please." A
feeling of tenderness and a sense of loss swelled, and she knew what
she had to say, something she had never said before, not to any boyfriend. "I love you," she whispered.

"How dare you," he said, his voice barely audible. "How dare
you." He issued a bitter chuckle that was so far from his usual gentle
snorts that it sounded like a new, awful side of him, a side she had
excavated from underneath his sweet exterior. He rose, and she tried
to walk with him. He put his hands on her arms like he was going to
kiss her, but then she felt his fingers dig into her tricep muscles and
she whimpered. He let go, and Evelyn wished he didn't have to bend
to pick up his shoe, as she knew it would make him feel more ashamed.
He walked toward the water and Nick.

"We can talk later?" she said. Her eyes were bright and she spoke
fast.

He didn't turn around.

She stood, watching him get smaller and smaller until he stepped
into a motorboat with Nick, and they went skipping along the lake,
Sachem bound. His fingers had left a painful kinetic imprint on her
arms, and the boats and the people moved around her, and it started
to get dark, and it started to get cold. She had been looking at, without seeing, the bow of a boat, and she blinked, then blinked again. It
read MILDRED's MOMS MANIA. Clutching at her phone so aggressively she almost dropped it, she shouted into it, "Yes, do you have a
listing for the Hacking residence in Lake James, on Mt. Jobe Road?
Yes, please connect me."

Bing picked up, almost causing Evelyn to drop the phone, but she instead deepened her voice. "Yes, Jean Hacking, please," she said, not that Bing would recognize her voice.

"Hello, is this Mrs. Hacking? Mrs. Hacking, it's Evelyn Beegan, from Sheffield. I'm well, thank you. No, no, I'm just over at the lodge with a group of people. I do, I really like the renovation. Preston? I was . . . I was planning on calling him, but it's been—he's been hard to reach. No, no, I have his cell phone. I actually hoped to talk to you. Listen, this is so forward of me, but I couldn't resist. I heard you were organizing a group for the Fruit Stripe tomorrow, and I just wondered, I love rowing so much, and if you need a last-minute fill-in. Yes, I rowed lightweight at Sheffield. I did! I did. Sculling? Okay, sure. I can scull. I will, I will definitely say I'm a Mildred's Mom. Really? That's fantastic. I can't tell you how much I miss rowing. Oh, that's just great, Mrs. Hacking. So seven A.M. tomorrow at the marina. I'll be there. I can't wait."

She pressed end. She would show them all. Scot would see her and change his mind. Camilla would see her and change hers. She had a vision of herself rowing into the dock, jumping out to claps on the back, and standing up on the porch of whoever was hosting this year and laughing as she toasted with her fellow racers, while Camilla looked on with at least interest and at most regret and Scot reconsidered. Evelyn was someone who had a rightful place in this regatta, in this world. They would all see.

CHAPTER TWENTY-SIX

Racecourse

The only room available at the Lodge at Lake James was the Moose Suite, and that cost $1,600 for the night. Though the receptionist at the Lodge had specifically asked for a credit, not debit, card, Evelyn thought it was highly possible that none of her credit cards, not even the Visa Pewter, were still working, and handed over a debit card instead, praying that there was enough cash in her account to cover it. When the woman successfully ran the card and handed Evelyn the room key, Evelyn told herself she just had to make it through the race Saturday and then she could figure everything out.

The Moose Suite turned out to have a spectacular view of the lake, but those picture windows also looked straight out to Sachem. When the glowing iris-blue sky of Lake James at dusk receded, replaced by blackness and stars, Evelyn could see the lights on the Rutherfords' camp.

She ordered room service and found she was watching Sachem like it was television, with her carbo-loading spaghetti laid out before her. A boat left West Lake, and she followed its pilot light as it skirted closer to Sachem, wondering if it had come from Shuh-shuh-gah. A light in the top of the main house winked on and off—was that the attic, or was that Souse's office? Then there were two more pilot lights, these from the same point on West Lake, moving toward Sachem, and she felt certain that the Hackings were headed there tonight for some pre–Fruit Stripe party, some event that Mrs. Hacking had not invited her to or even mentioned. She squinted at the lake, trying to detect movement on the island, Scot or Nick or Camilla, and opened the door to her balcony to see if she could pick up some sound over the water. She heard laughter from somewhere, and a few trumpet notes, but the acoustics of the lake made it too hard to tell where the sounds were coming from. Still, she could picture them at Sachem, lights on, fire jumping, Louis Armstrong playing, no doubt talking about her.

She felt better now that she had eaten. Her head was clearer than it had been in a while. Evelyn pulled out Camilla's bracelet from her duffel and fastened it on her wrist, pressing the pads of her fingers against the crisscrossed gold that made up the rackets' nets.

The next morning, Evelyn awoke at five-thirty with pillow creases on her face. She had not slept well. She trudged over to the marina, where the Mildred's Moms boatman helped Evelyn rig the single scull and take it down to the water. Evelyn hadn't been able to shake the sense that she was in a dream, and now, as she tightened the bolts and greased the slide and knotted her race bib, she was finding words and actions that had been gone from her physical and mental vocabulary for years resurfacing. Foot-stretcher. Oarlock. Gunwale. She looked down and saw she still had the racket bracelet on from last night. She thought of hiding it in the grass somewhere, but then left it on; it was irreplaceable, and she couldn't risk losing it.

Then she was rowing, still fogged with dreaminess. Sheffield's boats had been sweep boats, with each rower pulling a single oar on one side, and though the coach had the girls try sculling every now and then, flipping two oars and pulling them through the water wasn't a natural motion for Evelyn. She forgot, too, how tippy a scull was; a bit of extra depth on the oar, and the rigger would dip to one side, threatening to drag under and eject her.

Evelyn had thought this would be like the sailing Fruit Stripe, basically an excuse for onlookers and racers to drink before noon, so her lack of recent training wouldn't be a problem. The rowers looked meaty and intense, though, and their water bottles looked to be filled with water and not bottles of T. The implied irony she had banked on was not present in Lake James today. She heard a crackle on the shore and observed that loudspeakers on tall posts, which she had figured were for some sort of weekend concert, were actually for the narration of the race.

"Good morning, and welcome to the thirty-third annual Fruit Stripe Regatta," she heard a voice that sounded suspiciously like Bob Costas say. Hadn't she heard he had a place on East Lake?

The announcer reviewed the course as Evelyn warmed up: west of Turtle Island, another private island on the lake that was closer than Sachem, then the passage between Turtle and Sachem, around the buoy south of there, keep buoys on your starboard side, watch the rocks off Turtle's east side. The loudspeakers boomed as the first group of boats approached the line. "Robert Stimson, known for his annual Christmas party, is a three-time winner in the masters' doubles at Head of the Schuylkill. . . ." Oh, Evelyn thought. These were real rowers.

The officials were sending the boats off at two-minute intervals. The race marshal gave her a three-minute warning, and she pulled up to the line. Someone in the stake boat grabbed Evelyn's stern, and she was doing her best to stay lined up straight via small dips with the oars, but the wind was starting to blow her sideways. She heard the announcer saying she was Jenny Vinson, a Manchester resident and mother of three, with her eldest rowing for Choate; Mrs. Hacking apparently had not updated the bios. Then she heard, "Sit ready. Are you ready? Row!"

She was trying to remember rowing strategy as she pushed her legs down and swung her back backward. High pace at the start to lift the boat out of the water, right? Or in a head race, were you supposed to be slower and steadier?

People from some of the lakeside houses were starting to come out in boats to watch the race. One motorboat veered far too close to her, its driver apparently forgetting that the wake from the boat could send her scull onto its side, and she smelled eggs hollandaise over its gas fumes. The water felt heavy, and her body didn't remember how to get the oars through the water. Her hands were traveling too fast on the recovery, and her legs couldn't seem to push down correctly on the stroke. She was sweating, she hadn't brought anything to drink, and she had forgotten how long these head races took. Twenty minutes? An hour? A boat that had started two minutes behind her started to pull closer; the rower looked like he was visiting from the 1970s with his white-and-red-striped sweatband.

"Charlie Hawley is pulling up on our Mildred's Moms rower," she heard from the loudspeaker.

No, he's not, thought Evelyn. This time I'm not getting beaten.

She didn't know whether it was adrenaline or anger, and she didn't care. The rhythm was starting to come back to her—slam-swing-hands-glide, slam-swing-hands-glide—and her body remembered things that her mind didn't as she almost stood up off of the footboards and cracked her hamstrings down against the fiberglass. She made the water whoosh by as she sent her oar puddles flowing forward, and she was making the boat lift, lift, lift as though she could get it out of this water, out of the water and into the air. She was flying. "Jenny Vinson from Mildred's Moms is giving Charlie Hawley a run for his money," she heard from the loudspeakers. "What a great race this is becoming."

She passed the first buoy marking a turn and had to hold water with one oar and pull with the other one to get her boat angled around. She was now in the passage between Sachem and Turtle, Charlie Hawley getting ever smaller in the distance, and she slowed down her recovery a bit to gulp in a few breaths of air. Evelyn checked; she wasn't far from overtaking the next boat. She could win this thing.

Come in to the dock and raise that stupid Fruit Stripe trophy. Her hands felt hot and she could feel blisters forming, but she grabbed the oar handles tightly again and started getting her momentum back.

She heard the whine of a motorboat from the north, which didn't seem to be joining the other spectators at the shore. It was skipping straight toward her. Evelyn felt a surge of energy. Now she really began to row, forcing the blades through the water as she slammed her knees down. She was going. She was moving. She had the rhythm now. Slam, swing, hands, glide. Slam, swing, hands, glide. Now the seat did not seem to be trying to jump the tracks. Now the oars were understanding what she wanted them to do.

"Evelyn!" she heard from the motorboat. It was Camilla's voice, and Evelyn wasn't surprised to hear it.

Slam, swing, hands, glide. Shorter strokes now, pick up the pace, she heard the imaginary cox in her head shouting. That's it, you've got this, show them what you're made of. Slamswinghandsglide, slamswinghandsglide.

"Evelyn!" Louder now. About to explode.

One and exhale on the stroke, two and inhale on the recovery.

"What are you doing here?" Clipped, short. ("What is she doing here?" from the boat; Camilla had brought backup.)

Evelyn saw three heads bob at her from within the motorboat.

"Evelyn, what are you doing in the Fruit Stripe?" Camilla maneuvered the motorboat closer. Camilla didn't know yet that Evelyn was going to win this race. Didn't know that in about twenty minutes, Evelyn would get out of her scull, sweating and victorious, and be surrounded by well-wishers, Scot and Mrs. Hacking and Souse and everyone she had met along the way.

"Isn't that—" she heard Phoebe say loudly, and Camilla said what sounded like "The clematis is here," which made no sense. Then a third voice said, "We should get her disqualified." Evelyn twisted her head to see who it was, and it was Brooke. Back in. Which meant Camilla had replaced Evelyn, just as she had replaced Brooke after

Brooke's engagement, and Evelyn's attempt to get Brooke on her side had failed. Camilla would always hold the power, and Evelyn was the new girl with the goggles.

Evelyn looked at the tip of the motorboat, which was darting closer to her, and tried to press her legs down harder. Stand up against the footboards, the invisible cox yelled. Move this boat on out of here.

"Evelyn! Who invited you?" Camilla said.

Slamswinghandsglide. Camilla, looming over the steering wheel and demanding to see an invitation as though this were a private party that she was hosting. Slamswinghandsglide, slamswinghandsglide, but now Evelyn's back was hurting and she couldn't swing quite as far. She pulled in her stomach muscles and tried to shore up her back with those. Slamswinghandsglide. Her legs were burning. She needed to move away from this.

"Did you know she was racing in this?" Phoebe was saying.

"Obviously she wasn't. I mean, she was going to, with Mom's boats, but that didn't happen, clearly. This is some kind of insane scheme," Camilla said.

"Where is she even staying?" said Brooke.

"Maybe she's staying with the Hackings," Camilla said. "Anyone who'll take her in, right?"

Slamswinghandsglide. Evelyn had forgotten how good it felt to get a boat moving, once you got over the initial inertia. With a few heaves, she got it bulging out of the water and then half a boat length away, but Camilla followed.

"Maybe she's having kind of a breakdown. With her father and everything," Camilla shouted.

"Her father?" asked Phoebe.

"That trial lawyer who bribed people. It's all over the news."

Evelyn started to cough, then lustily hawked up a loogie and spewed it at the motorboat.

"Ew!" Phoebe cried. Camilla was saying something to the group, and Evelyn could hear that it was about her father's guilty plea.

"I can hear you!" Evelyn yodeled, and Brooke looked up, startled; Camilla, though, seemed to be expecting this and stayed erect at the wheel.

"Evelyn, what are you doing? I thought I made it clear that you were not welcome here," Camilla said, followed by a righteous "Hmmph!" from Phoebe.

"This is your lake?" Evelyn gulped in a breath of air, and realized this was a dumb tactical move, as it was certainly Camilla's lake more than it was Evelyn's.

Camilla didn't see the opening. "This is bizarre," she muttered to the ladies-in-waiting in the boat. "Nobody wants her here," Camilla added, loudly enough that it skipped across the water, and Brooke bleated, "It's crazy."

"With Jaime—" Camilla began, but Evelyn, for what felt like the first time in her life, interrupted Camilla.

"What, Camilla's mad about a boy? Camilla, who can sleep with anyone she wants, anytime she wants, is upset?" shouted Evelyn. "Did I disobey you? Do you get to make all the calls?"

"What are you trying to prove?" Camilla said.

"Maybe Evelyn should stop sleeping with people's boyfriends," Phoebe suggested.

"Maybe Jaime should stop sleeping with people's girlfriends, too, but we don't see him out here in the middle of ring-around-the-rosy, do we? Why do you have your little sister along for this ride, Camilla? What is this, a training session for her?" Evelyn shouted. "Maybe you should keep grown-up problems between grown-ups."

"I'm eighteen," Phoebe protested.

"Look, your lies about your father—" Camilla began.

"Oh, I'm sorry! I thought no one cared if people were indicted! Does that just apply to your New York circle, Camilla?"

"You lied about the donation, Evelyn. I'm sorry about your father—"

"Oh, can it, Camilla! You're sorry about my father? You don't give a fuck!" The "fuck" felt even more satisfactory than the loogie, popping off of Evelyn's lips with force. "You wanted Jaime for yourself! You're mad about a boy! That's all!"

"You think I'm mad about a boy? Do I look that uninteresting?" Camilla said.

"What is it, then? The dance? The three minutes that the spotlight wasn't on you? Sorry every photo wasn't of you, Camilla. That must have really stung."

"You didn't even deb, did you?" Camilla shouted. "The Bachelors' Cotillion? Guess what? My friend Morgan from St. Paul's was a deb there and had never, ever heard of you. Or your family. Shipping money? Really? You completely made it up. And for what? So you could be a handmaid for a bunch of teenagers? And your father? He was never going to be a donor for the Luminaries, was he? How long have you been lying?"

"You were going to eviscerate him at that lunch," Evelyn said. "You were going to parade him in there like some sort of freak. The Southern lawyer, ladies and gentlemen of New York City. He's so down-home that he didn't even get he was supposed to give twenty-five thousand dollars in exchange for people making fun of him. Does the mascot dance? Does Camilla get points for being so clever?"

"Oh, please. You're pathetic."

Evelyn gasped for breath as she tried to get away from the circling motorboat, but Camilla was upping the throttle and the waves were knocking the oar handles into her stomach.

"Yes, Camilla, you get to set the rules. You get to be in charge of everyone and everything. I forgot. Please excuse me." Evelyn had spent a not-insignificant amount of time reading up on where Camilla's fortune came from and had concluded the only difference between Camilla's money and her money was time. In her anger at being attacked, it was all spilling out. "The Hennings wouldn't even pay fair wages during the Depression, and the Rutherford banking fortune has some sketchy roots, so if you want to talk about background—"

"Oh, ladies, we have a stalker on our hands!" Camilla said, clapping, which meant her hands left the steering wheel and the motorboat nearly hit Evelyn's oar.

Charlie Hawley was pulling close, taking advantage of the fight. Evelyn tried to speed up. "Why don't you ask Brooke?" Evelyn said, but Brooke had turned to the side of the boat, apparently fascinated by Charlie Hawley's advance. "Brooke, you're not going to say it now? Fine. I'll tell you what Brooke said to me. Everyone has something to say when you're not around, Camilla, and it's not nice. We say you use people and throw them out. I'm saying it, but we talked about it. We talked about it."

"Brooke, did you say that?" Camilla said evenly.

Brooke shook her head miserably.

"I didn't think so. Evelyn, these are just more of your fantasies," Camilla said sweetly.

"I'm Evelyn and I was a debutante," Phoebe said in a loud falsetto. "I'm Evelyn and I like to sleep with men who are way out of my league."

"You're eighteen!" Evelyn said, sucking in air as her strokes got shorter and shorter. "Shouldn't you not be a major-league bitch just yet? Isn't that something you should age into, like your sister?"

Camilla brought the motorboat so close that Evelyn had to yank her oar in so she didn't hit it and get thrown off balance. She thought, for a second, that she had quieted Camilla, but then she heard, "Is that my bracelet?"

Evelyn shoved her oar back out into the oarlock and tried to row fast enough that Camilla's view of the bracelet would be blurred.

"You stole my bracelet, you freak?" Camilla shrieked. "It's been missing and I nearly fired our caretaker's wife because I thought she took it. You crazy stalker. I should've known."

Evelyn couldn't catch her breath, and she was going faster and faster, and then her starboard oar was sucked down into the water and the oar handle kicked straight into her stomach, and as the phrase "catching a crab" sprang to the front of Evelyn's brain and she realized that was what was happening, the water threw the oar handle over Evelyn's head and she plunged into the water. It was a jolt of cold and she was in the lake, which was freezing, how was a lake this cold in summer, and then there was her boat upside down with its pink rudder sticking up obscenely. Her clothes were clinging and dragging and she bobbed around, trying to get her breath and her balance back, treading water, then dunking underneath to get a break from the motorboat's surveillance. She looked toward the island's shore, but it was too far to drag the boat there, and she couldn't remember how to flip a scull. She clutched on to an oar, still fastened to her boat, that was floating innocently in the water like it had done nothing wrong when in fact it had ejected her. She had no idea what to do. She was just yards from the motorboat now, and Phoebe's sneering face was hovering over her. Brooke looked like she was about to cry. Evelyn coughed out water and moved to the upside-down hull, her legs kicking on the surface of the freezing lake.

Camilla brought the motorboat to the edge of the capsized boat, looking over its carcass to where Evelyn was trying to stay afloat. Phoebe started to say something else, and Camilla cut her off. "Be quiet, Phoebe," Camilla said. She looked at Evelyn, eyes glazed with fury. "My bracelet?" she asked.

Evelyn put her forehead down on the boat.

"Give it back," Camilla said.

Evelyn fumbled for the bracelet, then Camilla said, "No, stop. Stop. You're going to drop it in the water. Stop. Why did you lie about everything?"

"For me—" Evelyn looked up, her eyes stinging with lake water, one arm draped with a piece of lake grass, her other wrist bearing what was quite clearly Camilla's bracelet, her socks heavy in the water, her grand plans upturned. "I wouldn't have gotten here otherwise," she said finally, and quietly. She wasn't sure if Camilla had heard.

After what seemed like several minutes, she heard the crackle of a walkie-talkie. "Yes, it's Camilla Rutherford. I'm watching the Fruit Stripe. There's a capsized rower just off Turtle," Camilla said. Evelyn kicked her legs. "The racer? Yes, she looks fine. No one I know. I can't see a bib number, no."

Starting to shiver, Evelyn pulled herself up so she was draped over the flipped boat and partly out of the water. As she did, she saw Camilla raise a hand in a combination of a salute and a wave, and the motorboat moved backward with a kick. Camilla twirled the wheel with one hand, and made the boat skip off toward other racers, other friends, other lives. Evelyn put her cheek on the cold fiberglass hull and waited for someone to come and pull her in to shore.

CHAPTER TWENTY-SEVEN

Remaining Balance

Evelyn sat hunched in the train station, trying to work up the energy to buy her ticket on the 12:19. She had used up the little that remained of her willpower just now, as she'd forced herself to walk back to the Lodge at Lake James and pay the bill, which to her horror included a two-night minimum and came out to $3,936 after taxes. Once she'd withdrawn another $50 from the lobby ATM to pay for the lodge's car service to take her to the train station, the ATM had spit out a receipt whose numbers were seared into Evelyn's head: "Remaining Balance: $15.07."

She observed her feet, toes still polished a peppy magenta but dulled by the lake water and ashy from yesterday's long walk. It was so hot in the waiting room.

The door from the parking lot opened and shut, and she heard the wheels of a suitcase and the brisk rhythm of heels on the floor. "If you want to do the Hampton Classic next year, Geraldine, you have to take better care of your horse and not just depend on the stable to do it. Hold on for a minute. I just need to arrange my ticket. Fine. Fine. Good-bye." In a different tone, one that sounded reserved for the working class, Evelyn heard "One to Croton-on-Hudson, on the next train, please. What time will that be?"

"That's the twelve-nineteen," the female attendant said.

"Very well." Evelyn heard some beeps and papers shuffling, and then the woman was back on the phone, this time complaining about her assistant. Evelyn was trying to manage the uneasy feeling that this woman must be a friend of Evelyn's friends, but the feeling was growing. Evelyn peered up, but the woman was facing away from her, and she could only see blond waves. The woman hung up on that call, and then was on another one, a very loud one. Someone across the aisle gave the woman a dirty look, but it didn't have a quieting effect.

"So the girl invited herself up, and then wouldn't even take the hint? Souse. It is somewhat amusing."

Evelyn slunk down into her seat.

"Beegan? No, I haven't. Have you? Where are they from? Beegan? That's not a Baltimore name. Camilla's calling her what? Oh, I see. Clematis. A climbing vine. Once these girls from outside the city get a taste of fame, or even, really, acceptance—well, what they think is acceptance—it's just impossible. Of course, no one who's actually from here cares at all about all this." The woman had the tone of someone who'd given this advice time and time again. Conventional wisdom that applied to the thousands of kids from Duluth, from Mobile, from Detroit, who came to New York to try and rise above their stations.

Social clematis. That's what Camilla was saying in the boat. Evelyn had thought she was meant to be a part of this scene, but her mistakes had piled up so high that complete strangers could detail them in the train waiting station. Jaime. A girlfriend. That the girl had played field hockey at Yale. Scot. Her father. Her mother. Credentials that Evelyn didn't have. That Evelyn had just been faking all along.

"Train's coming in ten minutes. Have your tickets ready," the attendant said into a microphone.

Evelyn, feeling nauseated and still sweating, stood up and took the long way around the sitting room so the woman couldn't see her face. "One to New York, please," she said in a voice that finished in a whisper.

The attendant, pale with burst-capillary cheeks and a dyed red perm, typed in something. "That's a hundred seventy-five," she said.

"One-way?"

"Last-minute purchase. Only have business class available."

Evelyn used her forearms to support herself on the counter. Her head was whooshing so loudly she wondered if everyone could hear it. She opened her wallet and looked at the array of options that were no longer available to her. All these empty, useless cards filling her wallet.

The Visa Pewter. With the new terms she'd received. Maybe it would still work. She slid it across the counter. The woman ran it through and, as Evelyn had pretty much known she would, said, "Not going through, hon. Got something else?"

Something was wrong with Evelyn's breath. Or her heart. Were they changing the lights in the station? It was so gray. She thought she heard Scot's voice, and a hand extracted Evelyn's AmEx, and she knew there was something about the AmEx that she should be worried about, then Evelyn was surprised to see that the person's hand holding the credit card looked like hers. "Nope, not this guy, either. Hang on a sec," Evelyn heard, but the words were floating and bumping, not arranging themselves in any logical order. She heard Camilla saying "Clematis, clematis." Why had they turned off the air in here?

"The twelve-nineteen to New York City arrives in five minutes. Please gather your belongings and make your way to the platform for an on-time departure." Evelyn heard, then, "You got anything else, hon?" Evelyn must've responded, though everything was shape-shifting now, because she heard the woman say something about Barneys from very far away. She remembered the subway station next to Barneys from when she'd first arrived in New York, so long ago, when she thought she'd go into Barneys to buy a purse and didn't realize how expensive they were. She'd gone right back out, offended, and bought a purse from a street stand instead, a cute one, red, for something like twenty dollars, and had patted it as she'd gone to catch the N downtown to meet Charlotte for a movie.

She heard the roar of the subway train come and go, and she was on the Fifty-ninth Street downtown platform, which smelled of bile, looking across to the uptown platform, jammed with people in bright blue-and-orange jerseys. Groups of threes and fours were bright clusters of Mets supporters, everyone with individual allegiances proclaimed—PIAZZA 31, ALOMAR 12, ALFONZO 13. Triple claps broke out, and the whole platform would join in, "Let's go, Mets." They were all welcome, all part of something, all hoping the Mets would make the play-offs. Let's go, Mets. New York, New York.

Somewhere in the city, an orange cat finished chewing on a marjoram plant next to his studio apartment's door and leapt purring onto the shoulder of his owner, home early from work. Somewhere in the city, a young Chinese pianist sat down at a rehearsal hall and let his fingers play the first opening notes of the Emperor Concerto, notes that would envelop the small girl in row D of the Philharmonic that night in a shimmering cloud. A boy in Staten Island touched his finger to the lower back of the girl who had been just a friend until then. A woman in Hell's Kitchen stood in her dark attic garret, her paintbrush in hand, and stepped back from the painting of chartreuse highway and forest-green sky that had taken her two years to complete. A clerk in a Brooklyn bodega tapped her crimson fingernail on a box of gripe water, reassuring the exhausted new mother holding a wailing baby, and the mother's grateful smile almost made both of them cry themselves.

The rattle of the train announced its approach, the headlights sweeping as it careened into the station. The whole platform of travelers on the other side of her stamped their feet in unison; let's go, Mets; let's go, Mets.

"Go New York!" someone shouted in a deep Brooklyn accent as the train opened its doors.

New York, New York, a helluva town

The lyrics were rushing through Evelyn's head as someone jarred her backward. She was going to be late meeting Charlotte for the movie and wouldn't have time to get popcorn. Char loved Milk Duds with popcorn. "Excuse me, the train is here."

The Bronx is up but the Battery's down

"Are you all right?"

The people ride in a hole in the ground

She heard the shriek of wheels on the train track as the song changed keys and crescendoed:

New York, New York

"Ma'am? The train has arrived. Ma'am, do you need me to call a doctor?"

She seemed to be sitting. It was so hot. Why was she so cold when it was so hot? The song was so loud she could hear it even over the industrial fan in her ears.

It's a helluva town!

It took Evelyn a moment to discern that the words sounded so loud because she was singing them at full throttle. The blond woman—clematis, clematis—gave her a frightened glance. Evelyn gave her a wild-eyed look back, suddenly shooting out her fingers in a claw as if to attack. She didn't know where she was, and there was nowhere for her to go, and for just one moment, sweat pouring down her face, she felt free.

Part Three

CHAPTER TWENTY-EIGHT

Everybody Rise

Evelyn held the disc of grated old Parmesan, which she'd microwaved into a crisp, to the light. She had managed to get by for three weeks so far. The station attendant had insisted on calling her "loved ones," as the attendant had put it, ignoring Evelyn's insistence that she didn't have any loved ones. The woman had held the train as she called the "Mom and Dad" listing on Evelyn's cell phone to arrange for a ticket home and had the conductor load Evelyn onto the train and offer her water as she sweated and trembled; someone must've gotten her a taxi, and she woke up alone in her apartment two days later, the fever having passed. Under her door, she found another letter about the rent, this one giving formal notice that the company would pursue legal proceedings if Evelyn didn't remit the past-due rent immediately.

But there wasn't enough to remit. She had canceled her Internet and her cable. She'd gone through her closet, putting the dresses and the skirts and the shoes and the lingerie from that life that was now so far away into shopping bags. When she had bought the things, she had imagined the day when they would all sit in a proper and big-enough closet. The delicate silk items would be folded gently into lined wooden drawers and separated by tissue placed there by a maid, rather than rolled and stuffed into a fourth of one dresser drawer. The evening dresses she would have cleaned by Madame Paulette's and prepared for storage, so that her daughter or some other fuzzy beneficiary, perhaps Camilla's or Preston's daughter, of whom she would be the godmother, would be able to wear it at a funny vintage party thirty years from now. Evelyn removed the clothes from their hangers and drawers and folded them into the smallest squares she could possibly make, slowly halving them and halving them again. When they were arranged in bags in tight packets, she took them to a consignment shop on upper Madison when it opened one morning.

That had given her enough cash to make it through these weeks, on Cup Noodles and milk and bananas and Grape-Nuts, mostly, and Chateau Diana—which looked like wine but was actually a four-dollar "wine product"—when she was feeling desperate. She would walk only east to bodegas now, never west, and wondered whether the bodegas closer to the park also sold "wine product" and she had just never noticed.

She had thought about work, but she didn't have any real skills. What was she going to do, offer to introduce employers to all the right people, people to whom she was clematis? She had nothing to contribute. Nothing to offer. The New York rhythm was continuing without her, and she couldn't quite hear the beat. She didn't like to be on the street during the early morning or evening commute because it was so obvious she had no place among the people with jobs and purpose. She didn't fit in during the late mornings, when the mothers would borrow their children from their nannies and take them to to the exclusive music class to meet other influential mothers. She didn't fit in during the afternoons, when nannies would migrate east for Brearley and Chapin, and west for Nightingale and Dalton. She didn't fit in during the evenings, when people were heading home from work and rushing out on dates.

Without a place to be, Evelyn didn't want to be seen. She'd gotten one e-mail from Brooke before she stopped checking e-mail, demanding Camilla's bracelet, but she'd deleted it. She thought of calling Charlotte, but she didn't want to spark the lecture she was sure was waiting for her. Sometimes she looked at Preston's number, wondering where he was, and whether he ever wondered what his old friend Evelyn was up to. Her parents had called her a few times after the Lake James train-station incident, sounding concerned, but when Evelyn had said that she had just been feeling faint and hadn't eaten enough, they hadn't inquired further. She didn't want to call them, either; she assumed her father was angry with her after she'd ignored his guilty plea, and that her mother would just moan about how terrible her own life was. She did have some standby pals, the Barneys and the AmEx and now the Visa collection people, who had been calling daily, trying to trick her by calling from different numbers and at odd times, until Evelyn had powered off her mobile and unplugged her apartment phone.

Life was going to keep going on, that was the problem. She slept until eleven, then napped in the afternoon. At night, she sat up in bed, too panicked to go to sleep because she knew exactly what the next day would bring, more of the same, more monotony, and with each day she grew older, with each day she grew further from what she had wanted to be. Sometimes she pulled her hair back and forced herself to go to the dingy diner with Internet access around the corner, and she'd look through Appointment Book, seeing the parties she hadn't been invited to attend. How had she been so close to it all? How had she given it all away?

Individuals and families streamed by her on the streets, the days turned as they had so many times, her bodily processes became repetitive and futile. With nothing to mark one day as different from the next, her mind hurtled and her waist thickened and the little money she'd gotten for selling her clothes dwindled. She never slept through the night anymore. She would half wake, reach for the reassurance of Scot's forearm that wasn't there, and toss in tangled sweat-streaked sheets that she hadn't washed in weeks because she could no longer afford drop-off service and didn't want to have to sit, exposed, at a Laundromat.

She'd look out her window into the 3:00 A.M. darkness, which was filled with the kind of silence that can only happen on city streets, with a bodega clerk shouting in Korean over a pile of mangoes, and the beeping of a processed-meat delivery truck with a smiling pig face on the side. The worst part was realizing that the darkness would eventually be over, because that would mean another day was going to start soon. The sun just kept coming in the windows.

That morning (or yesterday morning, they all seemed the same), she had received yet another letter from the apartment management company. Evelyn found the letter stuck into her door when she opened it to take her trash down the hall; she didn't know how long it had been there, as she couldn't precisely remember when she'd last left her apartment. It read "Housing Part" at the top and looked like a lawsuit. Evelyn forced herself to read it, and though she had trouble concentrating long enough to interpret it, it was her management company calling her to court the following Friday for some kind of judgment. She had no money for judgment. She thought about calling her father for advice, but it would mean turning on her phone and she didn't want the credit-card people to be able to find her.

The sludge in her brain wouldn't let her think sharply. She reread the notice two more times. Friday. If she was gone by then, they couldn't do anything. They couldn't judge against her for not showing up at a hearing if she no longer lived here.

It was July 13, and Evelyn walked out that Friday having showered, which was something, though she didn't have the energy to dry her hair or even put it back in a ponytail. She wore Delman ballet flats that were worn through at the soles, and had underdressed for the weather, assuming the city was still as hot as it had been the last time she'd gone out. Now it was cold, almost autumnal, despite its being the middle of July, and she ducked her head to block the wind as she hurried down Third Avenue.

She turned right on Sixty-second, walking west to where the better town houses started. The skies were dark enough, with rain looming, that she could see inside the town houses clearly, stone-cold gray on the outside and inside the light, the parties, the drinks, the laughter, the figure in a suit moving purposefully from one frame of a window to the next, the tiny head of a child in an upstairs bedroom confiding in a doll. Her destination was the Colony Club on the corner of Park, and she stood across the street from it under some scaffolding that felt providential in its ability to cover her up.

The wind sliced past her, and Evelyn stepped behind a pole as she saw a leg, two legs, in camel stilettos, and a white coat, and the flipping backward of the long sandy hair. Camilla emerged from a taxi and said something to Nick, who was jogging after her. Then the heavy gait of Scot, following them out of the cab. Evelyn pulled back into the shadows, but they did not look her way. After giving them enough time to get out of the lobby, Evelyn walked across the street and entered the club.

"Excuse me," she said to the concierge, who was sitting at his desk with the little board behind him and the different-colored pins that showed which member was on which floor, the guide to his world, the guide to the world Evelyn had once hoped to master herself. "The party tonight, for Camilla Rutherford's birthday?"

"Yes, you are on the list? Your name, please?"

"No, I'm not," Evelyn said. She didn't think that they were going to welcome her back into the fold. She didn't even know if it was a fold she wanted to be welcomed back into. She just wanted to explain.

"Miss, if you're not on the list—"

"Just let me in for a minute, please."

"I'm sorry, miss, but it's a closed guest list, so I'm afraid I can't let you up."

"But I know all these people. They're my friends. Were my friends."

"If you'd like to call Miss Rutherford and have her add you to the list, I'd be happy to wait."

A woman in a pink suit wearing a necklace of large amber jewels, her osteoporosis so advanced that the jewels seemed to be pulling her neck to the ground, pushed past Evelyn. "Hello, where is Mrs. Hudson?" she demanded, and the concierge turned to look at the name board. "She hasn't arrived yet, Mrs. Bagley," he said.

"I can't call her," Evelyn said. "I mean, I can call her, but she wouldn't pick up. Things went really, really wrong between us. Have you ever had that? Where things just go off the rails, and you kind of know it's happening, but you don't really know how to fix it, and you just get more and more involved?" She realized she'd barely spoken to anyone in days.

He gave her a sympathetic look, but then inclined his head toward the exit. "Miss, if you will, I'm afraid nonmembers and nonguests are not allowed to linger."

The woman in pink returned. "I couldn't find her anywhere," she said, looking angrily at Evelyn. "There's something wrong; maybe it's tomorrow, but I can't come tomorrow, it's Saturday, and she knows I never dine out on Saturday. Have you seen her?"

Evelyn, uneasy, didn't answer. The woman listed back outside.

"Please," said the concierge, gesturing toward the door, giving no indication that anything unusual had just happened.

Evelyn's hand went into her pocket, and she started to say, "Could you just—" but the concierge was answering a phone call. Evelyn stepped back outside, freezing from the Colony's air-conditioning, and felt the wind picking up.

She smelled him before she saw him, sharp perfumed chemical notes, resin and the scent of black, and then Phil Giamatti said, "Beegs, what-what?"

"Phil," she said weakly. The lacquered banker whom she'd last seen at Sheffield-Enfield, back before any of this had happened.

"You going in? It's cold out here," Phil said, slapping her on the shoulder.

"What are you doing here?"

"They want my firm to invest in the fund. Along with my excellent party skills."

"What fund?"

"Nick Geary's. And some dude who worked with Greenbaum at Morgan."

"Scot? Tannauer?" Evelyn said.

"Think so."

"You know Nick and Scot?"

"I bring the money, honey." He rubbed his thumb against his index finger. "My former boss at Bear signed up as an investor, and he thought I should get in early, too."

"They're starting a fund?"

"What did you think this was?"

"I thought it was Camilla Rutherford's birthday party."

"Yeah, there's some chick's party mixed in, too. Social life and business mix these days, don't you know? The fund's gonna be H-O-T. Their angle is that the mortgage market's gonna implode. I guess they're trying to sign up rich widows here or something."

Evelyn shook her head. "There is—I want—can I just go in as your guest?"

"As my guest?" He patted his stomach.

"Please. Just tell the concierge I'm with you. I'll be in and out in twenty minutes."

"That's what she said," he said. "My date's coming any second. No can do, Beegs."

"I just want to—these were my friends," Evelyn said pleadingly.

"Never thought I'd see the day when Beegan came begging," Phil said with a guffaw. "Not on the guest list? What did you do?"

Evelyn saw someone with a purposeful stride coming from down the street and recognized Souse.

"Phil," she said, grabbing his hand. From her pocket, she took out Camilla's Racquet Club bracelet. "Give this to Camilla for me. Please."

"What's this?"

"Something that was hers that I tried to take. It's a long story. Please, just give it to her."

"What am I supposed to tell her?"

"Tell her—" Souse was bounding down the pavement at an alarming speed. Evelyn snapped her head from Souse to Phil, and pressed the bracelet hard into Phil's thick hand. "Tell her that I'm sorry. Tell her that I . . ."

"That you what?"

"That I lost myself. Tell her that I lost myself."

"You lost yourself?" Phil was saying, but Evelyn turned and started running, her flats slapping against her feet, running and running through the lights and through the honks and through the people. It was blue-black; the more reactive New Yorkers were already jamming their umbrellas up and out in anticipation of the first drops. Soon there would be sheets of rain that pummeled so hard it hurt. A swirling wind was picking up dirt from the street and hurling it at pedestrians' ankles along with leaves and Orbit gum wrappers. The wind whirled up and shook the tree branches, and the oblivious tourists continued walking in circuitous paths as the New Yorkers, who knew what was coming, crowded under awnings and behind the vertical plastic sheets protecting the fruit in front of bodegas, glancing at one another and at the troubled sky to measure how much time they had. A few kept moving, dueling with the umbrellas they had bought in the subway station from the Nigerian men who sensed the rain before anyone else did, as they hurried to wherever they were going so they could hurry to the next place after that. A single heaving drop of cold water burst on Evelyn's face, then another hit her knee. It went black, and the rain hit with a crash, slamming at her, her instantly soaked dress clinging to her legs and her shoes filling with water. She kept running. Sometimes she'd turn, when she hit a light, and several times she smacked straight into people who were running from the rain themselves, and she mumbled an apology and kept going.

Her lungs were filled with acid and she had big drops of water on her eyelashes when she stopped. She didn't know how long she'd been running, or what part of town she was in. She leaned over, hands on her legs, catching her breath. She needed a bathroom. She needed to dry off. She looked down the dark street: a closed nail salon, an open falafel place, and a red door with a neon sign overhead. A bar. That would be fine. She opened the red door.

The heat and the chord hit her at the same time. She knew those notes. Sondheim. It was the verse of—yes, now a man's tangy voice was singing it—Sondheim's "The Ladies Who Lunch." Her eyes adjusted to the room below her. It was small and wooden, as though someone had picked up an oyster house from 1700s–era Pearl Street and dropped it here in wherever she was, Midtown somewhere. Christmas lights crisscrossed the ceiling though it was July. There was a bartender and a small clutch of people gathered on stools around a piano, outfitted with a bar around it, where a man with ginger hair and glasses played.

The man who was singing was plump, swollen faced, with small hands clasped together, and wearing a worn brown sweater, the kind of man Evelyn would not have seen on the street if she passed him, but his eyes were bright and he had a gentle smile as he wended through the song. Evelyn felt she must be actually giving off steam in this roasting place, but she stayed at the top of the stairs, not wanting to go but not wanting to interrupt the singing with her presence. As she nudged the first notes of the next verse forward in her head, the music stopped.

"A customer!" the piano player shouted.

"A customer!" the Sondheim singer echoed.

She took a step backward.

"No, no no no no no no," the piano player shouted. "You! Come in!" He played a D^7, a chord of expectations.

"Me?" she said.

"Don't just stand there dripping. We're not interested in wet girls, are we, boys?" He played a G, the resolution to the D^7, as the people around the piano laughed. "Come. Here, the girls are beautiful. Even the orchestra is beautiful—" Now he was plucking out the opening notes of "Cabaret."

She took a few hesitant steps down to the wooden floor.

"His bark is worse than his bite," the Sondheim singer said.

"My bite is delicious," the pianist protested, his hands skipping along the keyboard with the "Ladies Who Lunch" chords.

"Do you know the words?" asked a man with a friendly long face, wearing a tweed newsboy cap.

"You can sit at the piano if you know the words," the pianist said. "Otherwise, we banish you to the corner, where the straights and tourists sit."

She looked at the room's perimeter, but there were no straights or tourists tonight to be seen. She took a breath. "I know the words," she said.

"She knows the words!" the Sondheim singer said.

"She knows the words!" the piano player echoed. "You can stand here, next to beautiful boy number three." This was a brown-haired man in a checked purple shirt and neat trousers, glasses, sipping a gimlet. "Please remember to tip the help, and I'll take requests if you make them politely and say 'please.' Don't drip on the piano. Pick it up with the next verse, fellows."

She did know the words and, for once, didn't care whether her voice sounded flat. She wanted to sing, and joined in with her clear soprano. She'd seen *Company*, a staged production with the Baltimore Symphony Orchestra, and had found it moving, watching the protagonist try and fail to connect. She had puzzled over "The Ladies Who Lunch" in particular, which chewed up one group of New York women after another: the girls who play wife, the girls who play smart. But weren't they all trying? Evelyn thought as she considered the lyrics, feeling the scarred wood of the bar with her index finger. Going to museums or making dinner for their husbands or sitting back and making wry comments—weren't they all just trying to survive New York?

Only she, the Sondheim singer, and the tweed-cap guy were staying on top of the third verse. One would smile at her, the other would nod to mark the next line, and when she fumbled, thinking of Preston or Scot or Camilla, they raised their voices just a touch and carried her through it. The group went into the final verse. When the end of the song came with "Everybody rise," to her surprise, all the men around the piano leapt to their feet, clinked glasses, and howled, "Everybody rise! Rise! Rise! Rise! Riiiiiiise!"

Then there was silence.

"You're very wet," the piano player said. "I don't think you'd want to touch the bar towels here. Why don't you—"

"Bathroom?" Evelyn said.

"Downstairs."

The bathroom mirror was carved with initials and some remarkably decent line drawings, but Evelyn could still see herself well enough. The final words of "The Ladies Who Lunch" were repeating in her head. Everybody rise, everybody rise, everybody rise. That was exactly it, she thought. Upstairs, and outside, and in every street and every avenue of Manhattan, everybody was getting higher on a tide of money and ambition, swimming frantically and trying not to drown. And she? She didn't have the energy to even tread water anymore.

When she came back up, the men were singing "Skid Row," from *Little Shop of Horrors*, and she bought herself two beers at once with the soggy $20 in her pocket, one of the final dribs of money she'd gotten from the consignment place. She allowed herself a few more songs around the piano as she drank, "Try to Remember" and then another Sondheim song, "Being Alive." The words and music made her sit still and be for just a moment as the room glowed red from the Christmas lights and the cracked red-leather barstools. The Sondheim singer in the brown sweater let his voice soar, and she could see the sad apartment he must live in, with the creaking old radiator with wet socks drying on it, and the wood floor so slanted that any button that popped off a cardigan would go skittering to a corner of the room. Not the life he imagined he would have when he came to

New York with that beautiful voice, she thought. Maybe not the life she had imagined, either, she thought, as she put her lips around the cold beer bottle. She had tried. She had fought. And she had lost.

She felt struck with tiredness. She made one final request, for "Corner of the Sky," putting her last $2 into the pianist's jar and remembering to say "please." She backed away toward the door as, softly, too softly for anyone to hear, she joined in on "Don't ask where I'm going; just listen when I'm gone." She slipped out the door without anyone noticing.

CHAPTER TWENTY-NINE

Marina Air

"Evelyn." Barbara didn't turn from her post in front of the coffee machine. "You're up early."

"Yes." The microwave clock read 6:05.

The only light in the apartment came from the dim bulb underneath the microwave. It was dark, and the Sheffield sweatshirt she had pulled from the box marked CLOTHES—EVELYN was on inside out and smelled of wood. Outside, in the parking lot of the Marina Air, a car's tires squealed.

Yesterday, after her train ride, bus ride, and taxi ride from New York to Sag Neck, she'd arrived at the house and seen it was as stripped as the Petit Trianon apartment she'd left behind, down to the dust balls and electric cords. There were light rectangles on the wood where the rugs had been and there was hair and dust detritus where the grandfather clock and tea table and chaise had been. Evelyn's room contained a sleeping bag, rolled up, and a shoe box full of old compacts and worn-down Lip Smackers that must have surfaced from some bathroom drawer. She looked into the front yard, which was when she saw the FOR SALE—SOLD sign.

Her father had walked in the door soon after. He looked folded into himself, like a Snoopy balloon after the Macy's Thanksgiving parade, and had nearly screamed when he'd seen Evelyn at the top of the stairs. They were awkward around each other, her father not asking what she was doing there, she not discussing what had happened in her life. He'd tried to summon some of his old cheer, saying that the weather was fine and her mother was already settling in at the Marina Air apartment. He had been surprised that Evelyn didn't know what this was: the apartment they had rented on the edge of town.

He drove her over to the Marina Air that night, a two-story structure with exterior stairs and exterior hallways located where Main Street gave way to Route 33. Evelyn thought it must have been a motel before it was converted to divorced-dad rentals. Barbara was inside apartment 2L, a dark four-room warren, unpacking boxes.

"What are you doing here, Evelyn?" Barbara had said. She looked like she hadn't slept in a long time, either.

"I left New York," Evelyn blurted. "I didn't call. I was just—I'm sorry."

"You left New York? Why on earth would you do that?"

"I left," she repeated in a small voice.

Dale indicated that she should sit on the couch, which took up most of the living-dining room. "Is this because of the case?" he said. "I appreciate you coming down, but there's no need to move here."

"Yes. No." Evelyn kept standing. "I was evicted from the apartment, or I think I would've been if I stayed. I lost my job. I lost my friends."

Dale considered this as Barbara slumped down in a chair in the corner, facing away from both of them.

"Okay. That's okay, Evelyn. People get into trouble," Dale said.

"I was trying to fix it all. Too late, I was trying to fix it all, but I was trying. I was always trying," Evelyn said. She looked at her father, who had balanced on the couch's arm. "This way I can be here for the sentencing. That's good. It wasn't like I wanted it to come to this. I ran out of money, and did what I thought was best. Maybe it wasn't. I was just trying to get through."

"It's all right," he said, intertwining his fingers. "It's all right."

Her mother stayed in the chair, and her father finally gave her a kiss on the forehead and said that she was always welcome, which was unexpectedly kind. Evelyn walked to the small bedroom that Dale said was to be the guest-bed-office-and-Evelyn's-room, where a framed Georgia O'Keeffe poster that Evelyn had bought at the Sheffield Shop her prep year, before she learned that all Georgia O'Keeffes were basically vaginas, hung a little askew. Evelyn wondered if her father or mother had hung it up.

The bedroom smelled of turpentine and Chinese plastic. Evelyn slept lightly and had been awake for an hour in the dark morning before she walked out to talk to her mother. Barbara still looked defeated, but at least she was speaking.

"You need help with the coffee machine?" Evelyn said.

Barbara swung the filter holder open and shut, and pressed a few buttons. "Your father always made the coffee."

"When is he moving in here?"

"I'm not sure what you mean."

"Once he's wrapped things up at Sag Neck?"

"Is he wrapping things up at Sag Neck?" This was one of Barbara's favorite repartee games, feigned confusion.

"I think so, Mom. I don't know. I'm not really in the mood to deal with this. Is he waiting to move here until the sentencing?"

"What do you mean?"

"I mean, is he waiting to move here until the sentencing? Do we have to do this?"

"Do what?"

"Mom?"

"Yes?" Barbara replied distantly, as though Evelyn were inquiring about tennis-court availability at the Eastern.

"Is Dad not living here?"

"No."

"Like, not planning on it?"

"I couldn't say."

"But you are? Here?"

"Evidently."

"But Sag Neck is sold."

"I am aware it is sold, Evelyn."

"So I thought he would come here until he has to go to prison, if he has to go. I thought he was just temporarily at Sag Neck. There's room for him here, right?"

"Can we all fit in this horrid apartment? Does the water go in this machine automatically?"

Evelyn ran her hand through her hair. "Can I have the car keys?"

"It's six-fifteen in the morning."

"Yeah. I'll be back. Later. Can I have them?"

"By the door."

Evelyn did not change her clothes, or brush her teeth; she just grabbed the keys and walked into the morning in her flip-flops and sweats. At Sag Neck, she heard her father crashing about upstairs.

"Hello?"

"Dad?"

"Evelyn. What are you doing back?"

"Just thought I'd make you breakfast. You need sustenance, right?" She held up the 7-Eleven bag she'd gotten en route, having found $5 cash in a junk drawer at the Marina Air, and put together cornflakes in week-old cream for him. She wondered how long he'd been here, alone, walking through what used to be fully furnished rooms, rooms where his family had lived. She couldn't bring herself to say much, but patted him on the shoulder when he was finished with the meal.

To parse out time, Evelyn gave herself two tasks a day. Monday: organizing the Marina Air bathroom, then making English-muffin pizzas at Sag Neck for dinner for her and her father. Tuesday: helping her father pack up books, then moving boxes to the storage unit. Wednesday: Laundromat, then using the Internet at the Jeremiah Regis Library on Main Street. She logged on to People Like Us and saw it had been redesigned and was running a discount on sports tickets on the homepage; she looked for Camilla's profile, but it had been deactivated. Her e-mail in-box held DailyCandy promotions, a sample sale at Theory, and an offer of tickets to the American Ballet Theater's fall gala. Her salesman at Céline e-mailed her to inquire as to why they hadn't seen her in a while. But, other than an e-mail from some Sheffield alumna asking her if she could help with an upcoming phonathon, there was not a single personal e-mail, not one from her former friends asking where she'd been or if she was all right. New York City was not only getting along fine without her, it didn't even notice that she'd left.

She returned home to find her mother fixated on a show about brides selecting wedding dresses. It was only one o'clock, and the afternoon stretched before her like one long taffy pull. Her mother sat with her mouth partly agape, like she lacked the energy to close it, as a man onscreen told a short woman wearing a cupcake silhouette that she looked like a child bride. "I'll be back in a couple of hours," Evelyn said to her mother, who did not look up.

She headed back to the Regis Library and found information on a temping firm in Baltimore. It might not be so bad, she told herself. Maybe a law or banking firm needed a temp, and she could have an office with a door and free pads of paper. At her appointment the next week, though, she was told she was not an appropriate candidate for temp work. The temp-agency interviewer had her sit at a greasy computer with the *g* and the *h* rubbed out for a skills test. The program looked to be from the 1980s, beeping like a Russian computer-chess game whenever Evelyn did something wrong. Beep, when she even clicked on the wrong cell in the Excel portion. Beep—beep—beep with each wrong formatting choice as she composed a business letter. When she backspaced, flustered, it would beep again, making her panicky. At the end, the interviewer, folding his arms, suggested she could be more competitive in the job market if she enrolled in a typing class at a secretarial school.

On the drive back, through the brown dust and the flat land, as the unrented billboards peeling at the edges got to be too many, she hit her hand on the steering wheel. Secretarial school? she wanted to shout. I went to Sheffield. I was the main photograph on Appointment Book. I am someone. I was someone.

By three days later, though, Barbara's depression covered the apartment like a giant version of the eyeshades Barbara had started wearing, and Evelyn decided she had to get out, and she had to make some money. There was no secretarial school in Bibville, but there were stores. She mentally reviewed the shops along Main. The new wine shop? She still couldn't figure out how to navigate cabernets, and they would probably reject her like the temp agency had. Bali High, but she couldn't see herself selling batik skirts with any success. The Caffeiteria, down on the wharf, wasn't the worst idea. Her summer friend Jane had worked there in high school and liked it well enough—the tips had been surprisingly good for a coffee shop whose food was little more than muffins and tuna salad on store-bought bread.

When she walked to the wharf, the Caffeiteria was in quiet early afternoon mode, with the windows shut and a PLEASE SHUT DOOR IT'S HOT OUT THERE! sign on the red door, which was thick with several generations of paint. There was no HELP WANTED sign. Didn't businesses like this put up HELP WANTED signs when they needed someone? She pushed open the door and a bell dingled, and from behind the counter, a man with a salt-and-pepper beard and rimless glasses and the bright concentration of a chipmunk looked up. He looked familiar; Evelyn remembered him being very strict about no free refills on iced coffee from her high-school summers.

"Hi?" she said.

"Hi, what can I get you?" he said, shaking out his newspaper, the *Bibville Tattle*.

"I'm actually—I wanted to see if you had any jobs available. Here, I mean. Working here."

He folded the *Tattle* away from him and smoothed the crease.

"I just moved back from New York, so I'm used to busy crowds," she offered. This sounded ridiculous. "Uh, and I can work any hours you need. I'm just up the street, so, really, anything last minute, or if someone doesn't show up."

He scratched his nose. "Who are you?"

She didn't know what he wanted to hear, so she threw out a bunch of answers. "Well, I was born outside D.C. but grew up in Bibville, out on Meetinghouse Creek, and my family—my mother, really—just moved into town—we sold our house, it was sort of an involved thing, so now we're at the top of Main, up by the park. By the Sunoco. I had been in New York until July, but I had some family stuff I had to deal with down here, and so I came down. My friend Jane worked here one summer, in 'ninety-six, I guess it was, back when you guys were the Early Roost, and liked it. So."

"I meant your name."

"Oh! Oh. Evelyn. Beegan."

"Evelyn. I'm Rick. I'm not going to shake your hand. Health inspectors could be watching. Do you have any experience?"

"I worked at a coffee place back in . . ." She stopped herself. To have to pretend like she knew how a commercial espresso machine functioned would end up with her spraying steam and milk all over herself and a lost job. "No," she said in a low voice. "But I can learn."

Rick put his paper down in careful parallel alignment with the counter. He intertwined his hands and put them under his chin and watched Evelyn as though he were waiting for a divining rod to tell him its read on her. Then, message apparently transmitted, he clapped his hands once. "Well, Evelyn, we do have to hire someone for the fall, since one of our workers is starting at Chesapeake, but you're not going to start at the top."

"Right. No, I understand. That's fine."

"You're not gonna get to touch this baby"—he pointed at the silver espresso machine—"until I say you can touch her. You can do drip and iced and the basic food service and the cleanup, and by cleanup I mean cleanup, okay, the mop and everything."

"I can clean," Evelyn offered, though it came out like she was asking herself the question.

"We pay a living wage here. So it'll be nine dollars an hour to start, plus tips."

How, Evelyn wondered, was $9 an hour a living wage?

"Come in Friday at six, and Mia'll show you the ropes. You don't show up, you get fired. You show up drunk, you get fired. Okay?"

"People show up drunk at six A.M.?"

"You'd be surprised." Rick picked up the *Tattle*, licked his finger, and with a brisk shake made the sports pages materialize neatly before him. Evelyn waited, wondering if he would give her a letter or have her sign something, but Rick was absorbed in the newspaper. She cleared her throat, and he looked up.

"Sorry—so—I have a job?" she asked.

He nodded, and turned the page.

So as not to disturb him and make him change his mind, she opened the door with the gentlest of force so the bell barely moved. She turned to look at the Caffeiteria sign, in a loopy cursive with an exclamation point. $9 an hour. In New York, she had occasionally thrown away dollar bills that had gotten wet or overly wrinkled because they grossed her out, and now she was going to be working for $9 an hour. She trudged back to the Marina Air and up the exterior stairs.

The apartment was dark with the shades down when she returned and had a sour smell to it. Barbara's door was closed. Evelyn walked to the living room window overlooking the alley and yanked the cord to pull the blinds up. She unlocked and shoved up the window, and moved into the kitchen to push open the tiny window there, to give the place some natural light and a little bit of air and outside sound. She cracked open the door to get a cross breeze going.

On Friday morning, after her alarm went off at the unbelievably early hour of 4:45 A.M., she was almost late because she kept swapping out outfits, having never noticed what people who worked at coffee shops wore. It felt good to shower and dress for work, and she chose a white tunic dress and sandals with kitten heels. By the time she got down Main Street, her feet were already hurting, and standing on those heels all morning made her feet scream.

Mia wore black pants, clogs, a nose ring, and a knit cap, and was clearly annoyed that Evelyn was such a novice that she didn't even know to cover her hair. Mia gave her a choice of disposable hairnet or dish towel; Evelyn went with the latter and thought that, paired with the white tunic, she looked like a manic midcentury nurse. As Mia made Evelyn grind beans, and as Evelyn then spilled ground beans all over the white dress and found that dusting it off just smeared in the mess, she wanted to throw the beans at the wall and run home, but running home would just mean Barbara in the dark. Evelyn stuck it out through her shift, limping up Main Street when it was over. Her left foot was bleeding by the time she got back.

In her room, Evelyn pulled out her bottle of Perles de Lalique, running her thumb over the smooth glass and the jeweled stopper. She spritzed it on her wrists and the back of her neck, smelling the pepper and dried-rose notes it always gave off at first. A few hesitant drops of rain tapped at her window. She could almost be back in New York, far away from the Marina Air and from any of this. Her iPod was in her night table, and she pulled it out and put on Judy Holliday. "'They've burst your pretty balloon and taken the moon away,'" Evelyn mouthed as Judy sang. She shut her eyes and sniffed her wrists.

Someone at the Caffeiteria this morning had mentioned the stock market was moving higher and higher and New York was celebrating. She wondered if it was raining in New York, too. She could see what all her friends would be doing. In Greenwich Village, Nick would be walking down Barrow Street, thinking with some glee about his fund with Scot. When a car came by, Nick would leap up onto a town-house stoop with the precision of a ballet dancer, sensing the exact moment he would need to move, as a thigh-high spray of water would hit the woman walking behind him. The woman, dripping, would let go of her cheap black umbrella, its metal prongs sticking out like an injured robot arm, a device unable to make it through even a single New York rainstorm.

In her living room, Camilla, who'd have zipped home from her reflexology appointment at the first sign of rain, would sip from a cup of tea and look at the Central Park Zoo below as the seals flopped around in the rain. The Style channel playing fashion shows might mention the stock market, and if it did, Camilla would turn it off. What did the fluctuations of the stock market matter to Camilla?

Scot was easy: He would be working at his hedge fund, whatever a hedge-fund office looked like, doing whatever people at a hedge fund did. Making money. Doing research. Getting frustrated that Nick was never around. Done and done, as Preston used to say.

Charlotte was easy, too: She'd be in an interior conference room packed with lawyers and would never know it had rained. She wouldn't leave work that night—she would barely sleep eight hours over the next three days—as her boss would've told her they couldn't time the markets, and if they didn't close this deal by the end of the week, it wouldn't happen at all.

Preston, where was Preston? He had tried to be a loyal friend to her, to warn her about the dangers of the circle she was trying to crash, the people she was trying to befriend: Bridie Harley, Gemma Lavallee, and, yes, Camilla Rutherford. She had repaid him by ripping him open, by making him feel like he couldn't rely on even his old friends.

She wanted to imagine Preston happy, so she placed him at the Greenwich Country Club on the eighth hole, carefully lining up his chip shot, wanting to finish the nine before the rain got up to Greenwich. A click, an arc, and his ball would drop cleanly onto the green. He would probably use the stock market high to buy more Florida condos or whatever it was he was doing for work. He would dart inside the clubhouse as soon as the rain really started, putting his spikes in his locker and changing back to his loafers, then sitting with his gin and picking pith off his lime slice as he watched the rain darken the course from the clubhouse's window. Was he lonely? Was he happy? Would he even know the difference?

Her alarm went off the next morning again at 4:45. Evelyn got up and walked to work with stiff legs and blisters, this time wearing a dark shirt and flats. Mia promoted her to writing out receipts and stacking them on a spike a few hours in, and the café was so mercifully busy on Saturday that Evelyn didn't have time to think about New York or the Marina Air. She was too busy shuttling muffins back and forth and handing out change and carrying over coffee orders. By Sunday, the job was fun in parts—since Mia didn't like talking to customers, Evelyn picked it up in her place. There was a dog walker whose charge, Hootenanny, a terrier with a wise gray beard, had developed a gimpy leg, but her owners were in Hong Kong for two weeks, and the dog walker wasn't sure whether he ought to take her to the vet. Another guy wore glasses that were literally rose colored and looked plucked from the Goodwill women's department. He did some job for Maryland Upper Shore Transit that required him to stand at the bus stop on the corner of Bay and Main and write something in a pad every time the bus passed, then cross the street to the bus headed in the other direction and write something else there. He liked his coffee with three Sweet'N Lows and extra hot (which meant, Mia said, she should microwave it for fifteen seconds but not let the customer see that was the trick).

At the end of her first full week, Rick gave her an envelope with a paycheck and a stack of bills that was her portion of tips in it. She tucked it at the bottom of her purse, checking that it was still there whenever she walked by the purse at work. On her way home, she deposited the check in her checking account. The ATM screen read "Current Balance: $315.19." It was the first time she had been to an ATM since Lake James, and seeing that she had shifted the balance up that far with her week of work made Evelyn give the blue screen a tiny smile.

She was reading a Sheffield-era copy of *The Magnificent Ambersons*, her old notes scribbled in the margins, when she heard the sound of the door, and her mother walked in, holding a McDonald's bag. (Having never tried fast food when she lived in Sag Neck, Barbara had discovered that she had a taste for Filet-O-Fish.)

"You're home," Barbara said; she was wearing a floor-length black kimono with little teahouses on it. Evelyn hoped she had used the drive-through. "You can set the table."

Babs was going to eat something made in a deep fryer, packaged in cardboard, and handed to her through a bulletproof window, but she would not deign to use a paper napkin, which made Evelyn smile a little. She got up and laid out the linen napkins and silverware and plates.

"Haven't you wondered where I've been for the last week?" Evelyn said.

"I don't know. All sorts of things are going on that I don't know about, I suppose." Barbara was listless and sat down and arranged her napkin in her lap, then pushed a lukewarm hamburger toward Evelyn.

"I've been working. I got a job. At the Caffeiteria. Out on the wharf, the cute little coffee shop. With the good lemonade?"

Barbara picked up her knife and fork, and cut a neat slice of fishburger. She chewed and swallowed so slowly Evelyn could practically see the fish descending down her throat.

"So," Evelyn tried again. "I'm saving some money, actually."

"Your hamburger's getting cold," Barbara replied.

The landline phone rang, startling them both, as no one besides telemarketers in search of uncomfortable conversations called anymore.

"Well? It could be important," Barbara said, dabbing tartar sauce from her mouth.

Evelyn picked up, but before she could say "Hello?" the voice on the other end began chattering. "Hello! I'm looking for Evelyn Beegan, and I hope I have the right number."

"This is a new number," Evelyn said.

"Is this Evelyn? Evelyn, it's Becky Breen, formerly Becky Aquino, from Sheffield. It's been ages."

Evelyn couldn't remember Becky's face but recalled she had been president of the Demosthenes Society, the classical-Greek group, and had given an endless oration at assembly their upper year in said classical Greek. "And an unlisted number," Evelyn said.

"Well, Sheffield doesn't maintain the highest giving rate among prep schools by just letting people fade away, fortunately or unfortunately. Now, listen, I want to talk to you about major gifts. As you know, our class is in the middle of a fund-raising drive, and we're so close to beating the class of 'eighty-seven—"

"Seriously, though, no one knows I'm at this number. Do you guys have the Mafia on your side?"

Becky laughed. "It's a prep-school development office. We're better than the Mafia. Remember Panupong Pradchaphet from Thailand? Came upper year, left after a term? We just tracked him down in the UAE."

"Did you get a major gift from him?"

"Recurring."

"Nice." Evelyn nodded. "So what's in your book on me?"

"I'm sorry?"

"Your book. I've done Sheffield fund-raising. I know you get a little book talking about everyone's giving history and potential. What's my listing in your book?"

"I'm afraid I can't disclose—"

"Becky, you just told me that Panupong Pradchaphet is living in the UAE, which is already a violation of the rules. Come on. I want to know what my listing says. What does it say? Here, I'll start. Evelyn Topfer Beegan 'ninety-eight, Beardsley dormitory, crew . . ."

"Uh, Le Petit Trianon—"

"And my job?"

"People Like Us. Director of membership."

"What's your target for me this year? I gave, what, a thousand last year?"

"Well, of course we're happy with anything you choose to give, but if you'd consider joining the Rising Gryphon Society and going up to twenty-five hundred—"

"Evelyn!" Barbara, who'd looked half asleep for weeks, was now alert, frantically waving her arms at Evelyn to get her to stop.

Evelyn covered up the receiver. "What?"

"Who's on the phone?"

"Sheffield. Alumni office."

"What do they want?"

"A donation. I'm just about to tell them that they're looking in the wrong place."

"Don't tell them that, Evelyn. There's no need to tell them that."

"Why not?"

"It's unseemly," Barbara said.

"Don't you think they'll figure it out when I can't give a major gift?"

"I don't think you need to debase yourself," Barbara said.

Evelyn stuck her tongue between her front teeth. She heard from the receiver, "Hello? Evelyn, are you still there?"

Evelyn put the phone back up to her ear. "Here's the thing, Becky," Evelyn said, her eyes still locked on her mother's. "Maybe you should put this in my listing. I've had a, let's say, an adjustment in circumstances."

"Ah."

"So if you could replace that 'membership' line with 'barista'—though that's overselling it, really, with just 'clerk'—'coffee-shop clerk'—that'd be better. Caffeiteria is my new employer. And I'd get rid of the Petit Trianon address. I'm now a temporary-but-it's-not-so-temporary member of the Marina Air apartments in Bibville."

Barbara was shaking her head faster and faster at the Filet-O-Fish box.

"Of course. I'll update the listing," Becky said.

"I assume the notes say something about my father, but he's probably going to prison, so the big gifts just won't be coming for a while. If ever. Can we do, let's say, three dollars?"

"Whatever you're comfortable with. It's participation, not amount. So I'll, ah, I'll make those notes."

"Three dollars doesn't get you the commemorative Scotch glass, does it?"

"No, I'm afraid not."

"What about a nice postcard? I'd like a Sheffield postcard. I can hang it in the coffee shop. I'm in charge of the bulletin board on alternating weeks."

"I don't think that should be a problem. If I could just grab the Marina Air address?"

Barbara had flattened the box by the time Evelyn got off the phone, and she was still shaking her head no. Evelyn took a giant bite of the cold hamburger. "Better to set expectations, I think," Evelyn said. "Did you get any ketchup?"

CHAPTER THIRTY

Sentencing Guidelines

"Mom? You have to get up. We have to be downstairs in forty minutes."

The fluorescent light in the bathroom of the Wilmington Friendship Inn was sputtering overhead as Evelyn tried to pat on concealer in the sallow bathroom. With no natural light, it was impossible to see whether the basic problem was that her skin was too ruddy for any makeup to cover it up, or whether the cat-sick light was at fault. Stepping into the room, with dark green carpet and dark magenta curtains, Evelyn looked at the twin bed across from hers. There was a sudden whoosh of breath from the lumpy figure under the covers.

"I feel just dreadful," her mother said, rolling away from her and toward the window.

When they had arrived last night, Evelyn had seen her mother planting the seeds for this when she announced wearily that she just didn't have the strength to have a bite of food, leaving Evelyn to get a baked potato from Wendy's on her own. Her father was already at the hotel, staying in a separate room, but had spent the last night discussing the sentencing with Rudy, his lawyer; Evelyn had heard

from him only in a brief phone call when he asked them to meet in
the lobby at eight-thirty.

"Mom, come on. You need to shower. It's not terrible water pres-
sure, and I brought some Kiehl's so you don't have to use the soap."
The water-pressure comment was a lie; she also knew her mother
would object to the thin, dingy white towels, barely thick enough for
Valeriya, wherever she was working now, to approve for dusting.
"Mom, please? Rudy said we had to be in the lobby at eight-thirty."
Evelyn moved back toward the bathroom. "I'll get the water started
for you, okay? It takes a minute to heat up."

Her mother raised an arm over her supine body, then let it arc
down heavily. "I feel just terrible. I can barely move. I think I must
have food poisoning."

"You haven't eaten anything since the sandwich you had in the car
last night."

"It was oozing with mayonnaise. Mayonnaise is swimming with
germs. I don't understand why people at these delicatessens put mayonnaise on absolutely everything. Valeriya never used to put mayonnaise on my sandwiches."

"You had Valeriya make you sandwiches?"

"It gave her something to do," Barbara said.

"Cleaning the house probably kept her occupied. But, Mom, you
get food poisoning, like, four hours after you eat something. It's been
overnight. I'm sure you're fine." Evelyn started for the bed, but stopped
herself; she didn't want to have to see her mother in her nightgown,
the outline of her aging body under the thin material, smelling of
morning and seeming far too vulnerable.

"Mayonnaise . . . ," Barbara mumbled, and drew the cover, a rough
paisley print, closer to her underarm. "Evelyn, please, turn off that
ghastly light."

"In the bathroom?"

"It's giving me a headache. I can feel a migraine starting to come
on, and I can't have any light when I'm getting a migraine. Evelyn, I

just don't think there's any way I can go today. You'll have to apologize to your father for me."

"What?"

"Don't say 'what,' Evelyn, how many times do I have to tell you? It's 'pardon.'"

"Mom, you have to. Rudy said it's really important that we're both there. It could help with the sentence."

"Well, you'll have to tell Rudy that I'm feeling just miserable. Your father has managed to do all the rest of this on his own so far. I'm sure me with a blinding headache standing behind your father as he does the perp walk will do no one any good."

"It's not a—I don't think it's a perp walk, Mom. Please get out of bed. You have to go."

Now Barbara had pulled the thin cover, a mélange in rust and orange, over her head. "Phowhit blan whaffle," she said.

"What?" Evelyn glowered at this creature. She could see the gray roots of her mother's blond hair above the paisley bedspread. Her mother was opting out, but opting out left all the responsibility on Evelyn's shoulders. Barbara was acting like a toddler at a moment when Evelyn badly needed a mother. Evelyn felt tears coming into her eyes but blinked to erase them; one of them had to stay stable, and apparently that had to be her. "Get up. Mom, get up."

Barbara moved the cover down to just below her mouth. "You don't know what it's been like, I was saying. All these people with their false concern: 'How is Dale?' What answer am I supposed to give to that?"

"I don't know, Mom. Please. Get out of bed."

"It's why I simply don't go out anymore."

"Today, you have to." Evelyn looked at the alarm clock, with its 1980s white-block lettering; 7:58 *thirrupped* to 7:59. "We now have half an hour. You need to get dressed. I don't care if it's the last thing you want to do. It will help with Dad's sentence and you have to do it. Please. Just get up."

Barbara was silent and Evelyn watched the clock flip to 8:00

and then 8:01. "I just can't get out of bed today," Barbara said finally. "Tell your father I feel nauseated and dreadful. I have tried, Evelyn—I came all this way. I can't face everyone like this. I need to rest."

Evelyn shut her eyes tight, then opened them and stalked over to the curtains and yanked them open wide, scraping the rings along the metal rod, eliciting a muffled moan from her mother. She returned to the bathroom and tried to slam the door, but the wafer-thin wood only gently puffed shut. She slammed down her hairbrush and threw a lipstick against the mirror so it left a chunk of pink wax dangling against the glass, then marched back to the room.

"One more chance," Evelyn said, her voice even and cold. "Do your duty."

Her mother laboriously opened her eyes. "Don't you think you should put your hair up?"

Evelyn's arms searched for something else to throw, but there was nothing nearby, and so Evelyn stamped her foot and let out a cry of frustration. Barbara's eyes were already closed. Her mother started to say, "Tell your father . . ." but Evelyn grabbed her purse and pulled the door to the room shut as hard as she could, getting out before she could hear the end of the sentence.

The elevator stank of instant coffee and cigarettes. In the lobby, a child was carefully peeling an orange into the steaming breakfast-buffet tin of scrambled eggs. She saw Rudy in front of the automatic doors, which were opening and shutting and opening and shutting as he waved his hands.

"Good, a couple minutes to spare. Your father's in the car. Get in there," he said.

She walked out and hoisted herself into the backseat of the SUV. Dale turned around from the front, looking up. He didn't smile; his forehead was creased in a new pattern. "Hi, there."

"Dad," Evelyn said.

Rudy grabbed the car door and stuck his head in. Evelyn could smell his cinnamon gum. "Where's Barbara?"

"Is your mom almost ready?" her father asked. He was neatly and subtly dressed, in a navy suit that was hanging off him. His jowls hung loose from his jawbone. He tried to grin a few beats after he had finished the sentence, but he couldn't quite achieve a full smile.

"She's not. She says she's sick. I'm sorry."

"What's that?" Rudy said.

"She says she's sick. My mother. She's not coming. She says she's sorry. I'm sorry."

"She's sick." Rudy chomped on his gum so that his lips smacked against one another with each jaw movement. "She's sick. Okay, so, what, she's bent over the toilet throwing up?"

Evelyn sat looking at the seat in front of her.

Rudy was working his gum into a saliva-filled lather. "She understands the concept here, right? You show up as an upstanding member of the community, your responsible wife and your pretty daughter at your side, judge is gonna look at you with a little more lenience than if your wife cares enough about you to go ahead and get sick the morning you're being sentenced for obstruction of justice."

Her father flipped down the visor mirror so he could see his daughter. "Evelyn, why don't you see if you can get her down here? Just go up to the room and see—"

Rudy chawed. "Yeah, hon, why don't you go up there and tell that mother of yours she'd better get down here, oh, five minutes ago? This car is going to leave and she had best be in it."

Evelyn turned to look at Rudy, spittle clinging to his lips, and then to her father. She took a breath. "Driver, you know where we're going, don't you?" The man looked in the rearview mirror and grunted. "Great. We'd better get going. Dad, are you ready? Rudy, if you're going in this car, I suggest you get in."

"Listen, sweetheart—" Rudy said.

"Evelyn. That's my name. Not 'sweetheart.' I'm not going back up there, all right? Don't you think I had this conversation with her already? If you want to go up there and slam the door and plead and cry and make a scene in the Friendship Inn hallway, go ahead. But I won't do it, and I think we'd better go. It's better to have his daughter there with him than just you. Right? Rudy?"

"Fuck!" Rudy shouted to the universe, then, a minute later, opened the back door and plopped down next to Evelyn.

The courthouse's exterior, to its credit, promised nothing. It looked more like a prison than anything, square, drab, from an era of Soviet-inspired cinder-block architecture. Rudy led Evelyn and Dale through the metal detectors and to a courtroom where the benches were already populated, some of the people, obviously reporters, holding notepads. The hearing started right on time, with the prosecutor and Rudy arguing over the sentencing-guideline calculations, then about $9 million in restitution, which was a whole lot more than Evelyn had thought her father would owe. Then the judge asked if Dale had anything to say.

He did. The back of Dale's neck was stretched long, his head seeming heavy. Then Dale stood up a little straighter. "Judge Nakamura, my respected colleagues in the legal profession, I just wanted to tell you all that I have thought seriously about what I did, and really faced some of my demons here, and I take full responsibility for it. I understand that it was wrong in the eyes of the law, however right I may have thought it was at the time, and however much I thought it helped my clients. I was always working for my clients, and I always believed I was doing right by them. Nevertheless, when the law tells you you're wrong, you'd better listen."

He sat, and the judge looked up at the room. The sentencing guidelines in this case were fifteen to twenty-one months, the judge said, and those guidelines were suggested but not mandatory. He had taken into account all of the factors, he said, including Dale Beegan's strong community support, his family, and his long work record that suggested this was an aberrance in behavior.

Evelyn saw the back of her father's head nodding. That was good; he always said he could read a judge better than anyone. Please, she thought, trying to send a message to the judge. Please. Probation with no prison time. Please.

The judge coughed, almost bronchial. However, given the state of Delaware and the current administration's stance on what was and was not proper conduct among lawyers, and the egregious nature of the scheme outlined by prosecutors, the judge said, it was important to send a message that the blind pursuit of money cannot be tolerated. Dale Beegan was hereby sentenced to twenty-nine months.

The courtroom blurred around Evelyn's father, who twisted his head to look at her. It was a look she'd seen only once in her life, when a blind man had been crossing the street and a semitruck driver laid on the horn and the man turned, terrified, his hands up, shaking, thinking these were the final moments of his life and he couldn't even see what was coming.

People were getting up now, the hearing over. Twenty-nine months? Almost double the suggested minimum sentence? Sending a message about the blind pursuit of money? Her father had messed up, but why were the consequences so severe for him? Companies were offering bribes to expand faster internationally, investors were scamming their clients, manufacturers were skirting environmental regulations, all to make ever more money, yet no one from those groups was in court. No one from there was going to prison.

Her father started to shuffle forward, and Evelyn thought of the boy with the flattop haircut who just wanted to show all those rich kids that they didn't run the world.

Rudy was opening the gate into the spectators' section to lead her father out, and Evelyn stumbled to her feet. "I'll handle this," she said.

"There's press outside. You don't know how to handle it," Rudy said.

"I do know how to handle it," Evelyn said. She pulled her father to the side; he was staring at the ground. She waited until the crowds had dispersed, then took the elevator down with him. Outside, she could see a few photographers gathered.

"I don't know . . . ," Dale began, but he was too stunned to finish.

Evelyn took his elbow. "We'll just head straight to the car, okay, Dad? You don't have to say anything. Just look straight ahead. I know photographers. Just follow my lead. We'll get through this."

She pushed open the courthouse door, passed the photographers clicking and running after them, and kept her eyes locked straight ahead as she escorted him to the car. As she opened the door for her father, he looked at her and said, his eyes still wide and frightened, "Thank you."

CHAPTER THIRTY-ONE

Self-Surrender

Dale's self-surrender date was December 19, and despite Rudy's pleas to push it back after the holidays, the Bureau of Prisons wouldn't budge. Before he left, Dale told Evelyn that he'd settled with her rental company; she'd forgotten he'd been the guarantor on her lease. When she'd said that she had a job and should handle it herself, he gave her the Bedazzler, which she hadn't seen in months. "Couldn't resist one last settlement," he said.

On December 19, Barbara walked out to the living-dining room with a cup of tea, wearing a St. John suit that Evelyn hadn't seen since Sag Neck and didn't think her mother had brought to the Marina Air.

"Your father's coming at ten?"

"Yeah. I think it's about a three-hour drive and he wanted to leave some time in case we got lost. I guess you don't want to be late reporting for prison," Evelyn said.

"What are they going to do if you're late? Send you to prison?" Barbara said, and laughed, a strange, sharp sound that Evelyn hadn't heard in a long time.

"Mom!" Evelyn said, giggling despite herself.

Dale rang the doorbell that morning, an uncommonly warm morning for a Bibville December, looking like he was about to go golfing, in a light khaki jacket, pink polo shirt, khaki pants, and tennis shoes. He was missing his usual alligator belt; Evelyn wondered whether that was the sort of thing that prison guards would take from one's belongings and sell.

"Hi, Daddy. You look nice." Evelyn wasn't quite sure what she was supposed to say, but the corners of his eyes crinkled a little bit.

"Thank you, honey. And thank you for driving me. I'll be the envy of all the fellows at prison with such a pretty chauffeur." The pads of fat that used to give him a chubby-cheeked grin were gone. He looked past her to her mother. "Barbara, hello."

Barbara's teacup was in front of her, but she hadn't had a sip. "Dale," she said, her voice trembling.

Evelyn waited a minute, then jangled the keys, trying to add merriment. "So, are you ready?" she said to her father.

"I just want to say good-bye to your mother," he said.

Barbara stood up quickly, nearly knocking over her cup. "I think I'll go with you," she said. "What are you both looking at me like that for? It's a nice day for a drive."

The parking lot at that hour was filled with people doing their daily exurban tasks: a woman lifted several huge plastic Lowe's bags with shelving poking from them out of the back of her SUV, and another screamed at her child that she was in charge of him and not the other way around. As Barbara and Dale walked toward the car, they looked like dolls of a different scale, her mother plumping out as her father caved in.

In the car, Evelyn put on a Hank Williams CD, one of her father's favorites. To her surprise, as she backed out of the Marina Air lot, she heard her mother's deep voice from the back, singing along to "Jambalaya."

"Mom? You're a secret Hank Williams fan?" she said.

"I've always hated my singing voice. It's flat," Barbara said.

Hank had moved on to "Half As Much," and the washed-out winter colors on the side of the road whizzed by.

"I'll get everything back," Dale said suddenly. "I have a plan. Once I'm out. I know I can't practice law anymore, but there's a whole list of things I'm planning on. I can't technically be a lawyer, but I can still be one heck of a consultant. I'm going to put both of you right back in Sag Neck."

"Dad." Evelyn looked at her father, who was staring out the side window. "You don't need to get it all back. It might not even be possible."

"It's always possible."

Evelyn looked at the road. She knew that wasn't true. A person can't re-create an old life with everything and everyone he once had. People react and interact, develop, and the puzzle pieces change shape and no longer fit together with a satisfying snap.

"Barbara," Dale said. "Will you be all right?"

She heard a click of a soda can opening from the backseat, and saw that her mother was now enjoying a Tab. "Vending machine," Barbara said by way of an answer. "I never supposed I would live somewhere with a vending machine, but it's rather useful, having a cold soda available at all hours. I've stopped making my own ice, in fact."

"Is that right?" Dale said.

"There's an ice machine right at the end of the hallway. It's all the ice you could ever want and I don't have to do a thing."

Evelyn glanced at her father, who had a little smile starting, then caught her mother's eye in the rearview mirror and gave her a respectful nod.

"And you, Evie? Are you going to be all right? You're not missing New York too badly?" Dale asked.

Evelyn watched the lane paint markers at the side of the car, thinking about how to answer that question. She owed so much on all of her credit cards. The Caffeiteria was a good step, and at least she was earning something, but her debt was so massive, always hovering gray around the edges of whatever else she was doing, that it wouldn't be enough. She could work there for years and still have bills looming.

She had been waiting, she thought. Always waiting. In New York, waiting for her life to be replaced by some other, more interesting life on offer. Waiting for money that she felt ought to be hers to flood in and elevate her position, from some male source, her father, Scot, Jaime. Waiting to be recognized and accepted in the social scene, starring on Appointment Book. When she thought about it, she had always imagined her future self in pictures with her face on others' bodies, in others' dresses, at others' parties, in others' poses. Now, back home, she had been biding time, waiting for some sign about what her life's goal ought to be. Maybe it didn't work like that. Maybe you had to change things step-by-step.

The fact that New York still existed was puzzling. It was disconnected from her present, this car and the prison drop-off. It was far from her feet, which tingled after standing all day, and her hair, which smelled like coffee even after multiple shampoos, and the tug of the espresso-machine filter handle, the turn of the frother dial, the cool splash of white milk against the metal cup. In Bibville, she looked different enough from how she had as a kid that old classmates didn't seem to recognize her, and her mother's former friends would order skim lattes and scuttle away, embarrassed for Barbara or her or themselves, she couldn't tell. Her twenty-eighth birthday was not too many months away, and she was living at home, working at a coffee shop, with a father who would be an inmate in a matter of hours and a mother who was not highly equipped for real life, and she was deep in debt. This was not the best set of facts, but as she put her foot on the gas, they just seemed like facts. No more, no less.

"Yeah," Evelyn said. "Yeah, I'm going to be all right."

When they pulled into the prison parking lot three hours later, Evelyn looked for reasons that it wouldn't be so bad. There was grass, and there were different brick buildings like at Sheffield, and the group of men in olive-green jumpsuits waiting to get on a truck were at least chatting with one another. Evelyn turned off the car's engine, and after they got out of the car she and Barbara gathered next to Dale. Evelyn looked around, wondering if a guard would come retrieve him.

"Do we go in with you?" Evelyn said.

"I don't want you to, honey. I have to go register with the officer and it'll take a while. I'll see you soon, okay?"

"I'll take your jacket," Barbara said. "I don't trust the federal system to get anything right, and they're certainly not going to lose a perfectly good jacket if I can help it. What about your ring?"

"My prison consultant said it's technically allowed."

"Those men inside will be melting it for money in a matter of seconds. I'll hold on to it for you," Barbara said.

Dale twisted his wedding ring off, and handed it to Barbara with a questioning look in his eye. Evelyn watched as her mother folded her fingers around the ring, then grasped Dale's hand and squeezed it tight. Dale let his head fall on her shoulder. Evelyn stepped a few paces back, behind the trunk, to give them some space.

She heard them murmuring, and a few minutes later, her father cleared his throat. "Evie?"

"Yeah." She joined them again.

"It's time to go."

She stepped forward and hugged him. "I should've asked: Are *you* going to be all right?"

"Dang straight," he said. He winked, and kissed a startled Barbara, then he was gone, inside a trailer on the prison grounds.

That evening, back in Bibville, Evelyn headed to the Regis Library, which was quiet, the computer kiosks empty. She sat down in front of one and Googled "Debt counseling Maryland or Delaware." Three days later, she was leaving an office in Wilmington with two strict budgets and a negotiated payment plan with her credit-card companies. One budget, for now, included a mandate to either increase her hours at the Caffeiteria or get a second job; she knew the Hub, the beer-and-burger place, needed a waitress. The other plan was for when she was, God willing, not living at her mother's apartment in Bibville and had a better-paying full-time job and was actually covering her own rent somewhere, albeit rent at the laughable level of $700 a month, which would translate into a fold-out couch somewhere in Queens. She was starting now on paying off the bills, some up front, some in steady monthly chunks over the coming years, a slow cleanup of the mess she had made.

CHAPTER THIRTY-TWO

On the Dock

Barbara pushed through the door holding bags from the Food Lion in Easton. Barbara had discovered Juicy Couture sweatsuits as of late and was wearing a peach velour hoodie and sweats, for apparently elastic waistbands were the one upside of being ousted from society.

The doorbell rang long and loud, surprising Evelyn. It was her day off, and she was still wearing pajamas though it was late in the afternoon, watching as Dorothy dissed Rose to Blanche. She couldn't remember the last time she had heard the apartment's doorbell. "Evelyn, will you see who's at the door?" her mother called from the kitchen.

Evelyn opened the door slightly, ready to shoo away the Jehovah's Witness or whoever it was, but there was a burp of cold air and she felt someone on the other side pushing against her. Through the crack of the door, the top of a head with messy light-brown hair appeared, and—

"Jesus Christ," said Charlotte, shoving open the door. "You're actually here."

Evelyn's left lip curled up in a smile. "Yes."

"What the fuck, Ev?" Charlotte lifted a hand as if to hit her. "Is that the *Golden Girls* theme song?"

"That's your first question?"

"No. No. Sorry. I was in Annapolis for work, and I thought—I didn't know where you went. I had no idea where you went, Evelyn."

Evelyn wrapped her arms around herself. "Did it matter?"

"Well, yes. Your cell phone was disconnected, your Bibville land-line didn't work, your apartment was emptied. What did you think I'd think? Bad shit happens to girls in New York and I was worried."

"Bad shit did happen to a girl in New York. How did you find me?"

"Alumni office. They once called me at a hotel in Dallas where I was working on a company integration, so it's really no surprise they found you at a fixed address. Meanwhile, didn't you think of men-tioning to your old friend that you were packing up and leaving the city?"

Evelyn moved to give Charlotte a hug, but Charlotte shrank back. "We didn't hug at graduation, we aren't going to hug now. I will bite you. With my sharp little canine teeth. My bladder is about to ex-plode; there are seemingly no bathrooms between Annapolis and Bib-ville. Can I pee?"

"Evelyn, dear! Who's at the door?" she heard from her mother's bedroom—her mother must have slunk in there when Evelyn an-swered the door—then a crash as her mother rounded the corner too fast. Evelyn turned her head to see her mother, resplendent in a caf-tan and a hair turban, looking like Elizabeth Taylor after one of her fat-camp sessions.

"Mom, can you give me a minute?"

Barbara apparently could not, and had not dressed for company for nothing. She peered over Evelyn, smelling of the vintage Babs leather perfume. "My goodness, Charlotte! What a delight. It was so nice of you to come all this way to see Evie. I quite like your hair out of those pigtails." She affixed her great claw, manicured, somehow not chipped despite the reality that she now did dishes and cleaning, to the door and pulled it open wide so Charlotte could enter.

Evelyn stayed where she was, her eyes flicking over Charlotte's as Charlotte took in the scene. For Charlotte, who had been to Sag Neck for several long weekends and Thanksgivings, it must have been like a game of Memory, Evelyn thought. Match the overstuffed couch wedged under the blinds to the one that sat in the piano room at Sag Neck. Find, in the stack of paintings piled against one wall, the one of a foxhunt that hung in the Sag Neck foyer.

Charlotte was standing uncertainly on the doorstep, her earlier bounty-hunting fire tempered.

"Mom," Evelyn said, more firmly. "I need to talk to Charlotte alone."

"I won't hear of it, after the long drive she must have had," Barbara said a bit too chirpily. "Charlotte, you'll have to forgive my daughter. I think she's lost her sense of propriety since leaving New York. Come in. Evelyn, will you get some cheese?"

Evelyn raised her free hand to smooth her eyebrows. "Some cheese," she repeated. "Sure. Let's see. We have some pepper jack, I think. Can I get you a slice?"

"I don't really need cheese," said Charlotte, pulling her blazer closer to her body.

"No. I'm sorry. It's cold. Come in. The bathroom's just down the hall, on your left."

Inside, Barbara was whirling around, straightening up stacks of magazines and removing items from the refrigerator. "We're just loving living downtown. It's a little more exciting than the old house, which had just gotten way too big to manage," she said as Charlotte passed her. "Can you imagine, being alone in that house at night? It was really frightening. I just hated going downstairs." Barbara placed a small stack of cocktail napkins monogrammed with BTB and— were those Cheez-Its?—on a tray that Evelyn hadn't been aware had made the journey from Sag Neck.

When Charlotte came back, Barbara set the tray in front of her. "I've found these delicious little cheese nibblies," Barbara said. "I'm sure they're loaded with calories, and we'll all have to do our penance at the gym, but since it's just a girls' outing, why not?"

Charlotte dutifully took two Cheez-Its and a napkin. "Mmm."

"It's so lovely to see Evie's old friends," Barbara said, smoothing her turban. "Just lovely, really. Charlotte, can I get you something to drink? We have some white wine, or I could look in the cocktail cabinet to see what I might put together."

"I think—Char, just give me two seconds to change, all right?" Evelyn said.

"Do you know, I'd just been thinking about Sheffield," Barbara began as Evelyn hurried to her room and threw on jeans and a sweatshirt. As she returned to the living room, Charlotte shot her an alarmed look; Barbara was saying ". . . and she won't talk to me about it, of course, but it seems like if Evie were just to extend an invitation to Camilla . . ."

Evelyn took a Cheez-It and hauled Charlotte from the couch. "We're going downtown!" Evelyn said, as Charlotte said, "Thank you for the snacks, Mrs. Beegan!"

Charlotte and Evelyn were silent for the first part of the walk, passing the bare-branch trees in the park, the closed-for-winter-outdoor-patio Thai place, and the small brick town hall, but as they passed the bank, Charlotte spoke. "So you've been—"

"Here. Yes. In a tiny apartment. With my mother."

"Roommates with the Babs. Jesus. Your dad?"

"Twenty-nine months."

"That's crazy," Charlotte said. "Do you think he did it?"

"I don't think the federal government brings cases that are made up," Evelyn said. "But twenty-nine months? What he did is hardly worse than what guys on Wall Street are doing daily. In the scheme of things, I don't know if he deserved what he got."

Charlotte kicked a stone. "I read he got a really good prison."

"Petersburg. His second choice."

"Is it like college? Where you have safeties and reaches?"

"I wouldn't be surprised. Did you know there's a whole prison-consultancy business? My father hired some ex-con to tell him about how to behave in the clink."

"For one, you probably don't call it the clink."

"Seriously. Don't cut in the lunch line seemed to be the main thing. It was interesting." Evelyn looked at the gray bay before her and thought that she would have liked a similar consultant to guide her through New York life. Don't try to upstage the alpha female; that was probably a rule that held both in New York and in prison.

Charlotte applied some Vaseline to her lips. "It's still impossible to see your father in, what, orange scrubs? Is that what they wear? Do you think they let him bring his pomade in?"

"He doesn't use pomade."

"I'm sorry, Evelyn, but it's time you knew the truth. That hair doesn't just happen. There is serious product involved." Charlotte swiveled her head to look at the HOT COFFEE sign on the ice-cream parlor. "Can we stop? I'm dying for caffeine."

"I can get you caffeine, but we're not going here," Evelyn said. "You'll be pleased to learn that I get an employee discount at the best coffee place in town." She cast it as a joke, unsure what Charlotte's reaction would be.

"You? You're working at a coffee place?" Charlotte squinted. "For real?"

"Yep. And in the evenings I'm a waitress at the Hub. You want beer and burgers, talk to me."

"Evelyn Beegan, a barista-slash-waitress?"

"Char, they're jobs, okay?"

"No," Charlotte said. "No. I actually think it's good."

"You're lying."

"I'm not. I think it's really good. You're working, for one. That's a good step, seriously."

It started to drizzle as they passed the Ioka, advertising *Knocked Up*, coming to Bibville months after it had been released elsewhere. The Caffeiteria's outside light shone yellow on the wharf, where the gray-blue sky now matched the water. Inside, the afternoon guy was wiping the counters and slipped Evelyn two free day-old almond croissants along with the girls' coffee. The rain was still just pleasantly speckling the ground, and Evelyn and Charlotte sat outside on one of the benches overlooking the winter harbor.

Evelyn tore off a corner of her croissant and wondered if she should bother trying to sound casual. "So how is everyone?"

Charlotte put her croissant in her lap. "That's one of the reasons I wanted to see you. Pres is in rehab, Ev."

"No." Evelyn had been bracing for gossip that made her feel left out, not severe life changes among her best friends; she had been hoping that Preston was doing just fine. Evelyn put her head in her hands. "The last time I saw him, Char, at Sachem," she said, looking at a piece of popcorn underneath the bench, "I told him everyone knew he was gay."

"Evelyn."

"I know. I know. I was drunk, which isn't an excuse, but he just, he just turned away and then ran down the steps and that was the last time I saw him or talked to him."

"God, Ev. What made you say that?"

"I think I hated it that he was calling me fake, and I felt like he was being so fake about this really core thing. I've thought about it a thousand times. If I could take it back, or handle it differently, believe me, I would. It couldn't have helped with his drinking."

"Oh, Ev."

"I had a scorched-earth policy when I left, I guess. When did Pres go in?"

"A month ago. He smashed into a tree when he was driving to Boston. I talked to him about it before he clammed up about the whole thing, and he'd swerved because he thought he saw a dog dash in front of his car. I'm not sure he really did—it was past midnight and a dog probably wasn't out then—but he kept saying the dog looked like Hamilton. He got a DUI, but the idea that he could've hit a dog when he was drunk, I think that's what made him check in and stay in."

"Oh, God, Char. That's so scary. He wasn't hurt himself? With the tree?"

"Bruised up, but air bags and seat belt. He paid for the tree's restoration, actually. It was some kind of prized elm."

"Char, I should've tried harder. After that scene at Sachem, I should've apologized, or knocked on his door, or done something. I just felt like he didn't want to see me—I'm sure he *didn't* want to see me—and then everything imploded. Pres. Jesus. Is anyone there with him? His parents?"

"They don't allow visitors during the first several weeks but I'm sure they check in on him."

"Has Nick called him? Camilla? Were they in touch with him during the accident and all that?"

"I don't think so."

"God. It's like a pack of hyenas. They don't have use for the weak. Have you gone up to see him?"

"No, it's still the no-visitors period. Even once he can have visitors, the best I can swing is one afternoon. Things are insane at Graystone. My boss is convinced the market's going to tank soon—the underlying economics right now are a disaster—so we're trying to wrap up a bunch of acquisitions. I'm only here, in Bibville, because I had to meet with a toy company in Annapolis this morning and don't have to be back in the city until tonight. And Preston needs, I don't know. Needs someone, something more. An afternoon of me dropping in for coffee isn't going to help that much. I'm still going to go up when I can, but I feel like he needs a real friend there. And you know Pres. He's never going to ask for help. I only know he's in rehab because he wasn't responding to my e-mails or calls after he told me about the accident, and finally I lost it—the island of the disappearing friends—and called Mrs. Hacking, and she gave me his number at this facility. It's some swanky place in Marblehead. I swear I wouldn't have known that it was a rehab place except Mrs. Hacking gave me the number for the main line, and the receptionist answered it, 'Seaview House, offering specialized addiction treatment since 1987, how can I help you?'"

"Since 1987, huh?" Evelyn kicked Charlotte's leg.

"I have a really specific memory. I remember thinking it must've started because all the traders were drinking themselves to death up there then. Plus ça change, plus c'est la même chose."

"Vraiment." Evelyn smiled sadly. "How long's he there for?"

"I think another month or so inpatient, then there's some extended outpatient treatment. I wish you two hadn't had your breakdowns simultaneously."

Evelyn lifted her head. "I'm sorry."

"Eh." Charlotte shrugged. "I moved to Brooklyn in September. How's that for change?"

"To get away from my haunting memory?"

Charlotte laughed. "Sort of, actually. Manhattan was getting ridiculous. *Sex and the City* tour buses overtaking Bleecker and condos left and right. Poor Jane Jacobs. Brooklyn's great. Lots of creative types. Do you want the updates on the rest of your crew?"

Evelyn took a deep breath. "Hit me."

"Nick and Scot's hedge fund is alive and well. Nick's greasing the palms for money, Scot's doing all the work. They're betting against subprime CDOs."

"Nick is betting against Wall Street?"

Charlotte laughed. "If it makes him money, right? I saw the prospectus. Nick has access to all these rich kids with money to throw around, and then Scot is doing the actual work. I've got to say, it seems like Scot got in at just the right time. Alan Greenspan said last month he thought housing was actually a bubble. I think it's going to make them a ton."

"Doesn't it ever stop?"

"On Wall Street? Not until it does, right? Anyway, if there is a crash, Scot and Nick are positioned to kill it."

Evelyn flicked a bit of crust out into the water of the bay. "Is he dating anyone?"

"Scot? Yeah, Nick set him up with this girl Geordie. She went to Princeton, a few years younger than us. She works in publishing. I think it's pretty serious."

"She's nice to him?"

Charlotte nodded. That hurt particularly badly; Evelyn did want Scot to be happy, and she knew they weren't right together, but she still missed him. After all her misplaced bets, it was Scot who was going to be a big winner, after all.

"What about Camilla?" Evelyn asked quietly. She still occasionally gave in to the impulse to Google Camilla and saw that there had been new additions to Camilla's social roster. She was dating someone from the Vanity Fair 100, a list of tech and media types, the founder of a voice-recognition start-up that Yahoo was rumored to be acquiring for a few hundred million.

"I see her here and there. She's gotten really into a couple of arts organizations, one with glass-blowing or something, and another with graffiti artists. It's pretty funny, actually. She's at downtown parties constantly now, and the last time I saw her she was saying she was going to move to the Meatpacking District."

Evelyn bit an almond sliver in half. They had all moved on so quickly, after she had done so much work to care about and get to know the first—and what she thought was the ultimate—elite circle. Charlotte was describing a Camilla-hosted party on the Soho House rooftop for the emerging artist Tayeb Idrissi, who took posts from something called Twitter and made them into word maps. As Charlotte began detailing Tayeb's installation at Storm King, Evelyn felt the almond's ragged edge against her tongue and felt, suddenly, that she couldn't hear it anymore.

"You know what, Char? Sorry. I know I asked, but I don't want to know. It doesn't matter. If it's not Tayeb whoever, it'll be something else, and someone else, and I'd always be playing catch-up. I was always playing catch-up."

Charlotte tipped her head back and closed her eyes for a moment. When she opened them, she asked, "What were you doing, Ev?"

"In New York?"

"In New York. You became sort of a bitch."

"Tell it like it is, Char." Evelyn flexed her toes.

"I'm sorry, but it's kind of true."

"With Camilla and everything, you mean? I guess it was that scene we were in—"

"I wasn't really in it, Ev. That was all you."

"Okay, fine. The scene I was in. It was just so much. The money it took. The competition over the invitations. The parties." Evelyn ran her hands over the wooden bench, grasping for how to explain this to Charlotte, who wasn't fazed by this stuff. "It sounds ridiculous, saying it out loud, because it's just parties, but it mattered to me." She was starting to sniffle, and wiped her nose and looked in some horror at the trail it left on her sleeve, then laughed. "New York made me crazy. I was just trying to make it."

"You were trying to make it in Edith Wharton's New York, Ev. That barely exists anymore. Look at the *Times* wedding announcements. It's 'She works at McKinsey and he's an economics professor.' It's all merit based."

"It is not, Char. I know the *Times* wedding announcements, trust me. It's all 'He's a director at Goldman and she's studying early childhood development at Bank Street School of Education and her father ran asset management at blabbity-blah, and they just bought a house in Cos Cob.'"

"Okay. There are a lot of bankers in there, but society isn't that closed anymore."

"Isn't it? Go to a deb ball and tell me that."

"Other people are throwing open the doors. The entrepreneurs and the artists and the whatnot—no, you laugh, but they make old money interesting. Why do you think Camilla's all of a sudden becoming a patron of the arts?"

Evelyn shook her head slightly.

"You wanted so badly to get in, when you should have been trying to get out," Charlotte said.

Evelyn cast her arm forward, sending the last bit of the croissant into the water, and it plopped with a satisfying splash into the bay. A lone Canada goose quickly honked over, gobbled it up, and flew off. Finally, Evelyn said, "Get out to where?"

"I don't know, exactly. That whole Upper East Side life, though— it isn't the only version of life in New York. In Brooklyn, there are all sorts of interesting people, the kind that New York used to have, writers, and graphic designers, and beer makers. . . ."

"Beer makers?" The raindrops were starting to fatten.

"Ev, I think . . ." Charlotte looked at the water, searching for the words. "What you were trying to be, wasn't that all about your mother?"

Evelyn looked down at her feet, taking time to put together her response. "Without my mother to report to, without her ideas of it, I'm not sure it would have been quite as appealing, yeah. But it was me, Char. It wasn't her up there attending debutante parties and going to benefits and stealing bracelets."

Charlotte pulled down her lower lip. "You stole a bracelet?"

"You don't know the half of it."

"I guess not."

"We don't even go to Cichetti's anymore, the grocery store on Main, because my mother is convinced that our fall from grace has tainted the neighbors' opinion of us so. She doesn't even see her old friends." Evelyn looked out across the gray water, which was starting to splash up against the dock.

"What is the plan now, Ev?"

"What, my *Gilmore Girls* setup with my mom isn't appealing?"

"I'm serious. You're young, you're pretty, you have money—"

"No. I mean, first of all, twenty-seven isn't exactly ingenue age. But money I do not have. My parents had to pay off the mortgage on the house, and the proceeds from the house sale are tied up in the settlement with Leiberg Channing, and there was a nine-million-dollar restitution to the government plus the legal fees. My mother still finds it uncouth to talk about money, so, trust me, I've tried to figure it out, but I don't think there's any money, at least not judging from the way she's barely spending it. I'm on my own."

"Wow. Well, at least you were down here to help out with the sentencing and all that."

"I should've been down here more. Helping them pack up, and hanging out with my dad, but everything in New York was such a mess and it seemed like if I could just get a little more time there—"

Her voice broke, and she felt tears coming, and as she started to blink them back reflexively, she wondered why. So she allowed them to roll, hot relief down her cheeks.

"Hey. Hey." Charlotte threw an arm around her. "You're still here, kid."

"I'm in Bibville," Evelyn said as she took a big, snotty inhale.

Charlotte squeezed Evelyn's shoulder. "Why wouldn't you say anything? About your dad, I mean? I tried to talk to you about it, and you were so, I don't know. Like it wasn't happening."

Evelyn looked at her friend, Charlotte's hair frizzing in the mist. "What could I have said, Char? I thought maybe no one knew or put two and two together. What good would it have done, really, talking about it?"

"Well, you might have fought a little harder to keep your job. And talking can lead to deeper connections. So my therapist said."

"Don't tell the WASPs," Evelyn said.

The raindrops started to spatter on the dock as Evelyn thought about the New York she had left behind, and the new New York that Charlotte, Camilla, and the others were discovering. She rose, and extended her hand. "Come on, Char. You're getting soaked. You're not used to the rains of the Bib. We'll get you a shower and a delightful Barbara Beegan monogrammed towel, and we'll have dinner at the Hub before you have to drive back. I'm rolling in money from tips and can afford extra garlic toast."

"I would not say no to extra garlic toast," Charlotte said, pulling her blazer tight. "Vámanos."

CHAPTER THIRTY-THREE

Northeast Regional

The train jolted Evelyn awake as it pulled past Trenton. She looked out the window for the passive-aggressive TRENTON MAKES, THE WORLD TAKES sign, but she had missed it this time. She had with her just a cheap red rolling suitcase, given to her as a going-away present from the people at the Caffeiteria. She was going back to Bibville the weekend after next, for another trip to Petersburg with her mother; she had promised to track down the e-mail address of a personal-finance guru whom Dale wanted to arrange prison seminars with.

About two months after Charlotte's visit, Evelyn told her mother she was leaving. Her library-computer excursions had turned up the addresses of several well-reviewed coffee places and restaurants in New York that might be hiring, and some Craigslist roommate-wanted postings that she could actually afford with a job like that. Preston's old cell-phone number didn't work anymore, and though she'd swallowed her pride and called Mrs. Hacking a few times, she'd gotten their answering machine and had just left messages that this was Evelyn and she hoped Mrs. Hacking would tell Preston she was thinking of him.

After being very cross on the drive to the train station and saying that she didn't have all day to chauffeur people around, Barbara had actually teared up when the train arrived. She patted Evelyn on the head and said that it had been wonderful having her little girl at home, that she didn't know what she would do without her.

"You know what? How many women, at your age, get a chance to start over? You're a free woman, for a little while at least," Evelyn said.

Barbara had pursed her lips, then smiled. "Perhaps," she said. She patted Evelyn on the head again.

"I'm just a train ride away if you need anything."

"Your friends will be happy to see you again, Camilla," Barbara said with a lifted eyebrow. Evelyn had been telling her gently, then insistently, that the friendship with Camilla was a thing of the past, but Barbara seemed to have decided not to hear it.

"Charlotte," Evelyn said pointedly. "Not so much Camilla."

"You shouldn't just give up friendships so easily, Evelyn."

Evelyn tilted her head, looking at the sun peeking out from behind the platform's railing. "Mom?" Evelyn said. "You have to let me make these decisions, okay?"

"Don't be condescending."

"I'm not, Mom. It's just my call now. Okay?"

Barbara looked around, as if she were going to see something that would change her daughter's mind, but she eventually looked back at Evelyn. "If that's what you wish."

Evelyn's rueful smile turned into a laugh. "That is what I wish, Mom. I'm going to hug you now, all right?"

"As if I would object to a hug?"

"Okay." Evelyn leaned in for a hug; her mother's breath felt warm on her cheek, and both of them pulled away quickly, patting each other's arms.

"Safe travels."

"'Bye, Mom."

"Good-bye, sweetheart."

Evelyn had been surprised to see that her mother waited on the platform once the train arrived, despite the chill, and raised a gloved hand in a farewell wave. Evelyn waved back from the inside of the smeared window.

The train scooted toward Manhattan. Evelyn had planned to crash at Charlotte's place in Brooklyn—Charlotte was visiting some textile factory in Georgia—for a few days while she checked out Craigslist apartment shares and hit the streets. Google said Brooklyn Heights had several good coffee shops, and while she pulled double shifts, she could look for a longer-term job, something in magazines, maybe, or e-commerce. As long as she earned $31,000 a year, and spent it on little besides rent and groceries, Evelyn could stick to the payment schedule she'd made with her credit counselor.

When the train pulled into Penn Station, Evelyn got out quickly but then stood on the dark platform as people pushed by her and up the stairs to the station. Brooklyn. Cheese makers and beer designers, or whatever Charlotte had said. The same song in a different key; her trying to create a life that other people had deemed worthwhile, Evelyn fighting to prove herself once again.

People were rushing off the train around Evelyn, who expected someone to ask her what she was doing here, or where she was headed, or what her plans were. Instead they barreled by, one hitting her with his backpack, another with his briefcase, and she realized she was now the irritating out-of-towner interrupting traffic flow. She started moving, dragging her bag up the stairs. As she reached the crammed waiting room, she read the Amtrak board. Adirondack, Carolinian, Crescent, Northeast Regional. Departing tracks 7E, 12W, 14W, 9W. An arrangement of travel brochures was displayed underneath the board, and she recognized the brochure sticking out of the top: *Boston—the City on a Hill.* The same quiet-looking city, the same pretty lights, that she had considered when she was waiting for Camilla in her final visit to Lake James. The same place where she had once been a good friend to Charlotte, to Preston. What was it that station attendant in his USS cap had said? Sometimes it's good to take a train somewhere else?

She pulled a brochure from the stand and, with a yank on her bag's handle, ran through a side door and along the hallway, her Tretorn soles squeaking as she veered around the corner to the Amtrak ticket counter. There was no line, and the clerk, a small woman with short gray hair so vertical and curled it looked like it had been through a fire followed by a washing-machine cycle, asked, "Where are you going?"

Evelyn held up the brochure. "Boston."

"Business or pleasure?" the woman asked.

"I guess both." She unzipped her money-belt thingy with her other hand. Her cash was stored in there, and she felt absurd wearing it, but she also wasn't about to get her Caffeiteria and Hub money stolen due to pride.

"Nice town, Boston."

"If you can make it there . . . ," Evelyn said, but the clerk didn't get the joke. "They do a lot of out-of-town tryouts for musicals there. People can get their footing," she explained.

"You an actress?"

"No. No. I'm not. I . . ." She pulled some twenty-dollar bills from her money belt, then looked up with her eyes bright. "I can work in theater, though. I mean, not onstage, but take tickets for Harvard musicals. I don't know. Sell ads for programs. Maybe stage-manage someday. Along with working in a coffee shop. But mostly I'm going to see my old friend."

The clerk shrugged. "One-way or round-trip?"

"One-way. Just one-way."

The woman handed over the ticket. "Boarding now. Better hurry. Northeast Regional. Track nine west."

Evelyn pulled her bag back through the Amtrak waiting room, flipping open her phone and trying to call 781-555-1212 as she ran, and pressing connect over and over again with no luck until she got to the bottom of a staircase that led up to Eighth Avenue, close enough to the exterior that she had a bar of coverage. "Hi, I need a listing for Marblehead. Seaview House. Yes, please connect me," she said. The phone rang twice, and someone on the other end picked up. "Hello,

Seaview House, offering specialized addiction treatment since 1987, how can I help you?" said the woman's voice.

Evelyn started laughing. "Was 1987 because of all the traders?" she said. "A friend told me that."

"I'm sorry?" the voice said.

"I'm trying to reach Preston Hacking. He was a patient there for a while and I think he's out now, but I need to get a message through to him," Evelyn said.

"One moment, please," the receptionist said. Evelyn checked out the "Boarding" status for her train and tapped her foot.

"I can't give out his number, but you're welcome to leave a message," the receptionist said.

"Thank you," Evelyn said. "Tell him that it's Evelyn, and I'm sorry for being out of touch for so long, and I'm sorry about everything, but I'm coming to Boston and I'm coming to see him. I don't know where I'm staying, or what I'm doing, but I'll figure it out, and I'll be there tonight, if I can see him. If I can help him. Even if I can't help him, I'll be there. That's it. I'll see him soon."

With her other hand, she pushed in the backing of her pearl earring so hard that she could feel the blood pulsing in her ears, and felt the comfortable discomfort of the even beats.

"Evelyn," the receptionist said kindly. "Very good. I'll pass on the message."

Evelyn gave the woman her phone number, then ended the call.

"Northeast Regional, please proceed immediately to the platform for boarding. Northeast Regional," said a loudspeaker overhead.

Glancing up the stairs to Eighth, Evelyn pressed the number now at the top of her favorites list and willed the other end to pick up.

"Hello?"

"Char?"

"Ev? You sound like you're in a cavern."

"Close. I'm in Penn Station."

"You made it to New York?"

"I did—I was going to—but then I realized—I'm going to Boston.

The train's about to leave. I'm going to go see Pres and drag him out of his solitude and try to be a friend. You can't do it, but I've got the time. Of course I should be the one to go."

"Northeast Regional," the loudspeaker said again, and Evelyn jiggled one foot.

"Charlotte?" she said.

"I think I'm about to cry, and I'm standing in the middle of a textile factory. Of course you should be the one to go," Charlotte said.

"Yeah?"

"Yeah. Go. Good luck. I'll call you tonight."

Evelyn sprinted to the gate, flapped her ticket at the attendant, and bounded down the escalator to the platform, her bag clanging over the escalator steps and into her calves. As she darted into a car and settled into a seat, breathing hard, she looked down to see she had a text from Charlotte.

"Nice to have you back," it read.

Evelyn typed out her reply: "Not totally back, but working on it." The train lurched, and when it pulled out into the harsh New York sunlight, she pressed send, and was on her way.

ACKNOWLEDGMENTS

I have loved books for as long as I can remember. To be writing one is a dream.

Elisabeth Weed, hereafter to be known as the dealmaking WASP, took this book and sprinted with it. She is a skilled editor, a tough negotiator, and a funny, frank, and delightful person. I lucked out with her. Dana Murphy at The Book Group is a smart, careful reader. I am glad to have the hardworking Jenny Meyer and Howie Sanders on my side.

Everyone I've dealt with at St. Martin's Press has been warm and wonderful. Charlie Spicer is witty, lively, and wise. Sally Richardson is a fierce—and glamorous—advocate for the book. Olga Grlic, Michael Storrings, and the art department created a stunning cover. Lisa Senz, Jeff Dodes, Laura Clark, Angelique Giammarino, and the marketing team have been innovative, and the salespeople are go-getters whose love for books is obvious. Dori Weintraub and Tracey Guest are total pros on the PR front. I am excited for this book to go into paperback because I'll get to work more closely with Jennifer Enderlin. April Osborn patiently answered my many irritating questions.

Elizabeth Catalano, Dave Cole, and the copyediting staff saved me from multiple errors.

The writing of this book was informed by dozens of authors and musicians. *House of Mirth* was the first adult book I fell hard for, and Edith Wharton's astute view of society and women's roles in it never ceases to impress and unnerve. I first read Booth Tarkington's *The Magnificent Ambersons* in my teens, and his tale of a family scraping to retain its status has been on my mind since. Theodore Dreiser's *An American Tragedy* showed how toxic social ambition can become. Louis Auchincloss's books provide an acerbic take from a Manhattan society insider; he should be more widely read. I have borrowed Camilla's Racquet Club bracelet from him; I like to think she could be the descendant of some of the women he wrote about.

From Stephen Sondheim, I borrowed not only this book's title but a particular view of lonely New York from *Company* and of dreamily ambitious New York from *Merrily We Roll Along*. Meryle Secrest's *Stephen Sondheim: A Life* and Sondheim's own *Finishing the Hat* were great reads and helped put his work in context.

Leonard Bernstein composed moving New York soundtracks that enriched my understanding of the city, and I refer to his and Sondheim's *West Side Story* and his (along with Betty Comden and Adolph Green) *Wonderful Town* and *On the Town* throughout. I have also used lyrics from *Annie, Bells Are Ringing, Evita, Cabaret,* and *Pippin.*

Lots of people helped me understand Evelyn's world—or, really, Camilla's world—from insight into the New York debutante season to old-money mores. They were generous with their time and I thank them soundly. Errors in how I portrayed their world are mine alone.

I learned how to be curious from great teachers, especially Tom Rona, Sue Hovis, Roger Hindman, and Ron Kim. I learned how to write from great editors, especially Dean Murphy, Jim Aley, Dan Ferrara, and Jane Berentson (I often thought if I could do my job with one-tenth the sass and intelligence of Jane, I was doing pretty well). Wendell Jamieson and the Metro editors have been not only terrific editors but supportive of letting me work on the novel while I work at the *Times*. It is a privilege to be part of the staff of *The New York Times*, and to be a part of an organization trying to observe and explain the world.

My friends were terrifically supportive even when I was frantic with anxiety about this book. Erin Autry Montgomery and Irene So Hedges are the kinds of smart, funny, lifelong pals one hopes to make in college. Robin Pringle is a devoted friend who makes leaning in look awfully elegant. Caroline Han has amazed me since the day we met. Katie McClurg Anderson is warmth personified. Megan Wyatt has been a stalwart since long before she wore a detergent box and I wore a cocktail dress to appear in our elementary school play about Northwest trees. Andrew Mandel and Scott Resnick sang me through some of my favorite moments in New York. Friends like Sarah Goldstein, Kayleen Schaefer, and Reyhan Harmanci make this city a place I love living in. There are many, many others whom I admire and adore (that's you! I see you!).

Several friends and acquaintances contributed directly to this book. Cynthia Collins Desai, a longtime, loyal, and hilarious friend, used her alarmingly good memory to help pinpoint hot spots in pre-financial crisis New York. They say it's hard to make lifelong friends after thirty, but Jessica Silver-Greenberg proves otherwise, I hope: She is a brilliant colleague, marvelous friend, and uproarious gal, and her feedback was invaluable. Julie Bosman has been a terrific guide through the publishing world and a paragon of graceful work-life balance. Olivia Wassenaar graciously answered my questions about Upper East Side life. Jennifer Pooley's feedback made this oodles better. Susan Bradanini Betz was a meticulous copy editor. Amor Towles, Nick Bilton, Tina Henry Bou-Saba, and Emma Frelinghuysen gave savvy advice about the book business and marketing. Courtney Sullivan, Maggie Shipstead, and Emma Straub kindly agreed to be early readers. Malcolm Gladwell's perceptive read was enormously helpful. David Carr helped me, like he helped so many other writers, feel like I had the gumption to do this thing. I really miss him.

My extended family is full of creative people and I am lucky to be a part of it. From dancing down Forty-second Street with Joanne to talking life and love with Denis to watching Missy paint, time with them has enlivened my world. My godmother, Mara Jayne Miller, is stylish, sharp, and a total original.

I have huge admiration for Lee Clifford and Jerry Useem, who are coolheaded parents, supportive spouses, fun to be around, and have propped me up when I'm down many, many times. I forgive Lee for telling Santa that "Stephanie has been bad, very bad."

My parents, Steve and Judy Clifford, encouraged reading and questioning, exposed me to art and music, and made me feel like I could take risks because they had my back. Their support and belief in me, and their enthusiasm for this book, has meant the world to me.

Thanks to Mac and Mabel, the best of writing companions.

Love and thanks to Steven, whose smiles in the morning show me that happiness needn't be so complicated. He is joy.

Finally, when Bruce Headlam encouraged me to keep going with this novel, he said that it doesn't matter what the end product is, but it matters that you try. He believes in living a creative, full life and works hard to make that a reality for us. While handling his extremely demanding job, he gave me time and space to write, he gave me advice, he let me vent when the book wasn't working, and then he helped me get back to writing. I love him, I thank him, and hope he knows how much he counts.

EVERYBODY RISE

Stephanie Clifford

About the Author

- A Conversation with Stephanie Clifford and #1 *New York Times* Bestselling Author Malcolm Gladwell

Behind the Novel

- Special Excerpt: "Barbara the Debutante": An Early Draft of an Unpublished Chapter

Keep on Reading

- Recommended Reading
- Reading Group Questions

For more reading group suggestions,
visit www.readinggroupgold.com.

St. Martin's Griffin

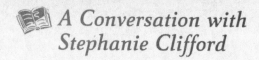

A Conversation with Stephanie Clifford

The following is an excerpt from a live Q&A between the author and Malcolm Gladwell.

Malcolm Gladwell: We're going to have a conversation about your marvelous novel, one of my favorite novels of the year. This is a book about class really as much as anything. I'm just curious what led you to write a book about class. That's a fairly unusual thing for someone to be writing about in America in 2015.

Stephanie Clifford: It is. It's a dirty word in the American landscape where people aren't supposed to discuss class. It's something we all know is there, but we try to pretend it isn't. I grew up in Seattle, where there are different levels of wealth, but not different levels of class, really. I went to a boarding school on a whim and had no idea what to expect. I showed up, and I had gotten these new gingham shoes that I was really excited about, and I was in my new Gap T-shirt. I was ready to go. Then I saw this girl from across the parking lot in a black business suit and a scarf and she was my year. I thought, "Oh my God. Where have I landed? What's happening?" I felt like an outsider, but it didn't frustrate me in the same way it frustrates Evelyn. I was interested in this crew and how they behaved.

MG: Evelyn's relationship to that world is really the core of the novel. It's confused. Talk a little bit about what you feel Evelyn's perspective on class is.

SC: She's somebody who has never fit in anywhere in her life. She doesn't really fit in with her parents. She doesn't fit in at school. So, she gets this chance to fit in, and it happens to be in this Promised Land of Adirondack camps and regattas. It could have been anywhere. It's that lure of feeling like somebody and feeling like you're finally seen.

MG: Her relationship with her parents is one of the things in this book that I found most interesting. When you describe Barbara and Dale, how do you imagine them getting together?

SC: They met when he was at law school. She thought he was going to be a great politician. She thought that would give them entrée into Washington society. Everybody said, "This guy's so ambitious. He can't lose." They were right, but it was not the version of ambition she was expecting.

MG: There's a poignant thing where two unformed people of great promise meet and their imaginations are running wild about their partner.

SC: They crossed at this one point where it made sense. At any other point, it wouldn't have. It becomes devastating disappointment to both of them, I think.

MG: To switch topics a little bit, you mentioned that Dale, the father, was pulled from your reporting. I'm just curious how being a *New York Times* reporter affects the kind of fiction that you write. In what ways are you a different fiction writer than if you had never had that kind of job?

SC: I think you look for the one telling detail. If you only have six hundred words to write a piece. You might only get one sentence to talk about how the person looked at their sentencing or how their mother screamed when she heard the guilty verdict. So, you look for that one thing that tells you more than any other detail, which is an interesting exercise. Is it the flowers? Is it the silverware? Is it the tablecloth?

MG: When you started this book, you were covering retail. When you finished it, you were covering the courts. There's a world of difference between those two beats. Did moving from one to the other change the way you wrote the book?

SC: It informed different parts of it. I was covering retail during and after the 2008 crash. It was really interesting to see. There was such a massive shift where the luxury purveyors, in particular, were hand-delivering things to people's houses or sending people home with plain bags. Nobody wanted to carry luxury bags on the street anymore. Little details like that, while they aren't actually in the book, set up the world that a lot of people are about to lose.

MG: I wonder how long that period of being aware of the social consequences of conspicuous consumption lasts. Six months?

SC: It stays with you. It keeps on going.

MG: There were a series of studies that came out, finding that regular reading of fiction of the sort you've written has quite a serious effect on your capacity for empathy. Fiction can do something that no other medium can do, which is provide an ongoing guide to the internal states of characters. You can't do that in nonfiction.

SC: Sometimes, the way to get people to care about something is through fiction.

Reprinted with permission from the authors.
Q&A courtesy of Barnes & Noble Booksellers.

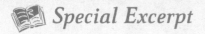 *Special Excerpt*

Reading
Group
Gold

"Barbara the Debutante":
An Early Draft of an Unpublished Chapter

Everybody Rise is my first book, and I wrote it in the early mornings before I went to work at the *New York Times*. I told hardly anyone that I was working on a novel. There are upsides to this approach: All that secrecy gave me space and time to finish the novel. One downside, though, is that I didn't realize how much of novel writing needs to be structural. I would write, edit, and revise entire chapters, then realize much later that the chapters didn't work in the book because of plot or backstory reasons.

This was one example: a chapter about Barbara's debutante ball. In this version, I had Barbara coming from a privileged background. She was rich, but she was angry: Her father had left the family when she was young, and, consciously or subconsciously, she was always trying to strike back at him. When I revised the book, I realized it worked better if Barbara came from a middle-class background, which would help explain the tremendous pressure Barbara puts on Evelyn: The daughter must succeed where the mother never could. That change meant, though, that Barbara would not have been a debutante, so this chapter had to go. I'm glad to be able to share it with you here.

—Stephanie Clifford

*Behind
the
Novel*

"Most decisions people can recover from," Barbara Trask Beegan once told her daughter, "but then there are some decisions that can set your life on a completely different course." For Barbara Trask, that moment was her debutante ball. Afterward, years afterward, when Barbara attended parties at Berry and Belle Buford's grand waterfront house, or saw their names on invitations to parties better than the ones she and Dale threw, she'd replay that June night, once, again.

Barbara grew up a pretty, spoiled only child in Baltimore; when she was a teenager, her father, Albert, left his meek wife, Roberta, to run off with his secretary, leaving Barbara with plenty of money and plenty of fury. She and her mother moved to Bibville, on Maryland's Eastern Shore, where she told her new neighbors that her father was dead, and pressured Roberta to say he was at least "departed."

The debutante ball became a fixation for Barbara after she read a *Life* profile of a New York society woman who'd attended prep school at Miss Damson's, come out at her Newport summer house, and now wore white gloves even when she visited tenement buildings as part of her charity work. Barbara soon enrolled herself at Miss Damson's, too. From Old Farms, Connecticut, Barbara sent enthusiastic letters to Belle, her best friend in Bibville, that described Miss Damson's customs without explaining them, used pet names for the Miss Damson's girls that Belle could never untangle, and added slang words (fream, grundy) that Belle tried, unsuccessfully, to import to Bibville High. When Barbara began writing to Belle, it was on lined notebook paper. By senior year, her letters were on engraved correspondence cards.

The ball was held at Sag Neck in June of 1964. Elsewhere, young people were starting to rail against Vietnam, and join radical student groups, and demonstrate for civil rights. At Sag Neck, Barbara was filling an upstairs table with her gifts: engraved silver cups and picture frames, little gold charm necklaces and charm bracelets, scarves that were filmy and romantic, scarves that were thick cashmere and sensible, tiny enameled boxes with painted scenes of a tiger face staring out of grass and a blue-capped bird balancing on a branch.

Barbara chose as her escort Berry Buford, who lived a few miles away from the Trasks, and was home from Georgetown for the summer. She had decided, without telling anyone, that she would marry Berry when the time came, and together they'd be the confident center of the Eastern Shore social scene.

Her guests started arriving on a Thursday morning, two days before the ball. Barbara put some of her Miss Damson's classmates in guest rooms at Sag Neck, and her other friends and some boys from Cheetam at the Marina Air Motor Inn in town. It seemed to work at first. She, Berry, and her friends from the North headed out to tennis during the day, in sun-slathered cars with the roofs pulled back, singing. At the beach, they ate picnic lunches of cold crab salad on thick slices of white bread, and the girls dashed into the ocean with little shrieks, silk scarves protecting their hairdos. The night of the ball, Berry gave a lovely toast that skillfully equated Barbara to the modern major-general in "Pirates of Penzance," and danced with her to "This Could Be the Start of Something."

However, about an hour into the dancing, Barbara realized that Berry was nowhere to be seen, and that drunken young men whom she didn't know were lining up at the bar. Twisting her head as she was waltzed around by a Cheetam pal to "The Blue Danube," and managing to keep her shoulders back and elbows pointed nevertheless, she saw one fellow was draped over the bar, with his backside in the air, kicking as he looked for something on the other side of it. On the next

turn, she spied Eaton McMaster, the fifteen year-old son of a neighbor, stuck in a large Chinese vase, drinking straight from a bottle one of the boys was sharing with him. She excused herself from her dancing partner.

"Who are you, and what are you doing at my party?" she demanded of the boys. Belle, who had been waiting to be assigned a role, hurried up behind her and looked at them accusingly. When she learned from the boys that Berry had invited them that day, Barbara grabbed the two bottles of champagne that they were drinking from and ran outside. She smashed the bottles on the patio as Belle gave little yelps.

She found Berry sitting on his haunches, on a part of the lawn hidden by trees, with some Cheetam boys and Miss Damson's girls, and a group of boys and girls that looked like they had just come from a drag race. They were passing around a bottle of gin, sloppily harmonizing to "Hit the Road, Jack."

"The lovely debutante!" Berry said, raising a bottle to Barbara. "You were a stunner tonight."

The past tense riled her, and she grabbed his collar. "Get up," she said. "You're supposed to be my escort tonight, which suggests you're supposed to be somewhere near me, and I've been alone for hours. In addition to that, you seem to have invited every piece of riff-raff on the Eastern Shore. Can you tell me just what you think you're doing?"

He giggled, tipping his head back to look at the moon as her hand pulled on his stiff white lapel. "Miss Trask, Miss Trask, don't be so angry."

"Who are these people?"

His gaze wandered to the group she was referring to, a few kids in leather jackets with slicked-back hair, and girls in high ponytails. He registered a look of surprise, as though he was just noticing them. "Oh. These guys. They're my new friends. They're from town. Say hi, new friends."

One that looked like Sal Mineo curled his lips and nodded his head toward the house. "Nice place."

"What are they doing here, Berry? This is a debutante party. Do you think I'm just anyone? That you can invite whoever pumps your gas to my party?"

Sal looked up, letting his eyes skate over her ivory dress. "I never met a real debutante before. Whaddaya know. Bet your daddy's real rich, huh?"

The moon was bright enough that she could see mud chunks on Berry's perfectly polished shoes. One of her Miss Damson's friends had grass stains on her pink-silk dress, and another had passed out and was snoring lightly. From the house, she heard the foghorn alto of a Cheetam friend's date, a girl from Back Bay, who was complaining that Maryland was a backwater.

Berry opened his fat lips and poured a stream of gin into them, and suddenly Barbara released her hold on his collar and watched as Berry toppled into the damp grass. "This was supposed to be," she said, and she stopped herself. She looked around at the strangers. "All of you. Get up. Get out. That includes you, Berry. You may take everyone out the side gate; do not come back in to the party."

"Oh, Barbara, that was so strong and brave of you," Belle was saying, trying to keep up as Barbara stalked back to the house. She stood, poised and pretty and lonely, through the rest of the dancing and the service of the scrambled eggs and sausage, through the guests' departures and the cleaners' roundup of grim napkins smeared with red lipstick and beef Wellington grease.

That night, Barbara pressed herself against the window

Reading
Group
Gold

Behind
the
Novel

seat in her bedroom, still wearing her dress and shoes, looking over the soft hills of the lawn and the water that looked gray in the pre-dawn light. She saw what looked like, and probably was, puddles of vomit near where Berry had been sitting. This was what she was left with, then, after all that. She had hoped something else would occur at the party—that someone fabulous would show up, or the band would be wonderful, or something would happen to make her father regret, just for a moment, that he had missed so much. But it hadn't happened, and now it was over.

She finally fell asleep with her back against the wall. When she woke up a few hours later, with a dry mouth and sore back in a wrinkled dress, Berry had already sent flowers. By the time she took a bath so hot that it pinched her skin to get into the tub, Barbara had decided not to respond to the floral apology. At the time, she thought she knew what the right call was: rejecting the flowers, and rejecting with them the life that the Berrys of the world offered. She thought she knew what that life would bring: a drunken husband, tennis dates at the Eastern, dominion over plain, admiring girls like Belle who would tell her how exciting her parties were. No glamorous nights at Washington ambassadors' residences or New York nightclubs, no piles of money to make the Trask name outrank other names for once. She would leave Berry to the dreary Belles of the world, girls with hair slipping from their settings and breath sour with champagne, destined never to leave this life, destined never to leave Bibville. Barbara would find something better than all of that. They would see.

When she heard the clatter of her Miss Damson's friends dragging their suitcases along the hallway floor, and their knocks at her bedroom door, she replied in a faint voice that she wasn't feeling well, and let them leave.

She met Dale four months later.

 *Recommended Reading*

Reading New York City:
Stephanie Clifford's List of Books for Further Reading

Louis Auchincloss, *A Voice from Old New York.* Though
Auchincloss's primary medium was fiction, this memoir
is captivating. Auchincloss, from an old-money New
York family, has enough distance from the society he
lived in to be an acerbic, engaging storyteller. I borrowed
Camilla's Racquet Club bracelet from this book—I
like to think Camilla could've been a descendant of the
people Auchincloss writes about. Essential reading if
you're interested in what "old New York" looked like
from the inside.

James Baldwin, *Notes of a Native Son.* Baldwin's essays
are sharp and moving. The ones he wrote while he lived
in Harlem are particularly thought-provoking—while
so much has changed since he published the essays in
1955, so little has, in some ways.

**Edwin G. Burrows and Mike Wallace, *Gotham: A
History of New York City to 1898.*** Written like a novel,
virtually every chapter of this book is a delight. I haven't
seen the city the same way since I read it.

Robert A. Caro, *The Power Broker.* If you want to work
in journalism or government in New York—or you just
like a good read—start this book now. This is the tale
of Robert Moses, who headed public works in the city
and state and made the New York landscape what it
is. Caro's reporting and research is a feat, and it gives a
fresh perspective on who really runs New York. (Bonus:
this book is heavy enough to double as a weight. Learn
and tone all at once!)

Dominick Dunne, *The Two Mrs. Grenvilles*. So. Juicy. I grew up in Seattle, where I discovered a copy of this book one summer when I was about ten. Seattle was all hiking, fleece, and pleasant talk about the Huskies. With this, I was transported to high-society New York City, and its money, sex, and glamour. I think this book was my mother's, but I never gave it back to her; I hid it away behind my other, more age-appropriate books, and promised myself that I'd try out New York myself someday.

Stephen Sondheim, *Finishing the Hat*. This is a coffee-table book, but a coffee-table book you'll want to read, not just flip through. Sondheim gives notes on his lyrics and shows, including why early drafts changed, how to deal with failure, and his gimlet-eyed view of New York life. I'm a huge Sondheim fan: The title of the book comes from his "The Ladies Who Lunch," and I played "Getting Married Today" over and over to amp up the anxiety as I wrote Evelyn's quasi-mad scene in the boat, among other Sondheim indulgences. Reading this helped me sharpen my own writing.

Edith Wharton, *The House of Mirth*. Why do we want what we want, and what happens when we don't get it? Lily Bart, Wharton's heroine, falls out of society despite her grasping efforts in this beautifully written book, which was a direct inspiration for *Everybody Rise*.

E. B. White, *Here is New York*. Whenever I'm feeling run over by the city—it's pouring, I'm covered in mud from a dollar van that almost hit me in a crosswalk, and my umbrella broke before my day even started—I turn to this lovely book. "No one should come to New York to live unless he is willing to be lucky," White writes; this book always makes me feel not just lucky, but in love with the city.

Isabel Wilkerson, *The Warmth of Other Suns.* New York City is one of three destination points in this history, which follows African American migrants leaving the South after World War I. This is not only an absorbing history book: Wilkerson has made the characters she profiles come alive, making this narrative nonfiction at its best.

Richard Yates, *The Easter Parade.* Yates captures mid-century American loneliness better than just about anyone. In this novel, two sisters navigate through their unhappy lives, each trying to keep up appearances. Yates is a spare and brutal writer who pulls you so deep into his world that to recover, you may need to have one of those three-martini lunches so popular among his characters.

*Keep
on
Reading*

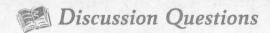 *Discussion Questions*

1. Why do you think Barbara has such specific
   expectations for her daughter? When does Evelyn
   successfully push back against these, and how?
   Why do you think Evelyn comes to hold some
   of the same values as her mother? How does the
   Barbara–Evelyn relationship shift as the novel goes
   on? Do you have sympathy for Barbara?

2. Evelyn considers, at one point, how easy it
   would be if she could marry Preston. Do you
   think this would be a good pairing? Can
   marriages of convenience like this work?
   Should Preston's sexuality, or Evelyn's
   assessment of Preston's sexuality, figure
   into her thinking more?

3. How porous is social class in America? Could Evelyn
   have made different decisions that would have
   allowed her to ultimately fit in in Camilla's circle?

4. At the end, Charlotte updates Evelyn and tells her
   that all her former friends are just fine. Still, the
   financial crisis is coming. How do you think the
   characters who stay in New York make it through
   that? Do you think they are as untouchable as
   Charlotte seems to think? Now, several years after the
   financial crisis, do you see certain groups who haven't
   been affected and certain groups who have?

5. When we first meet Evelyn, she feels overlooked:
   "But it would be nice to have a place for once,
   to have people look at her and think she was
   interesting and worth talking to, not to have them
   politely fumble for details about her life and get
   them wrong and instantly forget her. (Murray Hill,
   right? No, the Upper East Side. Ah, and Bucknell?
   No, Davidson.)" Why is that important to her?

Reading
Group
Gold

*Keep on
Reading*

Does she achieve this place she's looking for? Have
you struggled with a similar goal? What happened?

6. Why does Scot end up accepted by this group
   in the end? What does he bring to the table that
   Evelyn does not?

7. Did you find Evelyn likable? Why or why not?
   How important is it to you as a reader that a
   book's protagonist be likeable? What are books
   you've liked where the main character is unlikable?
   Do you have different expectations about likability
   for male and for female protagonists?

8. Do you think Dale committed bribery? Why or
   why not? How important is the question of her
   father's guilt or innocence to Evelyn?

9. Charlotte seems to see herself as a moral arbiter in
   the book. Do you agree with her moral stance? Is
   she a good friend to Evelyn? Are there ways that
   Evelyn is a good friend to her?

10. At one point Evelyn puzzles over why debutante
    balls still exist when young women are hardly kept
    behind closed doors until age eighteen. What's
    your take on this? Why do they continue to occur?

11. As Evelyn watches her father's sentencing,
    she wonders why he's receiving such a harsh
    punishment when others who have erred are not.
    "Why were the consequences so severe for him?"
    she asks. Is that something you see elsewhere in
    the novel—that rules apply to one set of people
    but not another? Are there current events where
    this applies? Or do you think she's making excuses
    for her father—and for herself ?

12. Is Camilla and Evelyn's friendship genuine? Why or why not? Have you had short-term friendships? Why didn't they work out? What makes for a real and lasting friendship?

13. Do you think Evelyn and Scot are well-paired as a couple? At the novel's end, after Evelyn has changed, would you see them working out?